PEACEMAKER

A GABRIEL WOLFE THRILLER
BOOK 15

ANDY MASLEN

TYTON PRESS

ALSO BY ANDY MASLEN

Gabriel Wolfe

Trigger Point

Reversal of Fortune

Blind Impact

Condor

First Casualty

Fury

Rattlesnake

Minefield

No Further

Torpedo

Three Kingdoms

Ivory Nation

Crooked Shadow

Brass Vows

Seven Seconds

DI Stella Cole

Hit and Run

Hit Back Harder

Hit and Done

Let the Bones Be Charred

Weep, Willow, Weep

A Beautiful Breed of Evil

Death Wears A Golden Cloak

See the Dead Birds Fly

Playing the Devil's Music

Detective Ford

Shallow Ground

Land Rites

Plain Dead

DS Kat Ballantyne

The Seventh Girl

The Unseen Sister

The Silent Wife

Other Fiction

Blood Loss – A Vampire Story

Purity Kills

You're Always With Me

Green-Eyed Mobster

To my family

'Character is destiny.'

—Heraclitus

PROLOGUE

SOVIET CLOSED CITY OF MIRAKOVO
19 FEBRUARY 1983

Shaking with horror at the obscenity he'd created, Comrade Professor K gulped down the tumbler of vodka he'd just poured.

They called it a weapon to end all weapons. A weapon to end all war. But it was a weapon of such horrific, calamitous, evil power it made nuclear bombs look like children's playthings. And now it was hours away from being shipped to Cuba.

On his cluttered desk, in a polished cherrywood presentation casket lined with red velvet, lay a gold-plated Makarov pistol. A personal gift from Comrade General Secretary Andropov. It was engraved, in typical Communist Party rhetoric,

For scientific services to the Union of Soviet Socialist Republics.
'A world without war is a world without fear.'

No more wars. Ever. That had been the dream for every

Soviet citizen after the end of the Great Patriotic War. Twenty-seven million dead. Countless others wounded. Who wouldn't want a world without fear?

But in Comrade Professor K's humble opinion, a world with this, this *thing* in it was a world that would one day be *ruled* by fear.

It was his job to prepare the device for shipment and its final destination aboard a submarine.

Russian men had never been afraid to weep. He wept now.

He poured another tumblerful of vodka and downed it, so drunk now that he didn't feel the rough spirit burning his throat anymore.

Fresh tears coursed down his unshaven cheeks. What had he done?

They called it *Mirotvorets*. Peacemaker. Such irony. Unusual for the Kremlin. Ha! Such jokers they were back in Red Square.

They should have called it *Koshmar*.

For Professor K had created a nightmare.

Not just for the Americans, though he could imagine all too easily the well-fed faces of the actor president and his advisers paling as they realised what they were up against.

No. Not just for them. Professor K had birthed a nightmare for the whole of humanity.

General Secretary Andropov himself had appeared in the facility the previous morning. He'd handed out vodka and Cuban cigars to the team before mounting an upturned packing crate and beaming at the assembled weapons technicians, nuclear scientists, computational biologists and engineers.

'Thanks to your tireless work for the Mother Country, the Americans and their allies will have no choice. They will surrender their entire nuclear arsenal or we will lay waste to them and their running-dog enablers.' The cold-eyed bureaucrat raised his glass. 'To Peacemaker!'

Cheering, they'd lifted their own glasses and swallowed the smooth, creamy vodka rumoured to have come from a pre-revolutionary stash discovered inside the Romanovs' Summer Palace.

Oh, Comrade Andropov was happy. His face shiny with Tsarist vodka. His reptilian features wreathed in the sweet-smelling blue-grey smoke of his Monte Cristo.

But Professor K could see further into the future than the next Strategic Five-Year Plan. And what he saw terrified him.

He was one of only seventeen people on the planet to have witnessed first-hand the devastation Peacemaker could unleash.

Andropov had requested a demonstration. They'd travelled nine hundred and five miles on a secret railway, all the way from Mirnakovo to another closed city.

Zarechinsk was a mining town. Uranium. But the seam was, like the group who arrived at its station, exhausted. The town was scheduled to be mothballed, its 250,000 inhabitants relocated at enormous cost.

In Andropov's words, 'Let's catch two wolves in one trap.'

The country saying revealed his proletarian roots, a source of amusement among the highly educated scientists who ran the Peacemaker programme.

Nobody felt much like laughing after seeing Peacemaker in action. White-faced, or green and waxy, if they had been vomiting, they quietly boarded the train back to Mirnakovo.

In their wake, they left a quarter of a million human corpses, or what was left of them. Men, women and children, mouths open in frozen screams, limbs twisted into bizarre knots. And that… that …degradation of the flesh. He retched at the memory.

The entire grisly business had taken eleven minutes and fourteen seconds from the moment Professor K's index finger had flicked the activation switch to the final shriek.

No explosion had rent the sky, shivering glass from window frames or blowing out eardrums. The whole thing had unfolded in eerie silence. Apart from the screams.

Birds had tumbled from the sky. Animals had collapsed, squealing, in the forest. And the human beings unfortunate enough to have been sent to Zarechinsk to work had died agonising deaths, of which their swiftness was their only redeeming feature.

Writhing, vomiting, voiding their bowels and bladders, clawing at their eyeballs as if they couldn't bear to see their own torturous ending, before their final and nerve-shattering transformation into the grisly residue that was Peacemaker's signature effect.

Andropov had been in high spirits on the return journey.

'No radiation! No fallout! No buildings damaged. Not even a fencepost out of place!'

That night, a great deal of vodka had been drunk. The politicians were celebrating, the scientists trying to obliterate the memories of Zarechinsk.

Meanwhile, 783 Tupolev Tu-22Ms flew due south from the Nagurskoye air base in Arkhangelsk Oblast. Once over Zarechinsk they dropped over 3,000 tonnes of high-explosive and incendiary bombs. It was said the orange glow of the fire could be seen in Moscow.

And now the professor was left alone in the research facility. The rest of the team had shipped out, their suitcases laden with souvenirs, their necks bent under the weight of the special solid gold medals struck to commemorate their work.

He took one final look at the shipment-ready olive-green steel casing designed to hold Peacemaker. Glanced out of the window at the oily smoke curling up from a fire. Picked up a photograph of his wife, Irina, and their son, Andrej, and kissed it. Returned it to the desk, face down.

Then he picked up the gold-plated Makarov, put it to the underside of his jaw and pulled the trigger.

1

SANTA ROSA, ATLANTIC COAST, HONDURAS

Gritting his teeth, the farmer swung the heavy-bladed sugar-cane knife. Unpleasant memories of bodies mutilated by similar weapons crowded his mind. He shook them free along with a spray of sweat.

The thick stem of the invasive weed they called, with typical Honduran irony, *El Alegre Gigante Verde* – The Jolly Green Giant – separated with a snap, releasing a pungent aroma of cat's piss.

He was clearing a patch of land in which he intended to plant Arbol chillies. The work was heavy, and painful, given the profusion of thorny, spiky or just plain poisonous scrub plants that had claimed this corner of his smallholding.

He was content. Not happy. Happiness was an emotion he thought of as belonging to his past. But here, tending his land, he could exist without wanting to kill himself with alcohol. Or anyone else, with whatever weapon – fists, feet, knives, broken bottles, guns, grenades – he felt necessary for the task.

Not that life was devoid of pleasure. He worked hard, growing mangos and papaya, corn and chillies, enjoying the physical exhaustion that a day tilling the rich red earth would bring.

Evenings were for reading or playing cards with his neighbours. He might spend some time with Pera, his one, true friend. Or play football with her sixteen-year-old son, Santiago. Go fishing. Or simply run from his home out along the beach, before swimming back. He meditated. And did a twice-daily yoga practice, essential if he was to keep his demons at bay.

And for the most part, all these activities – physical, mental, spiritual – enabled him to avoid thinking about his wife, and their unborn child who had died with her.

More than a year had passed. The people responsible were long dead. But for him, the ghosts of the past were ever-present. Hovering just out of view in the corner of his eye. Populating his dreams. And, at times of heightened stress, which he took pains to avoid, as real to him as if they had never died.

At the hum of an approaching vehicle, the farmer straightened, wiped the sweat from his forehead with a square of unbleached cotton and shaded his eyes against the harsh midday sun. The knife dangled by his side, though his grip was sure.

The 4x4's chrome trim sparkled like distant muzzle-flash. The black paintwork gleamed. No dust. Odd. Most farmers round here had trucks tinted a tawny brown by the soil they worked.

Visitors? Seemed unlikely. Most of his visitors arrived on foot. Or possibly horse- or mule-back. Even then, it tended to be in the evening, when the day's work was done. Everyone was hard at it during the day. Mostly on the land. Like him.

He tightened his grip on the knife. The *golok*, his subconscious renamed it, using the Malaysian word. The word they'd all used, back in the day.

The vehicle drew closer, slowing now. One man behind the wheel. Another in the passenger seat. A long-billed cap for the driver and, for the passenger, a broad-brimmed hat, casting deep shadows over their eyes. The lower edges of mirror shades rested on their cheekbones.

The farmer cast a glance over his shoulder. The house was two hundred metres away. His gun was two hundred metres away.

But not his safety. That, he carried with him.

He returned his gaze to the oncoming 4x4. A Lincoln Navigator. Space for eight. A squad.

His pulse ticked up to seventy. He breathed in and out, slowly, returning it to sixty. The men visible behind the windscreen were Anglos. So not cartel business, then.

It had been a year since he'd tangled with the Zinguizapa Cartel. Left them leaderless. Rudderless, you could call it.

Rumour had it the Rio Rosso had taken over territory, operations and supply chain. Not the human resources, though. That wasn't cartel style. The crocs in the Rio Grande had eaten well for a week.

The Navigator came straight towards him, its oversized tyres cutting furrows through his newly planted maize. The farmer scowled. Didn't they understand the care it took to raise the damn stuff to maturity? It was bad enough fending off the peccaries, who pigged out, literally, on the young plants.

No sense running. They could mow him down under the huge front wheels. No sense. But no chance, either. He was not a man to run from danger. Towards it, maybe. Which his old boss had occasionally upbraided him for, '*Old Sport*'. But away? No.

What happened next all depended on two factors. Numbers. And weapons.

Unarmed. Two on one? Four on one? Six on one? It didn't matter. With the *golok*, he was comfortable he'd send them on their way. Back where they came from. Or on to the great and final destination of every human being.

Armed, things changed. There was an old saying. 'Charge a gun, flee a knife.' He would get amongst them. Men wielding firearms were, on the whole, over-confident. Rush them and that self-assurance evaporated faster than spilled water on a desert floor.

You could inflict a lot of damage with a *golok* in the middle of a group of panicking gunmen, all fumbling for aim, snatching at slides and charging levers, trying to wield long-barrelled weapons in confined spaces without shooting each other. He'd seen it happen. Even ducked and let the bogies take a couple of their own side out before finishing the job himself.

But he was getting ahead of himself. Perhaps they'd come to sell him some young mango trees. Or equipment insurance.

He smiled to himself. Nice to know he still had his sense of humour.

He glanced up as a thin keening reached him. A black-and-white swallow-tailed kite soared on a thermal, describing vast, lazy circles over the land he tended.

The Navigator pulled up ten metres back from his position.

The front passenger door opened.

2

From the steep cliff of the Navigator's side stepped a man carrying a lightweight aluminium attaché case.

He was dressed like a Vegas hustler's idea of an oil baron. Cream suit cut in the western style with brown piping across the yoke, jacket buttoned across a corpulent belly. Oversized white cowboy hat with a black leather band bearing glittering engraved silver conchos. String tie. Trousers tucked into a pair of ugly snakeskin boots with silver tips. Quite the rig.

Maybe inside the Lincoln's air-conditioned interior the getup would have felt comfortable. But out here? Temperature in the 90s and a soupy humidity that the sea breeze did nothing to dispel? A mental shrug. *His problem, not mine.*

The farmer watched the driver. He remained in his seat. But he was doing something with his hands below the level of the dashboard. His right shoulder hitched and his weight shifted, first left then back to the centre again.

He might as well have hoisted a flag which read, 'I'm unholstering my sidearm.'

The man was of a breed he recognised. Ex-Special Forces.

American. Built like brick shithouses. SEALS, maybe. Delta Force. Made regular jarheads look like pencil-necks.

He and the lads used to joke that the Yanks spent more time in the gym than they did on the front line. Good fighters, sure, but unless you were planning to beat the enemy by winning a weightlifting competition, they just couldn't see the point of all that bulk. Just more weight to carry.

Stamina. That was the prize.

It was what took you up one side of Pen y Fan and down the other. Then back again. In two hours, forty. In the pissing rain. As your reward, you got to stand under the prized sand-coloured beret with the flaming sword of Damocles cap badge.

The oil baron approached him, stopping a metre or so back. His eyes, a brilliant green, flicked down to the blade in the farmer's right hand. Then back up. An incisive, analytical gaze.

His hands looked soft. Pale. Used to wielding nothing weightier than a fountain pen. At once, the farmer knew his profession. Lawyer.

'*Buenas dias, compadre*,' the lawyer said.

His accent revealed roots somewhere in the south. Texas, maybe. The farmer had had a friend from San Antonio. Dead now. One of many.

The farmer spoke English.

'What do you want?'

The lawyer frowned, no doubt surprised to hear an English accent all the way out here. Then he recovered his composure.

'Well, now. We've come a long way to see you. I don't suppose you could run to a glass of water?'

'None in your car?'

The man offered a broad smile that stopped well short of his eyes.

'Now that's not very friendly. I thought you Brits were all about being polite.'

'You just destroyed my crops when you could have taken the track around them. And your driver's carrying. Is that *your* idea of polite?'

The man held his arms wide.

'Hell, friend, this is bandit country. Gary there is just trying to protect me. And I'm real sorry about your crops. But, see, that's why we're here. Name's Lorne Packard, out of Houston, Texas.'

He stuck out his soft pale hand. The farmer ignored it. A shrug from the lawyer as he let the hand fall to his side.

'The man I work for would like to buy your little farm lock, stock and barrel. We're talking top dollar. *US.* How much land you got here?' He looked around. 'What, ten acres, twenty?'

'It's not for sale.'

The lawyer smiled, revealing the kind of dentistry that would have confirmed his nationality even if his voice hadn't already.

'Come now, friend, you haven't even heard my offer. Now, beachfront real estate on Roatán over there,' he waved an arm in the vague direction of an island known as one of the few tourist-friendly spots in all of Honduras, 'well, it goes for eighty-five thousand an acre. No offence, but this isn't Roatán. I mean, no yoga studios or juice bars. But it has development potential. My employer has authorised me to offer you, and, as a matter of fact, your neighbours, one *hundred* thousand an acre. Let's say you got some land I can't see from my vantage point here. Round it up to fifty acres and you're looking to clear five million US. Enough to buy a fancy place somewhere else with change to spare.'

The farmer breathed in and out, slowly. What the hell was going on? Development potential? For what?

The lawyer was spot on when he talked about Roatán. It did cater to tourists. But the mainland? No. There was a reason it stayed as agricultural land. The entire country was in the grip of the cartels. Either directly, or through their bought-and-paid-for politicians.

'I'm happy where I am, thanks,' he said.

'Oh, now, don't be a Stubborn Stanley!' The lawyer patted his attaché case. 'Got all the paperwork right in here. Including a cash deposit of a hundred thousand US as what you might call a physical gesture of goodwill. Rest to follow by bank transfer. I have all the necessary technical gizmos in my bag. You could have the money in your account before the ink's dry on the contract. Although, in this heat, it could be touch and go!'

He laughed. He sounded genuinely amused by his own, limp joke.

'Why?'

'The lawyer raised his eyebrows, as if nobody had ever questioned his motives before.

'Beg pardon?'

'Why are you offering a small farmer five million US for a patch of land that's worth no more than twenty thousand?'

The lawyer shrugged.

'Come now, friend, that's a strange attitude to a windfall of this magnitude. I would encourage you to accept my, very generous, offer. Because you know what?' He cast an eye over his shoulder at the driver. 'Maybe it won't be on the table all that long. And I can assure you the alternative is a lot less appealing.'

The farmer had had enough. He took a sudden step closer to the lawyer, forcing him to stumble back over a pile of chopped-down stems of the Jolly Green Giant.

'Let's get a couple of things straight,' he said from the midst of a fresh cloud of the tomcat aroma of the crushed weeds. 'One, I'm not your friend. Two, my land is not for sale. And three, I would strongly advise you not to threaten me.'

The lawyer held his hands up.

'I get the picture. You're happy on your little patch of scrub here, raisin' corn and beans or whatever the *campesinos* round here like to chow down on. Living off-grid or whatever you call this. But, see, there is such a thing as progress. And progress? Well, now, she's an unforgivin' kind of mistress if you take my meanin'. A man can no more stand in her way than he can hold his hands out to stop a tornado.'

'So you represent progress?'

'In a manner of speakin', yessir, I do. And, as I said, I have five million US to encourage you to join me.'

The farmer hefted the cane knife in his hand. Flipped it up in the air and caught it again after two complete rotations. Flipped it again. The lawyer's eyes followed its ascent and descent. Sweat crawled from under the brim of his hat and down into his eyes.

'Get off my land now, or I'll throw you off it,' the farmer said. 'Piece by piece if necessary.'

The lawyer backed up. The show of bonhomie gone. Replaced by a crocodilian sneer. He held up his hand and beckoned with two fingers.

'Gary!' he shouted, before retreating to the far side of the SUV.

The driver opened his door and climbed out. Only his lower legs visible beneath the black slab of metal.

'Boss?'

'He don't want my money. Show him the alternative.'

Grinning, the thickset man emerged from the shelter of the Navigator's door. In his right hand, a pistol.

3

The farmer could still identify most firearms in a split-second.

This weapon? A Beretta 92FS. A fine example of a nine-millimetre pistol. And a favoured sidearm of law enforcement, the military and criminal enterprises, from Honduras to Hong Kong.

He rushed it.

In the two seconds it took him to close the distance between him and the unfortunate Gary, several things happened at once.

Gary's eyes widened comically, exposing whites all the way round his pale-blue irises. His lower jaw dropped. And his brain instigated the complex set of muscular movements necessary to raise his gun arm to the horizontal.

While it was still pointing at the ground, however, the farmer reached him. It would have been a simple matter to remove his entire hand, pistol included, with the sugar-cane knife. But that would have been overkill. Instead the farmer spun the knife around until the thick, heavy back edge of the blade was downwards and hammered it onto the man's forearm.

Gary screamed as his radius bone snapped like a dry twig. The Beretta fell to the ground, sticking muzzle-first into the soft red earth. Eyes rolling upwards in their sockets, Gary followed it as the farmer dealt a lightning-fast uppercut that snapped his teeth together with a *clack*.

He bent to retrieve the pistol and stuck it in the waistband of his trousers.

The lawyer was fumbling with something inside his jacket. Might have been easier if he'd undone his button first.

The farmer stepped in close, took hold of the jacket's collar, pushed back and down, yanking the whole garment over the man's arms, pinioning them to his sides more effectively than cable-ties.

He reached inside and relieved the man of his own weapon, a chrome-plated subcompact 9mm pistol. He held it up before his eyes.

'Kimber Micro 9. Nice piece.'

The lawyer spluttered, his face now sheened with perspiration.

'Now, now, look, friend, I—'

'I told you already. I'm not your friend. So here's what's going to happen. I'm going to help you put Gary there into the back of your car. Then you are going to turn it around and get the fuck off my land. And don't come back. Like you said, it's a generous offer and, believe me, you wouldn't like the alternative.'

Five minutes later, the lawyer and his driver, minus two nine-millimetre pistols, were back inside the Navigator.

The lawyer swung the oversized black SUV in a messy circle, crushing more young plants and came to a stop a few metres away from the farmer.

He buzzed the window down. The reptilian smile widened.

'I guess that's the end of the pleasantries.'

Then he gunned the engine and fishtailed away, throwing sprays of red dirt high into the air where the finer particles mixed with the blue exhaust smoke and drifted left to right in an acrid cloud.

Something dark and slimy and heavy uncoiled in the farmer's stomach. Not fear. Far from it. He had lost his ability to feel scared of mere fighting along with his last remaining family.

This was the depressing realisation that his life was changing again. Without his consent.

Because *of course* he could send a lawyer and his thick-necked bodyguard packing with nothing more than a sugar-cane knife and a few well-aimed blows. But the sort of man who turned up offering five million US dollars for land worth a fraction of that wouldn't be deterred by such a pushback.

And next time he'd bring reinforcements.

With a yell of pure rage Gabriel Wolfe hurled the sugar-cane knife. It spun end over end before thudding, tip-first, into the rough bark of a mango tree.

Why couldn't people just leave him alone?

4

PORTLAND, OREGON

Roughly 2,900 miles northwest of the farmer's modest plot, Xander Kalt pushed his heels against the tight-strung steel wire girding his balcony. His lightweight aluminium chair canted backwards.

From his fortieth-floor vantage point, he had a superb view of the Old Town and the Wilamette River. Directly below him, the White Stag sign glowed red, white and green.

He owned every property on the city block but the council had dug their prissy, bureaucratic heels in when he'd pitched to buy the sign as well. Just because he wanted to amend the red neon OLD TOWN to read KALT OLD TOWN. Their loss.

He took a long pull on the straw sunk into the green super-smoothie. Seventeen fruits, vegetables, minerals and biological extracts. Each smoothie he sucked down increased his life expectancy by 0.017 percent. He calculated he was nudging 110 and he wasn't yet thirty-five. The plan was 150. Well, the plan was to live for ever. His cryonics division was on 24/7/365 standby if anything should happen to him ahead of schedule. Then he'd sleep at minus 75 until medical science caught up with his dreams.

His phone rang. The lawyer.

'Tell me you're making progress, Lorne,' he said by way of greeting, placing the smoothie on the stone tiles.

'Well, good evening to you, too, Xander.'

Kalt pursed his lips. He supposed he ought to observe the proprieties. Even though they just added noise into his pure-signal utterances.

'I'm sorry, Lorne. How was your day? Is the hotel all right?'

'Hotel's fine. Although they got a funny idea of what constitutes a medium-rare T-bone. But you don't want to hear about my dining disappointments and frankly I don't wanna relive them, either.'

Kalt struggled to keep his irritation from breaking out. Why did people have this compulsion to just *say* stuff? Why couldn't they just get to the point?

Lorne was still talking.

'As to my day. Well, I just got back from dropping Gary off at the ER. And I spent six hours toting a bag of cash around while a bunch of Mestizo peasants offered me homemade hooch and then politely told me to shove my money where the sun don't shine.'

Decoding what Lorne said took him a few seconds. The Texan's colourful turns of phrase were just more noise.

'Wait. They said no?'

'Like I said. Gave me all this BS about land being more important than money and how they all got this *com-YOU-nitty* going on. Anyways, ain't you going to ask me how come Gary ended up in the ER?'

Kalt hadn't been going to. He didn't know who Gary was. He wasn't really *interested*. He'd left the resourcing of the trip to Lorne. But to show willing, he asked now.

'How did he?'

'Some fucking Englishman dressed like a campesino broke his arm with the back side of a machete, is how.'

'What the fuck's an Englishman doing living in some Honduran backwater like Santa Rosa?'

'I intend to find out. People seem to hold him in high regard, for reasons as yet unknown. I got the feelin' while he was stayin' put, they was, too.'

'Lorne, I want that land. Everything I have planned *depends* on it. Now, I am paying your not inconsiderable fees because you told me, no, wait,' he gulped down the last of his smoothie, 'you *guaranteed* me, that you could get this done. "Ain't no bunch of illiterate, inbred beaners gonna out-negotiate Lorne Packard." Your words.'

'Now, now, calm yourself, Xander,' the lawyer said. Kalt heard the click of ice cubes down the line. Pictured the fat Texan lawyer in a hotel suite *he* was paying for, guzzling minibar whisky *he* was paying for. Probably running up a huge cell-phone bill, that *he* was paying for. 'I said I was gonna find out about the Englishman. And I will. Once I know who I'm dealin' with, I'll find his weak spot. Because let me tell you somethin', *everybody* has one. Then you just stick in your lever and push.'

'Well, you better push hard, Lorne. Failure is not an option.'

Kalt hung up. Threw his phone down in disgust.

Maybe he ought to go down there himself. Show Packard a different way of handling people. The same way he'd used to build Kaltium Corporation from a startup in his parents' garage to a one-point-five-billion-dollar publicly traded corporation.

Six out of ten companies on the Dow Jones ran their enterprise software on Kaltium systems. Half of those on the London Stock Exchange. From New York to Tokyo, Bangkok to Berlin, if somebody bought a purse or a golfball, a book or a tin of beans, chances were the transaction spent a few microseconds interacting with Kaltium.

Being rich was fun. Being powerful was better. But what Xander Kalt had in mind would beat both of those hands down.

He intended to be remembered.

And for that he needed Peacemaker.

5

Heart still pounding from the encounter with the lawyer and his hired goon, Gabriel strode towards the village. Full of misgivings, he used the twenty-minute trip to collect his thoughts and start planning for the next phase of the battle.

He frowned. *Was* it a battle? Was there *any* chance this was some misguided American businessman's clumsy attempt to acquire some coastal real estate?

Right. Because who wouldn't want to risk violent extortion, kidnapping and murder in order to build a hotel on the Honduran coast? Cuba offered a safer bet and they were still communist.

He'd humiliated the lawyer and broken the muscle's arm. There'd be some kind of blowback.

Wiping the sweat from his forehead with the back of his hand, he entered the village's bar, raising a hand in greeting to the middle-aged man behind the counter. He'd once been a soldier in the Honduran army, before returning to his home and a more peaceful life.

'Hey, Julio, how's your day going?'

'Good, Gabriel, good. Guifiti? Maria's just finished a new batch. Licorice root and ginger. Very strong.'

Gabriel shook his head. He'd been steadily cutting down his alcohol consumption since killing Eli's murderer. While beer was still on the menu, guifiti was off it. The local home-brewed spirit, for which every family had at least one recipe, could be used to fuel a car in straitened times. Gabriel was still trying to repair the damage to his liver it had caused him.

'Just a coke, please.'

Julio set down a fizzing glass. He ran a wedge of lime around the rim before squeezing a few drops of juice into the drink then dropping it in among the crackling ice cubes.

'Not like you to drop in mid-afternoon, Gabriel. What's up?'

He took a gulp of the sweet, cold liquid. 'Has anyone been in, asking about who owns the land around Santa Rosa? Americans?'

Julio shrugged. 'No offence, Gabe, but you're the only gringo crazy enough to want to hang around here.'

'Hey, Gabe!'

The voice, a papery rustle that spoke of too many cigarettes, came from a dark corner of the bar where two walls hung with native rugs met.

He made his way to the table where sat an old man in the universal farmers' garb of baggy unbleached cotton workpants and a smock top.

'Hey, Raúl, did you see any strangers?' he asked, taking the seat that the old farmer pushed out from under the table with a worn-down boot heel.

Raúl lit a fresh cigarette from the inch-long butt of the one between his lips before pinching it out between his fingertips. Nodded.

'Two Americans came to my house this morning. Early. One dressed up all fancy like some cattle rancher, the other looked like a soldier, you know?'

Raúl squared his shoulders, jutted his chin out. Not a bad impression of the muscle.

'What did they want?'

Raúl snorted, then coughed, sending streams of blue cigarette smoke pluming from his nostrils.

'The farm. Can you believe it? Offered me all this money, said I'd be a fool not to take the offer.'

'What did you say?'

'I told him I'd got to be eighty-eight behaving like a fool so I might as well carry on.'

'You weren't tempted?'

'Tempted? To move off the land that my father handed down to me and his father before him? And that I will hand down in my turn when it is my time? To leave Santa Rosa? Where am I supposed to go at my age? Teguz?' He used the nickname everyone in the country used for its capital, Tegucigalpa. 'Are you kidding? I'd rather die.'

A burst of tarry coughing racked his chest and he doubled over, hacking for a full minute before dragging himself straight again, wiping tears from rheumy brown eyes and spitting a gob of dark-brown phlegm into a beaten copper spittoon on the floor.

'So he told you you'd have to leave the town?'

'That's what I just said, isn't it? Crazy Yankee wants to buy the whole fucking town. Move the whole lot of us, every man, woman and child, off our own land.'

Gabriel thanked him then rose, signalling Julio to bring the old man a fresh drink. Time to make a few social calls.

Three hours later, Gabriel was sitting on his deck, staring out at the Caribbean and chewing the inside of his cheek. Because what his neighbours had told him painted a disturbing picture.

Out of nowhere, the Stetson-wearing lawyer had appeared in the village, offering suitcase-loads of US dollars to every landowner. Didn't matter whether your property amounted to a tin-roofed shack on the beach or a couple of hundred acres of forest you were turning to eucalyptus for paper pulp, the American wanted it.

And it was the same 'very generous' offer each time. An amount of cash equal to two hundred and fifty times what the land was worth. With a single proviso.

You took the money, you left town.

Specifically, you moved outside an exclusion zone stretching fifteen kilometres east and west along the coast and ten kilometres inland. Presumably, after winning over the farmers, the American lawyer would approach the business owners on the village. With no more customers, the money would seem like the sensible option.

Nobody had bitten. Sure, the inhabitants of Santa Rosa weren't the richest people on God's green earth. Cash-wise, at least. But the community was close-knit. Family helped family. If you didn't have family, then friends and neighbours would pitch in. Whether a storm had torn the roof off your house or those damn peccaries had treated your corn like an all-you-can-eat buffet.

As Gabriel sat on his deck and watched the sun set over the Caribbean, turning the water a shade of deep burnished gold, he sipped his coke and frowned.

What the hell was going on?

6

At 3:00 a.m., four days later, a voice whispered in Gabriel's ear as he drowsed in the crook of a tree, fifteen feet above the ground.

Gabe, darling, wake up. They're here.

'Eli?' he mumbled, as he woke. 'D'you hear something?'

In the three days since the lawyer and his ill-equipped, over-confident muscle had driven onto Gabriel's land, the ex-SAS man had been preparing.

A selection of single-shot, semi-automatic and assault rifles now lay in strategic positions around his property. In the house. The outbuildings. And in a hide he'd constructed from fallen branches and camouflaged with palm leaves. Other, more – *intense*, he thought might be a good word – defensive materiel could be brought into play, too. Should the situation demand.

Guns were useless without ammunition, of course. And in the early days of his new life in Honduras, Gabriel had spent time and money acquiring enough to withstand a small siege. He'd become, if not friends, then at least trusting partners with an arms dealer in Teguz named Óscar Ramirez.

For a long time now, sleep had stopped being a safe place for Gabriel. It came, when it did, in short bursts rather than night-long slumbers. Punctuated, still, by blood-soaked nightmares that left him drenched in his own, stinking night-sweat and screaming into the dark.

But one thing he had retained from his days in uniform was the ability to sleep anywhere. Swamps. Jungles. Deserts. Mountains. Didn't matter. So on each evening since the visit, he'd taken up a different watch position. Night-vision goggles by his side and at least one long gun plus a nine.

The SIG Sauer P226 had always been his favourite in the Regiment. He'd carried one on many missions for the now-defunct Department, the government black ops outfit run by his old CO Don Webster. He carried one still. Not around Santa Rosa. But for trips to Teguz, he felt it prudent.

His dead wife's form shimmered just at the edge of his vision. He kept his head still. No point turning to look at her. She'd just disappear. Like always. Mainly these days what he caught was that old, familiar scent of hers. Sandalwood and lemon.

'She' hadn't heard anything. But his subconscious sometimes liked to tease him by adopting her voice during the night. Waking him with warnings. Screams. Or just murmured endearments that would leave him unmanned and sobbing as her ghost flicked off like a burned-out bulb.

He closed his eyes and pushed his awareness out into the night. There it was. Below the high-pitched chitter of a million insects. The hooting calls of monkeys. The incessant creaking of frogs. The occasional throaty cough of a prowling jaguar.

He heard it.

A vehicle. No. Two vehicles. Large capacity engines kept under control with a feathered throttle. Heavy, too, to judge from the crackle and squish of vegetation crushed under big wheels and fat, heavy-treaded tyres.

The spectre of Eli's perfume was replaced by the gasoline top notes of exhaust fumes.

He took a breath. Slowed his pulse, which had ticked up to ninety. And lowered the night-vision goggles over his eyes. These were in a different league to the sets he and his comrades had used in the Regiment. Óscar had explained they'd been destined for a US infantry battalion. Until – the man had offered a shrug – 'You know, supply-chain disruption'.

One fewer pair of enhanced night-vision goggles wouldn't hurt Uncle Sam, but they gave Gabriel a profound sense of security now.

The old green glow was a thing of the past. In its place, softly flaring orange outlines for solid objects and bright turquoise for anything emitting a heat signature, from a bullet to a car engine.

He sighted through the scope of the rifle that he'd propped in the crook of the branches and cushioned on an old maize sack filled with sand from the beach.

Here they came. Two lumbering 4x4s, crashing through the brush on the edge of his land, flattening more crops, snapping stems, crushing fruits into pulp.

He ran a quick combat appreciation. Say six men per truck. Enemy force of twelve. They came to a simultaneous stop in the middle of a stand of mango trees. Turquoise plumes of exhaust smoke, orange at their point of origin, curled upwards through the branches.

The truck's outlines shimmered and shifted as Gabriel turned his head. Behind them, the trees and the sea beyond were also outlined, though the limited field of vision meant the horizon faded away to black on each side.

No moon.

That was in his favour. They'd be confident they couldn't be seen.

The doors opened and out they came. He counted the bizarre, cartoon-like outlines forming up between the SUVs. He'd been out by two. Ten enemy fighters. Each man toting an assault rifle. Hard to tell exactly which model, but not AK-47s with their distinctive curved magazines and ugly wooden forestocks. Some kind of AR-15 variants probably. He assumed fully automatic.

Immediate combat priority; defend his land, take out the enemy. Longer term, find the lawyer. He ground his teeth together, so that his bunching jaw muscles strained against the strap of the helmet.

Lawyers were bag carriers. They didn't make absurdly high financial offers on a whim. They made them because someone told them to. Nor did they launch night-time attacks on unprotected farmers because they'd watched everything worth watching on Netflix. They launched them because someone told them to. Their clients.

So. Deal with the insurgents first. Then find the lawyer. Extract from him the name of his client and then close this down once and for all.

At ground level, nine of the men were gathered in a semi-circle around a tenth. The squad commander.

A man about to become fully acquainted with the pressures of command.

7

Gabriel levelled his rifle.

There had been a time when he'd believed in a fair fight.

Not in parity of numbers. He was schooled in the doctrine of overwhelming force. But his military training had laid great emphasis on the Law of War. There were rules that governed conflict, and honourable men stuck to them.

But men who drove onto his land in the middle of the night, carrying automatic weapons? They'd made it plain by their actions that they had no more interest in a fair fight than he did.

Or were they here to replant the land the lawyer and his goon had churned up four days earlier? Tidy up the mess they'd made? Leave the farmer with his crops restored and his prosperity assured? A latter-day barn-raising type of thing?

Stranger things had happened. Just not in Honduras.

He squeezed the trigger.

Even with the suppressor, the rifle made one hell of a crack in the still of the night. The butt dug back into his shoulder and made his ears ring.

The target's ears weren't ringing at all. Mainly on account of them currently flying in roughly opposite directions, propelled outwards by an exploding cloud of brain tissue and several pints of vaporised blood. The lifeless corpse remained standing for another couple of seconds before toppling sideways.

Rendered in orange outlines, the scene took on a surreal air as his men scattered, diving for the ground, levelling their weapons and firing indiscriminately.

Not well trained, then. At least four burned through their magazines in the first few seconds. Two of them died where they lay, fumbling to reload as Gabriel shot them cleanly through the head.

He worked the bolt with practised fingers, muscle-memory still in perfect battle order.

But now he'd given his position away and some of the others were returning fire.

Time to move.

He slithered down from his sniper nest and moved across the ground, keeping low, and snaking between the maize, which was already waist-high.

Someone had stepped up to the command role. He was bellowing orders in a panicked shout in which Gabriel detected the rough edge of city-accented Honduran Spanish. Teguz gangbangers, then. Or their counterparts from that other inexhaustible source of violent young men, San Pedro Sula.

Gabriel heard the whine of a set of night-vision goggles being turned on. One set between ten? It hardly seemed fair.

The remaining insurgents spread out. One immediately flew skywards, in several large, ragged pieces, as he stepped on an IED set between rows of maize. More shouts, and screams as the noise of the explosion echoed off the nearby hills.

From beneath a tarpaulin he'd hand-painted in a camouflage pattern that perfectly mimicked the local vegetation, Gabriel pulled out a squat, green tube about the thickness of a man's thigh. He depressed a switch and pulled a lever. The tube extended until it was just over a metre and a half long.

He raised it to his shoulder and sighted on the nearest SUV's grille.

Depressed the trigger.

The rocket-propelled grenade streaked away, trailing a plume of white smoke, tinted turquoise by the ENVG-B's electronics.

The projectile slammed into the engine compartment and detonated with a deafening roar. Even through his squeezed-shut eyelids the explosion was bright as the sun. The shockwave knocked him off his feet. He landed on his back with a thump that temporarily winded him.

He opened his eyes. But something was wrong. He was blind. Shit. The ENVG-B's imaging software must've been fried by the explosion. He ripped the helmet off and tossed it aside. Ten grand's worth of high-tech military-spec hardware reduced to a conversation piece.

The SUV was ablaze, yellow and green flames twining through the dark like mating snakes. Sparks jetted out and fire spurted as different reservoirs of liquid burst from the heat, sending their contents flaming out in puffs of brilliant pink, cobalt and scarlet.

Gabriel yelled a command in guttural city-accented Spanish.

'De vuelta al camión!'

Back to the truck.

From his belt he unclipped an M67 fragmentation grenade. Pulled the pin, keeping the spoon in place with his thumb, and wedged it, just, under the front tyre. He retreated to the cover of the trees and waited.

The first man to arrive yanked open the door and hauled himself in. Two more followed. The first man started the engine and screamed for the remaining fighters to *'Muévanse, hijos de puta!'*

The only thing that moved, though, wasn't the motherfuckers still outside the cabin, but the SUV itself. Under the torque from the engine as he revved it hard, the big vehicle shifted by a couple of millimetres. Not enough to trouble a fit and agile fighter climbing in. But more than enough to dislodge a thin strip of metal standing between a detonator and an explosive charge.

Gabriel flattened himself to the ground and counted.

One, insurgent...

Two, insurgent…
Three, insurgent…
F—

The three men inside the SUV were killed outright as the 180 grammes of Composition B explosive shredded everything from the floor pan upwards.

Razor-edged shards of the grenade's steel casing spun outwards from the epicentre of the detonation. One of the insurgents screamed, dropped his rifle and clutched his right eye.

No need for high-tech military night-vision tech when your target stood silhouetted in the flames from two burning SUVs. Gabriel shot him centre-mass with a burst from a Colt M4 assault rifle that cut him in half.

From behind him, automatic gunfire. Bullets spraying in his direction. Pain lanced across his face and his nostrils filled with the sickening, burnt steak-fat stink of human flesh seared by a red-hot rifle round.

He clapped a hand to his cheekbone and ran for cover, heading away from the house.

8

The two remaining enemy fighters were swearing in the rough barrio dialect of Teguz.

Silence would have been the smarter strategy.

As it was, Gabriel didn't need the night-vision goggles to locate them. His ears would lead him straight to them.

A burst of automatic gunfire shredded the tops of a row of maize. The fattening heads of corn dropped like miniature bodies to the packed red earth. From a leather sheath on his right hip, Gabriel drew a knife. Not the agricultural weapon he'd used on the goon earlier in the week. A Fairbairn–Sykes fighting knife. Spearpoint blade with two cutting edges and a slim grippy handle.

In the flames from the burning trucks, a man stood perfectly silhouetted. He was swinging his assault rifle in a rapid semicircle.

Gabriel crept up behind him, not needing to worry about the sound of his boots, given the loud crackling and popping as the flames devoured the last two men's ride home.

He stabbed the soldier in the neck and jerked the blade down from jaw to collar bone. Blood jetted out, sizzling as it hit the red-hot metal sides of the flaming SUV. It was a killing blow, but

Gabriel punched the wicked little blade into his heart, liver and lungs anyway.

He turned just in time to see the remaining fighter levelling the barrel of his rifle. His face was spattered with his comrades' blood, glowing demonically in the firelight. White teeth gleamed from the scarlet, giving his face the look of a peeled skull.

Gabriel dived to his left as the guy roared in rage and opened up. Red-hot rounds spat from the muzzle, streaking towards Gabriel as the muzzle-flash underlit the shooter's face in a yellow strobe.

His left hip jerked round, throwing him off course as he scrambled round to the far side of the burning SUV. A bullet. Correction. *Another* bullet. He'd be visiting the sawbones in Bonito for a dressing at the very least, if not an extraction.

'Come back, motherfucker!' the last man standing yelled. 'I'm gonna cut your balls off and make you eat them before I kill you.'

Gabriel headed off down a narrow track, tripping over a branch as he went and swearing loudly.

Behind him, the remaining goon shouted in triumph. Heavy military boots crashed through the stiff stems of the crops, outlining his progress as he chased Gabriel down.

Gabriel took a bend in the path at speed only to find himself in a natural trap. Boulders blocked the path and thick, thorny scrub to either side would prevent even a tapir from breaking through.

His pursuer rounded the bend seconds later.

As he took in Gabriel's plight, he leered, revealing gold teeth.

'Not so fucking clever, now, are you, motherfucker?'

He raised his rifle.

'Just so's you know, I'm gonna do you slow – Sula-style – and film it for my boss, you fuck.'

He took another step forward.

Then he somersaulted upwards, rifle spiralling off into the thorn bushes.

Gabriel took his foot off the spring-plate that had triggered the simple loop-trap attached to a two-year-old mango sapling, and strolled over to where the disarmed merc now dangled from a couple of metres of rope.

Now who was so fucking clever?

He prodded him in the chest, setting him swinging.

On each return swing Gabriel shoved him again, harder, until the man was describing great, looping arcs between the trees.

From the man's lips, a stream of invective poured forth. Oaths familial, scatological, sexual, bestial, Biblical, and sometimes a combination of all five.

It was admirable, really, that a man, no more than a hired gun, could maintain such bravado, such aggression. His weapon was lost in the undergrowth. His comrades, if one could glorify a merely financial relationship with such a time-honoured word, lay dead. And his means of escape sat on burst rubber – engines, transmissions, control systems blown seven ways from Sunday.

Maybe he did it for love.

He swung forwards.

Gabriel hit him, hard.

The crack as his nose broke was audible in the still night air.

He screamed. Blood bubbled from his inverted nostrils. He coughed violently, spraying more red into the air. The swearing stopped. Hard to keep up the verbals when to open your mouth was to find it full of your own blood.

'You'll drown like that,' Gabriel said, steadying him by his shoulders. 'Two minutes, tops, I'd have thought.'

'Let me go.'

'Why?'

'Motherfucker! You have no idea who you're dealing with.'

Gabriel hit him again, over the site of the previous injury. The shriek of pain set off a pair of howler monkeys in a nearby tree. Ignoring their ear-splitting hooting, Gabriel leaned closer.

'More like thirty seconds, now. So, tell me, who *am* I dealing with?'

'He'll kill me if I tell you.'

'Yeah, but I'll kill you if you don't.' Gabriel tilted his head to one side. 'It's a toughie.'

'Fuck you, man. Fuck you!'

The upside-down mercenary spat blood at Gabriel.

Gabriel frowned.

Then he smiled.

'I respect your decision.'

He drew his knife.

'No, man, don't!'

'Then start talking.'

'OK, OK! So, there's a guy in Sula. A gringo. I don't know his real name. He goes by—' The man used a Spanish word Gabriel had to think about for a second. '*El Caiman.*' The Alligator. Original, he'd give him that. Another Spanish moniker floated down over the years to him. *El Bautista*. The Baptist. A cartel boss who'd enjoyed murdering his enemies by drowning. In a bathtub containing a few inches of water.

'And who hired The Alligator?'

'I don't know, man, I swear! Like, that's way above my pay grade. I just get paid to come out here, fuck up your farm and rub you out, you know? That's it.'

'That's it?'

'Yeah, man.'

'You don't seem very sorry about it.'

Gabriel wasn't sure, given his prisoner's inverted position, but he thought the guy shrugged.

'It's a job. Nothing more. So, you gonna let me go, or kill me? Because, tell the truth? I'm getting a headache hangin' upside down like this.'

And there it was. That particularly Honduran brand of macho. Balls the size of melons and sarcastic humour to go with.

Gabriel stepped in closer, and raised the knife.

The melons shrank to kumquats.

'No, man. No! Please. I—'

Gabriel reached up and grabbed the man's ankle. And, over his screams of protest, sliced through the rope suspending him over the ground.

The landing was a rough one. A face-plant. The third insult to his face brought forth an agonised moan that subsided to a bubbling cry.

Gabriel knelt by his side and gently lifted his head, turning it sideways so the blood would soak away into the leaf-litter, and not form a puddle in which he would, actually, drown.

He leaned down and murmured into the man's ear.

'I'm coming back in five minutes. If you're still here, I'll kill you. Slowly.'

9

He knew it was a risk.

Letting his man go like that.

But, however distant his sense of honour had become these last years, killing a prisoner was still a line he couldn't – wouldn't – cross.

Gabriel didn't think the man he'd let go would try for one, final, death-or-glory assault on the farm. He'd seen nine of his friends – well, co-workers was probably a more accurate term – killed by a target his employer had probably described as 'some gringo motherfucker'. Gabriel doubted the payday was big enough to compensate for a suicide mission.

More to the point, it wasn't the merc he was interested in. Now that the immediate threat had been neutralised, it was time to think.

Because in situations like this one, there was always a question. Who?

Who wanted the land around Santa Rosa so badly they were prepared to pay such an insane sum of money? Who would hire some fancy-dress Texan lawyer to make the initial approach? And who, when that failed, would resort to a bunch of gangbangers masquerading as trained fighters?

First things first. Two gunshot wounds to deal with.

He stripped off and stood in front of the pockmarked mirror in the little bathroom. Gingerly touched the flap of skin on his cheekbone. Turned out it was only glued in place by a clot of blood. Under Gabriel's gentle probing it unpeeled itself. A fifty-pence piece-sized patch of raw pink flesh opened up. He winced.

How about the wound to his side? The round that had spun him halfway round? He turned sideways on. The bullet had entered above his hip bone. His side was a mess. Bloodied and streaked with gore that his gear had smeared from hip to ribs. He rotated further and twisted his head over his shoulder, searching for an exit wound.

None present.

Shit.

So, somewhere in there, nestling among his organs, muscles and connective tissue, the blood vessels, nerves and sinews, lay like a toxic little lead parasite in its copper sheath.

He couldn't feel the pain. Not yet. Funny how the best cartel product could only imitate what the body could produce naturally when circumstances demanded.

You want that invincible feeling a good bump of prime Colombian coke delivers. Try adrenaline. Yours courtesy of two little blobs of tissues atop your kidneys weighing no more than a couple of ounces each. How about the blissful release from pain delivered by our old friend heroin? Yes, you could pay thirty dollars on the street in Teguz for a point-one gram baggie. Maybe get an unordered side of caffeine, laundry detergent or (if you're really unlucky) rat poison. Or just rely on your body's own bliss drugs: enkephalins and endorphins, manufactured deep in your brain by a pea-sized gland called the pituitary.

Right now, all that natural biochemistry was doing a fine job of shielding Gabriel from the effects of machine-gun rounds fired at close range at his soft tissue. But he didn't have long.

He called Pera.

'Oh my god, Gabe! Please tell me you're OK? We heard the shooting, all the explosions. Everyone was too scared to go out on the street.'

'I'm fine. And you did the right thing. Whoever's trying to buy us out of our land sent men to try and kill me.'

'And are they…? I mean, did you…?'

'They're all dead. Well, all but one. I let him go. Listen, I need a bit of first aid. Can you come over?'

'Stay there.'

The line went dead.

Gabriel had been friends with Pera – full name Esperanza – almost from the first day he'd arrived in Santa Rosa.

She was a kind soul with a big heart and would have helped a stranger, let alone a friend. But then he'd rescued her son from a local gang. And helped her make a long-wished-for career move from her old job, working in a brothel, to running a street food business out of a converted VW campervan. Now she would walk over broken glass for him. It was embarrassing. But he had so few friends left in the world that he gratefully accepted her loyalty.

While he waited for Pera, Gabriel put on a pair of low-waisted track pants. As the adrenaline left his system, the pain from the bullet wound in his side announced its presence via a series of sharp stabs that seemed to emanate from deep inside him. He kept his breathing shallow.

Damage assessment: well, he was breathing and although blood was oozing from the wound, it wasn't flowing, or worse, jetting, so no major blood vessels hit. Something of a miracle, but maybe he was due some luck. And the mess the first round had made of his face needed cleaning up. While *in extremis* he could do it himself, on balance he thought he'd prefer not to indulge in any regiment-style self-doctoring tonight, thank you very much.

He fetched his first-aid kit and unpeeled a dressing which he clamped over the entry wound.

From the other side of the wooden front door, Pera called out.

'Gabe! It's me. Don't shoot!'

She knew where he kept a key. Until recently he'd never

dreamed of locking his door. It was hardly as though he had anything worth stealing. Or nothing visible, anyway.

Yes, OK, there was a reinforced basement with enough weapons and materiel to start a small war. The recently dead gangbangers would attest to that. But try entering that little Aladdin's cave without knowing the security protocols and you'd be leaving the house as nothing more than a soul, if you believed in such things. Or, if not, a briefly lingering aroma of blood and tissue. Remnants of which would be bleached, bagged, buried or burnt.

Most of his neighbours felt the same way. But in the last couple of weeks, most had reluctantly begun using, or, maybe for the first time in their lives, installing, locks.

His now turned with a well-oiled click.

Pera rushed through the doorway, her face taut with worry.

She took one look at his face and compressed her lips.

'Those bastards! I hope they suffered before they died. Stay there.'

Gabriel had to smile, despite the pain, as she improvised a field hospital in his kitchen. From her woven rush bag, bright with red and green decorative strands, she took out disinfectant, dressings, a little black leather tool-roll and another smaller bag that rattled with pill bottles.

In a small agricultural community like theirs, people couldn't always afford to get medical attention from a doctor, always assuming they were in a fit state to make the trip to Bonito. Most people had rudimentary first-aid expertise. Some, like Pera, had made it their business to acquire a lot more. It worked for everyone, and meant that, in the phrase 'first aid', the word 'first' was doing a lot of work.

After scrubbing her hands for a good minute with hot water and soap, Pera dragged a stool over and sat facing Gabriel.

'What have we got? Apart from your face, I mean.'

He gestured to the dressing stuck over the hole in his side.

'There's a bullet inside me.'

She pursed her lips. 'It's bad?'

'Not sure.'

'I need to look.'

He nodded. Anticipating the pain. Because looking was where such interactions started. But never where they finished. After the looking came the probing. Then the pushing in of forceps, the groping blindly. The gripping. And, finally, the pulling.

Using the very edges of her fingernails, she pincered the edge of the dressing up and then peeled it away, discarding it in a bin she'd brought over from the sink.

Blood oozed from the wound, which was already blackening as the blood coagulated.

She leaned closer to his abdomen and very gently placed her ear, then her lips against the bruised skin. It was a curiously intimate gesture. They'd never been to bed together, except to sleep. But he felt with Pera he could be completely trusting, physically. In some ways, in *important* ways, what they had transcended sex.

'The skin's not hot. And I can't feel anything pulsing. You might be the luckiest man alive, Gabe. Looks like there's no internal bleeding.'

'Do I need to go into Bonito?'

She shrugged. 'Do you want to? The road's gotten a lot worse recently.'

'Not if I don't have to.'

She nodded. Offered him an appraising look.

'You have any morphine?'

'Sadly, no.'

'Pity,' was all she said.

Between them, they prepared.

He lay on his bed, after Pera spread out a clean white towel and covering top sheet.

She angled his bedside reading lamp so its conical steel shade directed the light at his side.

She placed a folded leather belt between his teeth.

He closed his eyes and silently began reciting the mantra

against pain his old mentor, Master Zhao had taught him a lifetime ago in Hong Kong.

Pain passes like clouds on a windy day.

Pain passes...

Pera took a pair of stainless-steel artery forceps from her medical kit and set them in a pan of water which she heated on the stove.

When her instruments were all sterilised, Pera took up the forceps. She leaned closer. Angled the blunt nose towards the clotted and blackened entry wound in Gabriel's side.

'I'm sorry, Gabe,' she said.

He forced himself to focus on the mantra, reciting it mentally, louder and louder, visualising the old, familiar words as soft blue neon writing.

And then she began.

10

Outside the house, hunting for its dinner, an ocelot paused by the seaward side of the house.

Barely larger than a domestic cat, the predator stilled its left forepaw mid-stride, its spotted and banded body quivering. The muffled scream from within sent it trotting away, into deep cover.

So much for mantras.

Gabriel felt keenly the impact of too much alcohol on his former talents for the eastern mysticism instilled in him by Master Zhao. Too late now.

As the forceps nosed their way into his side, he screamed again, driving his back teeth deeper into the leather.

It was like being shot all over again. Only this time, without the adrenaline of combat to numb the pain. He felt every nerve ending firing as Pera probed the wound track with the forceps. White-hot spears of agony tunnelled out from his hip through his viscera and into all four limbs. Why couldn't he succumb and pass out? Leave Pera to her bloody work in peace?

'Sorry, Gabe,' she muttered. Then, '*Madre de Dios!*'

He caught an unusual angle to her elbow as she guided the forceps deeper. He grunted in pain and his jaw cracked as his overstressed molars dug deep into the leather strap, so deep he tasted it, and the coppery tang of his own blood. Must have caught the inside of his cheek.

Something felt wrong inside of him. A strong pulse. He pictured hot scarlet blood hosing out of his side. Too reminiscent of battlefield injuries he'd witnessed up close in firefights from Iraq to Congo. Maybe he was going to die. That wouldn't be so bad. Not really. He'd be with Eli again. With Britta. With Mum and Dad.

Then a great black wave of agony rolled over him making him gag, and fearing he might vomit and drown himself in his own waste. His vision telescoped down to a small black circle and he moaned as razor wire flew out from the centre of his belly and encircled him in its slicing, stabbing steel thorns.

He felt a sucking pressure inside him. Then Pera swore, loudly. '*Hijo de puta!*'

A metallic tap and a clink. He rolled his head to the side. Pera had just dropped something – the bullet – into the small copper saucepan she'd placed at his side.

'I got it, Gabe,' she said. 'I'm gonna pack the wound then sew you up. It'll hurt some, but not as much.'

'Go for it,' he said, around the leather gag. His teeth were embedded so deeply it felt a part of his mouth, like a grotesque extra tongue.

The discomfort from the stitches was insignificant after the ripping pain of the extraction. Wasp stings.

Some time later, Pera nodded.

'We're done. Don't move. I need to clean you up.'

Jaw muscles creaking with the effort, he opened his mouth, and Pera peeled the leather strap away from his teeth.

'My god, Gabe, you almost bit it in half.'

'Could I have some water, please?'

'Of course. Hold on.'

She fetched a glass from the kitchen and cradled his head while he took a mouthful of the wonderfully cold water. He half-expected to see a jet of it spurting from his side like a cartoon cat full of holes. But it stayed where it was supposed to.

As Pera sponged more cold water over his side, he hoisted himself up onto his elbows and craned his neck to take his first look at Pera's handiwork. The wound wasn't large. Maybe half an inch in diameter. He counted five small, neat sutures in spidery black thread.

'You were lucky, Gabe,' she said as she patted his skin dry, making him wince. 'To be shot there and only get a flesh wound. You could have been killed.'

'Show me the bullet, would you,' he said, thinking the same thing.

Those mercs had been shooting M4s or something similar. That meant 5.56 mm NATO rounds. Capable of inflicting all kinds of damage from cavitation – huge pressure wave-generated cavities inside the body – to broken bones and pulped organs.

She handed it to him. A 9mm ball round. He'd been lucky. Whoever had shot him had been using a pistol. And now he looked closer, he saw the way the nose of the round had been deformed. It had hit something else before burying itself in his gut.

'You're going to need painkillers,' Pera said. 'Strong ones. And antibiotics to stop any infection.'

'I'll visit the doctor in Bonito in the morning.'

Pera's eyes widened, before she narrowed them at him.

'Oh, yes, of course you can! And you can split yourself open when that crappy old truck of yours hits a pothole on the road. I know, let me save you the trouble. I can shoot you myself and do the job properly this time.'

And then, without warning, she burst into tears.

Gabriel tried to push himself into a seated position but let out an involuntary yelp as something pulled inside him. He lay back down but held his right arm out wide.

'Hey, come here.'

She sat on the bed and then swung her legs up before cuddling alongside him.

'I thought you were dead, Gabe,' she said through her tears. 'When I heard all the gunfire. And then when you called and I saw that hole in your side. I didn't know if I could save you.'

He turned his head so he could look into her soft brown eyes, reddened now from crying.

'Well you did. And I am very grateful. Who knew a food cart lady could perform battlefield surgery?'

She laughed and sobbed at the same time. This brought forth a bout of hiccupping and then a violent sneeze.

'You live in Honduras long enough, especially working in a place like Frida's, you learn all kinds of useful skills.'

He smiled. Tried to reply but heard only nonsense-words coming from him. Fatigue settled over him like a weighted blanket. He closed his eyes.

Sunlight woke him. He checked the time. It was 2:45 p.m. He'd slept for almost twelve hours. No dreams, either. Just a blank between comforting Pera and now.

He hauled himself out of bed, wincing at the pain in his side and made for the bathroom. After relieving himself, he walked carefully into the kitchen and set the kettle to boil on the stove.

He took his coffee out onto the veranda and sat facing the Caribbean. Why had they come? He took a sip of the coffee. Not the mercs. That was obvious. The lawyer, Lorne, was it? He'd sent them. No, why had the lawyer and his driver come?

The land around Santa Rosa wasn't worthless. It was good, fertile soil, perfect for growing all kinds of cash crops as well as the staples the villagers relied upon. But it wasn't development land. Nobody would want to build a factory here, or a road.

He supposed a gajillionaire *might* conceive of building some kind of gated estate on the Caribbean coast. But in Honduras? Why not Costa Rica? Jamaica? Any one of a dozen safer places?

So if it wasn't the land itself they wanted, what else? One answer presented itself immediately. The sea. They wanted access to Honduras via the sea. For a coup? It was too far-fetched even to consider. The most likely source of anti-government sentiment was right here in the country. The cartels or the army. They were already here so why plan a seaborne assault? Honduras' neighbours, El Salvador and Nicaragua, could both mount attacks across their land borders.

But if a seaborne assault *was* the aim, why not land on the south coast? That convoluted hundred-mile stretch of coastline between El Salvador to the north and Nicaragua to the south offered a shorter distance to Teguz. Along better roads, too.

A high-pitched voice derailed his train of thought.

'Mister? Sorry, mister, but have you seen Rico?'

He turned. The owner of the voice was a small boy of maybe seven or eight. Straight black hair in an untidy fringe that drooped over wide, round, deep-brown eyes. He wore denim cut-offs and a Honduran national soccer team shirt about three sizes too big for him. He looked anxious.

'Who's Rico? Your friend? Your brother?'

The kid shook his head.

'My dog. He's missing.'

Gabriel shook his head. People did keep dogs as pets out here in the boonies, but the relationships could be best be described as casual. The canines, almost always mutts, came and went as they pleased, roaming free in spontaneous packs, returning home if the pickings were slim or the fun had run out.

'I haven't seen any dogs, I'm sorry. But I'll keep an eye out. What does he look like? Is he big, small?'

The boy swiped a hand under his nose and blinked fiercely, trying not to cry. *Machismo* was still a thriving masculine ideal in Honduras and they learned it young.

'He's little. Caramel and white. Kind of scruffy. He has a lovely face.'

Gabriel nodded, smiled what he hoped was reassurance.

'OK, well, I'll look out for Rico. Where can I find you if I see him?'

'I live over the cafe in the village. My mum runs it.'

He turned and ran off without another word, already calling out his dog's name.

Gabriel returned to contemplating the ocean. The dog would turn up. They usually did.

He took another mouthful of coffee. Watched a twenty or thirty-strong flock of pelicans swoop low over the water.

No. Not a coup. Nor some half-arsed Bay of Pigs-style plot involving deniable CIA-backed assets. The Americans maintained a small military presence at Soto Cano Air Base near Comayagua. And if Government spokespeople were to be believed, Honduras and the US enjoyed cordial relations extending to the latter being the former's main trading partner.

A couple of the pelicans had come up onto the beach and were clacking their beaks together in what Gabriel assumed was a mating display. Behind them, unseen, a small crocodile crept closer, its belly leaving smooth curves of swept sand in its wake.

One of the pelicans, its beak pouch flaring red, caught sight of the approaching predator and squawked in alarm before waddling away and slowly gaining enough speed to take off. Its mate followed, both of them clapping the air with their wings as the croc was left lunchless.

Gabriel stared after them. His forehead crinkled as he groped for the thought their rapid flight from the beach had spawned.

Lorne Packard's client didn't want Santa Rosa as somewhere to land people *from* the sea. He wanted it as a base for them to get *to* the sea.

He shaded his eyes against the sun, which was throwing bright-white reflections of the water into his face.

Something out there was worth killing for.

11

The following day, as Gabriel sat on his veranda, drinking coffee, nursing his wounds and pondering why some rich gringo wanted a secure base on the Honduran coast, a set of tin wind chimes he'd rigged to a loose floorboard tinkled.

He slipped a hand beneath the cotton blanket Pera had draped around his shoulders before going out for groceries. His fingers closed around the butt of his pistol.

He tensed. His injured side protested, but not nearly as much as his head would if a returning hitter put a bullet between his ears. He glanced at a shard of mirror he'd embedded in a wooden post at the corner of the veranda and relaxed, uncurling his fingers and letting the pistol lie in its hiding place.

'Good morning.' He called her *abuelita* – 'little grandmother' – a respectful term for any older woman. 'What can I do for you?'

The elderly lady who rounded the corner of the house and came to stand in front of him might have been seventy or a hundred. It was impossible to tell. The sun and, to judge from the vile-smelling roll-up between her lips, tobacco mixed with homegrown cannabis, had tanned her skin to the colour and texture of well-worn saddle-leather. Startling green eyes, as clear as a twenty-year-old's, twinkled from deeply creased lids.

'Not going to invite an old lady to sit? To offer a coffee? Or a *guifiti*?'

Gabriel smiled.

'Of course! Where are my manners? Coffee, then. I don't keep spirits in the house anymore.'

She looked down at him, those emerald eyes narrowing.

'There are plenty of spirits in this house, Gabriel Wolfe. People you lost but cannot let go.'

Gabriel's belly flipped. 'What do you mean?'

She grinned, revealing gappy front teeth the colour of burnt sugar cane, and tapped the side of her nose. Chuckled. A liquid sound that conjured up visions of lungs clogged with God-knew-what foul substances.

'You know already. I'll have a coffee. Strong. Lots of sugar. And something to eat. I'm hungry.'

Placing a worn carpet bag on the boards, she settled herself in the other chair, a beaten-up rocker. Took a deep drag on her homemade cigarette and blew a perfect smoke ring. Despite the warmth of the day she gathered the many layers of bright, woven shawls about her bony shoulders.

Wondering at the identity of his houseguest, and her reason for visiting him, Gabriel went inside to prepare coffee. Her unsettling remark about the spirits in his house suggested one possibility. She was a *curandera*, a healer. He'd read widely about his adoptive home since arriving the previous year. And of particular interest had been *curanderismo*, the system of traditional healing still practiced in rural areas and, if you knew where to look, urban centres too.

Perhaps because of his own unorthodox upbringing under the tutelage of Master Zhao, he didn't have the knee-jerk rejection of matters spiritual that many Westerners had. His old mentor had taught him to disappear from someone's conscious awareness so he could come right up to them and steal their wallet – or gun – without them noticing. To enter a state of deep meditation-induced calm that enabled him to withstand extreme pain – which recent events seemed to have shown he'd lost. And to respect the lives and the souls of all who had gone before him. He sometimes wondered if that was what lay at the root of his visions of dead comrades and lovers.

He tipped five spoons of unrefined cane sugar into the tiny coffee cup and stirred the sludgy liquid until he could no longer feel the grains through the tip of the teaspoon. He placed some small biscuits flavoured with honey on a plate and took it all out to the veranda.

The old woman nodded her appreciation and took a sip of the coffee. Gabriel looked on anxiously. Had he over-sweetened it? Would she spit it out like so much tobacco juice?

She favoured him with another grin, revealing those snaggled teeth.

'Not bad for a gringo.' She picked up a biscuit between thumb and forefinger and examined it. 'Who made these? Your girlfriend?'

'I don't have a girlfriend, *Abuelita*. I made them myself.'

She took a bite, closed her eyes and inhaled noisily through her nose before fixing him with a bright-green stare.

'Very good. Why no girlfriend?'

He shrugged as he lowered himself into his own chair and finished what was left of his coffee.

'I'm not in a romantic place, right now.'

She surprised him by shooting out a hand and grasping his in a tough, wiry grip. She pulled herself forwards until they were sitting knee-to-knee, and stared deep into his eyes.

'What was her name?'

A chill rippled across him, despite the heat of the day.

'Whose name?' he asked, knowing full well what the *curandera* meant.

'Your wife.'

He swallowed. 'Eli.'

She nodded. Sipped her coffee. Took another drag on her cigarette and blew the smoke out of the side of her mouth.

'Eli. Pretty name. She was a soldier like you?'

He'd fallen under her spell. No sense asking her how she knew these things. Maybe she'd heard about his skirmish with the mercs the other night. Of course! That was it. The whole village had heard it with their own ears. Who but an ex-soldier could pull off something like that?

'She was.'

'You love her very much.'

Present tense. Interesting.

'I do.'

'You think she wants you to be unhappy?'

He felt his temper rise out of nowhere like a summer storm, or a squall spinning up out of a calm sky over the ocean.

'Why are you here, *Abuelita*?' he asked, trying and mainly succeeding to keep the edge from his voice.

'You are hurt.'

He nodded. 'Someone shot me.'

'I know. And we'll deal with that in a minute or two. But you also have *susto*. You have it bad.'

'*Susto?*'

'An illness of the spirit. You are sad. I see it in your eyes. In how you carry yourself—'

'I just told you, I was shot.'

She ignored his interruption.

'You do not eat properly. You drink too much. Your eyes are dead, they have lost their spark. You do not dream, or if you do it is only to have nightmares. Your wife died and your spirit fled your body to escape your grief. Tell me, Gabriel Wolfe, am I wrong?'

He opened his mouth to protest, and then clopped it shut again. He knew what she was talking about. The *abuelita* called it *susto*. His old psychiatrist back in England would have called it depression.

He sighed.

'No, *Abuelita*, you are not wrong. But I am dealing with it in my own way.'

She pinched out the butt of her cigarette between thumb and forefinger and secreted it in the folds of her clothing.

'When you are ready to face your *susto*, come and find me. But for now, let me see your wound.'

Five minutes later, Gabriel was lying shirtless on his bed while the *curandera* bent over his torso and examined Pera's handiwork. He tried not to think about those nicotine-stained fingers touching such a fresh wound. He hoped fervently that Pera would arrive soon with the antibiotics.

'Pera is a good girl,' she pronounced. 'And she has done a good job here. Just like I taught her.'

Ah. Now he understood how the old woman had found her way to him. Maybe Pera had also shared a little of his history with her, too. No need for any *curanderia* spirit communication after all.

'She'll be back soon with medication,' he said, propping himself up on his elbows.

The old woman blew a raspberry.

'Fah! *Medication*.' She made it sound like he'd said, 'magic beans'.

Without another word, she hauled her carpet bag up onto the bed and unclipped the worn metal clasp. From its depths she produced a green stone mortar and pestle, and, incongruously, several Tupperware boxes. From the latter she extracted dried herbs and powders from them, mixing and grinding them into a paste with a little liquid from a vacuum flask. Finally, she chewed a little bunch of a fresh green herb for a few minutes and then spat the resultant green goo into the mortar.

Once it was mixed again, she used her fingers to spread the sticky green paste onto and around the entry wound. Gabriel flinched at the contact – the paste was cold – then relaxed as the expected pain failed to materialise. His nose twitched and he caught a strong scent of mint as the heat from his skin warmed the medicine.

'Turn onto your side,' she instructed him.

He did as she asked and felt her fingers massaging more of the paste into the soft flesh above his pelvis, roughly where the exit wound would have been if it had been a through-and-through.

Instead of hurting, the circular motion felt calming. Heat spread through his belly, relaxing him. He became aware of her voice, intoning a musical language he'd never heard before, maybe one of the many native languages still spoken in the Honduran hinterland. He smiled to himself. If she thought she could work some variant of Master Zhao's deep hypnosis on him, she'd reckoned without his own training.

'You can't kid a kidder,' he said to Eli, who was standing beside him on the beach outside his house, wearing a coral bikini, grains of sand sticking to her knees. Her lithe figure glowed a little in the noonday sun.

'She's right, Gabe,' Eli said, hands on her hips. 'I don't want you to be unhappy.'

'Who said I'm unhappy?' he said, grinning, pulling her to him.

'You're telling me you're not?'

He wanted to contradict her. To tell her he was fine. But when he opened his mouth to contradict her, those words wouldn't come.

'Oh, Jesus, Eli, I miss you so much,' he said instead. 'I wish I'd died on that shitty island instead of you.'

'Really?' Her eyes widened. 'You'd leave me a widow? Not very chivalrous.'

But her humour failed to make him smile. Instead, hot tears swelled behind his eyes and burst free. As he wept, she held him and he breathed in deep, inhaling that old familiar scent of lemon and sandalwood.

'What shall I do, Eli?' he gasped, freeing himself from her embrace enough to look into those grey-green eyes. 'I can't go on like this.'

'I know. You need to find your way, Gabe. Find your purpose.'

'The Department's gone. Everything turned to shit.'

'Not you, though, my honey, my soul. Not you! Find it. Find who you're supposed to be again. It was never about the Department. It was never about the Regiment, either.'

He opened his eyes. A ghostly afterimage of Eli floated in the room before him, her lips curved upwards into a tender smile. He touched his cheeks. They were wet.

He was alone. The *curandera* had left.

He swung his legs off the bed and sat up, tensing for the pain that would come as his stomach muscles clenched around the wound. But there was nothing. He looked down, half-expecting the stitches, and the hole itself, to have vanished. But no, they were still there, although the redness and puffiness had disappeared.

His eyes fell on a small tub of the green gloop sitting on his plain wooden dressing table. He rose from the bed and picked it up. A slip of brown paper lay beneath it, a translucent crescent marking it where some of the salve had transferred from the bottom of the tub.

It bore a short message in pencil.

Use when needed. Pay with peace. *Abuelita Leda.*

He supposed she meant peace for Santa Rosa. He'd do his best.

Footsteps sounded from the hallway.

Pulse racing, he grabbed his pistol.

12

Pera called out as she let herself into Gabriel's house.

'Gabe? It's me! I brought your medication. How are you feeling?'

He put the pistol down and had reached the door to the living room when she came in. Her eyes widened.

'What are you doing? You should be in bed, resting!'

He smiled at her and walked, steadily, but without pain, to the couch, where he sank into its collapsed but still comfortable springing.

'Did you send *Abuelita* Leda to see me?'

She frowned, two parallel grooves appearing each side of the bridge of her nose.

'*Abuelita* who?'

That was strange. Pera looked dumbfounded. But if it hadn't been her doing, how had the old woman known about Eli?

'Leda,' he repeated. 'She's a *curandera*. She was here earlier. Put some stuff on the wound, massaged me. I fell asleep. Now it doesn't hurt. I was sure you'd asked her to visit me.'

'Not guilty,' she said with a smile. 'But those people, Gabe? They have a gift, you know? Gringos don't believe in all that. Even in Teguz, they all want to be modern. They prefer this.' She held up the white paper bag of medication with its green cross and the name and address of the pharmacy in Bonito. 'But country people? They trust the *curanderos*. Not just for people, either. Livestock, too.'

He took the bag from her outstretched hand.

'I'll take this as well, but honestly, Pera, she really did work some magic on me. How much do I owe you?'

She shook her head. 'Nuh, uh. Nothing. It is my gift to you, although I wish I didn't have to.'

'Come on, Pera, medication like this isn't cheap. Let me pay you for it.'

She clapped a hand to her chest and widened her eyes comically.

'I am Esperanza Maria Sanchez Flores. An entrepreneur! CEO of Pera's Place mobile street food outlet. My business partner insults me by suggesting I am not successful enough to have the money to pay for some medication? Ha! I could buy and sell that *farmacia* ten times over!'

Gabriel laughed, which set off a twinge in his side. Typical Pera over-exaggeration, but he knew he'd have to concede the point. Her pride was at stake and he had no wish to hurt her feelings.

'I'm sorry, Pera. Of course you must pay and I am very grateful. Thank you.'

She grinned. Winked. 'Was that good? Did you like it? It wasn't too much?'

'Hilarious,' he deadpanned. 'But would you at least let me take you out for a coke?'

She pretended to think about it for a moment, staring up at the ceiling while tapping her lower lip, which she'd pooched out prettily.

'I suppose a coke would not be too insulting. Maybe I will even let you pay for some *buñuelos*.'

Now it was Gabriel's turn to pour on the mock scorn.

'Coke *and* mini doughnuts? You'll be back to Bonito to see the dentist!'

She rolled her eyes.

'I think I preferred you when you were wounded. Come on, let's go.'

Arm in arm, they walked up to the road and turned left towards the centre of the village. The temperature had climbed into the nineties and soon Gabriel was sweating, his shirt sticking to his skin. Ten minutes later, they reached the tree-shaded square that served as social hub, meeting place and venue for seemingly neverending chess tournaments among the older people. On the far side sat *Café Cielo Azul* – Blue Sky Cafe – its aluminium tables shaded by sun-faded umbrellas that might once have been azure and white.

They had just reached the centre of the small square when the roar of a stressed engine made them and everybody else present turn their heads towards the road entering from the east side.

A gleaming white SUV sped into the square, scattering chickens and small children who fled, squawking and screaming for the edges.

Gabriel instinctively reached for a sidearm that wasn't there. In his befuddled state after coming round from the *curandera*'s ministrations, he'd forgotten to bring one.

The SUV slowed, slewed in a sliding skid that brought the open passenger door round to face him and Pera. He pushed her to the ground and prepared to shield her from the bullets.

But no gunfire ensued.

The guy in the seat – black-clad, orange mirror shades, stubble – flung something straight out towards Gabriel. He swung away, flinching, before realising it was a dead animal. He caught ginger and white fur and a flash of white teeth and pink tongue as its mouth flopped open.

The door slammed, the SUV picked up speed and it slewed round before accelerating hard out of the square.

Beside him, Pera got to her feet, brushing grit off the palms of her hands.

She looked down at the carcass at their feet.

'*Madre de Dios*! What the fuck? Is that Rico? Oh no, it is! Hernando is going to be heartbroken.'

Gabriel squatted down. He raised the dead dog's head. It flopped unnaturally; someone had broken its neck. Its eyes were glazed and milky.

'Poor little boy,' he murmured.

He flashed on a moment almost ten years earlier when he'd received the news by phone that his own dog, Seamus, had been killed by a car. He swallowed hard as tears pricked at his eyes. He let them come.

Rico was wearing a simple collar of blue nylon rope. Gabriel frowned. Not really the style in Honduras. He rotated it, to see if it bore a name tag.

No tag. But there was a note, tucked through a couple of untwisted strands. He pulled it free and opened it.

Behind him, a cry went up. He recognised the voice. Hernando, Rico's owner. He stood and stepped back. In a blur of motion the little boy raced to his pet's side and squatted beside the inert body before picking it up and cradling it to his chest.

'Nooo!' he wailed. 'Rico, buddy, don't be dead! I love you.'

A plump woman in her late thirties came out from the cafe, drying her hands on a red and white tea towel. Her face was creased with concern. When she saw Hernando standing so forlornly with his dog's body in his arms she hurried forwards and squatted beside him, embracing both him and the dog in her strong bare arms.

She looked up at Gabriel.

'Who did this? Did you see?'

He shook his head.

'Two men in a white SUV—' He'd been about to say 'dumped him', but swerved the clumsy phrase at the last second – 'left him here.' He dropped his voice. 'I don't think they were from Roatán Rescue, either.'

Frowning, she got to her feet and ushered her son to the cafe, relieving him of Rico's floppy little corpse and carrying it with her free arm.

As soon as mother and son were safely inside, and the rumble of horrified chatter in the square had subsided to a buzz like a distant bee swarm, Gabriel read the note.

Email tpznx61b.foil@dyna.remail.com if you want to accept our offer. A month from now we will return and this time there'll be no money offered. Your village will be forfeit. For the greater good.

Pera looked up at him.

'What does it mean, Gabe? Forfeit?'

He knew only too well. He'd seen settlements 'forfeited' before. In places dusty with wind-blown sand, sweltering in year-round one hundred percent humidity, mountainous, below sea-level, wherever humans could gather to live together in relative peace until outsiders came. The results were always the same. And never pretty.

'It means I need to get reinforcements.'

13

Tech bros.

He wrinkled his nose. He hated the term. It conjured up completely the wrong image. Nerdy man-children on the spectrum who sounded off on social media and basically fucked society up the ass instead of using their immense wealth for good.

Not him, though. Not Xander Kalt. Xander Kalt was different. Xander Kalt was an unknown quantity. Oh sure, the editors of the finance papers knew his name. The *FT* in London, the *Wall Street Journal. Frankfurter Algemeine Zeitung.* But they kind of had to. Seeing as how he was both chairman and CEO of Kaltium and the company's shares were publicly traded.

But as for the general public, those little people who thought because they had an account on X or Telegram or Discord or whatever the latest rant-platform was, they had some sort of opinion that counted? No. They did not know who Xander Kalt was.

Not yet, anyway.

He ran his thumbnail down the final crease in the paper aeroplane he'd been constructing for the last twelve and a half minutes. Made a tiny adjustment to the ailerons. And, with a deft flick of the wrist, sent it airborne, where it executed a perfect banking turn that took in the floor-to-ceiling windows of his office before returning to land, silently, on his desk.

Satisfying.

Yes, once Project Peacemaker was in full swing, they'd all know his name. But not for some random retweet of a conspiracy theory. Or ill-judged remarks about a female executive.

He intended to leave a legacy. Something future generations would tell their children about.

He intended to end war.

Naturally it would be a selfless act. You couldn't play God with the future of humanity. But if the legacy powers decided that with such a figure available, maybe a strategic realignment of global authority was in order, well, he'd bend to their will. Of course he would. He permitted himself a tiny smile.

His intercom buzzed. His PA, Orianthi Stephens. Yale. *Summa cum laude*.

'Xander, I have Lorne Packard here to see you.'

'Does he have an appointment?'

'No. But he says it's urgent.'

Kalt sighed. How come everything was always urgent with lawyers when they wanted to see you, but you could never get them on the damn phone when *you* wanted *them*?

'Send him in, please, Orianthi. And bring us coffee.'

He picked up the paper plane and waited. This was going to require split-second timing. The door opened. He launched the dart. As Packard, clad as usual in a cream suit, entered, the plane passed a foot or so in front of his face, startling him for a second.

Kalt caught the flash of irritation, before the Texan pasted a smile on his jowly red face.

'Whoa, there, Xander. Nearly took my goddamned face off. You playing with paper darts now? Must be nice to have time on your hands.'

He drew out the visitor chair and stuffed himself down into it, puffing a little as the unyielding chrome armrests dug into his corpulent haunches.

Kalt observed his lawyer's discomfort with concealed amusement.

'So?'

Packard sighed. 'No time for small talk, huh? Well, given what I'm about to impart, y'all are probably right to get straight down to business. I've always admired that in you, Xander. Other powerful men, well, they tend to like the sound of their own voices, if you know what I'm sayin'. Y'all know there's a time and a place—'

'Which you apparently don't, Lorne. Spit it out. Did they bite? Any holdouts?'

Packard puffed out his cheeks, giving him the appearance of an out-of-breath beaver.

'All of 'em.'

Kalt smiled triumphantly. The mighty dollar had spoken.

'Excellent! So we can get moving straightaway.'

'No, Xander. Y'all got your saddle facin' the tail as we say down in Texas.'

Kalt doubted Texans said any such thing. Sometimes he wondered whether Lorne was even from the Lone Star State. All that y'all-ing came off as a bit too try-hard to his own Pacific North-western ears. But he was a good, if expensive, lawyer and not averse to the sort of grey-area activities that a man like Kalt needed in his high-ranking staffers.

'What do you mean?' he asked, suddenly aware that Packard was sweating profusely, despite the air-conditioning. The man was scared.

'I mean, Xander,' he drew a handkerchief from his display pocket and wiped his forehead, 'all of 'em are holdouts. There's this crazy hippie English dude down there called Gabriel. I have no idea why or how he washed up in that godforsaken corner of that shithole country, but there he is, plain as a piebald pony in a field full of Texas Longhorns. He's got 'em all riled up about how it's their birthright and they all lived there for generations and they don't need no money.'

'Did you offer *him* money?'

''Course we did! He threw it back in my face.'

'And did you try other methods of persuasion, like we discussed?'

Packard wiped his face again.

'Yes, sir, we did.'

'And?'

'And my monthly expenses statement will include the purchase of nine body bags.'

'Shit.'

'That about covers it.'

Kalt stared at the overweight lawyer opposite him. A thousand dollars an hour for services rendered. Sure, there were cheaper attorneys in Portland. Hell, there were cheaper attorneys in Manhattan. But that phrase 'service rendered' did a lot of heavy lifting.

Those white-shoe lawyers from the tony New York firms would be happy enough drafting contracts or litigating on some obscure point of commercial law. But organising and bankrolling paramilitary operations in Central America? Assassinating thorn-in-the-side English hippies? No, there, they would call it quits. And, quite possibly, the cops.

Trouble was, Lorne Packard was not rendering the services he was being paid for. And that made Xander Kalt angry. It made him very angry indeed.

'Do I pay you well, Lorne?' he asked, with a smile.

The lawyer shifted in his chair. It was pointless; he was never going to get comfortable. Kalt owned larger chairs, chairs without armrests. He owned Chesterfields you could park your fat butt on and disappear into those buttoned leather dimples like an anchovy in a shark's gaping mouth. He just didn't allow Lorne the relief of occupying one.

'Well, now, Xander, it's not about the money, is it? I mean—'

'Do. I. Pay. You. Well, Lorne? It's a simple question.'

'Yessir, yes you do. The terms of my remuneration are beyond generous.'

'Then why the fuck are you here, in my office, telling me your team of, what did you call them? Oh yes, I remember, "combat-proven, dogs-of-war, sons of bitches".' He paused for breath. Continued. 'Why are you, Lorne, here, telling me that I need to pay for fucking body bags, instead of down there in Hon-fucking-duras doing what I pay you for which is killing that fucking Englishman and securing my land?'

He wasn't shouting. Shouting was for losers and blowhards. Men whose power resided, if it resided anywhere, in their fists. Men who'd once been the jocks at high school who'd mercilessly bullied young Xander for his 'dweeb' name and even dweebier interests. Computers. Coding. Cyphers.

What Xander liked to do with subordinates who'd displeased him was to speak quieter and quieter, forcing them to lean in, to bring them closer. Because his power came from his money. His influence. His ability to unsettle the markets with a Tweet. To shake politicians out of their torpor with an email. And soon, very soon, he would make even that kind of power look as effectual as the jocks' taunts and head-flushings. He was going to make the whole world sit up and fucking listen.

Packard was sweating profusely. Partly because, out of the lawyer's eyeline, Kalt had moved a dial on an app on his phone and turned the aircon off. Mostly, because Kalt had developed a very precise sense of how to make people extremely uncomfortable in his presence.

'I'll sort it, Xander. I promise. I'll get some more men. Better men. I should never have used those guys. To be honest, it was Mason's idea. He recommended them himself. You just relax and leave everything to me, yes?'

Xander steepled his fingers under his chin. Nodded.

'OK, yes. So, basically what you're telling me is, this was all George's fault, you're innocent of all wrongdoing and I should just hand over more money. That about the size of it?'

'Well, not exactly, Xander. You know Honduras isn't America. It's like the wild west down there. This guy, Wolfe? He had all kinds of military-grade shit on his property.'

Xander placed his hands on the desk in front of Packard and eyeballed him for five seconds straight.

'Lorne, if Honduras was like America, I wouldn't need you and George, would I? Now, I need you to shut up for a minute while I tell you what's going to happen. You and George are going to take this Wolfe character into custody. Alive. And then I am going to fly my Lear down there and I am personally going to torture him until he tells me who's bankrolling him and why the fuck he won't take my money. And then, when's he's spilled his guts, I'm going to do it to him for real. Clear? Have I left anything out?'

The lawyer squirmed in his chair.

'Now, Xander, you know I have the greatest respect for your business decision-making. I mean, total respect. But that's a really bad idea.' He held his hands up. 'No, let me finish, goddamn it! OK, I called Wolfe a hippie, but that's just on account of how he looks. But we did our research on him, Xander. The guy's a ghost. He turned up about a year ago in Santa Rosa, growing mangoes and whatall. But back beyond that? Nothing. No digital footprint. No bank account, no credit cards, no employment history, no social security details in any major western country. The guy's a clean skin.'

Finally, Packard had something that Kalt found interesting. He leaned forward and tapped his mouse to wake up his PC. Started typing.

'He must have some internet presence. Even if it's a deleted Twitter account.'

'Nope. It's like the guy came down in a flying fucking saucer.'

Kalt scrutinised the results he'd just pulled up from a dark web search engine.

'Huh. How about that?'

Lorne leaned forwards. 'As far as I'm aware, and I checked this out with George as well, the only kind of man who has a blank slate like that is a spook.'

'OK, so he's what, a former British agent, is that what you're telling me? Big deal. The key word is "former". The plan still stands.'

Kalt intended that to be a dismissal, but the Texan lawyer stayed in his seat. Maybe he was jammed there, was Kalt's mocking thought.

'He's dangerous, Xander.'

Finally Kalt's anger erupted, like a whale breaching in the Pacific Ocean, eighty miles southwest of his HQ at Depoe Bay.

'*I'm* fucking dangerous! Christ, this is one man, Lorne. One man! You obviously didn't look hard enough. I'll do my own research. I'll find out everything about him and then you and George will do whatever it takes to capture him and take him somewhere secure, do you hear me?'

'Loud and clear.'

Xander had had enough of his lawyer and his excuses. He dismissed him and instructed him to close the door behind him, enjoying the whipped-dog expression on his sweaty red face.

Alone in his office, he crossed the expanse of thick woollen carpet he'd had flown in all the way from Wilton, in England, a custom design featuring his company logo that he'd designed himself, and opened a safe.

From its cold steel cavity he retrieved a simple cardboard box file, a mottled grey pattern on its exterior. He took it back to his desk and lifted the lid. Beneath the spring clip were documents. They were the only copies and they had no existence in the digital realm. He was literally the only person in the world who could gaze upon them.

And what documents!

Journals, Politburo memos, reports, research notes, blueprints, a submarine's pre-launch mission briefing including maps. And, crucially, the transcript of the final encrypted radio transmission from the doomed research and special operations submarine *Ozersk*.

Acquiring the cache of documents had taken thirteen years and cost Kalt three hundred and eighty seven million dollars. Then he'd had to build, launch and target a satellite and position it in geostationary orbit above the Caribbean. Where, finally, at 3:41 a.m. one cold January morning, his phone had bleeped with an alert. The satellite's AI-guided detection systems had located an anomaly forty metres down in a fissure in the Mesoamerican Barrier Reef off the coast of Honduras.

Kalt had immediately deployed the salvage research boat he'd had on standby. Within thirty-six hours they'd located *Ozersk*. Of course Kalt couldn't allow that kind of knowledge to escape him. He deployed a second vessel. No research technology on board. Just six very well-paid and ruthless men armed with automatic weapons and a serious quantity of C4 plastic explosive. No questions asked beyond, 'what's the target?'.

Peacemaker was waiting for him, Xander Kalt, to liberate it. To put it, finally, to use. It was too deep to be accidentally stumbled upon by pleasure divers, and thanks to the satellite, he knew nobody had been near it. Anybody who did would meet a similar fate to the captain and crew of the *Aurora* salvage ship.

But to get his hands on Peacemaker, he needed the perfect team, and he was starting to have serious doubts about Packard and Mason both.

If the two of them couldn't deal with one retired English spook, maybe he should look elsewhere.

Maybe at the spook himself.

14

LIVERPOOL, ENGLAND

Still jetlagged from the flight, Gabriel had the taxi drop him at the corner of Seel Street and Slater Street, a narrow road teeming with shoppers, students and tourists.

Bars and fast food joints lined both sides of the road. The Liverpudlian accent abraded his ears after a year or so living amongst Hondurans with their rapid-fire but melodious Spanish. Mixed into the sound was a babel of foreign languages amongst which he identified at least seven, including Hausa and Cantonese.

Maybe there *had* been a summer to write home about, but September had clearly decided enough was enough. Ten degrees and a light but steady rain chilled him to the bone. He regretted not packing a waterproof jacket for the trip.

He stopped to buy an umbrella from a man pushing a cart festooned with the things. Three pounds each or two for a fiver. He couldn't work out why anyone would want two.

Fifty yards further down the street, when a gust of wind blew his umbrella inside out and then snatched the canopy away to send it whirling skywards like a mutilated crow, he understood.

Shaking his head, he ducked into a shop and returned to the street beneath a sturdy golf umbrella big enough to shelter at least three men. Almost a patrol, he thought wryly.

He reached his destination, squeezed between a kebab shop, AbraKebabra, and an Irish pub called Shaky McDowell's. He looked up at the fascia: Ink Squad, in ornate red, blue, gold and green lettering. The windows were full of tattoo designs, body jewellery mounted in black velvet display cases, and a selection of deactivated ammunition, from dinky little .22 cartridge cases right up to a Russian RPG. Each painted with more designs, giving the former munitions a funky, counterculture vibe.

He went inside. An acoustic guitar mounted to the ceiling emitted a loud, resonant chord as a plectrum on the door strummed its steel strings.

Heads turned. Mostly shaved. A couple of mullets. Apart from a heavily tattooed young woman behind the counter, the place was full of men.

He approached the counter.

'I'm looking for Jerry. Is he around?'

'Is he expecting you, love?'

'Nope. But if you tell him Wolfie's here, that should do the trick.'

She actually rolled her eyes. Clearly his old nickname was as impressive to this twenty-something as it had been to him when the guys in the Parachute Regiment had bestowed it on him.

'Wolfie,' she repeated. Like he'd said 'paedo'.

'Yep.'

She turned and sauntered off, disappearing through a side door. As it opened he caught the click of hard balls on baize. The pool room was still operational then.

Jerry 'Can-Can' Myers and Gabriel had served in the SAS together. Jerry had mustered out, returned to the green army and then taken his honourable discharge. He'd moved to Liverpool and opened a tattoo parlour. It had become an unofficial hangout for current and former soldiers, especially those with mental illnesses. PTSD mostly, like Jerry and Gabriel. But Jerry was pretty accepting. Depression, anxiety, addiction: nothing was a bar.

He had a single rule. No trouble. And his clients – friends, really – respected it. Civilians were welcome to get their skin inked. But the pool room, and the little bar serving coffee, tea, soft drinks and cakes was off limits to them. Inside, men could let their hair down. Cry if they needed to. Talk. Reminisce. Basically, keep their shit together.

The young woman returned, chewing gum. She tipped her head towards the pool room door.

'He's in there.'

'Thank you.'

Heart fluttering, Gabriel pushed through into the inner sanctum.

'There he is! Wolfie! Come here, you tart!'

Jerry, a wiry eleven stone, grabbed Gabriel in a tight hug, clapping him on the back, then released him.

'How are you, Can-Can?'

Eyes suddenly hooded, and a shade or two darker blue, Jerry nodded.

'Good days and bad days. More good than bad, thank god. You?'

'About the same.'

Jerry glanced at Gabriel's left hand. Grinned.

'Fuck me, you're not going to tell me you persuaded a real, live woman to actually marry you?'

Gabriel's heart hitched in his chest.

'I did. But—'

Jerry's face fell. 'Oh fuck, mate. I'm sorry. Never did get myself on a sensitivity course. It wasn't a divorce, was it? I can tell from the look in your eyes. What happened? Actually, let's get a couple of coffees then tell me what you've been up to all this time.'

Coffees made, Jerry led Gabriel to a corner table. The other guys in the room glanced their way, but if Gabriel was with the boss then he was clearly sound.

Jerry took a sip of his coffee, eyeing Gabriel over the rim of his mug.

'So?'

'It's a long story.'

'I like long stories. Hear them every day. Sometimes I think I'd make a pretty good trick-cyclist.'

Gabriel smiled. One of the things he liked about Can-Can was how he didn't mind what he said or who he offended. It all came from a good place and if people couldn't take it, that was on them. But where to begin?

There could only be one place. The hard, awful truth.

'I got married eighteen months ago. She was pregnant. Then she was murdered. I left the country. I'm living in Honduras now.'

Jerry nodded. It was as if Gabriel had said, 'I'm living in Birmingham now.' People like them, who'd seen and done what they had, suffering the way they did, well, you did what you needed to survive. You wanted to fuck off to the arse-end of nowhere – no offence to Honduras, sure they're lovely people – that was what you did.

'Murdered.'

'I took out the people responsible.'

'Make you feel better?'

'Not really.'

'No, 'cause she's still gone.'

'Yep.'

'You're keeping it together. Out there in Honduras.'

'Pretty much. Or I was. The village where I live has become a hot property for some rich guy in the US. He sent mercs to kill me because I wouldn't sell up. Now he's given us a month before he sends more men to wipe the place out.'

Jerry finished his coffee. Signalled to the girl behind the counter for another.

'Police?'

Gabriel twisted his face up.

Jerry nodded. 'Let me guess. Bought and paid for.'

'I don't know for sure, but I'm not waiting for blue lights to save the day.'

Jerry regarded him coolly. Gabriel could see he'd realised why he was there.

'Meet fire with fire, then. That's the plan.'

'I need some men. Good men. Special Forces. Marines. Paras.'

'You know, some of the guys here, they're not doing so well. Not really. They're holding on, but I don't want you talking them into some half-arsed remake of the Magnificent Seven. They'll do it, you know they will. For the rush. But they need to be out of that life, mate. You know it.'

'I do. And, believe me, that's not what I want either. But if there are guys here, or who you know, who are fit mentally as well as physically, I can pay well – double the market rate – all expenses covered.'

Jerry frowned.

'You're loaded.'

'In both senses of the word.'

'How?'

'Which?'

'Both.'

'Inherited some stuff, took some untraceable bearer bonds off a corrupt biotech executive, the usual.' Gabriel permitted himself a half-smile. 'Spent some of it with a man in Tegucigalpa who doesn't use Klarna.'

A hint of suspicion blossomed behind Jerry's eyes. 'You didn't go into consulting after you left, did you, Wolfie?'

A speeded-up slideshow rattled in Gabriel's mind's eye. A trail of corpses stretching back ten years, splayed on jungle floors, desert sands, underground bunkers, villas, hotels, African streets, cult compounds, remote Scottish islands. The guilty…and the innocent.

'I thought I was doing the right thing, Can-Can. Only now I'm not so sure.'

Jerry leaned back, spread his ropy arms, dark with ink, along the back of the battered brown Chesterfield.

'As long as you were trying, mate, that's all you can ask for. Tell me about the gig. Opposition forces, terrain, civilians, gear. You have a plan, I assume.'

Gabriel nodded. 'Which will survive everything except—'

'— a boot up the arse from Dame Fate, yeah, I know. Tell me anyway.'

Over the next two hours, Gabriel talked, drew sketches, answered questions and speculated on those items where he lacked knowledge.

They concluded with Jerry telling Gabriel to come back in three days.

'I'll see what I can do.'

15

Compared to the simplicity of life in Santa Rosa, Liverpool felt overwhelming.

Too many vehicles, too many people. Too much harsh, industrial noise. And the stink of the vast urban machine itself: a noisome blend of car exhausts, fast food smells and the shed cells, bodily secretions and breath of several million humans going about their business.

He felt an outsider. And, despite having travelled to the UK on a false passport, always at risk of discovery. He had no idea what sort of state security apparatus might have taken over from the Department, or whether anyone was still interested in him. But it paid to be careful.

He found a cheap hotel. Ate a depressing room-service dinner. Burger, fries, coke, vanilla ice cream. A strange restlessness took over him. He switched on the TV, flicked through a dozen channels and switched it off again. His room had a small balcony, but when he tried the door, it opened only a few inches before ramming up against a metal stay. He swore.

His meal sat heavily in his stomach. Too much processed food since getting back to England. Without realising, he'd adopted the

Honduran way of life to such an extent his diet was mainly fresh vegetables, home-baked bread, fish or beans for protein with only the occasional bit of meat, usually if a neighbour was having a *fiesta*.

The room was too hot. He suddenly felt anxious. Cooped up like a chicken on one of the smallholdings back home.

Back home? Really? Was that how he thought of the tiny coastal settlement on the Caribbean coast? Strange kind of home for a man born in the home counties of the UK, raised in Hong Kong and matured in the British army in bases all over the world.

He grabbed his key card and left the over-hot room. Maybe a walk would clear his head and settle his nerves. He looked up and down the corridor, half-expecting to see Eli waving from halfway down its undifferentiated expanse of brown and beige carpet. But, apart from a cleaner pushing a cart laden with fresh linens and guest toiletries, who waved, it was empty.

The hotel was in a quietish neighbourhood, off one of the main shopping streets. Rather than heading towards the lights and the noise of the main drag, he turned away, seeking quiet and the space to stride out.

Dusk had fallen, and a few streetlights were flickering on, pink first, then orange. As he turned a corner, he caught a glimpse of the Royal Liver building down the steep-sided concrete canyon that led all the way to the docks on the river Mersey. It was lit a vibrant electric purple apart from the two patinated copper birds atop its twin clock towers, which glowed an unearthly greyish-green.

He hooked a left, then a right at random. At the far end of the street, a pub, lights blazing. The swell of drunken cheering piercing the evening calm. A football match. He'd seen a news vendor's sign earlier. Liverpool were playing at home to Millwall, a London team notorious for the alleged ferocity of its fans.

He passed the pub on the far side of the road. Easier, since the whole of the corner was occupied with men clutching pints, sometimes two pints, and festooned in red-and white. Liverpool fans, then.

One guy called out to him, drunkenly.

'All right, lad? Coming in for the match? We're gonna smash it tonight.'

'Sorry. Not a fan.'

The guy's eyes popped open comically. Unable to comprehend how a male of the species in Liverpool on match night couldn't be interested.

Gabriel rounded the next corner and encountered company.

Here were five men who looked very much as if they were fans. Just not of Liverpool Football Club. All aged between twenty and thirty five. Dressed in variants of the same uniform. Navy T- or polo shirts emblazoned with 'HUSKI chocolate', Millwall's sponsor. Beige or stone chinos. Trainers.

They had hard expressions. He'd seen that look. On men in combat. Not before: then there was a tightness around the eyes, a wariness, in gaze and posture. Even the most experienced trooper couldn't completely quell the nerves before contacting the enemy. But in the middle of a firefight. When adrenaline was doing its job, transforming anxiety into energy and excitement, the blood was up and the warrior within had been unleashed.

They all registered his presence in the deserted street at the same time. And in that split-second, he knew it meant trouble.

Five against one.

No. Make that one against five.

He needed to stop this before it got started.

Changing course to avoid a middle-of-the-street confrontation would only goad them, so he slowed and aimed for a gap between two of the men. Numbers four and five as he looked at them reading the group left to right.

It was a move born of confidence. Might make them think twice.

It didn't.

The gap vanished.

He stopped.

The five men stopped.

Did they have weapons? Nothing obvious. No bats, chains or

pistols. He smiled. Pistols? This wasn't Teguz, where every minor criminal carried, from gangbangers to street kids. A vision sparked behind his eyes. A snot-nosed little waif who'd shot a woman in cold blood right in front of him. Her face had broken into a smile straight afterwards because she'd been given a lollipop by a doctor and told she was brave.

'The fuck you smiling at?'

Three was glaring at him, thin lips drawn back in a snarl. Heart, spade, diamond and club tattooed onto the right side of his neck.

Gabriel breathed easily. Pulse sixty-five.

'A memory. Excuse me, I need to get past.'

One, Two, Four and Five were eyeing him with casual grins. Fists clenching. Eyes flicking to their leader for the cue to go in.

'You a football fan, mate?' Three asked.

Distance between them. One yard.

'No. In fact, I was just telling—'

'Shut up! Why not?'

'Pardon?'

'Why. Aren't. You. A. Football. Fan? Cunt.'

Colour had left Three's face. Blood diverted to the muscles. A big predictor of violence to come.

Gabriel shrugged. 'Never seen the point. I mean, what kind of idiot watches a sport where twenty-two people can play for ninety minutes and nobody scores a single point?'

Three put his hands on his hips. The right slid down into his pocket. The knuckles bunched, distending the fabric. Fingers curling around the hilt of a knife.

'Think you're pretty funny, don't you?' Three said. 'Think you'll be laughing after we fuck you up?'

Gabriel frowned. Folded his arms. He didn't have time for this.

Three's forehead crinkled. Not how these things were supposed to go.

'Let me ask you something,' Gabriel said in a conversational tone of voice. 'How do you imagine, I mean, when you visualise it in your mind's eye, things are going to stand between us in the next, what, three minutes? Am I on the ground, lying in a puddle of my own blood? You and your mates here strolling off to get into it with the Liverpool fans round the corner? That's a bold move, isn't it? I mean, you know nothing about me yet you're preparing to attempt murder. You do know that's how it could go down, don't you?' He paused. 'If your little fantasy plays out the way you think it will, that is.'

'Nobody's murdering anyone, you prick,' Five said, finding his voice. 'He's a trained MMA fighter.'

'Shut up, Dave,' Three said. 'He doesn't need to know that.'

Gabriel shook his head. He'd forgotten the woeful level of preparedness of the average British hooligan. If they put a tenth as much effort into their fighting skills as they did into their bluster, the scene about to play out would look substantially different.

'Actually, that's quite interesting,' Gabriel said. 'I've done some cage fighting myself. In Tegucigalpa. Do you know where that is?'

Three frowned again. 'How the fuck should I know?'

It didn't matter. Without him realising, Gabriel had just taken control away from him.

'No reason for you to. It's the capital of Honduras. That's where I live. Anyway, my last bout? I broke my opponent's neck and then castrated his corpse with a sugar cane knife. I'm telling you this not to boast – I can't say I'm especially proud of it, although the dead man was a rapist so, you know, reap what you sow and all that. Where was I? Yes!' He clapped his hands loudly, making Three blink. 'Not to boast, but as information. Have you killed anyone?'

'No,' Three said.

Beside him, his four accomplices were looking decidedly unsettled, shifting their weight from foot to foot. Probably wondering how they could escape this lunatic unscathed.

'I have. A lot. So best we part as friends, yes? Let me through.'

Three was thinking about it. He'd lost face in front of his mates. A lot of face. That could make people act irrationally. And from his chosen way of passing a weekday evening, it was clear he was not a deep thinker.

'Five of us, one of you,' Three said. 'Nobody's letting anyone through. We're going to do you then we're going to find some Liverpool scum and we're gonna fuck them up, too.'

Gabriel held his hands up. One final attempt to secure peace.

'You're right, you do outnumber me. And so, in your head, I can see how this looks. Overwhelming force. You all pile in together, kicks, punches, slashes with that blade you're holding in your pocket.' Three blinked again, as if the bunched fist in his pocket wasn't such an obvious clue to his intentions. 'But, and I'm not being rude here, you guys are amateurs. You might be *talented* amateurs, but that's all you are. I'm a professional. Was, technically, but it doesn't matter. Not here, not now. So, if you *do* start something, I am going to inflict a lot of pain, damage and distress on all of you. It won't be life-threatening, but it won't be pleasant either. I wish I could find a way to show you what I mean, but that's the whole point. That's what I'm trying to avoid. So, are you going to let me through please? Try your luck round the corner?'

The hand holding the knife came up at speed. A red, steel-bodied Stanley knife. The boxcutter was the football hooligan's weapon of choice. Capable of inflicting horrific, yet superficial wounds. Lots of blood, little chance of hitting something important. Like nineteenth-century German students dealing each other duelling scars.

Its wicked little triangular blade was arcing in towards Gabriel's eyes. But unlike the Prussian undergraduates, he had no leather mask designed to protect his sight.

And then it was in his left hand, as the right twisted Three's wrist over until it broke with a loud snap. He pushed him away, tripping him as he went down in a tangle, colliding with Two and Four as they jumped back in surprise.

Time was, Gabriel might have barked at them to stop. Instructed them to carry their leader away. But times were different now. Very different.

Five swung a meaty fist glinting with the blued steel of a spiked knuckleduster. Gabriel side-stepped the punch, which otherwise would have removed his front teeth if not broken his jaw, and kicked him hard in the left knee. Ligaments separated with a pop like bubble-wrap being stamped on. He shrieked in agony and fell to his side, landing on top of Three who was nursing his broken wrist and maintaining a stream of curses only marginally less inventive than you'd find on the backstreets on Teguz.

Gabriel turned to face the remaining men.

Two held a dagger with a serrated top to the blade. Serious weapon. He obviously hadn't got the memo about duelling scars. One brought out a little kitchen knife. Four a length of pipe. Must have had a specially sewn pocket in his chinos Gabriel thought, stepping inside his swing radius, relieving him of the pipe, and chopping him hard in the soft place below his Adam's apple.

Continuing the swing of the pipe, which was now gripped by his fist, Gabriel brought it down on Two's right wrist. The knife clattered to the cobbles and, as Two looked down, horrified, at his dangling hand, Gabriel delivered a kung fu kick to the side of his skull – long-banned in competition – that knocked him out cold. His head was saved from a potentially fatal encounter with the cobbles by Three's thigh.

That left One and Four. They'd closed ranks. Stupid move. He almost wanted to stop the fight to explain to them where they were going wrong. Two against one, you split up, move to your enemy's twelve and six, or three and nine, give him two targets, two places to look, instead of one. Game over.

Four wasn't really a threat at this point. He was leaning against a black and gold cast-iron bollard, his face beet-red, clutching his injured throat, eyes bulging out of their sockets as he struggled to draw breath. Gabriel would leave him until last.

But One was a different story. One was passing that wicked little boning knife from hand to hand like a pro. Odds were he'd only practised in front of a mirror in his bedroom, but you never knew.

'Put it down now,' Gabriel said, 'and you can walk away from this.'

One grinned, revealing sharp little teeth.

'Fuck you. I'm going to open you up. Show you your own guts.'

He feinted low, then swerved the tip of the knife up towards Gabriel's ribcage. A nice little move and one that would find a less experienced opponent staring at his ribcage in horror as he tried to compute the presence of a knife handle sticking out of his chest.

The knife passed harmlessly a couple of inches from Gabriel's torso. Gabriel lanced out a fist, but the guy parried it with his arm, jolting Gabriel's wrist, and followed up with a hard blow, catching Gabriel across the right cheekbone.

Gabriel stepped back, out of range. The guy had some moves of his own. As he brought the knife up again and launched himself forward, blade upraised, Gabriel grabbed Four from his temporary cast-iron support and swung him bodily into One's path. The knife came down. Gabriel lost sight of it as Four's body blocked his view. Then Four folded forwards, grunting out the precious breath he'd managed to suck down, and collapsed.

The knife in One's hand was smeared red. He looked down at it in puzzlement, then down at Four, who was clutching his bloody torso and moaning. Gabriel's fist must therefore have come as a surprise as he drove it down hard directly over a spot on the back of One's neck where a bundle of nerves passed close beneath the surface.

Gabriel checked his clothing for blood. He was clean.

Now what? He could hardly leave five men in various states of physical distress in the middle of the road. Maybe if they'd been Honduran cartel enforcers and this was Comayaguela or San Pedro Sula, yes, that would be an option. But this was Liverpool.

He looked up and spotted the cameras mounted on lampposts and the sides of buildings. The most-surveiled country in Europe, wasn't it? The men would need help but he had neither the time or the inclination to give it.

An idea occurred to him.

He jogged back round the corner to the pub.

The guy who'd called out to him was still there, draining a pint of Guinness.

'Hi,' Gabriel said. 'Listen, there's five Millwall fans round the corner. I think they were fighting among themselves. I don't suppose you could take a couple of your mates and go and see if they're all right, could you? I would myself, but, as I said, I'm not a fan.'

As he left, the guy was already roaring. A posse of red-and-whites detached themselves from the crowd drinking the pub dry and tore off towards the corner, screaming bloodcurdling threats. The battle cries were choked off mid-scream. They'd found them, then. Someone screamed, 'Call the bizzies! They're fuckin' dyin' here!'

Gabriel reached his hotel without further incident. He felt calm. No way would the Millwall call the police. So without a complaint, even if the CCTV cameras had picked him up, what would the cops do about it? Five armed men against one? He doubted they'd lose much sleep trying to track him down.

All the same. He showered and let the hot water course over his face, softening his beard hair as much as possible with copious squirts from the tile-mounted soap dispenser.

In the steaming bathroom, a towel wrapped around his hips, he cut it as short as possible with scissors, then shaved.

He watched a movie. Slept dreamlessly. Woke refreshed, and headed to Hereford, pausing at a barber's for a dramatic cut that left a mound of long black hair speckled with silver on the floorboards.

He caught sight of himself in a shop window.

Hello, stranger.

16

Gabriel rode his thumb to Hereford, and the base of his old outfit.

There, he discovered that the man he'd come to see, Johnny 'Sparrow' Hawke, had also left the Regiment. He was running a training company just over the border in Wales.

With the address in hand, Gabriel hitched his way to Crickhowell, a small, pretty town in the shadow of the Brecon Beacons.

Borderlands Training occupied a black-painted converted barn on the northern outskirts of the town. The company's name was affixed to the clapboard side facing the small gravelled carpark in artfully rusted steel lettering.

Gabriel went in and approached the reception desk. The forty-ish guy behind the counter looked fit, white crows' feet fanning out from his eyes, interrupting what looked like a proper outdoorsman's tan.

'Hi. Welcome to Borderlands Training. How can I help?'

'Is Johnny in? I'm an old friend.'

The guy smiled.

'He's leading a trek at the mo. Be back about,' he checked his watch, an olive-green Casio G-shock in a ruggedised rubber case, 'eleven? Eleven-thirty? Depends on how the group's doing. Got a bunch of HR executives from Jaguar Landrover doing a team-building weekend. Not the fittest bunch we've had through the doors.'

Gabriel checked his own watch: 10:05 a.m.

'I'll come back if that's OK.'

The receptionist smiled. 'Of course. Who shall I say called?'

Gabriel sighed.

'Wolfie.'

But the guy just nodded. Jotted it down.

'No problem. If you're looking for a coffee or something to eat, try The Bear on the High Street.'

Gabriel nodded.

'Thanks, I will.'

* * *

In the end, Gabriel grabbed a takeaway coffee from a small independent cafe and took it to a grassy slope overlooking the training company's building.

With a warm breeze blowing and a rare splash of sunshine in an otherwise dreary few days since he'd landed, he leaned back on his elbows and closed his eyes.

Was this really going to work? Assembling a crew of elite soldiers, OK, *former* elite soldiers, and flying back to Santa Rosa to defeat, what? Another ten-strong crew of cartel muscle rejects and pensioned-off contras? More? Americans, this time? The Honduran army? Why not? Whoever was behind the odious lawyer had seemingly unlimited funds.

The trouble was, it *had* to. Gabriel wasn't a private contractor, with his own outfit, hundreds of blokes on call. He knew men who'd chosen that path. One was the genial, overloud CEO of Kagiso Group, based in Mokolondi in Botswana. He'd assisted Gabriel and Eli when they'd been hunting down the plotters behind the assassination of a princess on her wedding day. With more time, Gabriel could have mustered a larger force, but time was the one thing he didn't have.

He must have drifted off. Laughter and good-natured banter floated out of a dream. Of Eli, naturally. Smiling at him in Botswana, with that blazing overhead sun throwing crisp, dark shadows onto the hard-packed red earth.

Descending the hill to his left, on a straight line to the barn, were eight people. Six clearly relieved to be back, despite their smiles, and two, one fore, one aft, who looked as though they'd just popped out for the paper. Lean, moving easily, Bergens on their backs. Gabriel recognised Sparrow at once. His blonde hair was paler still. Maybe a life lived outdoors had added sun-bleach to his natural colour. Or was it actually hints of silver?

Gabriel got to his feet. Presumably Sparrow would need a few minutes to sign his walkers back in before attending to whatever it was training company bosses did. He'd give it five, then saunter down and ask his question.

17

Inside the building again, Gabriel saw his old friend and comrade chatting to a couple of his car company clients. They both had walking poles and brightly coloured jackets that looked brand new.

Gabriel caught Sparrow's eye over the shoulder of the female walker. Sparrow smiled, nodded and then finished up his conversation.

Once the two walkers had left, he strode over, arms wide.

'Mate! It's been too bloody long. How are you?' he said, enfolding Gabriel in a hug.

Gabriel offered a tight smile. He realised this was going to be a story he'd be repeating for the rest of his life unless he broke off all contact with everyone he'd ever known. Although hadn't he already done that? No time to think about that now.

He gave Sparrow the shortened version.

His old comrade looked down then back into Gabriel's eyes. When he did, Gabriel saw a sadness there he hadn't noticed when they'd hugged.

'I lost Beth two years ago. Breast cancer. It's a bastard, Wolfie, I tell you.'

'I'm sorry. How long had you two been married?'

'Seven years. Best years of my life. I know it's a cliché, but that's genuinely how I felt – feel – about the time we had. It just wasn't enough. Not nearly enough.' Then he shook his head. 'Shit, what am I saying? You and Eli weren't even married a month.'

'It's OK.' *It's not OK!* 'The time we did have was good. I just … you know, it's not been easy.'

'Of course it hasn't. What are you doing to cope?'

'That's kind of why I'm here, actually. I've got a little bit of trouble at home and I need some help straightening it out.'

Sparrow narrowed his eyes.

'I'm assuming we're not talking about a leaky tap.'

'More like paramilitaries aiming to raze my village to the ground so their employer can build some kind of base there.'

Sparrow had always been sharp. Used to sit under the camo netting doing cryptic crosswords while they were standing by to stand by.

'And you're back here raising a small private army. A few trusted guys, certain skill-set, combat experience. You want me to join them?'

'I want you to lead them.'

That did catch Sparrow by surprise.

'Me? Why not you?'

'I'll fight, don't get me wrong, but I also need to go after the moneyman. I need to sort out proper defences, rig the terrain with IEDs. I think we're going to have to train the villagers as well if they're to stand a chance. They're mostly farmers so they've got long guns. Shotguns, mostly, but a few hunting rifles. You might even find a few handguns: Honduras is a dangerous place.'

Sparrow rubbed a hand over his jaw. He hadn't said no. That was a good sign. But as Gabriel looked around he realised the error he'd made. Sparrow was thriving in civvy street. He'd built up a business. A successful one to judge from the large calendar whiteboard mounted to the right of the reception desk. He was hardly going to walk away from it to be a merc, even for a couple of weeks.

Following his gaze, Sparrow looked over at the whiteboard. Gabriel prepared himself for the disappointment. He realised he'd been relying on Sparrow saying yes to bring the plan to fruition.

'Do you remember Congo?' Sparrow asked.

Gabriel looked out the window. But instead of lush green grass dotted with sheep and the soaring mountains beyond, he saw thick forest. Wide brown rivers. Rebel encampments bristling with Kalashnikovs and misted with blue-grey cannabis smoke. And blood. A lot of blood.

'How could I forget?'

'That ambush. Twenty or so of them caught you, me and Smudge down by that fishing pool.'

Gabriel's nostrils filled with the firework smell of burnt propellant and the sour, metallic odour of red-hot brass shell casings. His ears with the bark and rattle of small arms fire. His mouth with the taste of blood, where he'd bitten his tongue.

The three troopers had fought the onrushing militia to a standstill, the bodies piling up on the far bank. Those that had fallen into the water being snatched and rolled by the enormous crocodiles that prowled the country's inland waterways.

With the numbers almost even, and therefore the fight almost over, a squad of lean, crazy-eyed enemy fighters had circled round, approaching the three SAS men from behind. If they hadn't been stoned, their ambush-within-an-ambush might have succeeded, but the lead man couldn't resist yelling a battle-cry.

Sparrow whirled round: the movement saved him his life. The huge, ugly machete sliced into his helmet instead of the back of his neck. But the weight of the blade, and the force behind it, knocked him off his boots. He fell back, his head struck a rock and he was out cold. The enemy fighter screamed triumphantly and raised the machete for another slashing blow that would either have fetched Sparrow's head off his neck or opened his torso up like a gutted fish.

But before his muscular arm could descend, Gabriel drew his Fairbairn–Sykes fighting knife and plunged it into the attacker's throat, opening his neck like a can of beans and spilling his blood onto the boggy ground. Two more thrusts into his ribs and he went down, gasping and gurgling, scarlet bubbles foaming from his slack lips.

Smudge still had ammunition and despatched the other two with bursts from his M4 carbine.

Gabriel snatched up a Kalashnikov and, between them, they forced the few remaining guerrillas into a retreat, taking out three more before they disappeared into the forest.

The trees faded. The screams subsided to a distant high-pitched whine in his ears. The stench of blood and shit and the rotten leaves lying in the shallows dissipated.

Jesus, these flashbacks weren't as scary as they used to be, but they were definitively more vivid.

'You saved my life that day,' Sparrow said. 'And not for the first time.'

'You did the same for me.'

'Well, I didn't but OK, I know what you mean. Anyway, I'm not the one asking for help, you are. So, the answer's yes. I've got a capable number two.'

'And he can handle things here for a week or two?'

'*She'll* be fine. Actually come and meet her. I think you'll like her.'

Sparrow led him to an open-plan area where ten or so staff sat at desks or conference tables where large-scale maps were spread out.

'Sal! Come over here, there's someone I'd like you to meet.'

A woman in her mid-thirties detached herself from a group poring over a 3D model of the Beacons and came over. Up close, Gabriel saw she was older than he'd first thought. By maybe a decade. But she had the lean frame of someone who spent their life active, not slouched over a computer.

She smiled.

'Hi, I'm Sally. Bowles. No relation.'

Gabriel introduced himself and shook her outstretched hand. Her skin was dry and callused.

'Army?' he asked.

'Sheep.'

He frowned and this made her laugh, a salty cackle that had her colleagues looking over and smiling.

'Sorry. My family farm sheep. I grew up here. I know these hills like the back of my hand. I guess Johnny needed someone to stop the corporate types getting lost.'

Sparrow smiled.

'Sal's being modest. She's part of the local mountain rescue outfit and holds a bunch of climbing records.'

She shoulder-bumped him.

'Stop it! So, Gabriel, you *are* army, I take it? Or ex?'

'The latter.'

'And, like Johnny here, I assume you absolutely, definitely did not have anything to do with a certain little group of ruffians just over the border?'

He knew Sparrow wouldn't have told her, or anyone, which precise regiment he'd served in. None of them did. It was one of the fail-safe ways they had of spotting the Walter Mittys. The fantasists and wannabes who claimed to be ex-SAS for pub-boasting points, to impress women (God help them) or just to patch over some deep and obvious chasms in their sense of self-worth.

He shook his head.

'Nothing so glamorous, I'm afraid.'

'Shame. I go for those rugged do-or-die types. How long are you staying in Crickhowell? I'm assuming you *are* staying.'

He glanced at Sparrow, who nodded fractionally.

'Probably a night. I hear The Bear's good.'

'Yeah, definitely your best bet. The beds are great, I hear.' She fished in her pocket and presented him with a card. 'If you strike out at The Bear, give me a call. I've got a spare room.'

Suddenly, Gabriel felt hot under her probing gaze. Sparrow rescued him.

'Leave the poor man alone, Sal. Come on, Gabe, let's have a chat in my office.'

Over coffee, Gabriel filled Sparrow in on the details of the op, much as he had with Can-Can. As he talked, he felt a sense of relief spreading over him.

It was starting to look like it might actually work.

18

SANTA ROSA, HONDURAS

Can-Can had come good.

Ranged in a straggling line on the beach outside Gabriel's house were five men Can-Can had screened personally for both experience and their own mental wellbeing.

An enthusiasm for combat, a healthy respect for, but a willingness to ignore, risk, and total commitment were considered must-haves. A lack of dependents, conversational Spanish and no criminal record in the UK were nice-to-haves.

Gabriel surveyed the team. Beside him stood Sparrow, clad, as they all were, in jungle greens.

'Tiny' Tim Christie. Special Boat Service. Six foot four. Broad as a battleship. Says little.

Austin 'Paddy' Gauntlet. Irish Guards. Former mortar operator. The flame-red hair and beard of a Kerryman. Born in Canterbury, Kent.

Marco 'Bullseye' Bishop. SAS. Once shot a militiaman

through the right eye from 900 yards. Was unhappy about the shot. Had been aiming for the left.

Lucas 'Kylie' Minogue. Parachute Regiment. A joker. Also a first-rate field medic.

Scott 'Bilbo' Bagley. Royal Marine Commandos. Kind to animals. Less kind to people trying to kill civilians.

Not a bad crew. Three SAS, one SBS, an infanteer and a Para. Action seen and survived in hotspots ranging from Iraq and Afghanistan to Mali, Syria, Nigeria, El Salvador and Kyrgizstan.

Gabriel pointed up the beach. In the distance were the rotted spars of a beached fishing vessel, sticking up from the fine white sand like the ribs of a long-dead beached whale.

'There and back. The veranda rail's the finish line. Last one to touch it does it again with a seventy-pound Bergen. So if—'

Kylie broke ranks, sprinting away from the others, whooping a strangulated battle-cry.

'Fuck!' Tiny said, before charging after him.

The other three set off in hot pursuit. They saved their breath for running.

Shaking his head, Sparrow turned to Gabriel.

'You think we'll be doing much beach-fighting?'

'Nope. But I want them to bed in together as a unit.' He gestured towards the house. 'Come on, you can help me get some of the gear out here for when they get back.'

He led Sparrow into the kitchen and rolled up a native rug, pushing it to the edge of the room and revealing a trapdoor in the wooden floor.

He hauled it up by the iron ring, swung it through its arc of travel and lowered it gently onto the floorboards.

Sparrow peered down into the dark.

'Wine cellar?'

'Come and see. It's all pretty recent vintage.'

Gabriel descended the robust slatted wooden steps, pausing to throw a switch that bathed the underground room in bright-white light. Behind him, Sparrow whistled.

'Well, if Blackwater ever go out of business you could probably pick up the slack.'

It was an exaggeration. But outside of the cartels, the military and the police, Gabriel reckoned he had one of the bigger arsenals in Honduras. M4 carbines were racked on one wall. Two sniper rifles, one British, one Russian. Pistols. Knives and bayonets of varying sizes. Boxes of M67 fragmentation grenades. Claymore anti-personnel mines. Hinged steel boxes containing M112 C4 demolition blocks. Stacked on the floor, four long wooden boxes, stencilled in yellow over their olive-green paint: FGM-148 'Javelin'. Anti-tank weapons.

Ammunition crates occupied one corner. A workbench below wall-mounted tools sat opposite.

'If we don't have it, we can make it,' Gabriel said. 'I've got triggers, detonators, everything, really.'

Sparrow rubbed a hand through his thinning blonde-silver hair.

'What were you expecting when you bought all this stuff, Wolfie?'

Gabriel shrugged. It was a good question. Nobody had known he was here. And his intention had been to disappear quietly. *How's that working out for you?* a sarcastic inner voice asked. But somewhere, deep down where his subconscious fear lay, never far from breaking through to the surface, he'd wanted to know he could take on anyone and anything who came looking for him.

He shrugged now.

'Forewarned is forearmed.'

'More like forty-four armed if you ask me.' Sparrow wandered over to a rack of sidearms and took down a silver-barrelled revolver. Straightened his arm and aimed the monster piece at the wall. 'Do you feel lucky, punk?'

'It's not very practical, but it puts the fear of God into people if you stick it in their faces,' Gabriel said.

Sparrow sniffed the muzzle.

'Ever used it?'

Gabriel nodded. 'I shot an alligator with it last July. Bastard was taking goats from one of my friend's farms. It had got a taste for them. Sort of like an all-you-can-eat buffet. Took three rounds to finally stop it. It was like shooting a tank.'

'Bet it made a mess.'

'Yeah the skin wasn't exactly in what you'd call saleable condition.'

'So what are we taking topside?'

'An M4 each, a sidearm. Then I suggest we let the boys loose down here to pick up whatever else they fancy. There's some non-conventional stuff in that locker.'

Sparrow raised his eyebrows.

'And when you say "non-conventional"?'

'Come and have a look.'

Gabriel flipped the catch on the large battered steel trunk then stood back to allow his number two to get a better look.

Sparrow squatted in front of the trunk. He reached in and pulled out a coil of thin steel wire twisted at each end around short wooden handles fashioned from sawn-down lengths of broom handle. He placed it on the ground beside him. Reached in again. Retrieved two brutal-looking brass knuckle-dusters, not a million miles away from that wielded so ineffectively by the Millwall fan in Liverpool. A foot-long, black, tactical tomahawk with a razor-sharp edge that glinted as it caught the light. And then he let out another low whistle.

'You are joking.'

His hand emerged, wrapped around the haft of a short wooden weapon that terminated in a pair of iron gears, welded into each other at right angles, their teeth filed or ground into lethal points.

He stood, swung the implement in an experimental semi-circle. Grinned.

'A mace?'

'I took it from a gangbanger. The workmanship's good, isn't it?'

Sparrow turned the weapon in the light. Tossed it from hand to hand. Flipped it into the air and caught it mid-rotation.

'Nice balance. Not too heavy.' He peered at the intersection of the two gearwheels.

'Oh god, that's not brain, is it?'

Gabriel frowned. He kept his materiel clean and tidy. No way would he have missed something like that.

'Let me see.'

But as he stepped closer, Sparrow swung the mace wide before bringing it round Gabriel's throat and clamping his left hand on the haft.

'You're dead, Wolfie,' he said, before releasing his grip. 'You're getting too trusting out here in paradise. You've lost your edge.'

Gabriel stepped back, rubbing his neck. Sparrow had a point. But then, that was why he'd recruited him.

'That's why you're team leader,' he said ruefully. 'I want those guys…' He angled his head up to the open hatch. '…remembering everything they ever learned about combat. So far I've met rent-a-muscle, then some trigger-happy thugs from SPS. The next lot aren't going to be such a pushover.'

Sparrow nodded. 'Let's get this stuff upstairs then. The boys should be back soon.'

* * *

With the gear topside, laid out on the veranda, Gabriel fetched two cold cokes from the fridge and handed one to Sparrow. They popped the tops off and each took a long, satisfying swig.

Sparrow shaded his eyes against the sun and gestured up the beach.

'Here they come.'

Kylie was leading the pack, arms pumping as his feet kicked up rooster tails of dry sand behind him. But Bilbo was gaining on him, yelling obscenities as his arms pumped by his sides like tattooed pistons.

They were only fifty yards from the finish line now. Kylie looked over his shoulder, already crowing with victory. A mistake. Bilbo dodged left, then right, feinted left again, like a winger in the Rugby Sevens Gabriel had played as a boy in Hong Kong.

Instead of turning back and sprinting for home, Kylie tried to block him. Then, disaster. He caught his leading foot under a thick strand of seaweed, the type the locals called *cuerda de sirena* – mermaid's rope – and with a yell of frustration, plunged headlong into the white sand.

With a high-pitched war whoop, Bilbo leaped over his fallen crewmate, punching the air as he landed.

Thirty yards to the finish line. And then, powering forward as if someone had injected adrenaline directly into his heart, Tiny, all six foot four of him, barrelled past Bilbo, slapping his hand down on the rail of the veranda.

Gabriel exchanged a look with Sparrow. *Didn't see that coming.*

He patted the giant's heaving back before fetching another coke for him. He whacked the top off on the rail Tiny was now using for support. Sweat streamed off his back in rivulets, dropping to the sun-bleached wood and turning it a deep grey before fading again as the midday heat dried it.

Bilbo came next, then Kylie. Bullseye next. And, red-faced, clutching his ribs as if stabbed, the last man in, Paddy.

Cokes handed out, Gabriel nodded to Sparrow who barked out an order for the men to fall in.

Chests heaving, the men's faces had turned various unattractive shades from puce to cherry. Apart from Tiny, who, suddenly a waxy green, spun suddenly and ran a few steps down the beach before bringing back up the coke in a fizzing brown stream.

'Good,' Sparrow said. 'Tiny, you won so you get first pick on the personal weapons in the cellar. Off you go. Everybody else, you can follow him down once you've selected a long and a short.'

Paddy was first onto the veranda, already reaching for a camouflage-painted M4 carbine.

'Not you, Paddy,' Gabriel said.

Paddy straightened. His forehead furrowed.

'What?'

'You came last. Grab the Bergen from inside and then do it again.'

Paddy put his hands on his hips.

'You're not serious, Wolfie? Come on, it's bloody boiling out here. At least let me finish my drink and cool off for ten minutes.'

Gabriel made a few minute adjustments to his posture. Mentally thanking Master Zhao, whose teachings he'd been striving to recapture these last few weeks. Paddy fell back by half a step. If you'd asked him why, he'd have been unable to explain. It was instinct.

'First of all, from now until the end of the mission, it's "Boss".' He raised his voice to be heard over the ratcheting of charging levers and slides being racked. 'That goes for everyone. Sparrow is Skip. Second of all, yes, I am serious. You think Cartel soldiers or CIA-trained mercs are going to wait for you to get your breath back? Let you have a nice cold coke before they resume the fight? No. You came last, Paddy. Do it again.'

The two men stood facing each other for ten seconds. One breathing heavily, the other calm. One flexing his fingers as if wanting to curl them into fists, the other with arms loose by his sides.

Paddy broke eye contact. Looked down for a second then flung his half-drunk coke into the greenery that fringed the beach. He stomped inside and returned two minutes later, holding the huge green Bergen by one of its straps. By his little finger. His grin stretched across his face.

Gabriel smiled. Just fractionally.

'When I said a seventy-pound Bergen, I meant its capacity. You don't think I'd actually load it, do you? You'd die from heatstroke.'

'You pussy, Paddy,' Bilbo crowed, slinging an M4 over his shoulder and heading inside. 'Lucky the boss cut you a break there. Or we'd have been down to six before dinner.'

Paddy dumped the Bergen on the sand.

'Really? I'm a pussy? OK, you weaselly little Hobbit, watch this.'

He fell to his knees and began scooping sand into the rucksack. Five minutes later, he was hoisting it onto his back and snapping the waist belt around his middle.

He turned and jogged off. As Gabriel had known he would.

It took Paddy forty-three minutes and fifteen seconds to complete his second return trip to the rotted-out hulk up the beach. When he returned and threw off the sand-filled Bergen to tumultuous applause, Gabriel walked up to him and ceremonially presented him with the mace.

'You earned this, Paddy. Well done, mate.'

Even though his chest was heaving, and his lungs must have been bursting, Paddy threw back his head and yelled a defiant scream of aggression up at a passing V of great brown pelicans. He swung the mace and brought it down on a chunk of driftwood, shivering it into a mass of flying sawdust and splinters.

He stood, arms akimbo, feet planted wide apart in the soft white sand and pointed the mace at his crewmates.

'I am Paddy Gauntlet of His Majesty's Irish Guards, and a proud Kentish man. Behold, Skullsplitter. Now get the fuck out of my way. I need a drink.'

Over the general laughter, Paddy mounted the steps of the veranda and, ignoring the firearms left for him, went inside and drank two pints of water from a jug on the kitchen table.

Gabriel joined him.

'Impressive stuff, Paddy. I'm glad we've got you.'

Paddy turned, wiping his chin. 'I'm glad I came. Boss.'

19

Café Cielo Azul was buzzing.

Los Chicos de Gabriel, as the villagers had immediately dubbed them, were surrounded by the village council of Santa Rosa, plus, in a secondary ring, the rest of the village's able-bodied men. Beyond them, the elders, the women and at the very edge the children. A traditional hierarchy. Gabriel had thoughts about that, but for now he was keeping them to himself.

A large, hand-drawn map of the village lay spread out across the wooden tabletop.

Tiny stabbed a thick finger down onto the map.

'One road in and out. That's good.'

The council chief dragged a finger in a looping curve around the village's southern side. He spoke in Spanish, which Gabriel translated.

'Here is scrub. It's thick and thorny. Sharp as the Devil's tail. They won't try and come through there.'

Kylie looked across the map at Gabriel. Both thinking the same thing.

'If we were attacking your village, sir,' he said in a respectful tone of voice, 'that's exactly the way we'd come. You wouldn't be expecting it. Probably wouldn't be guarding it.'

'We don't need guards when we have those thorns,' the councilman said. 'Those fuckers are three inches long. The tips break off under your skin and you get blood poisoning.'

'Could they drive through?' Bilbo asked the councilman in Spanish.

The older man shrugged. 'In a tank, maybe? You think they will have tanks?'

Gabriel shook his head. He was relying on a gut feeling plus a sense of the way unofficial fighting was conducted in Honduras. In other hotspots, too. Senegal, Afghanistan, Moldova. Government forces had the heavy armour. Insurgents, rebels, militias, terrorists, call them what you will, tended to Toyota Landcruisers and Hilux pickups, captured jeeps and assorted civilian vehicles up-armoured in a scrapyard by a welder with ready access to steel panels.

'We'll take precautions,' he said, turning to Sparrow. 'Let's get a few IEDs laid in there. If they try to push through with an SUV, it'll blow and they'll back off.'

'Have you got any anti-tank stuff, boss?' Tiny asked from the far end of the table.

'Javelins. Couple of RPG-7s.'

Tiny nodded, apparently satisfied. Unsurprised, too, as if all one's friends might have stores of military anti-armour munitions in their understairs cupboard.

Gabriel got to his feet and stood on his chair to address the crowd.

'Tomorrow, we need to start training you. I want every adult who can shoot to assemble in front of the cafe at 7:00 a.m. Bring your guns.'

A barrel-chested man in his forties, thick black beard and piercing dark eyes, shouldered his way to the front.

'You mean every man who can shoot, of course.'

Gabriel had been expecting this moment. Honduran society was still governed by a strict, age-old code of *machismo*. Women could work, sure, preferably in low-paid jobs. Better yet, stay at home to raise children and tend the home. Things were changing, slowly, in the cities. But out here, on the coast, far from Teguz with its gradual loosening of traditional social and business customs? No. Here, things were very much the same.

'I mean everyone,' Gabriel said loudly, eyeballing the speaker first, then the crowd at large.

A murmur swept through the cafe. Deeper male voices grumbling, female voices raised in opposition. Gabriel held up his hands to quell the voices.

'Your village is under threat. The people who are coming won't care who they shoot to take your land out from under you. To defeat them, we need as many fighters as possible.'

'Women cannot fight wars,' an old man piped up in a reedy voice. 'They don't have the strength. The killer instinct.'

This pronouncement met with a ripple of assent from the men and the older women in the cafe, and catcalls from some of the younger women. Once more, Gabriel raised his hands for silence.

'You've all heard of Russia?' Nods, murmurs of assent. And derision. *Of course. We're farmers, but we're not idiots. Who does he think we are?* 'Well, when their country was threatened in war, women picked up rifles, grenades, drove tanks and they killed their country's enemies. In Vietnam, women and children fought.'

'Are you suggesting we send our children to fight mercenaries now?' the piercing-eyed man shouted.

'No. But even they can play a part. They can carry ammunition. Bring water.'

'But they could die!' a woman shouted, clutching her baby tight to her breast inside its woven cotton sling.

'That's the last thing I want,' Gabriel said. 'But if, when, these mercenaries come, they will be ruthless. The youngest children should be taken away. To relatives in other towns if possible. But otherwise kept indoors. In cellars if you have them.'

'I still say women can't fight,' the old man grumbled, lighting a clay pipe and sticking it between toothless gums.

'Hey!' someone shouted. A woman. Gabriel recognised her

voice. Who else but Pera Flores, his true friend, field medic and, it now appeared, spokeswoman. 'You think all a woman can do is lie on her back for you, huh? Cook your meals, tend the chickens, pull beans from the earth, clean up baby sick? Huh? Do you?' She turned to Gabriel. 'Give me a gun and I will blow the head off any motherfucker who comes here looking for trouble. Am I right, ladies?'

People, men mainly, started shouting and cursing. Much shuffling and stumbling. In a wedge formation, as if they'd been practising infantry tactics on their breaks, the girls from Frida's, the brothel on the outskirts of town, arrived at the front of the crowd.

Frida herself led the charge. Eyes blazing, she turned to speak.

'Me and my girls are used to strangers coming through Santa Rosa with their,' a beat, 'little weapons. I'm not scared of them and I'm not scared of these mercenaries either. This is my town and if Gabriel says we need to defend it, then I will. Give us guns, Gabriel, and we'll shoot those motherfuckers' balls off, won't we, girls?'

To cheering, ribald insults aimed at strangers and their *pistolitas*, and some good-natured banter back and forth between the women and the rest of the townsfolk, the matter was settled. If you could hold a gun and were able or willing to learn how to shoot it, you were on the front line.

Then a new voice rose above the hubbub.

'I'll fight, too. And my friends.'

Gabriel saw a head bobbing above the rest. A tall teenaged boy, missing an ear, made his way to the front. His heart sank. It was Santiago. Pera's son and only child. At fifteen, already a man in his own eyes and half the village's, too. Children grew up early here.

'Santi, you can be useful carrying ammunition,' Gabriel said. 'Your friends too. There are going to be casualties, too. We'll need a first-aid post. People to treat the wounded.'

Santiago's eyes widened. 'Let the grandmothers treat the

Peacemaker

wounded! I am fit, I am strong. Gabriel, you've seen me shoot. My friends, too. It's our home, too.'

Pera laid a hand on Gabriel's arm. 'Let me speak, Gabe,' she said softly.

Thank god. She was going to talk her son out of it. Gabriel couldn't have Santiago's death on his conscience. It was overburdened as it was.

Pera climbed onto the chair.

'My son, Santi? Well you all know him. He's headstrong.' A few chuckles. 'He's got a temper, for sure. But ever since he came kicking and screaming into this world, and *Abuelita* Maria gave his little red arse a slap, he's been a fighter.' She looked down at Santiago and beckoned him to stand by her side. She laid a hand on the top of his head. 'This isn't the men's fight. This isn't the women's fight. This isn't Gabriel's Boys' fight. This is Santa Rosa's fight. So, yes, I give you my blessing, Santi. Fight for Santa Rosa. Fight and win!'

The cafe erupted into cheering, boot-stamping, whistling.

Gabriel stepped back and shared a look with Sparrow.

'Henry the Fifth didn't say it better,' he mouthed.

Grim-faced, Sparrow mouthed back. 'Game on.'

20

From his vantage point above the village, Gabriel looked back at the tiny coastal settlement he'd made his home.

And he sighed. Because, whatever the outcome of the looming battle for Santa Rosa, he knew one thing as surely as he knew his own name. His residency in Honduras was over.

Yes, they might triumph. So far it was two for two, and with Sparrow and the boys and an entire village of trained guerrilla fighters it could be three for three. But there would be casualties. His conscience would be bearing a lot of grief, his own, and others.

People wouldn't blame him. Not directly. But there'd be murmurs. Maybe they should have taken the cash. With the kind of money being offered they could have recreated Santa Rosa inland or further up the coast.

And he knew, deep down, beyond the place where he needed words to clarify his thoughts, that eventually those voices would start to whisper about him. How life in Santa Rosa had been peaceful until the gringo turned up. How he'd brought trouble with him as surely as a north-westerly brought storms to the coast.

The sun was already high in the sky despite the early hour and he adjusted the broad-brimmed straw hat to shade his eyes. He'd dressed like a *campesino*. Loose-fitting unbleached cotton smock, baggy trousers and scuffed brown leather shoes. Harmless, it said. Yes, it made him prey for bandits, but what could a poor peasant have to offer them? Money? Ha! A few Lempira? Hardly worth it.

They'd let him pass. And if they didn't? Loose garments weren't only good for allowing air to circulate over the wearer's skin. They could conceal as well as cool. In Gabriel's case, the items in question included a compact nine, two spare mags, his Fairbairn–Sykes fighting knife and a home-made garotte. He'd give fair warning. *One* fair warning. But time wasn't on his side. If they didn't back off, they'd pay.

The decision to hitch a ride instead of taking his truck had been hard. Time was short, so driving made sense. But if the lawyer or whoever was paying him had decided to take Gabriel off the board then he needed to stay as far from the playing surface as possible.

In the distance, a plume of red dust. The signature of a vehicle negotiating the red-dirt roads that connected all the local settlements.

He stood at the roadside and waited for the vehicle to make an appearance.

An old Ford three-ton truck hove into view, its slatted wooden load bay stacked with watermelons. Gabriel raised his hand. The driver slowed to a stop beside him. A spindly home-made cigarette dangled from his lower lip. The pungent smoke drifted down to Gabriel. He sniffed, experimentally. Coughed. Jesus! The guy's lungs must have been black from throat to diaphragm.

'Where you headed?' the driver asked. Friendly, but cautious. Despite the campesino rig, this was clearly an Anglo.

'San Pedro Sula. How far are you going?'

'La Masica.'

It was better than Gabriel had been hoping for. Halfway there. He nodded.

'Thanks.'

'Get in, then. I haven't got all day.'

* * *

Three and a half hours later, feeling as if his kidneys had been put through a blender, Gabriel stepped down from the cab in the market square in the centre of La Masica. He thanked the driver and the truck wheezed away, the driver's hand raised in a laconic farewell. Gabriel had asked during the journey whether the man had heard any rumours about foreign mercenaries or fighting men.

Nada.

Two bars flanked the square. One with red and white umbrellas, one with green and yellow. He picked the former just for the slight connection to the flag of St George. When the waitress arrived, he ordered a beer and a couple of *baleada* specials, the hot tortillas rolled around pulled pork and charred pineapple.

Two men at the next table were eyeing him. One fat, one thin, both in grease-stained denim overalls. A Honduran version of Laurel and Hardy. Their gazes looked like curiosity rather than anything malign. He nodded to them.

'Hi. Your beers are almost finished. Can I buy you fresh ones?'

They nodded their appreciation. No smiles. People in this part of the country were trusting, but they weren't pushovers.

Gabriel caught the eye of a passing waitress and ordered three beers. She brought them over almost immediately and the three men clinked the long brown necks together before drinking.

'You're Gabriel, aren't you?' the older of the two asked after putting his condensation-speckled bottle down on the table.

Gabriel's pulse flickered upwards. 'I am. How did you know?'

'I met a guy from Santa Rosa the other week and he told me this wild story about a crazy Englishman living there. He said this guy, right, well he was some sort of ex-soldier hiding from his enemies. He described him.' He pointed a nicotine-stained finger and grinned. 'He described you.'

Gabriel smiled. At least the American lawyer hadn't put out a contract on him. An image flashed before his eyes. An old-time

Wanted poster printed in crude black block capitals on cheap, yellowing paper, bleached by the sun. A bad pen and ink drawing of his face. WANTED DEAD OR ALIVE.'

'Yeah, well, that's me.'

'What are you doing in La Masica? Shopping for guns?'

He winked at his companion, who roared with laughter. Maybe the beers Gabriel had replaced weren't their first of the day.

'Just passing through,' Gabriel said. 'Though maybe you can help me with something. Have you heard anything about some American lawyer? A big, fat man in a suit. Big white cowboy hat on his head.'

Both men shook their heads. A little too quickly, Gabriel thought.

'How about a wounded man? Honduran, but more like from Teguz or San Pedro than round here.'

Two more shakes of the head.

'La Masica's a quiet town,' the older man said. 'I think we'd have heard about someone like that. Most excitement we get is when Raúl the fish man comes through.'

His companion nodded animatedly.

'Oh, man, that snapper he had last Monday. My wife cooked it in butter and garlic with some chilli and lime. I thought I'd died and gone to heaven.'

Gabriel got to his feet, suddenly tiring of their double act.

'Nice to talk to you.'

He crossed the square to where a couple of traders were lounging against the side of their pickups, both white, dusty and much-welded.

'Any chance of a lift?'

'Where you headed, friend?'

'San Pedro.'

He shook his head. 'Sorry. I'm headed the other way.'

'Yeah, me, too,' the other guy said.

Gabriel shrugged. Looked back towards the bar where he'd

left his drinking companions, thinking he'd ask them where best to try for a lift. At the cafe table, Ollie was on the phone.

He left the square, not looking back. The main road heading for San Pedro Sula resumed just beyond the network of tiny winding alleys that tangled around the western edge of the market.

The buildings here, faced in white or yellow stucco, were squashed tightly together. The streets running east–west were bright with mid-morning sun, but those crossing were shrouded in deep shade.

Cats prowled along the gutters, birds sang from rusting wire cages suspended from balconies. Scarlet geraniums overflowed window boxes.

Men appeared from a side street.

21

The trio who stepped out of the shadows were armed with pistols. Shiny new nines. Not battered old Colt 1911s their grandfathers had brought back from some foreign war.

The looks on their faces suggested they didn't want to talk. And he doubted they were random muggers pouncing on a poor *campesino* from out of town.

The man in the centre stood a foot in front of the others. The boss, then. He had a triangular bleached soul patch under his bottom lip. The other two were clean-shaven but sported an array of facial tattoos. MS-13 was Gabriel's assessment. Members of one of the most-feared gangs in Honduras.

Gabriel didn't waste time. He turned and sprinted down a narrow alley scarcely wider than his shoulders. Shots echoed in the confined space, blowing chunks of plaster off the walls.

Was that all of them? Or were there reinforcements? He darted left into a wider lane then doglegged immediately right, vaulting a pile of trash bags knotted at the tops but still emitting a putrid reek.

He had plenty of ammunition, but he didn't want any more

noise than he could help. Not if Huey, Dewey and Louie were only the advance guard.

Down here, at street level, he was at a disadvantage. Ahead, a fire escape. A hinged contraption featuring a great many ladders and half-landings attached to a three-storey apartment building. He leaped for the lowest rung and hauled himself up and onto the first landing. The whole structure groaned and creaked as rusty metal parts ground against each other.

Behind him, shouts.

'Down here!'

'Get him!'

'Gringo bastard!'

He swung himself up and onto the next landing then scrambled up the final ladder and vaulted the low parapet that surrounded the roof.

He ran over to the facing side and looked over the edge. Saw two of the men running down an alley. Where was the third man? Behind him, the fire escape creaked and groaned again.

He raced back and slid down to crouch behind a small hutch that housed a couple of rickety-looking air-conditioning units.

Boots crunched on the gritty bitumen roofing felt. He strained to catch a sound of further attackers, but it sounded like just one man. Good.

The footsteps drew nearer. Cautious, spaced out. A man not about to blunder into a trap. The bang when he shot at the hutch was deafening, even without high walls to funnel and reverberate the report back on itself.

The round slammed into the air-conditioning unit behind Gabriel's shoulder blades with enough force to jolt him. Thank God for Japanese engineering. It was lost somewhere inside the mechanism.

'Come out, motherfucker,' the man shouted, loosing off another two shots, this time into the air. 'I've got you, so stand up and die like a man.'

On balance, Gabriel thought he'd rather crouch down and live like one. But the gunman was getting closer. Gabriel had no desire to be shot where he sat. He drew his knife, holding it point uppermost. Opinions varied on the best grip for a fight. Some said an overhand, point-down grip was better. Others, the reverse, the better to drive the blade under an opponent's ribs and into their vital organs. Gabriel was agnostic. Whatever worked.

Which, in this case, meant a hard, fast, curving slash that sliced through the guy's right Achilles tendon as he drew level with the hutch and looked down at Gabriel.

'Motherf—' was as far as he made it into the traditional, if threadbare, insult. Before he could fire again, the knife had ripped a clean-edged cut deep into the inside of his left thigh, opening his femoral artery from groin to knee. Blood hosed out in high, parabolic arcs, spattering the bitumen for six or seven feet.

Gabriel stamped hard on his right wrist, breaking bones. The pistol clattered free. He knelt on his chest and pushed his face down towards the dying man.

'Who do you work for?' he hissed.

'Fuck you!'

He drew in a huge breath, ready to call for his friends. To give away Gabriel's position. Gabriel couldn't allow that.

The Fairbairn–Sykes's needle-sharp tip punctured the soft flesh inside the point of his jaw, speared his tongue to the roof of his mouth and continued upwards, bursting one eyeball before breaking through the thin floor of his brain pan and lodging in the squashy mass of greyish-pink porridge that constituted the home of his few remaining thoughts. His undamaged eye rolled upwards and he died emitting a strange series of dove-like cooing noises that subsided into a phlegmy gurgle.

Gabriel went to the edge of the roof and listened. The two men at ground level were calling to each other. Had Pepe seen the gringo? Where was Fred? Should they split up?

The gap to the next building was only five feet. Gabriel barely needed a run-up. He tracked the men as they quartered the little neighbourhood. Finally, they did decide to split up. By now Gabriel had located one of them. He looked down at him as he paused in the lee of a fruit shop to light a cigarette. Pretty relaxed attitude for a hired killer. Perhaps he was confident they'd catch their quarry without too much trouble.

Trouble descended from above, landing directly on the smoking man's shoulders, breaking both with loud snaps from splintering clavicles and drawing an unearthly scream as the tendons connecting his skull to the now-useless bones stretched to breaking point.

His neck seemed to double in length as Gabriel's feet drove his ruined shoulders down onto the top of his ribcage. He collapsed to the ground, howling, his pistol never having reached the horizontal. Gabriel stabbed him through the right wrist, pinning it to the ground, before grabbing the nine, a Glock 19. He had time to think and stuck it into the back of his waistband.

Then he slapped the man viciously across the mouth to shut him up.

'I killed your friend because he wouldn't talk. You can make a different choice. Who hired you?'

'Take me to the hospital, man. You broke my fucking neck.'

'Who hired you?'

'Hospital first. Then I'll tell you.'

Gabriel shook his head.

'Don't worry. Your neck isn't broken. I can fix it.'

He lifted the guy's head and cradled it in his arms. Wrapped his right arm under his chin.

'OK, take a deep breath in.'

The guy complied.

And then his neck *was* broken. Two down.

As Gabriel slipped back into the shadows he glanced back at the corpse. He'd felt nothing when he killed either man. Was that normal? Was it natural? Always before, he'd felt at least a passing sense of transgression. Thou shalt not kill. But if thou dost kill, thy conscience should prick thee. Just a little.

No. His conscience was quiet. Since he'd lost Eli and their unborn child, he'd lost a part of himself. The best part, he thought. Now, if people came after him, he showed no mercy.

Their cause, their reasons, their circumstances? Of no concern to Gabriel. They made their decisions. He made his.

His trousers were sticking to his legs as he slipped down the dark alleyway. He looked down. They were wet and heavy with blood from the man he'd bled out on the roof. He'd need new clothes. And a ride. He'd grown tired of hitching, and it clearly hadn't worked to keep him under the radar.

So Dewey and Louie were down. Where was Huey?

He wouldn't be shouting out anymore. Or not for long anyway. Once he got nothing back he'd figure it out. And then what? Continue alone? No. Men like him were cowards. Once their numerical advantage was lost they'd call for backup.

Gabriel turned a corner and stopped dead. Ahead of him, two children, a boy and a girl, were petting a kitten. Its mottled grey and black tail flicked back and forth, but its loud purring suggested it was enjoying the attention.

Gabriel crouched down and called softly to them.

'Hey, children?' They looked round and their eyes widened as they took in his bloodstained clothing. He held up his hands. 'It's OK, don't be frightened. I cut myself chopping peppers.'

'Do you need a doctor?' the girl said.

'No. It's fine. It looks a lot worse than it is, really. But listen, I'm looking for my friend. He's about my height, with a little beard under his mouth like this.' Gabriel sketched a little gesture at his own chin. 'He's got a first-aid kit in his car. Have you seen him?'

The little boy nodded shyly, not quite making eye contact.

Gabriel smiled before checking behind him, desperate to find his man before his man found him.

He pulled out a five-dollar bill from his pocket.

'I will give you this money if you tell me where you saw him.'

The boy stuck out his arm, while the other continued to stroke the kitten. He slowly extended his index finger, pointing to a gap between a bodega and a laundrette.

Gabriel nodded. 'Down there?'

His informant nodded again. Gabriel extended the note

between his first and middle fingers, releasing it the moment the little boy darted out a hand to pluck it free.

'Thank you,' Gabriel said, getting to his feet. 'I like your kitten, by the way. Does it have a name?'

The girl piped up. 'Eli.'

Gabriel swallowed hard as a flash of anxiety streaked through his body.

'What did you say?'

'Her name is Bella.'

Gabriel blinked. Fought to regain his equilibrium as stars flitted around the edge of his vision. He thanked the children a second time and headed towards the alley where Huey had taken refuge.

22

Gabriel slipped into the alley.

Ahead of him, footsteps echoed off the high plastered walls that hemmed in pursued and pursuer.

Gabriel drew his pistol. Noise had ceased to be an issue. He looked back at the entryway to the alley. A tall sliver of light. Nobody following. Ahead, darkness. Maybe the alley was a dead end. That would suit his purposes.

Flattening himself to the wall, the plaster cool against his back, he edged along, not wanting to present a target for Huey.

Stinking water ran into a central gutter. A smooth rippling flow. Then it changed. A V-shaped wavelet progressed towards him. Someone had disturbed the little stream.

Gabriel looked up. No fire escapes to help him this time. But as he took another cautious step forwards, his hand edging along the cool plasterwork, his fingertips encountered a door, set flush with the wall. He gave it an experimental push and it swung inwards. He slipped inside.

His eyes took a few seconds to adjust to the gloom. An abandoned workshop. Maybe for a potter. An old wheel lay at an angle, a sack of rock-hard clay canted over beside it. Broken jugs, mugs and cooking pots lay in a pile. In the centre of the room a big cuboid structure constructed from cinder blocks, standing on short steel legs and connected to the wall by thick electric cables. A kiln.

And a door.

An idea came to Gabriel. He pulled the door and it opened into a further derelict space. And another door. He entered the third room and caught his breath, darting back into the shadows.

Outside, through a glassless window, he saw Huey, backing up the alley, his gun up.

He lifted his own pistol. Took aim through the window. His man had a cat's sixth sense for danger. He spun round and fired wildly into the workshop. Bullets slammed into the back wall, splintering a shelf-full of finished but abandoned pots. Razor-edged ceramic shards whickered through the air.

He had to move. Huey was at the window, firing constantly, though thankfully without aiming.

Gabriel returned fire but Huey was already on the move, sprinting away. Maybe he didn't like working solo.

Time to finish this. Gabriel climbed out through the window, checking that Huey wasn't waiting to kill him in a turkey shoot from further up the alley. The coast was clear. At the end of the alley, he emerged into a little courtyard. Above him, a woman was pegging out terry cloth nappies on a line slung between opposite apartments.

She looked down at him. He returned her frank, appraising stare.

'There's a man. A gangster. He tried to kill me. Which way did he go?' Gabriel asked her, his voice, though quiet, reverberating in the enclosed space.

She inclined her head toward the far corner of the square then retreated inside.

A huge terracotta pot housed a lemon tree. Behind it, almost hidden, an arched doorway. With a yell, Huey emerged from behind the tree, brandishing his weapon. He strode across the square towards Gabriel, gun tipped over sideways in the style gangbangers loved. Gabriel felt sure they'd imitated it from American movies in a case of life imitating art.

Gabriel ducked inside one of the other three doorways leading off the square, his own pistol raised. Breathing heavily.

He counted five shots.

He got to his knees, then his belly, and rolled into the open doorway, firing upwards. Three shots in a fast volley. *Bangbangbang*. A single continuous eruption of sound that added its echoes to Huey's gunshots. He had just enough time to catch sight of the man ducking back behind the lemon tree.

Huey returned fire. Ten more rounds in two five-round bursts. Silence. An oath. Gabriel crouch-ran across the twenty yards of open cobbles and flattened himself against the curved belly of the pot. He registered the click and scrape of mags been ejected and inserted. The slide being racked.

Huey was right-handed. He'd leave his cover on his right side. Gabriel hunkered down and eased his heels underneath him then shuffled silently round to his left. Just a little. He didn't want to come face to face with his opponent. Not yet, anyway.

Boots scuffed on the cobbles. Huey stood, sprang up and out to his right. Commenced shooting. Into empty space.

'What the fuck!'

Gabriel rounded the pot and stood behind him. He dug the muzzle of his P226 deep into the man's neck, right over the knobble of the sixth cervical vertebra.

'Move,' he murmured. 'I dare you.'

Then he withdrew the pistol so the man wouldn't know where to aim for if he turned and tried a fancy disarming move.

'No? Drop the nine. You fuck around, you die.'

The man opened his hand and the Glock clanked to the cobbles.

'Kick it away. Nice and hard. No tricks.'

A combat boot teed up to the Glock and flicked it across the cobbles to the edge of the courtyard where it clinked against the wall.

Gabriel drew his arm back and smacked the butt of his pistol into Huey's right temple. He went down in a heap, his head hitting the cobbles with a dull crack.

When he came round it was to find himself bound to the pot containing the lemon tree. Gabriel had rented the washing line from the woman upstairs. Twenty dollars. Enough for ten more.

Gabriel crouched in front of him.

'The question I'm about to ask you, I asked your two friends. They told me to fuck off. So I killed them.' He nudged the muzzle of his pistol into the top of the man's nose, sending him cross-eyed as he focused on the barrel. 'I'm going to ask you now and I want you to think very carefully about how you answer. You've got a big, important choice coming up. Understand?'

'Yes, I understand,' he answered nasally, unable to tear his gaze away from the gun deforming his face. 'I'll tell you what you want to know. Just ask your question.'

'Who hired you?'

'The Alligator.'

'Yeah, I figured that much out for myself. I want to know his real name.'

The man's eyes jittered left and right, finally able to focus on something other than the muzzle of Gabriel's pistol.

'If I tell you, you'll untie me?'

'Yes, I will. But you'd better tell me now. I'm losing my patience.'

'His name is George Mason. He's American. Ex-CIA.' Now the guy had started talking, he couldn't stop. Maybe it was a relief to drop the macho act. 'He's been in South America for years. Training rebels, insurgents, whatever. Anyone who hates communists, leftists, socialists, whatever they call themselves these days. Those guys like to come down here and treat our countries like a training ground. Now he's in business for himself.'

'Who does he work for?'

'All kinds, man, I don't know!'

'Who does he work for *now*? Who's paying your wages?'

'I don't know, man! I swear on my mother's life. That's all I know. Please.'

'Where can I find him?'

The man nodded frantically.

'Yeah, OK, I can tell you that. His office is in a warehouse on Avenida New Orleans. Where it crosses Calle 7. Got this chica painted on the side in her underwear smoking a cigarette. You can't miss it.'

He was telling the truth. Gabriel had an instinct for it.

'Hey, man! You gotta untie me. You said you would.'

Gabriel nodded at the man sent to kill him. 'You're right. I did.'

He took the muzzle away from Huey's face. And shot him cleanly through the heart.

Gabriel stooped and untied him. Wiped the white plastic clothesline down, coiled it over his elbow and returned it to the lady on the second floor.

Now he had a name. George Mason. Ex-spook. Paramilitary branch. He knew the type. Their souls seared away by too much double-dealing, too much 'enhanced interrogation', too many political assassinations and murders of trade unionists. Too many bombings, kidnappings, disappearances.

He wouldn't be the guy at the top of the tree. Just another intermediary between the gunmen and the ultimate paymaster. The person who wanted Santa Rosa as some sort of private naval base.

And Gabriel was going to find him.

23

Gabriel entered a little general store set just back from a market square.

The owner's wiry eyebrows elevated as this blood-soaked figure entered the blue-white, neon-lit interior of his shop. But he was too polite, or maybe too worldly, to say anything.

'I need some clothes,' Gabriel said.

'Clearly,' the man replied. Worldly, then. 'I have shirts, jeans, boots. Even some underwear if that,' he gestured at Gabriel's trousers, 'has soaked through.'

Five minutes later, a less gory, though still baggily dressed Gabriel emerged from the store. He crossed to the cafe and entered the bar. The woman at the counter glanced up. She'd served him his lunch earlier.

'What can I get you?'

'A coffee and the answer to a question.'

She regarded him coolly as she made his coffee.

'American?'

'English.'

She raised thick black eyebrows that met in the middle. Set a tiny white china cup on a saucer in front of him. Pushed a sugar pourer closer.

'English? Do you know Princess Kate?'

He shook his head. 'Not personally, no. I hear she's very nice, though.'

She snorted. 'Of course you don't know her! Do you think I'm some ignorant peasant woman? But you're polite, I'll give you that. So tell me, it's none of my business, but what is an Englishman doing in La Masica?'

One of his mother's phrases popped into his head. Not one his paymasters in the Regiment and certainly not the Department had favoured. *Honesty is the best policy.*

'I'm on my way to San Pedro Sula to find the man who sent gangsters to kill me.'

She tilted her head on one side. Considering.

'Because you're English?'

Another worldly resident of this small town. He liked her.

'Because I wouldn't sell him my land.'

She picked up a bar cloth and started drying glasses.

'A man's land is very precious. How come you've got some here, though?'

Honesty was still the best policy. And it helped to talk, he'd found.

'My wife was murdered. She was pregnant with our first child. I had to get away from everyone and everything I knew from before.'

She stopped polishing the glass in her hand.

'Oh, Mother of God, I am so sorry for you, my love.'

'Thank you. May I ask my question?'

'Of course, of course! Whatever you need to know, if I can help I will.'

'I had lunch here earlier, outside. The *baleada* specials. They were delicious.'

She smiled. 'My grandmother's recipe.'

'I was drinking with two men at the next table. One was fat, one thin. Do you know them?'

'Oh, I know them. Rafi and Hipó, he's the fat one. He owns the garage on Calle de la Revolución. If your car has broken down they're the only game in town. But watch out. They'll try and fleece you if they know you're English.'

Gabriel finished his coffee.

'Thank you. I'll be on my guard.'

Outside, blinking in the sunlight, he headed towards Stan and Ollie's garage.

He wasn't the one who'd need to be on his guard.

24

The sign – red neon, half-on, half-off – proclaimed *La Ingenieria de Hipólito*.

Engineering? Seemed a bit high-flown. Gabriel reckoned if they couldn't fix it with a screwdriver, a lump hammer or a monkey wrench, they'd be out of ideas.

Two gas pumps out front. Faded Shell livery that looked pre-war. A pile of bald tyres in a corner of the yard, home to a huge ginger cat that eyed this interloper with malevolent yellow eyes. A handful of vehicles sitting beneath a hand-painted sign reading 'Previously-loved' – by a great many suitors, to judge from their condition. And, sitting among them, like a pedigree stallion in a field of spavined nags destined for the knackers yard, a gleaming black Chevy Suburban. Not a speck of road dust on its acres of glittering chromework or deep, glossy paintwork. Probably not a farmer's vehicle, then.

Gabriel slouched, pulled his hat brim lower and limped onto the forecourt. The tomcat raised itself into a magnificent inverted U, its fur spiked up into a malevolent bottle-brush, and hissed as if it were the Devil himself.

Hands in pockets, he approached the open hatchway that led to what he supposed Hipó would call his engineering workshop.

Sitting in the shade in a couple of beach chairs were the two men he'd bought beers for earlier. On home territory, they seemed even more relaxed than they had at the cafe. Hipó got to his feet as Gabriel entered the gloomy space and walked up to the pair.

'Help you, friend?'

Gabriel straightened. Removed his hat. The effect on Hipó was profound. He stepped back hurriedly, tripping over the frame of his beach chair and stumbling into his skinny friend, who exclaimed in annoyance then zipped his lip as he saw who'd come a-calling.

'Yes, you can help me,' Gabriel said, pleasantly. 'You can tell me who you were calling when I left you at the cafe.'

His eyes flicked down to his friend. Gabriel raised a hand in warning to him. Stay down. He stayed sitting. Wise.

'I wasn't calling nobody.'

Gabriel shook his head.

'I watched you make the call. Who was it? Those men who were after me? Did you think I'd be dead? Is that why you looked at me like I was Lazarus?'

Hipó held his hands out wide. 'Look, man, I don't want no trouble, OK? I'm just a simple man. I fix a few cars, I sell a little gas. It's a quiet life. It's all I want.'

'Yes, well that's what I want, too. But every time I try, someone tries to spoil it. So, Hipólito, let me ask you again, who were you calling? If it helps sharpen your memory, those three men? They're dead. I killed them.'

The fat man, sweating profusely now, opened his mouth.

His skinny friend chose that exact moment to leap from his chair and swing a wrench at Gabriel's head.

'Motherfucker!'

The crunch when it hit bone was sickening.

Rafi uttered a low, disorientated groan and fell to the floor clutching his dislocated left shoulder. Gabriel pointed the wrench at Hipó.

'See what I mean? Now talk. Quickly, before I adjust one of your ball-joints as well.'

'It was the guy with the little beard, here.' He touched his chin just below the lower lip. 'He was telling all us guys the same thing. Let him know if we saw the Englishman. Fifty US. I'm sorry, man, but times are hard. I got to eat.'

Gabriel looked over his shoulder. At the Suburban. Back at the garage owner.

'That Chevy. It's his?'

'He left it here. Said he'd collect it when he was done kil—' He reddened. 'I mean, you know, when he was finished with his business here.'

'Give me the keys.'

Hipó frowned. 'But...'

'Give me the keys or I'll kill you. I don't want to, but I also don't care. Your choice.'

Hipó shook his head violently. 'No, no, it's all good. Hold on. They're on the board.'

He hurried to a dark corner of the workshop. Gabriel watched him the whole way. If he came back holding anything larger than a Chevy key fob he'd be discussing poor life choices with Huey, Dewey and Louie in a flame-licked waiting room.

Sensibly, he puffed his way back across the oil-stained concrete with a chunky black plastic fob in his hand. He held it out for Gabriel to take.

'Thank you. Now, let's fix your friend Rafi. Bring me a length of rope.'

'No, man, please! I did what you asked. Don't hang him!'

'Bring it!' Gabriel barked.

Once Hipó returned with the rope, Gabriel looped it under the prostrate man's shoulders, ignoring his howls of pain, then wrapped it in a figure-of-eight over and under both biceps. He held the paired ends out to Hipó. 'When I tell you, pull. Hard.'

Gabriel pinioned Rafi to the ground and eased the heels of his hands down onto the dislocated shoulder. He looked across at Hipó.

'Now.'

The fat man squeezed his eyes shut and yanked on the rope.

Gabriel pushed down in a forceful jerk, dropping his upper-body weight onto the joint. With a pop, and a scream from Rafi that bounced off the corrugated-iron roof, the joint reseated itself.

He left them struggling to get Rafi back into his chair. Outside, the temperature had risen by a few degrees. On the western horizon, thunderheads the greenish-charcoal-purple of day-old bruises were massing.

He unlocked the SUV and climbed up into the cabin. Inhaled deeply. Leather and pungent human sweat, overlaid with aftershave. It was a choice between sealing himself into the noxious interior so the aircon would work, or boiling, humid air and a release from the nausea threatening to envelop him.

He cracked the windows and pulled away.

Next stop, San Pedro Sula and an appointment with an alligator.

25

Gabriel slowed the truck and pulled off the highway into a stony lay-by pitted with foot-deep potholes and studded with cacti.

A black and green lizard eyed him from a rock. The reptile had to keep lifting alternate pairs of feet in a strange dance designed to stop its feet burning down to the bone.

La Masica lay seven miles to the east. Far enough for him not to be worried about a tail.

He punched in the number. One of maybe three he'd committed to memory. The other phone burred distantly, long, drawn-out tones during which he almost decided to hang up before it connected. But then—

'Hello. Who is this?'

'Tara, it's me.'

She screamed.

'BB! Oh my god! Where are you? What happened? I thought you were dead. I've had people looking for you all over the world. Talk to me, big bro! I've been going out of my mind.'

'Whoa! Slow down. I will talk to you if you let me.'

'Talk then. You fucking owe me an explanation.'

HIs sister's voice sounded odd. Like she was recovering from a bad throat infection.

He drew in a deep breath. Why did it never get any easier?

'Eli's dead. She was pregnant, too. Murdered. Agents of the British state.'

As he spoke the awful words, that heavy black sadness descended on him once again. As if every single bad thing in his life, every loss of a friend in combat, or afterwards, even Seamus being hit by a car, had collapsed into a black hole of despair at the centre of which lay Eli's inert body, bleeding out on the floor of that bullet-riddled cottage on the Isle of Scalpay in the Hebrides.

When she spoke again, Tara's voice was low. He could hear her grief in the thickening tone.

'BB, I am so sorry. I mean, you know, I am devastated. For you. And for Eli. And the baby.' She paused and he heard her choke back a sob. She resumed in a halting voice. 'Did you get them?'

The question revealed much about his sister. That she had formed a deep bond to Eli, despite only meeting her once, at the wedding in London. That she had depths of compassion Gabriel felt he was missing. And that her first question was about vengeance.

Maybe she was now a legitimate businesswoman. But Gabriel knew a truth about her many of her current investors didn't.

Chinese agents had taken Tara as a child and trained her as a ruthless assassin. A hideous woman nicknamed 'the Crane' had instructed her charges to kill in a hundred ways, only a few of which involved conventional weapons. After escaping, Tara had become a Triad enforcer, eventually ending up running the whole operation.

So, on being told government agents had murdered his wife, the question was not whether they'd been caught, tried and jailed. It was whether he'd killed them.

'I did.'

'All of them?'

'All.'

'How high did it go?'

'To the top.'

'Shit, BB. I'm sorry.'

'What's done is done.'

'No! Don't say that. I know you, remember? How are you coping? Where are you coping? Are you still in England? No, you can't be. Not after that.'

'Honduras. It's why I'm calling. And I'm sorry I didn't call before. I really am. I've not been in a good place. Not for a long time.'

'Hey, it's fine. You're calling now. So, what's up?'

The story took longer to tell this time. He had more details. More ideas. More suspicions. When he finished speaking, Tara didn't speak immediately. He listened to her breathing, a light, steady whisper down the line from Hong Kong to a gritty, pockmarked lay-by in the middle of nowhere in Central America.

'You want my help?'

'Not straightaway. I'm in the middle of a trip. Gathering intelligence on whoever's behind this whole thing. But when I get back to Santa Rosa. How long would it take you to sort out a flight from Hong Kong?'

She laughed bitterly.

'I don't live there anymore. I had to get out. The Chinese government is cracking down on what it calls 'triad-linked organisations'. They were starting to dig around and I figured it was time to liquidate my assets before they stole them from under me.'

'So the business?'

'Dissolved. It was a bugger, BB. I had employees, I had offices. Shit, I even had a fucking marketing department, can you believe it? All gone. So the biggest gang in East Asia can pretend it's running a corruption-free country.'

'So where are you now?'

'Paris. I bought an apartment on Avenue Montaigne in the eighth arrondissement. You know it?'

'I know that's an impressive French accent, but the avenue? No.'

'My block is sandwiched between a Dior boutique and a Ferrari showroom. One of my neighbours is a French movie star.'

'Not bad. So you're a woman of leisure these days.'

'Yeah, and I'm bored stiff, so your offer is a welcome relief. But listen, BB—'

He caught it, then. A note of anxiety in her voice. The way she tailed off. Something was wrong.

'What is it? What's wrong? Are the Chinese still after you?'

'Bloody hell! Are you a mind-reader? Not as far as I know. But there are always rumours in the expat community. Especially, and I'm not boasting, BB, among the rich ones, there are rumours we're all being watched.'

She didn't have to say by whom. It would be agents of the Ministry of State Security. Oh, the Russians always got the headlines, thanks to the current president's taste for flamboyant murders on foreign soil. But the Chinese were content to leave the limelight to others. Those who knew, knew. The MSS was every bit as ruthless, every bit as deadly as the FSB or the GRU. And because they still served an ideology, rather than a single man, they were far less corruptible.

'So what's the problem, Tara?'

She sighed deeply.

'When I got here, I wanted to disappear. Completely. I had a new identity, that wasn't hard. But the MSS are past masters at ferreting out people they want to talk to. I couldn't risk it. I found a surgeon.'

Now he understood. Tara had paid to have her features altered. That was OK. Why the fuss?

'It's fine. I understand.'

'No, BB, you don't! I had everything done. Facial remodelling. I even lost the epicanthic fold. The western look's very popular now among China's super-rich. We all look like *gweilos* now.'

'Listen, you did what you had to do.'

'I haven't finished. They broke my jaw, repositioned my ears so the facial recognition software wouldn't ping on me.' She was crying now. 'Oh, god, Gabriel, I felt like I'd died. Every time I looked in the mirror there was this total stranger looking out at me.'

'Is that why your voice sounds odd? Did you do something to your vocal chords?'

'It wasn't too bad. They just tighten them, or loosen them, I don't really understand. Then they sort of induce scarring to add a bit of grittiness.'

'I can still tell it's you though. You're literally the only person on Earth who calls me BB. Actually, it's a relief. The guys I hired all call me Wolfie.'

She laughed.

'Wolfie? That doesn't sound very tough. When I get there we'll have to sort out something better.'

They agreed he'd call again when he was back in Santa Rosa.

Back in the SUV he cranked the air-conditioning.

It sounded like Tara had been through the mill in her escape from incarceration. But he had no illusions what the Chinese government would do to someone like her. If changing her looks and even her voice was the price of freedom, who wouldn't do what she had done?

Mainly what he felt was relief. After losing Eli and their child, he'd been drifting in a fog of grief, alcohol and emotional numbness, distracting himself any way he could. It was good to speak to his sister. Even if the next time they met he'd have to relearn how she looked.

He shrugged. When he looked in the mirror, which he seldom did these days, he didn't see the man he'd been looking back at him, either.

Maybe reconnecting with Tara was the first step to regaining his old self.

For the first time in a very long while, he felt able to smile, even if it was only a grim twist of the lips.

Things were going to get better.

26

Gabriel rolled into El Progreso at 3:43 p.m.

It wasn't a huge town, but compared to La Masica it was like London. He filled up the Suburban, paying in cash, then sought out a clothing store.

There had been a time, it seemed like another life entirely, when Gabriel had cared quite deeply about clothes. He'd chosen well-cut suits, fine cotton shirts, silk ties. Handmade shoes. He'd worn an expensive watch, a legacy from his father. When that had been lost, buried beneath the oozing red mud of a Cambodian killing field, he'd replaced it with another.

Why had he bothered? Really? The last time he'd worn a suit had been on his wedding day. Even then, he'd been targeted. Seeing signs of impending loss nobody else saw, not even Eli.

Shoving the memory down before it could take him too deep to function, he walked into *El Hombre Bien Vestido*. He had no intention of emerging sharply dressed, but the peasant rig had served its purpose.

The salesman's sceptical glance quickly turned to one of ingratiating charm as Gabriel spoke to him in deliberately high-register Castilian Spanish, emphasising his English accent.

'Good afternoon. I would like your help choosing an outfit. I have very specific requirements.'

An hour and ten minutes later, having made use of the store's inhouse alteration service, whose queue he jumped using an additional hundred dollars direct into the salesman's pocket as a launchpad, Gabriel left wearing a fresh suit of clothes. Anonymous, yet not shabby.

A black T-shirt. A thick grey cotton jacket, now with a concealed pocket high up on the left. Heavyweight jeans complete with a deep, slim pocket stitched down the right thigh and reinforced with leather. A pair of expensive brown leather boots with thick ridged soles, billed as 'biker' but actually just very high-quality hiking boots. A navy baseball cap. A pair of Ray-Ban Aviators with mirrored blue lenses.

On his way back to the Suburban, which he'd parked a little way up the street, Gabriel handed the bundle of clothes he'd bought in La Masica to a homeless guy pushing a supermarket trolley.

Reaching the SUV, he spent a few minutes rubbing and scuffing the boots on the kerb. Once he was satisfied with their newly worn-in look, he removed the jacket and rubbed it against the dust-caked door before dropping it to the ground and grinding it into the tarmac. He shook it out and put it on again. Much better.

The P226 went into the inner pocket freshly constructed by the store's seamstress. The Fairbairn–Sykes slid down into the scabbard stitched into the jeans. The gangbanger's Glock 19 had gone into a drainage ditch long since, but the Luger 9mm ammunition chinked in one of the jacket's outer pockets.

It took barely fifteen minutes to find the junction of Calle 7 and Avenida New Orleans. As described by Huey, one corner was occupied by a warehouse that presumably had once dealt in cigarettes.

Like a poster for *Attack of the Fifty-Foot Woman*, a faded advertising mural occupied the entire road-facing wall. A busty blonde in 1950s-style corset and stockings performing an act on a lit cigarette that could charitably be interpreted as 'smoking'. Flowing beneath her high-heeled feet, a slogan on a blue ribbon. 'She smokes London Lady'.

On the corner opposite was a tyre place. Orange-painted metal gates, shutters, brickwork, even the roadway leading inside. Gabriel drove in and booked the Suburban in for a fresh set all round. The technician looked sceptically at the existing rubber.

'They're fine, man. Got thousands of kilometres left on them.'

Gabriel shrugged. 'My boss wants new ones. What am I gonna do?'

With a knowing smile, the technician directed him to the reception area where he could get a coffee.

'It's gonna take a couple hours, man.'

Gabriel waved a hand to say, no problem. One working stiff to another.

With the car in secure parking, he wandered into the reception and then out through the street door. His outfit wasn't quite complete.

Four blocks from the tyre place he found what he was looking for. The building site sprawled over a vacant lot. No workers in evidence. That was Honduras for you. Unguarded, because who would want to steal some red and white traffic cones and a couple of bits of safety gear discarded in the bucket of a backhoe?

Across from the cigarette warehouse, ten or twenty motorcycles and scooters were parked haphazardly outside a Yamaha dealership. On the edge of the grouping was a manhole cover. Gabriel set up the traffic cones at the corners and strung some tape between them. He dragged a white plastic chair over from outside the neighbouring bodega and sat down.

He adjusted the yellow hi-vis jacket over his shoulders and pulled the peak of his scratched green hard hat down over his eyes. His uniform was the blue-collar equivalent of a clipboard and lanyard in an office environment. With the right kit you could go anywhere and yet be seen by no one.

He had a perfect view of the cigarette warehouse. Only one

entrance, on Avenida New Orleans, where he was now ensconced on his lurk.

For the first hour, all Gabriel got for his troubles was a nagging sore throat and a persistent cough from exhaust fumes. After ninety minutes a man in a leather jacket and pressed blue jeans came out of the Yamaha dealership and asked him what was going on.

Gabriel shrugged.

'City council work order. I gotta wait here for a crew.'

'What kind of crew? I'm running a business here.'

Gabriel shrugged even more vigorously.

'How should I know? My boss says I gotta wait, I wait.'

The guy shook his head and ran a hand over luxuriant black hair glistening with product.

'Motherfucker!'

But he was smiling in that typical Honduran style when confronted with the vagaries of officialdom. A loose translation: 'Eh, waddya gonna do?'

Gabriel returned to staring across Avenida New Orleans. It wasn't the worst lurk he'd ever been on. For a start he had a chair. And he wasn't waist-deep in swamp water. So no leeches. Or hunkering beneath camo netting on a rocky desert escarpment beneath a broiling sun while his skin burnt to a crisp.

Another hour passed. Still nothing.

He caught movement at the side of the building. A door opened inwards, cutting a perfect black rectangle into the washed-out pink stucco. Framed in the rectangle a man stood, talking to someone on the inside. He wore a turquoise short-sleeved shirt over white trousers. A wide-brimmed straw hat with a black band.

He turned away from the person he'd been addressing and checked the traffic. The lights changed, as he took advantage to trot across the four lanes, jinking left and right between cars, bikes and trucks.

His path brought him within a few metres of Gabriel's position.

He was an Anglo. Hooded eyes in a craggy face shaded by the

hat's wide brim. The lights changed to green and the traffic moved off. A tall-sided van blew past and his shirt flapped in its slipstream. Beneath the cotton, a pistol in a black nylon belt holster. The shirt settled over his hip again.

Was this George Mason? It was easy to draw conclusions. American. Nice clothes, in that distinctive style that screamed 'CIA paramilitary doing casual'. A concealed firearm. But easy conclusions were for amateurs. And, though he hadn't been official for a long time, Gabriel was still a professional.

What he had was a lead. Nothing more.

But the great thing about leads was you just had to keep hold of one end and see where they took you.

27

Gabriel tailed the American for a block, keeping around a hundred yards back, enough for a dozen or so locals to provide cover.

The target took a left turn and disappeared from sight. Unworried, Gabriel picked up his pace a little and turned down the same street twenty seconds later.

His man had gone. Vanished as if whisked away under a magician's cape. All kinds of street hustlers worked the Calles and Avenidas in the big cities of Honduras, but as far as he knew, people who could make other people disappear were not yet a reality. Although, on reflection, there were plenty of cartel and gang members who could do a pretty effective job. If you didn't mind a certain amount of residue.

He walked a few hundred metres further, looking left and right. Where had the American gone? Convinced now that the man he was following was George Mason – *El Caiman* – he wasn't giving up just yet. So how would Gabriel lose a tail? Duck into a doorway? None in evidence. Alligators loved sewers in urban myths. So drop down a manhole cover? No, lifting one of the heavy cast-iron plates embossed *Ciudad de la SPS* would take too much time and make too much noise.

He skirted a pile of rubbish only for a grimy human hand to emerge from the stinking mess of rags and old newspapers. Another of the thousands of homeless who drifted through the city looking for work, or, as here, a handout.

Gabriel fished around in a pocket and drew out a crumpled 200-Lempira note. About eight dollars. He passed the colourful banknote with its design of two scarlet macaws to the homeless man.

As their fingers brushed, Gabriel felt an immense shudder pass through him. For a moment Eli appeared before him surrounded by a blazing corona of white light. His brain boiled in his skull and as he collapsed onto the sidewalk his muscles seemed to be trying to twist free of their attachments to his skeleton.

Something smothered his nose and mouth and a sickly, sweet smell like overripe melon invaded his nostrils, his brain, his consciousness.

The light faded. Eli disappeared.

28

The homeless man straightened up from the prostrate form on the sidewalk in front of him.

He took off the filthy raincoat, stained with road dirt, dogshit and the grease from a nearby *baleada* stand and dropped it onto the pile of crumpled newspapers under which he'd recently been hiding. Scratch that. Not hiding. Waiting.

The battered ballcap emblazoned with C.D. Marathón, a city soccer club was next, along with the greasy grey wig beneath it.

He took out an iPhone 15 Pro Max. Spoke in English.

'I've got him.'

Seconds later, a minivan pulled up at the kerb. A dusty grey Ford Econoline. George Mason nodded. It was twenty years old and still going strong. You couldn't beat the old blue oval, the working man's ride.

A burly Honduran man jumped down from the driver's side and together they hauled the body into the back, slinging it in unceremoniously with a shouted '*Uno-dos-tres!*' in unison. And laughter.

Mason climbed in after his captive. The interior was plain metal, the floor scraped in many places and stained with dark-brown splotches here and there. With brisk, efficient movements he zip-tied Wolfe's wrists together and then his ankles, finally lashing him tight to bars welded onto the side panels.

He stood, keeping his head bent – he was tall, and had lacerated his scalp more than once in similar situations – and kicked Wolfe in the back, over the right kidney. And again, over the left.

It wasn't strictly necessary. He just felt like it. OK, he *enjoyed* it.

Maybe his flair for causing pain had tipped over into enthusiasm some years back, but his paymasters hadn't seemed to mind. At least not until that case of mistaken identity in Bogota. Man, that had been a monu-fucking-mental clusterfuck. Heads had to roll. After the French journalist's, that was. Mason's was first onto the chopping block.

Relaxing in the passenger seat, he called his current client.

'I got him.'

'He's alive? Please tell me you didn't kill him, George.'

Jesus, the guy was such a Prissy Pete.

'He's fine. I Tasered him and gave him a jolt of the old sleeping juice, but he's basically fine.'

'Basically?'

'He fell as me and Jorge were loading him into the van. Might have caught something on the bumper.'

'Find out what he's been up to in Santa Rosa.'

'You don't want me to just kill him?'

'No! I already said, what if he's put counter-measures in place?'

Mason laughed. Probably not the ideal client-management protocol with a billionaire but hey, he was in Portland and Mason was in San Pedro Sula, so he had some leeway was how he figured it.

'Countermeasures? What, you think he's set up a cordon sanitaire? Got some goats wired with infra-red cameras and—'

'Shut the fuck up, George! Just shut up. I pay you to take my orders, OK? *I* pay *you*! If this Englishman makes one more attempt to derail my plans I will come down there personally and kill him. Then I'll kill you and then I'll kill every single one of your employees, associates, casual day-rate guys and your pet fucking gerbil!'

Mason smiled at Jorge as he held the iPhone away from his ear. Kalt really was a piece of work. Mason fantasised about taking him to the warehouse and showing him what violence looked like in the flesh, not threatened down the phone by some Yale dropout in a plush office.

'Relax, Xander. I'll find out everything. Trust me, when I'm done with him he'll be begging me to ask for his Apple ID, his credit card PIN and his inside fucking leg measurement.'

'Really? *Trust* you? Trust *you*, George? Like I trusted you when you sent in your, what did you call it, your *kill team*? Oh, OK, because that worked out so well, didn't it? Oh, wait. No. It did not. It was a fucking trainwreck. He killed them all.'

'Actually he left one alive.'

'I don't care!'

Kalt was screaming now. Mason wondered whether a man could give himself an aneurysm making that much noise. He'd never seen it happen, but there was always a first time. Maybe today would be his lucky day. Not Kalt, obviously. He was the money man and, as such, Mason felt he could put up with a certain amount of bratty play-acting.

No, not Kalt. But Wolfe.

Wolfe was another story.

29

Wake up, my honey, my soul. Wake up.

Her voice is so sweet, he wants her to keep talking to him. Even though it must be a dream.

A steely, metallic taste sours the inside of his mouth. His ears are ringing. And, oh, Jesus, a deep, nauseating pain in his kidneys spreads out in all directions, stretching slimy agonising tentacles into his legs, his groin, his belly, and up into his chest.

He knows the signs. A beating. Not a bad one. But professional.

A portent.

30

Light burst into his brain. So bright he saw the outline of the bare bulb through eyelids that felt suddenly insubstantial, filmy. Not up to the job of keeping the light out.

He opened his eyes. Took stock.

How long had he been out for? He looked down at the front of his trousers. He hadn't wet himself. So maybe a few hours. A little longer since he hadn't been keeping himself hydrated properly. Must fix that. Drink more water. Not *guifiti*. Terrible stuff. All those weeds floating in it like—

The light crackled through his brain like lightning. He opened his eyes. Looked down. A large deep-blue stain spread over the front of his jeans. This was bad. Losing time. Mason had Tasered him. He'd been shot before. Stabbed. Bludgeoned. Never Tasered. A first, then. He hoped there wouldn't be a second.

He was in a cell. No need to pace it out. Five-foot-high ceiling. Four feet to a side. Classic dimensions so that incarceration itself became torture. He couldn't lie down. Nor stand.

On the plus side, he was alive. So Mason had a need that only

Gabriel could meet. On the minus side, that meant torture. Or what did the spooks like to call it? Oh, yes. Enhanced interrogation techniques.

The tiny space smelled of his own urine and, below that, a sour reek of vomit and shit.

Some unfortunate previous occupant had painted a graffito onto the soft white plaster in deep-brownish red ink.

Desaria estar muerta.

I wish I was dead.

He visualised nails ripped out. An agonised prisoner daubing their own blood onto the wall. *Her* own blood. Because *muerta* was the feminine form. Fuck. This was not good. Not good at all.

A tiny hatch in the door slid open with a grating noise that set Gabriel's teeth on edge. A plastic tray slithered across the floor. On it a plastic bowl containing some greyish mess that might have been porridge. No spoon. A small bottle of water rolled in after it.

Another hatch, higher up the wall, opened. Brown skin, stubble, a broken nose.

'You're in deep shit, gringo. You know where you are?'

'Enlighten me.'

'Ever hear of Battalion 3-16?'

'No. Is it a soccer team?'

'You wish. Counter-terror unit. We cleaned out the communist filth infesting Honduras. Leftist politicians, lawyers, journos, civil-fucking-rights activists, trade unionists. We used to take'em right off the streets. Bring 'em here for a little refresher course in Honduran culture. Then the new government disbanded us. But guess what, they never found all our prisons.'

'Your friend George. Did he train you? He's ex-CIA, isn't he?'

'What he is and what he ain't is nothing to do with you. But I promise you this, gringo motherfucker. By the time he's done with you, you'll know all you need to know about him.'

The hatch slammed shut. Gabriel considered what he'd learned. Most of it was bad. He'd fallen into the hands of a torturer. Worse, a torturer who'd trained one of South America's notorious secret police-slash-army units. But the guard was talkative. That might prove useful. And they'd have to take him somewhere to interrogate him. No room in here for much more than him and the tray of whatever that was in the bowl.

His stomach cramped suddenly. When had he last eaten? He couldn't remember. He cracked the top on the bottle of water and took a long drink. The unbroken seal meant nothing. Plenty of ways to introduce drugs into a bottle of water, from a micro-thin hypodermic needle to simply pouring it in and using a recapping machine. Yours for a few bucks if you knew where to look.

But he was thirsty. So he drank. Oblivion would be welcome right now.

He stared down at the gloopy porridge. A foamy blob stared back at him. Saliva. He shuddered, dipped his finger in and hooked it out. Flicked it to the floor.

He'd need as much strength as he could muster for what was to come. He scooped up a blob with his fingers, put it in his mouth and swallowed. He retched, but fought the vomit reflex down. Took another little scoop. Ate it. His belly squirmed under the onslaught but the food stayed down and he finished all of it.

He picked up the tray. Placed it in the corner between the wall and the floor at a forty-five degree angle. Lifted his right boot and kicked out at it. It splintered into a dozen pieces with a satisfying crack.

From the debris he selected a dagger-like piece with a wicked point and a serviceable edge. He ripped a strip of material from his T-shirt and bound the fatter end to make a hilt. Nodded. A dagger. He stuck it into the waistband of his jeans. Then remembered his custom tailoring and replaced it in the side pocket sewn down the outside of his right thigh.

To pass the time, he sat cross-legged, closed his eyes and began a deep-breathing sequence designed to calm the mind. He focused on a series of mental combat exercises Master Zhao had drilled into him when he was fifteen. Visualising an enemy's body and plotting every single vulnerable spot as a red cross. Planning the most efficient strike at each one to disable, maim or kill. Master Zhao had not believed in pussyfooting around.

As he ran through the training exercise, he placed a digital clock in the top-right corner of his mental screen and set it running. An hour passed. Two.

Then the door opened.

Broken-nose was back. And he was grinning. In his hand, an ugly length of black rubber piping.

He lunged forwards and grabbed Gabriel's ankles in meaty fists like backhoe buckets. Gabriel went limp and let his man drag him feet-first out of the cell. Physically tiring and mentally confusing.

Why wasn't the prisoner struggling? He'd find out soon enough. Gabriel pulled his right arm close to his body and grabbed the hilt of his improvised fighting knife.

Any second now.

31

Gabriel's head bumped over a metal sill in the doorway. In that moment, he contracted his stomach muscles and jerked his torso upright. In the same flowing move he drew the dagger and raised his fist ready to stab deep into the man's biceps, ripping the brachial artery open.

The bat appeared out of nowhere, whistling around in a low arc and connecting with his elbow. He shrieked in agony as a jolt as stunning as the Taser disabled his arm from shoulder to fingertips.

The plastic dagger clattered to the ground. The bat returned for a second swing. Bright-white light exploded in Gabriel's brain. A tearing sound like a train braking filled his ears. His own scream added to the hellish soundscape. And the lights, mercifully, went out.

The water was icy. He coughed and moaned in a single choking breath as it hit him full in the face, charging into his nostrils and open mouth.

Facing him were the two men he'd already met. Broken nose and George Mason himself.

Gabriel spat onto the ground at Mason's feet.

'Hi, George. I'd shake hands only mine are out of commission.'

He looked up at the iron hook screwed into the ceiling and the ropes that descended to his wrists. So far the pain was bearable. Everyone from the Romans onwards knew you could torture someone extremely effectively just by leaving them dancing like this.

Toes just able to touch the ground to take a little weight before the fatigue got too much and you slumped. Your arms pulled your ribs up and stopped the muscles around your lungs, the intercostals and the diaphragm, from working properly. You'd get short of breath first, then panicky and light-headed. You'd start to strangle and you'd frantically push yourself up again to snatch a precious gasp of oxygen.

A variation on crucifixion. Only without the nails, obviously.

Shit. Why had he thought of nails? He flashed on another secret prison. This one deep in the bowels of the Iranian Ministry of Information and Security on Delgosha Alley in Tehran. He'd escaped, but not before sustaining a horrific injury to his left hand.

Mason turned to face him, coming close enough Gabriel could see the pores on the skin of his smoothly shaven cheeks. He smelled of soap. A harsh almost disinfectant smell in contrast to the musty, bodily aromas emanating from the walls of this hellish prison.

'Who are you, man? I mean, really. Who even *are* you? We've put a lot of effort into establishing some basic background and there's nada. There are aliens at Roswell we know more about.' He chuckled. 'Joking. Actually, not joking. Anyway—'

The blow drove deep into Gabriel's solar plexus, driving every scrap of wind out of him in a gasped-out groan. Mason stood back and watched as Gabriel writhed in agony. He felt sure he'd pass out, but Mason was an old pro. Unconsciousness was the prisoner's friend. And George Mason had no time for friendship.

Finally, Gabriel's paralysed diaphragm relaxed and he was able to suck in a breath.

'Who are you?' Mason asked again.

'My name is Terry Fox.'
'Your name is Gabriel.'
'My name is Jack Lang.'
'Your name is Gabriel.'
'My name is Eyal Abarbanel.'

Another punch. To the groin this time. Gabriel retched as the pain exploded in his balls. He didn't bother turning his head aside. Mason stepped back smartly, but not before a blob of vomit splashed onto the toe of his shoe.

'Mother*fucker*!'

'Must have been something I ate,' Gabriel grunted.

Mason fished a white cotton handkerchief from a pocket, startlingly clean in this barbarous space, and mopped the toe cap of his shoe.

'Let's start again. You're English. According to the *campesinos* you've been palling around with for the last year or so, your name is Gabriel. You have some righteous combat skills that I'm willing to bet you didn't learn as a grunt. And you have a number of scars that to this old operative's eye look like they were sustained in a military context. How'm I doing so far?'

'Let me down and I'll show you.'

Mason shook his head. 'Not just yet, old boy.' This last in a cod-British accent that made him sound like a bad sitcom actor.

'Now, where does an English vet learn to make IEDs, rig booby traps, fight ten mercs down to one? Gotta be special forces right? So, SAS or SBS. Maybe MI5, but I'm just getting this vibe off you. Let's say SAS. Which sabre squadron? F? G?'

'I have literally no idea what you're talking about.'

Mason turned his head fractionally. Blinked. Broken-nose thundered a fist into Gabriel's back, directly over his right kidney. Gabriel couldn't help himself. He shrieked as the agony coursed through him, lighting him up with blinding white-light pain that felt as though his whole body was being ripped in two.

Black curtains swung shut over his eyes.

A wave drenched him. How was he even afloat in the Arctic sea? He blinked, coughed. The room swam back into focus.

How long had he been out? A minute? An hour? He flexed his fingers. They were numb. And the pain in his armpits had receded to a distant ache. As had the spot over his kidney, though his insides felt off, somehow, rearranged. A while, then.

Mason rose from the chair in which he'd been sitting. A cigarette smouldered in a pressed tin ashtray sitting dead-centre on a basic metal table.

'Welcome back, trooper,' he said. 'I've been thinking about you while you were unconscious. Sorry about that, by the way. Fernando doesn't know his own strength. I specifically told him *not* to knock you out. I picture him as this really big baby, you know? Made his poor mama scream the house down when he was emerging from between her legs.'

Gabriel twisted his head around. Broken-nose was gone. He faced Mason again. The ex-CIA man was too smart to get within striking range. Gabriel's chance would come if he was left alone with Broken-nose. Or Fernando, he supposed he should call him now.

He needed to get Mason to the point he'd give up temporarily and hand over to the Honduran.

Talk, then.

'What do you want from me? I mean even if I told you everything about myself, what would you have? Really?'

'My employer wishes to know who's been stymying his plans. Call it intellectual curiosity.'

'And who exactly would this person be? In fact, don't answer that. Let me repay the favour and do a little character study for you. He's immensely wealthy. You're ex-CIA and we're in Central America, so I'm going to say he's American. Given his actions so far, and his way of going about them, he has no shame. So he's not old money. And he wants a stretch of the Honduran coastline all to himself as a secret seaport-slash-naval base.

'He could be an old-school oil-type, but I'm picturing one of those horrible little tech bros. You know the type, bullied at school, probably by someone very like you, George. On the spectrum.

Someone else has already built a space rocket so he wants to do something out at sea to leave his mark. How am I doing?'

Mason clapped laconically. Five percussive pops in the hard-edged, flat-walled space. He picked up the cigarette and drew a lungful of smoke down, holding it for a second before expelling it in a thin stream towards the ceiling.

He came close. Took a series of short puffs. The tip glowed red-hot with each breath. Gabriel stared into Mason's soulless eyes. Waited for what was to come.

Mason held the cigarette up where Gabriel had no option but to focus on its glowing red tip. Then he moved it out of his eyeline, around to the side of his head. The pain as he inserted it into Gabriel's left ear was excruciating. Once again, Gabriel let out a howl but he mixed this with an oath, directing all his energy into cursing Mason back to whatever torments hell reserved for psychopathic ex-spooks.

Eyebrows raised, Mason took a step back, dropping the crushed butt to the ground and swivelling his toe to kill it.

'Now, that is unkind, Gabriel. I'm just doing my job here. A job I could end right here and now if you'd volunteer a little information about yourself. You know, something I can take to the big man.'

Gabriel nodded, his thoughts disordered by the searing pain pulsing inside his left ear.

'OK. Tell him,' he gasped, 'tell him I'm going to stop him. Tell him I'm going to save Santa Rosa. And George?'

Mason smiled indulgently. Took a half-step closer, though calibrating the distance between them so he was in no danger.

'Gabriel?'

'Tell him I'm going to kill you.'

Mason laughed. He seemed to find it genuinely funny.

'Oh, man, I wish we could bottle what you got. That kind of chutzpah? We could sell that online and make ourselves rich.' He turned and headed for the door. 'I'm going to ask Fernando to step back in. I'll see you later.'

32

Like all expert torturers, Mason used every tool at his disposal.

Amateurs thought only in terms of their instruments. Car batteries, buckets of water, knives, batons. Professionals used the intangibles as well. Space. Light. Sound.

And time.

An hour passed before the big man finally made his appearance. He was wiping his mouth and a blob of red stained the front of his shirt. Gabriel could almost hear Mason instructing the Honduran to, 'Wait a while. Go get something to eat.'

'Hi, Fernando. How was your breakfast?'

The Honduran paused in his walk across the room. Frowned.

'Idiot. It's lunchtime.'

Thanks, Fernando. Now I know what time of day it is.

'What did you have? Spaghetti? Barbecue?'

'Soup.'

'Soup. Any good? Did you bring it from home? Did your wife make it for you?'

'Shut the fuck up.'

'Sorry. Just making conversation. So you work for George, huh? Is he a good boss?'

A derisive snort.

'My boss is the police chief of San Pedro Sula. And he's an asshole. George and me got this private enterprise thing going on.'

'Oh, right. A side hustle. Good for you.'

Fernando grinned crookedly, exposing large yellow teeth.

'Sure, good for me. Not for you, though.'

'Let me go.'

The Honduran's eyes widened.

'The fuck?'

'I can pay you. I'm rich. Richer than George. Whatever he's paying you, I'll double it. No! Wait, I'll triple it.'

Now he frowned, his massive brow folding and crinkling like expensive leather. Was he actually considering it? This could be easier than Gabriel had thought.

Fernando shook his head. 'He'd kill me. And my family.'

He dragged the table closer to where Gabriel dangled from the rope. Dug into his pocket and brought forth a delicate little switchblade which he opened with a metallic snick before laying on the plain metal top. A pair of pliers followed. And, finally, a brass knuckleduster. Old school. No electricity or mains water for Fernando.

He turned and jabbed a thick finger into Gabriel's chest.

'I'm gonna fuck you up. George said I can do whatever I like, long's you don't die. Oh, and I gotta leave your mouth alone so's you can still talk.'

He turned away and fingered each of the torture implements in turn.

This was going to hurt.

Gabriel tensed his stomach muscles, pouring every ounce of his strength into tautening his core, ignoring the reawakened pain in his kidney that brought sweat to his forehead.

Fernando picked up the knife and held it up to the light. Gabriel waited. Imagined that wickedly sharp, slim blade slicing through skin, muscle, viscera.

Fernando shook his head and grunted disapprovingly. Put the blade back down and grabbed the pliers.

And Gabriel convulsed.

His legs came up so high his knees were right under his chin. Silently, despite the soul-sapping effort it cost him not to cry out, he shot his legs out and scissored them around the Honduran's neck. He locked his ankles over each other and squeezed his thighs tight, choking off the man's air supply. Now, Gabriel did scream. He threw his head back and howled like a banshee.

'No! Please, I beg you, no!'

The big man's heels scuffled on the concrete floor for purchase and he reached up with his hands to try and prise Gabriel's legs away from his throat. But physics dictated this was a poor move. The principles of leverage gave Gabriel the advantage. His legs were more powerful than Fernando's arms. And squeezing in was infinitely easier than pulling apart.

Maybe Fernando could have dropped to the floor, trying to enlist gravity on his side. It might have worked, his deadweight dragging his body free of the strangling grip. But it took a surprising amount of training and self-control to go limp when every fibre of your being was screaming at you to fight. To regain control.

And then again, it might not have worked. The fall might have resulted in a broken neck.

His struggles were weakening. Gabriel tightened the scissors, clamping down on the big man's carotid arteries as well as his windpipe. His grip on Gabriel's legs slipped. He scrabbled to dig his fingers between Gabriel's legs and his own throat.

Choking him to death would take too long. Five minutes at least. Gabriel didn't have the time. Or, had Fernando realised it, the strength. His own arms were burning as if immersed in acid as Fernando's struggles hauled him left and right.

Time to end it.

With another scream of genuine agony, Gabriel arced his whole body and then twisted clockwise, like a crocodile spinning with its prey caught fast in its jaws. The snap as Fernando's neck broke was audible above the scuffling boots on the concrete and Gabriel's hammering pulse.

He dropped in a crumpled heap, his skull bouncing off the floor with a woody clonk.

Panting, Gabriel looked up at the rope binding his wrists and looped over the iron hook. No way would he be able to flip it free. But George, or more likely Fernando, had been careless. The rope around Gabriel's left wrist was tight against his skin because of the acute angle as it dug in. But the knot hadn't been tied close enough to his wrist.

There was room for his hand to pass through the loop. Or there would have been but for the bony protrusion at the base of Gabriel's thumb. It acted like a stop-knot, preventing his hand from slipping free.

No time for the mantra against pain. Mason could be back at any minute, though Gabriel hoped he would be relaxing somewhere, content to let the hired muscle work over the prisoner before reporting back.

He crunched his core muscles once more and hauled his feet up to his hips, then swung himself upside down, shooting his feet up until he was fully inverted. The pain in his shoulders was like being burnt. White-hot steel blades lanced inwards towards his heart making him gasp. At least he didn't have to keep quiet. Screams of pain only added to the enjoyment as far as people like Fernando and George Mason were concerned.

Blinking through tears that turned the ceiling lights into six-pointed stars, Gabriel placed his boot heel against the base of his left thumb. Took a deep breath. Held it. And kicked.

The edge of the heel scraped a swathe of skin free and Gabriel screamed in pain. But the bones stayed stubbornly knitted into their appointed positions.

Gritting his teeth, he repositioned his boot heel and tried again. He threw his head back and yelled his defiance but again the wounded digit refused to part company. It dripped blood into his eye as he lined up for a third attempt. Blinking, Gabriel sandwiched the insulted joint between both boot heels.

With a groan that rose into a full-throated scream of genuine, debilitating pain, he shot both feet up towards the ceiling.

His thumb dislocated with a loud snap. It folded in on itself as Gabriel's bodyweight dragged down on the rope. And it slid through the loop around his wrist, wriggling obscenely as if a separate organism from the rest of the hand.

The newly freed end of the rope flew upwards over the belly of the iron hook, whipping up to slap the ceiling before snaking down as Gabriel plummeted to the ground.

Groaning with the effort, he got to his knees and stretched over Fernando's corpse to grab the flick-knife. He sliced through the loop around his right hand.

He looked down at his thumb. It hung out at a disgusting angle. No time for niceties. He summoned a memory of a course held in the mortuary at University College Hospital in London. Eight of them, plus the pathologist and four corpses. He gripped his thumb, warm, unlike that of the corpse he and Smudge had practised on, gritted his teeth, then simultaneously shoved and twisted.

Once more he let out an animalistic howl of pain as he relocated the thumb. He cut a strip of fabric from the dead Honduran's shirt and bound his wounded hand tightly to protect it.

Before he left, he threaded his fingers through the holes of the knuckleduster. The pliers he had no immediate use for, but he took them anyway.

Time to go.

33

Gabriel slipped out through the door to the torture chamber.

He half-hoped he'd meet George Mason. With the element of surprise on his side, he'd enjoy disarming the ex-spook before sending him on his way. But the corridor was empty.

Knife held point uppermost in his knuckle-dustered right fist, Gabriel strode along the narrow hallway. From the sounds echoing down towards him it seemed they'd been interrogating him at ground level.

He approached a dog-leg. Cigarette smoke caught in his nostrils. His pulse skyrocketed as he doubled back. Two men, laughing, bantering, were coming the other way.

'If my wife cooked *baleadas* like that, I'd divorce her.'

'Yeah and be a bachelor the rest of your life, man? I mean what woman would have you now? Look at that gut.'

Gabriel flattened himself into an alcove. It was barely a foot deep, a quirk of the prison's architecture. The men drew closer. Fit and well, and armed as he was, he would normally be confident in his ability to best them. But right now every part of him was either aching, burning or sparking with pain like electric shocks.

He gripped the knife tighter. Prepared himself.

Then the footsteps halted. He heard a bunch of keys being manipulated. Plenty of them to judge from the tinkling. They fell to the floor. Were swiped up again.

'Where is that motherfucker?'

'Why don't you have the office key on a separate ring? That's what I do.'

'"That's what I do",' the keyholder repeated in a mocking parody of his partner's voice. 'There! Got it! Come on, the match starts in two minutes.'

Gabriel waited. Football commentary blared into life, the TV pundit opining on the strengths of SPS's new striker.

Walking fast on the balls of his feet, Gabriel hurried past the closed door and on towards the main door.

Whatever kind of operation George Mason was running in San Pedro Sula, it didn't extend to front-of-house staff. Gabriel simply walked across a ten-metre expanse of scuffed brown linoleum and out the street door.

He closed the switchblade and slid his fingers out of the knuckleduster, placing both in his pockets. The street was busy with shoppers and Gabriel merged into a knot of pedestrians heading towards the market. Head down he scanned his surroundings, looking for what he needed.

He spotted them across the road. Two young men in tracksuits, faces tattooed, necks hung with gold chains, lounging on an ageing cream Mercedes. Drug dealers most likely. But low-level cartel enforcers was also a distinct possibility.

He broke away from the market-bound shoppers and zig-zagged across the street, threading his way between the slow-moving traffic to end up ten metres ahead of the two gangbangers.

He started gesticulating, throwing his hands around and staring, wild-eyed up at the clouds. He muttered about God watching over him, twitched his whole head from side to side and then took a couple of hopping steps towards the gangbangers.

They pushed off from the bonnet of the car and stood

watching him with amused smiles on their tattooed faces. He tripped just as he arrived, pitching forwards directly into the left-hand guy's arms. He jumped back, pushing Gabriel away from him.

'The fuck, man! Get the fuck offa me, you crazy motherfucker!'

Gabriel shook his head. 'They're coming, you know? They're coming! The lizard people. That's why Papa Jesú is watching over us. You, man. Your friend here. Me. All of us need to give praise to Sacred Baby Jesú. Come on, Man. Join hands. We gotta pray.'

The guy Gabriel had fallen against shook his head and looked up and down the street.

'No we don't, bro. I tell you what you gotta do, though. You gotta get the fuck out of my face before I cap you. OK? Fuck off! Now! Fucking loony.'

Gabriel held out his hands.

'No offence, bro. I sorry. I real sorry. Praise be to Holy Baby Jesú. He gonna keep you safe man. And your brother here.'

He stumbled away from them, arms aloft like a worshipper in a revival tent, memorising some of the more colourful phrases that followed him down the street. Who knew when they'd come in useful.

He rounded a corner and picked up his pace, dropping his arms to his sides. Ducked down an alley and ran to the far end. By the time he emerged he'd emptied the guy's wallet of its contents. Two hundred dollars and an equivalent amount in Lempiras.

He looked both ways as he emerged onto a shopping street. No sign of the gangbangers. It was a fifty-fifty call on whether they'd go after the madman who'd relieved one of them of his money. Not good for the image and they had looked like they were on either sentry duty or waiting for a meet. Better to just stick up some poor citizen and repeat the process.

Ten minutes later, a cheaply dressed peasant under a new but battered straw cowboy hat emerged from a phone shop, pulling a pay-as-you-go phone from its packaging, entering the code and slipping it into the pocket of his denim jacket.

Ahead, a dozen people were clustering around the doors to a blue and white bus as it wheezed noisily at the kerbside. Gabriel checked the destination on the front.

Aeropuerto Internacional Ramón Villeda Morales
La Lima

Perfect. If the gangbangers were looking for him, no way would they imagine the lunatic who'd robbed one of them would head for the airport.

As the bus clattered away from the stop, Gabriel swayed up to the back and slumped low in a seat in the centre of the back row, equidistant from the windows. With his hat pulled low over his eyes, he affected sleep, though ironically, he fought with every fibre of his being to stay awake. To be caught, literally, napping would not make a good end to his day.

At the airport, he disembarked from the bus and transferred straight onto a second, this one heading for La Progreso. As it rumbled away from the stand, finally, he had no option but to give in to sleep. He awoke in the town he'd passed through on his way into San Pedro Sula.

Six hours later, he climbed out of the load bay of a farmer's pickup, waved goodbye and walked into the centre of Santa Rosa, massaging his back. The journey had done nothing to ameliorate the pain still pulsing outwards from his kidneys. Nor his dislocated thumb. The cigarette burn in his ear was probably the least troubling of his wounds.

First things first. Coffee. And painkillers.

He was lying on his battered sofa under a woven throw in muted earth tones of brick red, yellow ochre and dusty green when the front door banged wide and Pera rushed in. She knelt next to the sofa, her eyes brimming with tears

'My god, Gabe, what happened to you?'

How much to tell his friend? That he'd been outwitted, captured, brutalised and tortured by George Mason? That he'd killed Fernando before mugging a pair of gangbangers to escape San Pedro Sula dressed as a peasant? He settled for part of the truth.

'I found the man who hired the mercenaries. I'm hoping I can use my contacts to find out more about him. Maybe get a lead on whoever's behind this whole thing.'

The look Pera bestowed on him would have cut armour plating.

'You found him?' She pointed at his burnt ear. At the bruises on his face. At his bandaged hand. '*You* found *him*? Oh, really? Because from where I sit it looks like *he* found *you*. You're mad, Gabe, going after him on your own. You could have been killed.'

How could he tell her, that sometimes, in his darker moments, he felt like being killed wouldn't be the worst thing that could happen to him. Fighting one battle after another, against a seemingly endless supply of evil people. Was that to be his life evermore? Was he never to escape his fate, always to be rescuing other people and their loved ones, while his lay in an unbroken series of coffins stretching all the way back to his little brother?

Instead, he raised himself on his elbows, wincing as the bruises over his kidneys complained.

'I'm here, aren't I?'

'By the grace of God, yes, you are! Now, lie still while I fetch some things. I'm going to patch you up properly. Then I'm going to make you something good to eat.'

34

Xander Kalt tapped the screen to bring up Mason's call. Finally. Wolfe had buckled and Kalt had his tame Brit SAS man to add to his tame CIA guy.

Outside, rain such as he'd only before seen during monsoon season in Uttar Pradesh hammered on the widows. He dragged a slider with his fingertip to boost the audio.

Mason's tanned features filled the screen. He did not, in truth, look as happy as Kalt had imagined he would after breaking Wolfe. The insight flashed through Kalt like a spark. He was good at intuition. Probably nobody in the company was better. Nobody in the *country*.

Mason hadn't broken Wolfe. Mason had killed Wolfe. After Kalt had given him *explicit* instructions.

'Talk to me, George,' he said. 'And you'd better have some good news.'

Mason didn't speak straightaway. Which was like massively disrespectful. But it did at least give Kalt the opportunity to review the biometric data scrolling down the side of the screen. It was a super-cool algo he'd personally designed that measured all this shit like tension in all twenty facial muscles. Saccadic movements of the eye, those little jerky flicks when someone was looking at stuff. Skin tone, which was a really great predictor of anxiety and/or rage 'cause it related to blood flow. Basically a load of data points that you could use, if you were a genius at reading people like Xander Kalt was, to figure out stuff. Like if a person was happy or sad, or anxious or whatever.

George Mason was not happy. Kalt could tell.

'Wolfe's gone.'

Kalt sighed. 'I told you—'

'Not dead, Xander,' Mason interrupted, which was also super-massively rude. 'He escaped. He killed one of my guys and disappeared.'

'What the fuck, George! I literally gave you an order that wasn't even that hard and you fucked it up anyway. Are you sure you were in the CIA?' He looked up and put the tip of his finger to this chin. 'Oh, wait. Yeah, you were. You were in the Central Idiot Agency.'

That was a zinger and no mistake. The biometrics were going wild. Kalt didn't even need to study the turquoise and amber dials. He could read Mason like a book. Not that he read books. Ink on paper? Get real! That was literally dead dinosaurs on dead trees. Mason was feeling guilty for letting Kalt down. Guilty, and afraid.

Mason inhaled slowly, probably trying to fight down his fear.

'I'll find him. And when I do, I'll find out everything about him, and then I'll kill him. Fernando was a friend.'

Kalt stared at the screen. Friend. Pfft!

'No you won't,' he said, timing it perfectly, another of his skills.

'What?'

'I've changed my mind. My strategy, I mean. I want Wolfe here. With me.'

'What the fuck do you mean?'

'He could be useful. And he escaped your clutches, George, didn't he? Maybe *he* could be my point man. You could concentrate on, you know, logistical support.'

George's biometrics were really going crazy. He was pissed.

Kalt nodded to himself. He'd be extra-motivated to impress him now.

He ended the call and returned to the work he'd been doing before George called. He'd suspected that CIA methods might not work on the mysterious Englishman. And anyway, they were so old fashioned.

Whereas he, Xander Kalt, sat astride the bleeding edge of AI technology. And he'd been using it to track Gabriel across half the world.

On the dark web, obviously. Although it was amazing how ordinary people thought it held all the answers. When often what it gave you were the details of people you could hire to do stuff for you. Then they'd find out the answers. Russians. Germans. Syrians. Israelis. Turks. All kinds.

Kalt had started from a simple premise. English people usually start off in England. Anyway, they certainly aren't born in Honduras. So Gabriel must have flown to Honduras from somewhere else. And, at some point, he must have flown out of England.

In the old days, like the 2010s, turning that genius-level insight into useable intel would have taken years. Maybe decades. But not now. Not when companies like Kaltium had brought quantum computing into everybody's lives, whether they knew it or not.

Yeah, they thought it was pretty cool to swap faces with one of their idols, but AI was capable of so much more. In the right hands.

Hands like Xander's. He'd begun with a simple piece of analysis. Tracking the flight manifests for every single plane leaving the UK in the last five years. Running the passenger lists against the British government's passport database, census data and electoral roll. Screening out all the women and girls. Then everyone under thirty. Tracking each flight through every layover and connecting flight. Overlaying the one essential datapoint: Honduras.

Guess what?

Xander had spotted anomalies in the flight data relating to five people. Brilliantly, he'd labelled them A, B, C, D and E. According to his analysis, those five people couldn't all exist at once. Or not in a single universe. It was impossible.

A had vanished somewhere between London Heathrow and Charles de Gaulle in Paris. B had blinked into existence but disappeared again as his flight crossed into Spanish airspace. Hello C, you tricksy little dude! Oh, bye. Guess you fell out the window into the Atlantic. D landed in Miami. Did a Jimmy Hoffa. And E landed in Tegucigalpa. Elapsed time, thirty days.

Trouble was, you could tell people your name was A, or C or E and you could certainly buy fake IDs to prove it. But your face stayed pretty much the same. Facial-recognition data was a wonderful thing nowadays. And so accessible. So Xander was able to deduce that A thru E were a) all the same man and b) a man with a name.

From there it was child's play to put a full dossier together.

Gabriel Wolfe was born in Surrey, England. He grew up in Hong Kong. Joined the British Army's Parachute Regiment when he was eighteen. Then the SAS. Was awarded the Military Cross. Then left for the private sector. A year or two working as a security consultant to business executives. Then…

…then the AI fell on its face. Much to Xander's irritation.

It was as if Gabriel Wolfe had just stopped being. Clearly he was alive, because Xander had identified him as the man thwarting his plans for Santa Rosa. But between leaving the SAS and, like, now, there was no data. Weird.

No, scratch that. It wasn't weird. It was *wrong*. People could disappear as far as other people were concerned, But from AI, and systems such as those built by Kaltium, no, they fuckin' couldn't. It was so lame.

Well, maybe when Gabriel was working for him, Kalt would ask him.

35

The morning sun was already bristling with fierce heat as the sharpshooting team shot at targets two hundred metres distant down a field.

Under Marco 'Bullseye' Bishop's tutelage they were racking up impressive scores. One of the shooters caught his eye. Santiago. He shook his head. It would have been pointless trying to stop him signing up to defend his own village. Gabriel would have done just the same at his age.

He walked down the line of prone shooters and stood behind Santi. The boy turned his head and grinned up at Gabriel.

'Watch this,' he said.

He worked the bolt on the long-barrelled rifle and laid his cheek against the stock. No telescopic sight. These were hunting weapons. Handed down from father to son. Accurate enough to knock a bird out of a tree five hundred metres away. *If* you knew how to shoot.

Santi's ribcage rose and fell, rose and fell.

One more time it rose, and, as it fell, it stilled. Good lad. Gabriel could almost count the heartbeats.

He squeezed off the shot and then inhaled again.

Downrange, the target, a metal disc no bigger than an orange, spun. The distant clink reached Gabriel's ears a split-second later. He shook his head. No. He must have imagined it. Too much gunfire to perceive it.

'He's a natural.'

Gabriel turned. Bullseye had come up on him silently. Not hard, given the noise made by a dozen rifles. But there had been a time when nobody but Master Zhao could have mastered that feat.

'Keep him out of the hot zone, OK? Overwatch.'

Bullseye pursed his lips.

'From what you told us, isn't the whole place going to be hot?'

'All right, tell him to set up a nest somewhere he can cover the whole village.' Gabriel scanned the curve of hillside that cupped the landward side of Santa Rosa. 'That'll put him on the hill there.'

'He won't like it, boss.'

'He's fifteen, for god's sake! Give him an order. I don't want him in the middle of things.'

Bullseye nodded. 'Got it.'

'Where are the others?'

'You'll like this. Head up the coast road about half a click. Just watch your step.'

'Shit, they haven't mined it, have they?'

Bullseye rubbed his chin, furry with a couple of days' stubble.

'They can't. Too much friendly traffic. But they've gone one better.'

* * *

It took Gabriel nine minutes to walk the five hundred metres. He frowned with irritation. He should have done it in five. But the toll his injuries had taken on his body had slowed him up.

Not wanting his senses any duller, he'd forgone all but the mildest painkillers. As a result, his attention flicked from one physical insult to the next. His left thumb, professionally bandaged by Pera now but still swollen. The region over and around his kidneys, which felt as though a large dog had chewed on them. And his ear, which continued to throb beneath the plug of herbal salve Pera had applied.

The road curved left in a gentle bend, ascending over a shallow rise at the same time. Heat shimmer rendered the hills on the far side hazy and mirage-like, wavering in the heat. Gabriel sniffed the air. A sappy, sawdust aroma drifted towards him on the breeze. And the buzz of chainsaws.

Cresting the rise he looked down on two teams of men led, one each, by Kylie and Bilbo. Shirtless, they shouted commands and when they weren't doing that, yelled insults at each other across the red dirt road.

Each team was working on a tall mature eucalyptus tree that flanked the road. Fast-growing they had reached thirty metres in only a handful of years. The residents had nicknamed them Carlos and Carlita, after two characters in a popular cartoon.

He ventured closer. Now he understood why the air smelled like a timber yard. Each team was cutting a wedge out of the trunk, about a foot from the ground. Pairs of ropes were slung into the branches and lashed to posts driven down into the ground some ten metres away. Were they felling them? Surely that would block traffic, even if it wouldn't destroy it?

No. The ropes were holding the trees in place.

Then he saw it. Nodded with satisfaction. He'd made a good choice bringing these boys out to Honduras.

Having cut the wedges in the sides of the trunks facing out into the countryside, the chainsaw operators sliced upwards into the roadside wood. These narrow cuts rose at an angle to end just below the innermost part of the wedges. A classic lumberjack's cut to ensure a tree would fall in a predictable direction.

With a final growl, the chainsaws fell silent. The trees leaned in towards each other at a barely perceptible angle. Just enough to ensure that when the ropes were cut, they'd crash earthwards across the road.

Gabriel walked over to the nearest team. Bilbo stood, wiping sweat from his face with a wirily muscular forearm.

'Boss! You're back.' He pulled his chin back. 'Blimey! What happened to you?'

'I met a middleman in less than ideal circumstances. Ex-CIA thug called George Mason. Probably a paramilitary agent back when he was legit. He's the one hiring and training the mercs.'

'And yet you're here. Can I assume this Mason character now sleeps with the fishes?'

'Sadly, no. But I made him a promise I'd do him in and I intend to keep it.'

'Good for you. So.' He turned and waved a hand at the men in his crew who were now arranging brush at the foot of the tree to disguise the lumberjack's cuts and twining vines along the ropes. 'What do you think?'

'It's impressive. Deadfalls?'

'Pretty much. We'll station a couple of guys at each tree. When the enemy hits the mark they axe the ropes and bring the buggers to a halt. Then we blow the vehicles with a couple of those charming Javelins. A fire team'll clean up anyone left standing. Who knows, we might not need anything else.'

'Yeah, I wouldn't bet on it. Mason's seen what I did to his first crew. I doubt he'll be that careless this time.'

'Tell me, Boss, how are we going to know when they're coming? I get that they said a month, but what if they come early?'

Gabriel nodded. It was a good question, and one he'd pre-empted before setting out for England on his recruitment drive.

'Everyone round here has family spread out among the towns between here and San Pedro Sula. Friends, too, people they trade with, buy supplies from. We've got a bush telegraph set up. The mercs are going to be easy to spot and if I'm right, they'll be coming in a fleet of pickups or SUVs. We'll get word when they're still three or four hours' drive from here.'

'Nice. You don't think they'll come by sea? Or by air?'

'It's unlikely, but they could. Not that our ultimate target is short of money, but it adds complexity and expense. Plus the people who they could hire for this kind of work have their own ways of working. The cartels are the biggest example and they do like to drive.'

'Fair play. Just asking.'

'Of course. I'm going to see Tiny and Paddy next. They're working on our sea defences, just in case.'

36

Tara double-locked the front door to her apartment and wheeled her suitcase down the hall to the gleaming brass concertina gates for the lift.

The block was old but when her company had acquired it, she'd had it refurbished, all according to the strict Parisian planning laws. The descent still carried that frisson of danger as the rickety workings, refurbished, yes, but still over a century old, clanked and ground as they lowered the car from the top floor. On the sixth floor the car stopped and one of her elderly neighbours stepped in. Tara smiled at her.

'*Bonjour, Madame Huppert. Ça va?*'

The neighbour, resplendent today in a cerise Chanel suit trimmed with black, nodded, offering an eloquent shrug as only the French could. It communicated so much more than the brief, '*Pof! Ça va un peu.*' Literally, 'It's going a bit.'

The old lady switched to English.

'My advice, Tara? Do not get old. Die young while you are still beautiful and your bones don't ache like the Devil fucked you all night on a brick mattress.'

Tara burst out laughing. Madame Huppert had been a TV star in her prime, offering French housewives advice on etiquette. She doubted Madame's producers would have been as amused by her colourful turn of phrase as she was now.

'I intend to live until I am at least as old as you, Madame,' Tara replied. 'And if I am still half as beautiful as you I shall be happy to sleep with the Devil as payment.'

Madame Huppert smiled. Took a cigarette from a silver case and inserted it into a tortoiseshell holder.

'Flatterer! Not that I mind. At my age you take your compliments where you can. So,' she glanced at Tara's suitcase, 'where are you off to? Somewhere exotic, I hope. Fiji, perhaps? Zanzibar? Djibouti?'

'Honduras.'

Madame Huppert's brows, already plucked into fine arches, lifted further.

'Honduras? *Mon Dieu!* Why on earth would you go to Honduras? It is full of cartels and gangsters, no?'

'My brother called me. He lives there now.'

'Is he mad?'

Tara shook her head. 'No, not mad. Maybe sad, though. He lost his wife a year ago.'

'Oh, well, then of course you must go. Family, eh? It is the most important thing.'

They continued to chat, although the topic moved onto more neutral ground until they were both on the street. Madame Huppert crossed the street to the bakery, waving a gloved hand and using the other to light her cigarette.

Tara hailed a cab. As she climbed into the back seat she thought about Madame's words. Yes, family was the most important thing. And she and BB were all each other had now.

'Where to, miss?' the driver asked.

'Charles de Gaulle, please.'

She leaned back as the driver pulled away. Traffic was never heavy on Avenue Montaigne, but the moment they turned left onto Avenue des Champs-Élyseés their smooth progress stalled. They crawled up to Place Charles de Gaulle, formerly known as Place de l'Étoile for the huge star-shaped junction at which twelve major roads intersected in manic, fender-bending fashion.

Employing a very specific Parisian form of courage, in which outsiders always thought they could detect insanity, the driver ploughed onto the junction without looking right or left. He hit the horn immediately, adding the ageing Citroën's reedy voice to the cacophony of hooters honking like squabbling geese on the crowded junction.

Tara gazed out of the window. A twelve-pointed star designed as the cutting edge of urban traffic management, now a free-for-all in which fortune favoured if not the brave then at least the brash. This thought led to another. A four-pointed star. The Four-Point Star triad, a onetime rival of the White Koi, the triad she herself had led. The male leaders of the other triads hadn't accorded her the respect they would normally for a male rival. Using a variety of methods, she'd ensured they changed their opinions of a woman triad boss. A *South China Morning Post* headline floated down through the years.

BLOOD ON THE STREETS: TRIAD WAR TAKES HEAD OF FPS

That had been a day to remember. Although not for Tam Tang, the erstwhile leader of the Four-Point Star, whose memories, if they persisted after death, were contained in the roughly six kilograms of skull and brain tissue police divers recovered from Kowloon Bay.

And now she was on her way to another conflict. With, from what BB had told her, another powerful man with no respect for others.

Finally, the taxi drew up at the stand at Charles de Gaulle.

After paying and retrieving her case from the boot, Tara turned to be greeted with a uniformed porter towing a huge suitcase on a trolley.

'Mine's small enough,' she said in French. 'I can manage.'

He nodded. 'OK, miss. Have a good flight.'

37

Gabriel found Paddy on the beach. The former Irish Guard was stripped to a pair of shorts and battered sneakers. He was pushing a Claymore anti-personnel mine's spikes down into the sand. Ten more stretched out along the beach, wires leading away to the handheld detonators known as 'clackers'.

Gabriel flashed on a memory of Scalpay, the Hebridean island where he'd lost, and then avenged, Eli. The rogue Department agent Kevin Bakker had killed himself with one, hugging it to his torso and blowing himself to pieces to avoid capture. He squeezed his eyes shut before Eli could appear before him, stepping out of memory and into hallucinatory reality.

Paddy looked up as Gabriel walked down the beach. Sand stuck to his chest which, as Gabriel's did, bore the pockmarks and ugly gnarled scars of combat.

'Hey, boss, you're back.'

'Paddy. All good?'

Paddy swept a hand in a broad arc to encompass his row of mines.

'Any fucker tries to land here's gonna get a ball-bearing facelift.'

Gabriel smiled. Shouldn't really, given what Paddy was describing, but that was what soldiers did. Like cops and firefighters, paramedics and pathologists. It was a coping mechanism. Although, maybe, in Paddy's case, it was just the man had a twisted idea of what was funny.

'Where's Tiny?'

'Oh, you're gonna love this, boss. He's turned one of the fishing boats into a pinky.'

Gabriel turned seawards, shading his eyes against the bright sun bouncing off the water, searching for the fishing boat. Back in the day, the first SAS members had welded general purpose machine guns and Vickers K .303s to jeeps, turning them from general utility vehicles into ferocious fighting machines capable of laying waste to entire airfields crammed with German planes. Experiments showed that pink was the colour that best blended with the desert where they were fighting behind Rommel's lines. The camo hadn't lasted, but the nickname had.

The distant chug of a marine diesel engine rose in volume as a blue and white fishing boat rounded the headland and made headway towards them.

Gabriel recognised the vessel. Jerome 'Papa' Ortiz, eighty-five and still out on his boat every day, fished inshore for spider crabs and lobsters plus the huge, succulent prawns locals called *conenose de mar* – sea rabbits. It must have cost him to surrender a lifetime's habit. But everyone knew this was no idle threat. A month's lost fishing versus an end to a way of life? Who wouldn't make the necessary sacrifice?

Tiny had made good use of Gabriel's armoury. 'Bárbara', named for Papa's wife of sixty-eight years, drew nearer, her gunwales bristling with black machine-gun barrels.

The bear-like former SBS man hove to and dropped anchor. He hoisted himself over the side and swam the fifty metres to shore in a powerful crawl stroke. He emerged, a modern-day Poseidon, his combat fatigue trousers clinging to his thighs.

High-pitched giggling from behind him made Gabriel turn. A group of local women, all in their twenties, were covering their mouths and pointing at Tiny as he shook his head like a dog, flicking salty spray into the air.

'Looks like you've got a fan club,' Gabriel said with a grin.

Tiny nodded. 'They've been hanging around since I got here.'

Gabriel raised a hand in greeting.

'*Buenos días, señoritas,*' he called. '*Quieras venir a ayudar?*'

'What did you say?' Tiny asked, frowning.

'I asked them if they wanted to come and help.'

Blushing furiously, Tiny swiped a meaty palm over his face.

'Oh, man, really?'

But it was too late. One of the women, long black hair tied back, called out to Gabriel.

'*Tiny es muy guapo. Está casado?*'

At this her friends shrieked with laughter, covering their mouths.

Gabriel grinned. 'She says you're very handsome and she wants to know if you're married.'

Tiny's blush deepened. 'Good god, man, I'm up-armouring a bloody fishing smack here. Give me a break.'

But Gabriel had no intention of letting the giant SBS man off the hook that easily. After the trials and tribulations of the last couple of days he felt he was owed a little fun.

'*Lo siento, le ha dado su corazón a Bárbara,*' he called out.

The young woman mimed crying, screwing her fists to her eyes before turning and saying something into the ear of the woman nearest. Then she sashayed down the beach towards Gabriel and Tiny.

Tiny looked panicked.

'What the hell did you tell her?'

'I said I was sorry but you'd given your heart to Bárbara.'

The young woman arrived. Up close she was beautiful. Wide-set eyes sparkling with mischievous wit. A full mouth curved upwards in a half-smile.

'*Buenos días, Tiny. Te ves ardiente. Te traigo una coca?*'

Gabriel translated. 'She says you look hot.' A beat. 'I think she means literally. Can she bring you a coke?'

Tiny managed to look the young woman in the eye for a second and nodded.

'*Sí, por favor.*'

She beamed at him, revealing even white teeth. '*Un momento!*'

Tiny held up a hand as she turned to leave. He murmured to Gabriel, 'I got that. Tell me how to ask what her name is.'

Gabriel whispered back. Tiny nodded then cleared his throat.

'*Uh, señorita, cómo se llama?*'

She nodded and spoke slowly and clearly.

'*Me llamo,*' she touched her chest, '*Julimar. Pero puedes.*' She reached out and placed the flat of her hand on Tiny's pectoral muscle, '*llamarme Juli.*'

'She says—'

Tiny nodded, his eyes not leaving Juli's. 'I got it.'

He put his hand on his chest where her palm had so recently rested.

'*Pero puedes llamarme Tim.*'

'Tim,' she repeated. 'Is nice name. Better than Tiny. From now on, I call you Tim.'

And then she spun round and ran back to her gaggle of friends. They screamed with delight as she regaled them with the details of her conquest.

'She bloody well speaks English!' Tiny complained, though to Gabriel's ear there wasn't a great deal of genuine grievance in it.

He left Tiny to his job transforming a humble pocket trawler into a gunboat.

38

Gabriel scanned the arriving passengers, trying to ignore the squirming in his gut. Would he even recognise Tara, given the amount of plastic surgery she'd been forced to undergo?

Most of the passengers towing their wheeled suitcases or pushing luggage carts were South American. A few Anglos. And, as everywhere these days, Chinese. Mostly in business suits, but a few in tourist garb.

A group of businesswomen in their thirties emerged from the white-walled corner where the arrivals lane doglegged. His pulse stuttered. Was that Tara, at the back? He caught her eye but in return received only a puzzled look before she bent to her phone.

The stream of people became a trickle. Then just isolated travellers, wearier than the rest, perhaps, or having paused at the restrooms to freshen up.

His anxiety mounted. She'd texted to say this was her flight, and the boards had been clear: Copa Airlines, AF4511, had landed on schedule.

As he was pulling out his phone, intending to call her, he heard the loud rattle of a misaligned suitcase wheel on hard marble tiling. He looked up and saw her. He didn't recognise her at all. Her face was that of a stranger. But her gait. That nobody had been able to change, even by the addition of a few centimetres to her height. Her right toe still turned in as she lifted it before landing perfectly straight. And something about the way she transferred her weight as she walked.

He broke into a smile, relief mingled with a sudden and unexpected surge of happiness at seeing his only remaining blood relative.

'Tara!' he called out.

She looked up and her face split with a wide smile.

'Gabriel! Oh, my god, it's really you!'

She ran over, the loose wheel of her suitcase beating out a frantic tattoo on the marble floor tiles. She slammed into the Perspex barrier and let go of the suitcase handle to throw her arms around him.

'Oh, Gabriel, I never thought I'd see you again.'

He felt wetness on his neck. His own eyes were pricking and they stayed locked in a tight embrace, while a new batch of passengers and their family, friends or business associates arrived.

Finally, Tara let him go and hurried around the barrier to greet him all over again.

As he looked into her westernised eyes, he searched for the sister he'd only come to know a few short years before. Although every feature had been altered, and the fine lines of her surgery were still visible – just – below her foundation, he sensed his sister there, anyway. The way she cocked her head. The laugh as she regaled him with a funny story about a child on the plane, even if delivered with a rougher edge than he remembered. Just some sort of essence that surgery could never eradicate.

He led her to his truck, which he'd parked in a corner of the outside carpark that served both arrivals and departures. He noticed that as she walked, there was a hitch in her step. The result of the painful surgery to lengthen her legs and further confound the MSS agents.

Tara stopped dead and put her hands on her hips.

'Wait. That's what you're driving these days? You used to have such great taste in cars. The Maserati. The Camaro. The Jaguar. What even is that?'

He took her case and heaved it into the load bay of his battered sky-blue pickup.

'It's a classic. Vintage, you might say. Ford F100 from 1953.'

'Does it work?' she asked, pulling open the passenger door, which yielded with a metallic squawk.

'Well, I didn't push it all the way here, if that's what you're asking.'

He climbed in next to her and stuck the key in the ignition. She reached out her hand and stayed his in the act of starting the engine.

'Look at me,' she said.

Gabriel twisted round in his seat. Focused on her eyes, still the same shade of brown as before. Although since that went for at least ninety-five percent of the mainland Chinese population, not a reliable predictor of identity.

'I'm looking.'

'Do I look…' She bit her lower lip and her breath hitched as she spoke again. 'Can you tell it's me?' She circled a hand around her face. 'Under all this, I mean.'

'Of course I can. I recognised you the moment you came round the corner in the arrivals hall. I'm trained, remember. We learned to recognise the enemy whatever kind of disguise they'd assumed. Some things are beyond faking, Tara.'

Her face fell.

'You don't think they'll be able to, as well, do you?'

No need to clarify who 'they' were.

He shook his head and took her hand. So small, yet, as he'd witnessed, so capable of killing men twice her size.

'You're my sister, remember? They're just trained goons of the Chinese state. Honestly, you look totally different. Whoever you used, they did a great job.'

She smiled ruefully.

'You should have seen me straight afterwards. You wouldn't say that then. I looked like a cross between the Mummy and a burns victim. I had to learn to talk again, walk again. Even eat. I don't know what exactly they did to my mouth but I kept poking my chopsticks into my top lip.'

'We do what we have to, to survive. I left my whole life behind.'

'What about the job? Wasn't that hard? Leaving, I mean. You loved it.'

'I *used* to love it. But even before Eli died, they'd shut the Department down. I'd had enough.'

'That's fair enough. It's partly why I wanted to reshape the White Koi. Remember when Fang Jian was going to have me kill you?'

'I remember the look on his face when you stuck that sword in his belly.'

'How about Africa? With Stella. She and I having to strip off in that horrible gambling den in Gaborone so they could search us?'

Gabriel shook his head and twisted the key in the ignition. 'I don't want to think about that anymore, Tara. Come on, let's go. I'll brief you on the drive. I have to warn you in advance, she doesn't like going much above forty.'

On the road, Gabriel surveyed all the other traffic, not just on the roads they took, but on side roads, too, at intersections, up in the hills. Always on the lookout for heavy-looking SUVs or pickups driving in convoy.

'How did you know the Chinese were coming for you?' he asked on a long, boring straight stretch of road fringed with cacti, agave and not much else.

'It all started back when we were already semi-legit. My second-in-command was hit. They could easily have made it look like a rival. Used a knife or a gun. Taken his ring finger. But they used nerve gas. That was a pretty clear sign that they were coming for us. Then after I completed the transition, they began infiltrating the group. They were good, but we were better. In the end, I got word from someone I trusted completely that the MSS had put a contract out on me. I had to run. Seoul first, then Hanoi. Berlin, London, then Paris.'

'I'm sorry.'

'Don't be. Fighting the CCP is like trying to hold back a tsunami. You just drown. And now I'm here with you, so it's all good. I mean, things have worked out for the best.'

'You might not say that when Mason and his men turn up in a couple of weeks' time.'

Tara shook her head.

'People who walk into the dragon's mouth seeking treasure find only fire.'

Gabriel smiled grimly.

'Sounds like the sort of thing Master Zhao might say.'

'How is he?'

Gabriel whipped his head round.

'What?'

'How is he? Master Zhao?'

'He's dead, Tara! How could you have forgotten?'

'No! I mean, I didn't forget. Sorry, it was a very long flight and I'm jetlagged. I meant are you still holding him in your heart?'

'Oh, well, yes. I think about him a lot.'

Sometimes there was no need to think, what with his old mentor still putting in an occasional appearance at his house. Sitting on the battered sofa next to Smudge. Or standing leaning on the rail outside, looking out to sea.

He pointed to a sign in the distance.

'We take the coast road there. Then it's another two hours and we're home.'

39

He picked up the pistol. It was surprisingly heavy. Squinted along the barrel at a monkey in a nearby palm tree. Tightened his finger on the trigger. Until it clicked.

'If you want to go hunting, we can pick up a couple of rifles. This place is swarming with game,' Mason said from the neighbouring rattan chair.

'It's a fucking nature reserve, George. Jesus, have some respect.'

Kalt shook his head. However many times he'd tried to explain to Mason how his plan for Peacemaker was going to work, all the thick-necked Floridian seemed to pick up on was the opportunity to shoot at people. It was as if he didn't care that Kalt was going to achieve world peace single-handedly.

Mason took a pull on his beer.

'It's hardly respectful to bribe the governor of Yucatán Province so you get to build a compound inside La Reserva de la Biósfera Sian Ka'an.'

Kalt valued Mason for his tactical skills, organisation abilities and contacts. But he found it impossible to stomach the man's constant attempts to undermine him. Why couldn't he understand that he was an employee? In fact, not even that. A contractor. No better than a fuckin' freelance coder. When Wolfe was on board, Mason would be out the door. Kalt grinned. In fact, given what he now knew about Gabriel Wolfe, maybe out the window was a more appropriate exit route for George.

'Something funny, Xander?'

Kalt turned the pistol over in his hand. Shook his head.

'Just boring HR stuff.'

Mason gave him a weird look. Without the biometric readouts, Kalt found it hard to interpret. Probably envy that he was so low down the food chain.

'On which subject, I pulled together the last few men we need in SPS. Wolfe won't know what's hit him. He'll be dead before he's fired a shot.'

Kalt slammed the gun down on the table between them, cracking the glass top and toppling Mason's two empty beer bottles.

'Wolfe doesn't die! I want him, George. Fuck, how many times do I have to tell you?'

'And how many times do I have to tell *you*, he won't come over. I don't know who he is, but I know the type. You could offer him millions, hell, billions, and he'd laugh in your face. Guys like him, it's all about honour. He'll never come work for you. Not in a million years.'

Kalt regarded the ex-CIA man with a mixture of feelings. If pushed, he'd say one of them was probably disgust. But there was a lot of disappointment in there, too.

'You're right, George,' he said carefully, enunciating every word as if talking to a five-year old. Which, compared mentally to Kalt, Mason totally was. '*You* don't know much about Wolfe. Despite torturing him. But guess what? I do. While you were playing in your private little Abu Ghraib down in Honduras, I was using more modern methods. Wolfe is ex-SAS, ex-Parachute Regiment. He has a sister called Tara who used to run a triad called the White Koi. After leaving the SAS he went into business for himself, which, by the way, shows really entrepreneurial spirit, as a private security consultant. And he was married. Not for long but yeah, he tied the knot. An Israeli citizen named Eliyah Schochat. Ex-IDF. Ex-Mossad.'

Mason was shaking his head all the way through Kalt's speech, which was totally inappropriate. Fine. It only hardened Kalt's reserve to replace him first chance he got.

'You a betting man, Xander?'

'What do you mean?'

'I mean I'll give you a hundred to one Wolfe will spit in your face if you ask him to join you. Let's say a thousand dollar stake.'

Kalt eyed his hired gun with the curiosity of a scientist. Mason was a fool. And a braggart. But it was his loss.

'Do you have a hundred grand to lose, George?'

'Won't need it, Xander.'

Kalt tutted. 'Yes, but do you have it? Otherwise you're just posturing.'

'Yeah, I have it. Do you have ten bucks for when you lose?'

'Funny.'

'So, we on or what?'

'Yes, George, we're on. Not that I need an extra hundred grand. According to Forbes my net worth is—'

'Yeah, yeah, Xander, I know what you're worth.'

Kalt shook his head. And for once, decided to let the impertinence go. With the hold he had over Wolfe now, he'd be begging to work for Kalt. And taking a hundred thousand off Mason would merely be the icing on the cake.

He turned to Mason.

'Don't you have a plane to catch?'

40

Horrified, Gabriel looked down at the sheet covering his body. It was soaked in blood. The surface was shiny with it. Bubbles popped wetly, releasing fine sprays of scarlet that floated in the air towards his face until he inhaled them.

He threw the squelching sheet back. Eli lay beneath it, her abdomen ripped apart. Somewhere a baby cried.

He sat bolt upright, screaming. Scrabbling to get away from the bloody corpse of his wife. But the bed was empty. The sweat-soaked sheet lay in a twisted rope on the floor. He jumped out of bed and ran into the kitchen, gulped down a glass of water then fled the house for the veranda.

Breath coming in ragged gasps, Gabriel stared out to sea, following the silvered line of broken crescents that led away to the moon.

Gripping the worn wooden rail with both hands, he threw his head back and moaned loudly.

Dry wood cracked at the side of the house. Instantly alert, he dashed back inside and emerged a few moments later with a pistol.

A voice came from behind him. Calm, unhurried. In command.

'Put it down, Gabriel. Put it down right now. One twitch and I'll cut you in half.'

Gabriel didn't hesitate. He dropped the pistol onto the decking boards and kicked it to the edge of the veranda.

'Turn around. Slowly.'

Gabriel complied, to find himself staring down the barrel of a Colt M4 carbine. Holding it was the man who'd so recently tortured him in the Battalion 3-16 secret prison.

'Are you here to kill me?'

Mason shook his head. 'My boss wants to talk to you. Sound good to you, Trooper Wolfe?'

So he knew about Gabriel's service in the Regiment. How? The British Government never released that kind of information. And Gabriel had never volunteered it.

'Do I have a choice?'

'Sure you have a choice. You can come with me or I can kill you right here. Believe me, that would be my preferred option. Only, the man paying my not inconsiderable wages has other ideas. So what's it to be?'

'Where is he?'

'In my car. I'm parked on the outskirts of town. You don't mind a little walk, do you?'

'I need some boots.'

'Nah, you really don't. Let's go.'

Gabriel knew plenty of moves to disarm an armed opponent holding you at gunpoint. But as he walked in front of Mason, the ex-spook showed he knew them too. He hung back, out of range. Gabriel faked a stumble and slowed right down. Drawing Mason in. Trying to kid a kidder.

Mason's voice was sardonic.

'Think I should come closer? Maybe give you a good old prod with my rifle? Sorry, buddy, I do krav maga, too. Bunch of us trained with the IDF. How about you? Did that wife of yours teach you? Eliyah, wasn't it?'

Gabriel whirled round, teeth bared, fists clenched, his heart pumping wildly, battering against his ribs.

'Don't you fucking dare say her name!'

Mason was standing ten metres off, gun levelled at Gabriel's midsection. And he was smiling.

'Whoa, whoa, whoa! Steady, there, cowboy. Never make a man holding an assault rifle nervous.'

Every fibre of Gabriel's being wanted to launch himself at Mason, claw his eyes from their sockets, tear his tongue from his mouth, strangle, punch, kick, debilitate, kill. But what use would rushing the gun be if he ended up dead? Santa Rosa would fall and everything he'd fought to protect would be gone. He forced himself to take a breath. To level a cold gaze at Mason.

'Let's just go.'

Twenty minutes later, his feet bleeding from contact with sharp rocks and loose cactus spines, Gabriel spotted a black SUV pulled off the dirt road and hidden from view behind a stand of scrappy trees.

'Get in,' Mason said.

'Which side?'

'Passenger. Front.'

Front? That was odd. Gabriel assumed Mason's boss would be up front.

He climbed into the front passenger seat. Looked over his shoulder. He was alone in the cabin.

Mason got in behind him. The muzzle of the Colt poked him in the back of the neck, slotted by Mason between the chromed steel supports of the headrest. He spoke close to Gabriel's right ear.

'Turn on the ignition to the second position.'

Gabriel leaned over and twisted the chunky plastic key. The lights on the dashboard lit up and the huge central infotainment screen glowed brightly.

'Tap the Zoom icon,' Mason said.

Gabriel tapped the screen and, realising what was planned, followed the onscreen instructions.

A man's face appeared on the screen. Smooth-cheeked. Dark hair curling around his face. He looked to be in his early thirties. The single most arresting feature was his thick black eyebrows, so heavy they appeared to have been imported from a different face altogether.

'Hello, Gabriel. I'm sorry for all the clandestine business. I hope George has been respectful. My name is Xander Kalt. I expect you've heard of me?'

'Actually I haven't. What do you want?'

'You haven't...' The eyebrows crawled upwards like caterpillars seeking food. 'I'm surprised. I founded and still own Kaltium?'

'Also, no. What do you want?'

Kalt looked annoyed. Probably unwise to wind up a predator intent on destroying an entire village. Gabriel resolved to hold his temper in check. He could negotiate, after all.

'OK, we'll leave the backgrounder for later in our relationship. All you need to know right now is this. One, I am a very, very rich man. Two, I have a plan, a truly *brilliant* plan, that will end war on this planet for ever. And three, I want you to help me bring that incredible transformation of the human race to fruition. *You*, Gabriel. I want you to come and work for me.'

Gabriel said nothing. Was he dealing with a madman? The guy sounded delusional. As he'd been speaking, his eyes had seemed to gleam and his speech had taken on a messianic fervour.

'End war?' he said after several seconds.

'For ever. Imagine it, Gabriel. All that human potential released. All those lives put to more profitable use than killing or being killed. You were a soldier. You know the human and economic cost of war. I am inviting you to imagine a world in which human beings worked together, in pursuit of common goals. We can solve the climate crisis within a generation. Hunger in the global south? Eradicated inside a decade. Colonies on distant planets? I have people drawing up plans as we speak.'

Gabriel nodded thoughtfully. Not because he agreed. Xander

Kalt, whoever he was, was clearly insane. Because he needed to buy time while he worked out how to negotiate with a lunatic.

'Those are admirable aims. And yes, as a former soldier, I do know the cost of war. Can I ask you a question?'

Kalt nodded rapidly, almost feverishly.

'Yes, yes! Ask me as many questions as you like. That's why I'm here, Gabriel.'

'People have talked about ending war before. But they're still raging all over the globe. How are you different?'

'Oh, I'm not different, Gabriel. I'm just a man. But when I get what I am searching for, they'll have to listen. I'll say, "Lay down your arms," and they will. All of them. From machineguns like the one George is unfortunately having to point at you to thermonuclear bombs and kinetic weapons.'

'Why?'

Kalt frowned. 'Why?'

'Yes. Why will they do that? How are you going to convince them? You're very rich, I get that. But these are nation states we're talking about. You can't buy the Russians or the Americans, or the Chinese or the Indians, or the Pakistanis.'

Kalt tapped the side of his nose. It looked like an amateur dramatic move he'd learned before playing a secret agent.

'Come and work for me, Gabriel, and I'll explain everything. I'll pay you whatever you ask. In fact, no, wait.' He giggled. 'You name your price, and then I'll double it.'

'Why do you want me? You've tried to kill me at least twice so far.'

'A strategic error, Gabriel. I apologise. I want you because those peasants in Santa Rosa respect you. If you persuade them to take my offer, we can avoid all the bloodshed. All the killing. Which, by the way, I totally do not want to happen, but it's for the greater good, you know? I know you worked in the private sector after the army. Surely you picked up a few negotiation skills along the way?'

Gabriel dearly wanted to tell Kalt to go fuck himself. And to tell whichever psychiatrist was keeping him just this side of reality to get his patient sent to a secure institution.

But he wanted to find out more about Kalt's plans. Because whether or not the man was lying, delusional or both, Gabriel agreed with him on one thing. He wanted to avoid bloodshed.

'Look, can I call you Xander?'

Kalt beamed, his face breaking up momentarily as the signal faltered.

'Of course, Gabriel! Call me Xander. The first step in building trust, am I right?'

'You are. But this is a big deal. I need a few days to think about it. Clearly your plan is at the genius-level but I need some time to process all the implications. Not just for Santa Rosa, but for the world.'

Kalt had started nodding as soon as Gabriel answered. By the end of the flattering speech that had Gabriel wondering if he'd overdone it, Kalt's head was threatening to detach from his neck altogether.

'Take a couple days? Sure. But don't think too long, Gabriel. I hate to remind you, but there is a deadline in place and one thing I've learned from running the world's most successful quantum computing platform is you have to meet your deadlines.'

He held up a hand.

'Ciao for now.'

The image froze. The app burbled. Then faded out.

Gabriel sat, bemused by what had just happened. A jab from the Colt's muzzle snapped him back to the present.

'Get out.'

Gabriel swung round in the padded seat.

'Not going to offer me a ride back to my house?'

'Get the fuck out before I shoot you.'

'Hmm, George, not sure Xander would take too kindly to that. Seems like he's keen to have me on board. Maybe I'll end up telling *you* to get the fuck out.'

Mason's finger whitened on the trigger.

'One…'

Gabriel got out.

Behind him he heard Mason exit the vehicle and get back in. The driver's door slammed shut and with a roar Mason spun the big vehicle around, sending a shower of stinging grit and choking dust Gabriel's way.

Without a backward glance, Gabriel set off back to Santa Rosa.

41

Mason stalked along the hotel corridor to his room. He thrust the key into the lock with such savagery the cheap brass bent and he feared it would snap off in the mechanism. But it held. And he was inside.

He twisted the cap off a bottle of guaro – foul stuff, but he'd finished his stash of Jim Beam the previous evening – and took a slug straight from the neck. Coughing as the sweet yet harsh liquor scorched his throat, he filled a glass and took it out onto the narrow balcony.

He rested his forearms on the steel railing and stared down at the street. Fucking Honduras. Fucking Gabriel Wolfe. And, most especially, fucking Xander Kalt.

His 'genius-level' plan, as Wolfe had cleverly called it, was pure, unadulterated, unfiltered bullshit. Mason had worked in intelligence his whole adult life. And what he'd seen, on every side of the ideological divides that separated human beings more effectively than mile-deep, mile-wide canyons, had convinced him of one thing.

People enjoyed war.

Oh, they *claimed* to be appalled by human suffering. To want to live peaceably with their neighbours. To focus on improving the lives of their citizens. Curing cancer. Saving the ice caps. Protecting pandas and whatever else floated their boats. But give them a reason, no, give them an *excuse*, and they'd be spending all that hard-won tax revenue on drones, cluster munitions, nerve gas, rail guns and all the rest of it.

His ex-wife had accused him of being a cynic. And he'd retorted that he was simply a realist. To secure a lasting peace, all Country A had to do was cede a few hundred square miles of barren scrubland. And in return, Country B would open a trade route through its territorial waters. But, no. They'd rather feed the flower of their young manhood into the meat grinder.

So, sure, if Xander could really end war, more power to him. Have at it, Xander! It was just, he couldn't. Even if he had found a way to direct Peacemaker's infernal energy signature down every fibre-optic cable, copper wire, mobile data, Bluetooth, WiFi and satellite signal, who'd believe him?

A test would only work if he took it all the way to the touchdown line. Anything less and the big powers would laugh at him. Send teams to eliminate him. He laughed bitterly. Probably the only time you'd ever see the Russian, Chinese, North Koreans and Americans collaborate on anything.

But he paid well. So well, that George had acquired a plot of land on New Zealand's south island. When the inevitable happened, courtesy of Xander Kalt or his enemies, George intended to be so far off-grid, he would make preppers look like they were holding up, 'SOS. WE'RE HERE!' signs.

His phone rang, interrupting a pleasant daydream about swimming in the pool below the hundred-foot waterfall that sat dead-centre on his slice of Eden.

He sighed.

'Yes, Xander. What is it?' *Now*, he felt like adding.

'How do you think it went with Gabriel? Give me your honest assessment. From an intelligence standpoint.'

'My *honest* assessment?'

'Nothing less, George. You know how much I value your opinion.'

'He's playing you, Xander. He just took your dream, amplified it, and fed it back to you. He just wants to find out about Peacemaker so he can destroy it. Let me neutralise him.'

Seconds ticked by. Mason was content to wait. Below his balcony, a gangbanger was slapping a woman around. She wore a white micro-mini and neon-green stockings. Pimp plus prostitute. He aimed a finger down at the crown of the man's head. Pow.

'I'm sorry, George. Were you even in the car with Gabriel? I mean, did you not hear the same things I did? All he was doing was showing he understood my ideas. It's human communication 101. He's buying time, of course he is. But that's because he thinks I need pressurising to pay him more. Once he realises money's no object he'll come over. I know it.'

George shook his head. Wow. His current employer was living in another world. Just then, at street level, the pimp pulled a knife. The girl screamed and retreated until her back hit the wall of the hotel.

He yelled down a simple warning.

'Hey, amigo. Vete a la mierda!'

Literally, get to shit. But the Spanish equivalent of Fuck off.

The pimp stared up, straight into the barrel of George's Glock. Wisely, he fled, shouting a string of oaths over his shoulder.

The prostitute looked up at him. Her face tear-steaked.

'Gracias por nada, idiota!' she screamed before running after her pimp.

Xander was repeating himself over and over in George's ear, like a particularly annoying mosquito. God, he'd be glad when this job was over.

'George, are you there? George, are you there? George, are you there? George, are you th—'

'Yes! For fuck's sake, Xander, I'm here.'

'You need to remember something, George,' Xander said, using a particular tone, part patronising, part prissy, that always had George wanting to kill something, preferably Xander. 'In this relationship, I am the organ-grinder and you are the monkey. Now, you're a very talented monkey, otherwise why would I be paying you all this money? But at the end of the day, a monkey you are and a monkey you'll remain. So when I ask you what you think of Wolfe, what I am expecting is your honest opinion that he is the missing piece of the puzzle that will enable me to bring Peacemaker out of the ocean and into the offices of every world leader. He bested Lorne once. He bested you twice, including your, quote-unquote, "hand-picked team of badasses". So he has shown that he should be on my side of the fence. Are we clear?'

Time was, George had meditated every morning. But that habit had died at roughly the same time as his second marriage. So he was pitifully short of mental resources to cope with the flood of cortisol that had his vision doubling and his hands clutching convulsively around a non-existent throat.

'Clear,' he choked out through a windpipe narrowed with rage.

Xander was gone.

On the plus side, in two days, the deadline would expire and he could launch the final assault on Santa Rosa. With a bit of luck he'd get to kill Wolfe personally.

He smiled and poured himself another glassful of guaro. Stared down at his Glock.

Wondered idly whether he should go out and track down the pimp.

Or his girlfriend.

42

Gabriel drove into Bonito for medical supplies.

He hadn't replied to Kalt yet. It was a delicate balancing act between maintaining the village's readiness for a threatened assault and finding a way to change Kalt's mind. The latter was the least worst option, but Kalt had shown every sign of being delusional. So, preparations continued.

He emerged from the *farmacia* laden with white plastic carrier bags stuffed with antibiotics, painkillers, dressings – the hundred and one items their improvised field hospital in the village hall would need. The bag's wire-thin twisted plastic handles were already digging into his curled fingers.

When he rounded the corner where he'd parked his truck, he stopped. Not again.

'Kalt's sending you in the wrong order,' he said. 'I've already had a visit from the ghost of Christmas yet to come. What's the ghost of Christmas past doing here?'

The overweight Texan lawyer stared at Gabriel dumbly.

'I ain't no ghost, Gabriel,' Packard said. He grinned and patted his corpulent belly. 'In fact, y'all could say I'm a little too much of the flesh. Now, before y'all say anything, I bring what you might call salvation for the good folks of Santa Rosa, who I know are close to your heart.'

Gabriel was suspicious of the lawyer's folksy act – all those "y'alls"s had to be fake, surely? Even Sean Cunningham, a long-dead friend and a true native son of the Lone Star State, hadn't gone in for them with such profusion. 'I already told your boss, I'm thinking about it.'

'Yes, indeed you did. But, see, Xander's kinda getting a little antsy on account of how the deadline is the day after tomorrow. He thinks maybe what y'all need is a little actual face time with him. IRL as the kids say nowadays.'

Well, this was new. Gabriel had his doubts, though. He'd be walking into the lion's den. No doubt unarmed. But then he thought of Santiago with the rifle. Positioned in a sniper's nest. The moment Mason realised they had a guy on overwatch, he'd send men up to kill him. Gabriel saw Pera's grief-stricken face as clear as if she'd been standing next to him in the sun-baked square. He'd never be able to live with himself if anything happened to Santiago.

'Kalt's here? In Honduras?'

The lawyer hauled his belt up and resettled it around his middle.

'So you'll meet him?'

'Yes, I'll meet him. Where is he?'

'Close. Somewhere private. No interruptions, guaranteed. You're in?'

Gabriel nodded.

'Y'all going to have to leave those bags behind, then. Come with me.' He pointed at the bags swinging from Gabriel's hands. 'Maybe the shop delivers.'

* * *

Packard drove fast along the country road leading away from Bonito. Every time the truck hit a pothole it lifted clear of the ground before ramming back down hard. Gabriel clamped his jaw against the pain from the injuries Mason had inflicted on him.

Packard turned to him.

'Now, before you go into your meeting with el heffay, Gabriel, I just want to make sure we're all on the same page regarding Xander's offer.' He shifted his weight. 'It ain't wildly complicated. We need Santa Rosa, that goes without saying. And I won't insult your intelligence by telling a pack of lies about how we could just pack up and find what we need somewhere else. It has to be Santa Rosa and the land either side. That's a non-negotiable, as we lawyers say.'

'Go on.'

'We need, well, Xander needs, to know what y'all got planned up there. In terms of defences and so forth. He knows y'all won't go down without a fight, so, whatever it is, you're gonna have to tell him.'

'And if I do, what happens to the villagers?'

'Well, Gabriel, it's like in every conflict. You get an acceptable level of civilian casualties in pursuit of your strategic objective. Sadly, Xander's come to the conclusion that negotiatin' with them is a waste of his time. Seems like they have got this notion into their heads that if they stick together, he'll just throw it over and walk away. But as I said, that ain't going to happen.'

'So Mason and his men are going to massacre them.'

Packard shifted his weight again. 'Oh, Lord, Gabriel, "massacre" is a real ugly word. It's collateral damage, sure. But this ain't gonna be no My Lai situation. And after all, it ain't as if they are your people. I mean, you're British, right? They're just little people. *Campesinos*. I think when you hear exactly what Xander's prepared to offer you, y'all will see things in a new perspective.'

The truck hit another pothole, sending both occupants floating out of their seats for a second before thumping down. The distraction gave Gabriel just enough time to stop himself from killing the lawyer. Mason's offer to spare the residents of Santa Rosa was just another spook lie. They wanted nothing less than a full-blown betrayal. Not just of the village he'd made his home, or the friends he'd made. But the six men who'd agreed to come out to Honduras to help him defend it.

He pictured Santiago's face. That of a boy, still, but still with that spark of manhood glowing brighter with each passing day. And Pera's on the day she'd taken delivery of her food truck. He conjured a vision of the six former soldiers, hard at work training the villagers, finding humour despite the bleak prospects looming just over the horizon.

'You're right. When I think about them, I can see exactly what they're worth to me. Let's go and talk to Xander.'

43

Gabriel tore off the black cloth hood Packard had apologetically insisted he don a few clicks back up the road.

Gabriel had counted the left and right turns since that point in the journey, but in the end he'd given up. Wherever Kalt was hiding out, it would no doubt be heavily defended. And what Gabriel had planned required subtlety, not force of numbers.

Facing him was the man he'd only seen on an eight-inch infotainment screen so far.

Xander Kalt.

In the flesh the eyebrows were less dominant, but still impressively dark and thick. He smiled widely and advanced, hand stuck out in front of him on a straight arm. The move seemed unnatural, forced, somehow.

Gabriel shook hands anyway. Kalt's skin was unpleasantly cool to the touch, reinforcing the image of his being not quite human.

Kalt spread his arms wide.

'Welcome to my temporary home, Gabriel. *Mi casa es su casa*. I hope you'll make yourself at home during your stay.'

An hour later, during which time Gabriel had been shown to a guest room in the single-storey hacienda and invited to 'freshen up', he found himself sitting on a deck looking out at rainforest, sipping a gin and tonic. Bowls of stuffed olives and macadamia nuts sat on the table between him and Kalt, who was sucking a vibrant green liquid through a straw. Gabriel caught a faint whiff of spinach.

No sign of any goons, but he was sure they'd be around.

'Ever had pre-dinner drinks with a billionaire before, Gabriel?'

Gabriel sipped his drink before replying. The Russian industrialist Tatyana Garin and he had shared more than one sundowner over the years, ever since he'd retrieved her Birkin bag from a pair of North London chancers. And Tatyana was definitely a member of the nine noughts club.

'Can't say I have, Xander.'

'Well you'll be doing it a lot from now on, I hope.' He raised his own glass. 'To the future.'

'To the future.'

Kalt grabbed a handful of the creamy-fleshed macadamias and tossed one into his mouth.

'Let's cut to the chase, Gabriel. Are you going to join me and help save the world, or not?'

Gabriel eyeballed the madman sitting opposite. And with as much quiet sincerity as he could muster, said, 'Xander, I thought a lot about what you said. And Packard was on the money when he asked me what use I had for a bunch of Honduran peasants. So, yes, I'm in.'

Kalt punched the air.

'Yes! I knew it! You just needed to meet me man to man. I tell you, Gabe, when they write new history books, because believe me, they're gonna need to, this meeting is going to be talked about as the pivotal moment in everything that followed. You know your military history?'

'A little. I studied—'

'Of course. So, this is gonna make the Geneva Convention look like, I don't know, like, a, a, fuckin' playground handshake! Imagine! I am going to bring the world to its senses and you'll be standing right beside me.'

'Not George? Not Lorne?'

Kalt shook his head violently. Leaned towards Gabriel and dropped his voice to a conspiratorial murmur.

'Not telling tales out of school, Gabe, but those guys? They have their uses, but they're just hired help. Spooks like George? Lawyers like Lorne? They're a dime a dozen. Whereas you? You're a true man of the world. Like me! You grew up with this old Chinese dude who taught you all this righteous, mystic eastern shit. I would never tell them this, Gabe, but they're dispensable. With you, though, I sense something. And I am probably one of the best readers of people in the world, so believe me when I say you have something special.'

'So, all I need to do is brief you on how I've defended Santa Rosa and I get the full welcome package?'

Kalt smiled broadly, ate a handful of macadamias and spoke through the debris.

'That's all. Well, that and help me secure the whole area and proceed to the next stage of my plan.'

'Can you tell me what that is now I'm on board?'

'Of course, of course. I just need you to sign this.'

He reached down to his left side and pulled a plastic folder from a bag. Inside was a thick document stapled in one corner.

'What's that? My employment contract?'

'NDA. We'll do the contract later. Gotta sort out the financial package, too, my man. Have to keep the newbie happy, am I right?'

Gabriel smiled accommodatingly.

'Do you have a pen?'

Kalt frowned. 'Aren't you going to read it?'

'No need. The only people who read NDAs are the ones who want to break them down the line. I have no such intention.'

'Awesome. Use this.' He proffered a beautiful lacquered fountain pen. 'It's Lalique. Made from glass taken from the tomb of Nefertiti. Used to belong to Marilyn Monroe.'

Gabriel signed the NDA with a flourish. He could afford to.

What he had planned would involve no breaches of confidence. Nothing so legalistic.

Kalt snatched the stapled sheets away as if he feared Gabriel might change his mind.

'So, Xander, now you have my silence guaranteed, what's so interesting about Santa Rosa you were willing to pay millions over the odds to acquire it?'

Kalt smiled crookedly. For all the world, he looked like a guilty schoolboy caught sneaking porn into class.

'My great-grandfather was a Russian scientist. Technically a Soviet scientist. You know the Soviets revered science, right? They got rid of God and they had to replace him with something. Dudes like my great-grandfather were fuckin' rockstars. Anyway, he'd been working on this weapons project. In Russian it's *Mirotvorets*. Know what that means? It's—'

'Peacemaker.'

A flash of annoyance darkened Kalt's boyish features. Then it was gone.

'Smart guy. I guess you learned Russian in the SAS, huh?'

Gabriel shrugged.

'I was always good at languages at school. Something of a model student.'

'Whatever. So, my great-grandfather, who by the way was called Vladimir Kaltrov, he designs this device. Basically a Doomsday weapon. So powerful, once the Soviets revealed it, the rest of the world would have had to fall into line. Surrender their nuclear arsenals. I came into possession of his private journals. He should never have written them. They'd have sent him to Siberia if they'd found out. Or shot him.'

Gabriel frowned, genuinely interested in this bizarre tale.

'What happened? The Soviets didn't have anything like that. I'd have read about it.'

'Oh, they had it all right. Old Vladimir went to witness the first and only test. They tried it out on one of the secret cities. Guess how many people died?'

Kalt's eyes were shining unpleasantly. Gabriel had seen that look before. On the faces of men, and, occasionally, women, who revelled in human pain and suffering. Unaware of, or unable to countenance, the idea that other people might have feelings different to their own. The feeling, for example, that living was preferable to dying.

'I'd prefer not to.'

'Two hundred and fifty thousand, eight hundred and seventeen,' Kalt said, eyes wide. 'Sticklers for accurate record-keeping, the Soviets. Only the Nazis were more meticulous. My great-grandfather was hazy on the details, but he wrote this one passage that really stuck with me, Gabe. I've memorised it. He said, and I quote, "Compared to their agonies as Peacemaker wrought its devilish havoc on their bodies, the horrors of the Great Patriotic War were like a child's squabble in a kindergarten. At its height, I wanted to put my own eyes out so I could stop seeing that awful degradation, pour molten lead into my own ears to block out those screams of human beings suffering, cut off my own nose with a bayonet so I could no longer smell that indescribable stench. I have visited Hell. May I never return." What do you make of that?'

Gabriel didn't say anything at first. The unusually poetic phrases seemed like something from the writings of a mediaeval divine rather than a hard-nosed Soviet scientist. What kind of weapon could have so horrified its own creator?

'Did he give any detail about the weapon itself? How it worked?'

'No, and that's a real pain in the ass. But the reason you never heard of it? It went down in a sub. It was sailing to Cuba but freak weather conditions meant the captain diverted into the Caribbean between Cuba and Honduras. Something happened and the sub was lost.'

Now it all became clear without Kalt having to explain further. Some tech billionaires spent their money building alternative universes, or sending people into space. Xander Kalt had spent a portion of his tracking down this literally indescribable weapon.

'You know where it is, don't you? It's off the coast near Santa Rosa. You're going to use Santa Rosa as a base for your salvage operation. Bring it ashore there in total secrecy. And then what?'

Kalt laughed. 'Oh, Gabe, your face! Don't worry, I have no plans to deploy it. No, I'm going to follow through on what the Soviets had planned. I'm going to call a press conference and announce I have it. Then I'll give the nuclear powers a deadline to disarm. I'm going to end war for ever.'

'They'll never do it. They won't believe you. Unless—'

Kalt rolled his eyes.

'OK, you got me! Unless I demonstrate it. So, maybe there will be a small, and I mean totally *trivial* loss of life. I mean, in the context of the lives I'm saving, it's like rounding error.'

Gabriel sat with that piece of information for a minute. Could a decades-old Soviet weapon that had gone down on a sub still be operational? Would Kalt know how to operate it? Where the hell would he test it? On whom? The whole thing was ridiculous. And yet the grinning billionaire sitting opposite him seemed to think it was anything but.

The stakes had just increased exponentially. Saving Santa Rosa was important. But getting to Peacemaker before Xander Kalt did was essential. And killing him would do no good at all. The weapon needed to be destroyed. And only Xander Kalt knew its precise location. The long game, then. But in less than three days, a band of merciless killers would descend on Santa Rosa and the people Gabriel had come to regard as almost family. Most especially Pera and Santiago.

Kalt interrupted his whirling thoughts.

'You know, Gabe, I have to say, now you're on board? You got kinda lucky that first time down there in Santa Rosa.'

'Oh? How do you mean?'

'That team George assembled? It was short notice. Just a bunch of lowlifes who couldn't even get a job with a cartel. But the guys he's curated now? Man, you wouldn't have stood a chance. We're talking sixty ex-Nicaraguan Contras, El

Salvadorean mercenaries, even some Honduran cops with links to Battalion 3-16.'

'That's an impressive line-up. I'm glad I'm going to be on the winning side.'

'You bet! Jesus, the poor *campesinos* won't know what hit 'em. So, time for you to fulfil your side of the bargain. What have you got going on down there? Brought in some buddies of yours from the SAS?'

Gabriel kept his gaze level. How had Kalt guessed? He shook his head, glad that, on top of the training, they'd also instituted a widespread sentry system out in the countryside around Santa Rosa. Anyone trying to get close enough to spy on their preparations would have been spotted immediately and dealt with.

'It was all a bluff. They've got their shotguns and hunting rifles, but all I could do in the time available was give them some basic combat training. We sent the women, children and old folks away, but you're looking at a bunch of farmers. I was hoping my presence might deter you, if you thought I was planning some serious armed resistance.'

Kalt nodded as if he'd been aware of the strategy all along.

'I see. Kind of a psyops type of thing. You know, I've read Sun Tzu's *The Art of War* like a hundred times. I bet nobody's read it more than me. When you're strong appear weak, when you're weak, appear strong. That's one of my favourites. So you're weak and you were trying to look strong. I get it. I mean, it was a smart move, given your woeful HR situation, Gabe, but I'd have seen through it anyway.'

Gabriel shrugged. 'That's what I figured. It's why I decided to take you up on your offer. I like to be on the winning side, Xander.'

'Of course you do! And believe me, Gabe, you will be. You will be.'

Gabriel nodded. 'I have no doubt.'

44

After a dinner of venison – 'shot it myself' according to his host – Gabriel accepted Kalt's offer of a bed for the night.

At 2:30 a.m., he rose from the floor, where he had been sitting cross-legged, eyes closed. Fully dressed. He moved to the bed without making a squeak, thanking some Honduran carpenter for doing such a professional job on the floorboards.

Before leaving, he wadded up some spare bedclothes and a pillow and arranged them under the top sheet into the semblance of a sleeping human form. It was an old trick most people thought only happened in the movies, but done right was surprisingly effective.

How about a weapon, though? He looked around the room. Nothing so convenient as a gun cabinet or wall-mounted display case full of knives. He looked at the wardrobe where he'd found the spare bedding. It had a hanging rail.

He lifted the wooden rail off its u-shaped brass supports. It was half an inch in diameter and three feet long. He slipped it between the mattress and the bed base and snapped it in half with a muffled crack. When he withdrew it, he had a serviceable dagger with a long, razor-edged tip of bright bare wood.

The hallway outside his room was floored in bare planking covered by a central runner. Keeping to the edges, he made his way along the corridor to the top of the stairs, where he paused to listen for sounds.

A murmur of voices floated up from the ground floor. Kalt must still be up. And with a second man. He crept a third of the way down and scanned the square ground floor hall. Nobody there. So the two men were in one of the reception rooms. Gabriel strained to identify Kalt's companion. But whoever it was, he was speaking in a low voice.

He descended to the ground floor, wooden dagger, point uppermost, in his fist. The conversation was issuing from behind a closed door to his right, halfway down another long, narrow corridor, also floored in bare planking covered with a brightly patterned woven runner.

Exfiltrating immediately was a decent option, but Gabriel wanted to leave with every last possible scrap of intel. If Kalt was discussing tactics, then Gabriel wanted to know what they were.

On sliding feet, he covered the few yards from the foot of the stairs to the closed door. Willing his pulse to settle – its insistent throb was noisy in his ears, especially the left, which still hurt from time to time from the cigarette burn – he bent his head to the reddish wood.

At once he recognised Kalt's companion. It was the lawyer. Packard. He couldn't hear every word but then Packard barked out a place name.

'Nottingham?' Gabriel's heart froze. But the Texan hadn't finished. 'Where the fuck's that?'

Gabriel blinked. Surely they couldn't seriously be planning to deploy Peacemaker in the UK? How would they even transport it? Then he cursed his own naivety. Xander Kalt was a billionaire. For men like him, rules were optional extras. There'd be a hundred different ways he could smuggle a weapon of mass destruction into any country he chose.

Then an even more horrifying thought struck him. He'd been assuming it would need to be on site. But what if it worked remotely? Some kind of beam weapon, maybe. Or an as-yet-unknown technology that went down in that Soviet sub, now to be resurrected to deadly effect.

This was international terrorism on a grand scale. Yet with no allegiance to any of the usual state and non-state actors, Gabriel was willing to bet Xander Kalt would get a free pass from all the world's intelligence agencies. Christ, he probably rubbed shoulders with their bosses at Davos.

Chair legs scraped. The lawyer coughed.

'Well, now, I need to go shake hands with the unemployed. Be back in a little while.'

Gabriel ran for the front door. Outside, the coast was clear. Parked a few yards away were three black SUVs. He ran for the closest one and tried the door, but it was locked. So was the second. The third, set back a way from the other two, was his last chance, then. He approached the driver's door, praying the driver had been less security conscious than the others.

He lifted the door handle but it stopped well short of the reassuring clunk of a lifting latch.

'Hey! What the fuck are you doing?'

Security. Gabriel spoke without turning.

'Xander asked me to get his briefcase from the backseat. I don't suppose you've got the keys, have you?'

'Oh, sure. Hold on.'

Gabriel waited until he heard the chink of the keys, then he turned. A shit-eating smile on his face. He pointed upwards at a sky milky with billions of stars in which a full moon hung like a giant silver dollar

'Thanks, buddy. Hell of a night, isn't it?'

The guard peered into the window, and frowned. He turned to Gabriel, who'd taken a step back.

'There's no briefcase in there,' the guard said.

Realisation dawned. The hand holding out the keys to the SUV dropped and instead the other, wrapped round the butt of a pistol, swung out. The arm didn't stop when it was level, though. Assisted by a thrust from Gabriel's left hand, it continued arcing upwards until the only person in danger of taking a bullet was the Man in the Moon. He still managed to squeeze off three closely-spaced shots, though, their deafening reports a klaxon that would bring the rest of the guards running.

Gabriel's right hand lanced up, catching the guard under the chin. Even in the absence of a weapon, the strike was deadly. But when it propelled six inches of sharpened wardrobe hanging rail into the soft flesh behind the mandible, up through the tongue and into the brain-case, instantly fatal.

Gabriel snatched the keys up from beside the dead guard and opened the SUV. He was inside, with the door closed and the engine spinning up just as five men converged from different points around the house.

Each carried a sidearm and one held a Heckler & Koch submachine gun, whose charging lever he was scrabbling to drag back.

Gabriel put the SUV into Drive and launched directly at the guy with the H&K. The impact sent the man skywards, tumbling through the air, broken limbs flexing unnaturally mid-flight, to land somewhere in the brush.

He hit the narrow curving track that led away from the house and back to the highway doing fifty and still accelerating. Gunshots behind him told their own eloquent story. Several hit the car, one smashing the rear windscreen, making Gabriel flinch and hunch his shoulders in instinctive recoil. Then they stopped. He knew why.

They hadn't given up. They were climbing into the remaining SUVs to give chase.

45

He didn't have much of a lead on the two pursuing SUVs. Maybe four hundred metres. Once they hit the open road, it would be game over. No way could he outrun them both.

He hit a bend, barely slowing, then hauled the wheel over and smashed his way into the thick green undergrowth that fringed the road on both sides. Branches and tall fern-like plants thrashing at the windscreen, he slewed the big vehicle round in a circle and came to rest facing the road.

He dropped the wide window. And listened as the roar of the following SUVs grew louder.

He caught a glimpse of the lead car. Twenty metres off. He stamped on the gas pedal, driving his foot down into the mat beneath. The SUV lurched forwards, engine screaming, the four-wheel drive system scrabbling for grip.

He broke out of the undergrowth just as the lead car was passing and struck it amidships with a deafening bang. Gabriel's car lifted at the front, throwing him back against the seat. The airbag detonated with a secondary explosion, filling the cabin with white powder and temporarily blinding Gabriel. The front wheels crashed down and Gabriel kept his foot on the gas, ramming the other car into the brush where its sideways-travelling wheels lost grip and sent it into a roll.

Gabriel leaped from the still-moving vehicle. Seconds later, the other pursuing SUV swerved around him before coming to a stop. The first car's petrol tank ignited with a whoomp. A column of bright-yellow flame burst out of the undergrowth, lighting the scene with an unearthly chartreuse glow. Men screamed.

No time to even consider saving them from immolation. The second car's two occupants were out and shooting wildly into the darkness.

Gabriel circled round behind them as they went to investigate the burning SUV. It was a natural response to tragedy. One not just forgivable but laudable in civilians, perhaps arriving at the scene of a motorway crash. But in supposedly trained security staff, a fatal error.

Gabriel stole up behind the trailing man and threw his right arm around his throat, locking it in place with his left. A deadly hold that not only choked off the air supply to the lungs, but the blood supply to the brain. He was unconscious in ten seconds and dead three after that, when Gabriel broke his neck with an efficient and brutal jerk.

'It's too late, they're dead,' the lead man said, turning.

Then his face contorted as he tried to make sense of the scene confronting him. His gun arm came up, but far, far too slowly.

Gabriel closed with him and stabbed rigid fingers deep into his eye sockets, closing his hand into a claw and yanking his man forwards. Screaming, the man tripped over Gabriel's outstretched foot. His chin connected with an up-jerked knee, shattering his front teeth and sending him into unconsciousness. Gabriel pulled his fingers free of the man's ruined eye sockets and wiped them on his trousers. No time for compassion. He prised the man's pistol free of his fingers and shot him once, cleanly, through the chest.

He had to drag both bodies off the road before he could take the remaining SUV and drive away from the carnage.

The highway lay several miles ahead and then the long drive back to Santa Rosa. But would he be in time?

46

Gabriel arrived back in Santa Rosa at 5:45 p.m. that day.

He found Tara at the cafe, talking earnestly to Bilbo and Tiny.

She jumped up when she saw him walking across the village square and ran to hug him.

'Gabe! You're back. Oh my god, what's the deal? Who is the money man? What does he want?'

Gabriel glanced over at Bilbo and Tiny. Would it help or hinder the plan to save the village if he told them about Peacemaker? He decided to keep that piece of information to himself for now. It would just muddy the waters. But Tara should know.

'He's a billionaire. Some sort of tech genius. Name's Xander Kalt.'

Tara's newly tweaked eyes widened.

'Xander Kalt's behind all this?'

'You know him?'

'I don't *know him* know him, but I know who he is. My god, Gabe, he's the CEO of Kaltium. Their software basically powers the web these days. Why does he want a piece of the Honduran coastline?'

Gabriel spoke in a low voice.

'I know this is going to sound hard to believe, but he's trying to retrieve a Soviet Doomsday weapon aboard a sunken sub. Claims it's so horrifically effective he'll be able to force the world's nuclear powers to give up their nukes.'

'He sounds crazy.'

'I know, but regardless, he's hell-bent on getting his hands on it and that means trouble for us.'

'How much trouble?'

'Sixty paramilitaries, for start.'

'Shit, Gabe, are we really ready for that?'

He frowned. Why did Tara keep calling him Gabe? Pera used the nickname. Eli had, too. But Tara? She always called him BB. A thread of doubt unwound in his brain. He looked at the woman facing him. *Properly* looked.

She was taller than Tara. She didn't *look* like his sister. She didn't *sound* like her. She had plastic surgery scars, but that proved nothing. Maybe they were just makeup. Or superficial cuts made to look like operation scars.

Yes, she knew all kinds of stuff about his past, from the cars he'd owned to the incident in a club's ladies' room in Gaborone, Botswana. But then she'd asked him how Master Zhao was doing. She'd explained it away as jetlag but Tara knew how important Master Zhao had been to Gabriel. And how much his death had hurt Gabriel. Would she really have forgotten such an event?

Cold fingers gripped his heart. Squeezed. People like George Mason knew how to extract information. Had he worked on Tara? Had Xander Kalt ordered his sister's kidnapping to get leverage over him and then sent a ringer in her place?

He forced himself to smile.

'Let's go and talk to the boys,' he said, gesturing towards the cafe table where Tiny and Bilbo sat waiting for them.

Coffees ordered, Gabriel turned to the others.

'Has my little sister been making herself useful? She used to run a triad, you know. Worked her way up from the ranks as an enforcer.'

'Kudos,' Bilbo deadpanned.

Gabriel turned to her. Forced himself to smile. Laid his trap.

'They gave her a name when she was little. Wei Tao. It means "beautiful peach".'

Tara nodded and smiled at Bilbo.

'I used to have better skin when I was younger.'

Gabriel slung his arm over her shoulders. Sprang the trap.

'Nicknames were always a thing in our family. I call her Peachy, she calls me Pidge, because I used to shoot pigeons off the roof at school with my airgun.'

'Pidge had righteous marksmanship skills even then,' she said, grinning.

Gabriel took a sip of his coffee and looked at her. Feeling suddenly sick, he stood.

'I have to go and see Pera. You three carry on. Tara, you can brief me later OK? See you back at mine?'

'Sure, Pidge. Laters.'

His mind spinning, he continued along the dusty street, hardly noticing the waves and greetings from the people he passed.

The mission had just mutated again, taking on a third, vital, personal dimension. Protect Santa Rosa. Destroy Peacemaker. Rescue Tara.

Mind whirling, and praying for Tara's safety, he started looking at ways to use Kalt's spy against him.

47

Pera was at home, cooking, when he knocked on her front door. Still trying to process what had just happened in the square, he kept the fact of Tara's kidnapping to himself. No sense adding to Pera's worries.

'Oh, Mother of God, you're back in one piece,' she exclaimed. 'Come and sit down. Do you want a coffee? A cold drink?'

'I'm good, Pera, really. But could you take a look at my injuries?'

Gabriel took his shirt off to let Pera examine his wounds. The long drive back to Santa Rosa had left him aching and sore.

He winced as her probing fingers found a tender spot.

'Hmm, you have the luck of a street dog, Gabe. No infection, everything healing up nicely.'

'No luck needed, Pera, just the finest nurse on the northern coast.'

She smiled but it was a tight, mirthless expression. He knew why. Her son was perched high above the village in a sniper nest. A high-value target in trade parlance. He sought to reassure her.

'He's in a good spot. Way away from the fighting. I'll try to keep an eye on him.'

A tear leaked from her eye.

'He's my baby. What if something happens to him? I couldn't live without him, Gabe.'

A sob broke free from her then, a cracked sound in his wood-framed house that connected to all the grief he'd brought into it from England. He sat up and drew her into his arms.

'Hey, hey, come on,' he murmured into the top of her head as she wrapped her arms round him. 'Santi's going to be fine. He's an excellent shot. It's the people in his sights you should be worried about.'

She pulled herself away from him and looked straight into his eyes.

'Swear he'll be OK, Gabe.'

'Pera, you know I can't.'

'Swear it!' she insisted, fresh tears breaking free.

'He's his own man, you know it. He wants to help defend his home. I'll do my best, but I—'

'If they kill my boy, I'll die!' she wailed.

'They won't, Pera. I won't let them. I swear.'

Her face brightened.

'You mean that? You swear it?'

'I do.'

Her eyes searched his, looking for a sign he was only saying what she wanted to hear, he assumed.

'I know you can't really promise that, Gabe. But thank you, all the same. I love that boy better than my own life.'

'I know. I...' He paused. Was he really going to say it? He closed his eyes and just let the words come, whatever they might be. 'I love him, too.'

He opened his eyes to find her close and looking deep into his eyes. And then she did something that took Gabriel entirely by surprise. She clasped his face between her hands, pulled him close and kissed him full on the lips.

He neither pulled away nor deepened the kiss. He just went with it, keeping his eyes closed. But confusion swirled through him. It didn't feel like a good-luck kiss before battle. Finally, Pera ended the embrace, letting him go.

'Oh my God,' she said, her cheeks crimson. 'Such bad timing. I've wanted to do that for such a long time, but you were hurting from losing Eli. I'm sorry, Gabe. Forgive me.'

He shook his head. 'Nothing to forgive. But, Pera, you're my true friend here. My only real friend. I just don't think we should change anything.'

In truth, the kiss had awakened physical feelings he'd almost totally forgotten could exist in him. But no sooner had he admitted this to himself than a memory of Eli's smile flitted across the back of his eyes. He pushed it down, and all the other feelings as well.

Pera looked down at her fingers, intertwined between them.

'Is it because, you know, I used to work at Frida's?' she murmured.

He lifted her chin gently.

'No. It isn't. Nothing about you, nothing you do or have ever done, is wrong or bad, Pera. You are beautiful and smart and loyal and you make the best *baleadas* in Honduras and I count myself lucky to have met you.'

She smiled sadly. 'But I'm not her, am I?'

He swallowed down a lump in his throat.

'Nobody is, Pera. Nobody is.' He got to his feet. 'I need to go.'

* * *

Gabriel found Sparrow on the landward side of the village. On the walk out there he'd formulated a whole new plan. One that would use Kalt's play against him.

Sparrow was supervising a gang of village men who were pouring petrol into deep, narrow trenches lined with slit-open polythene feed sacks.

Sparrow looked up, sensing his old comrade's arrival, and waved.

'Not bad, eh, my captain?' he asked when Gabriel joined him on the lip of one of the trenches. The air around them was thick with the heady stink of the petrol. 'The fire trenches'll keep them away from the centre, hopefully. The plan is to ignite them all at once. I've got some det cord rigged in a daisy chain. Should be quite a show.'

'It's good. But it's not enough. They've got sixty fighters drawn from some of the nastiest outfits in Latin America. All heavily armed. These aren't your dime-a-dozen cartel thugs. We're talking disciplined combat troops against us seven and a bunch of farmers armed with shotguns we're expecting to move from shooting game to men.'

Sparrow nodded. Rubbed his chin. He didn't respond at first. Just looked along the trench and shouted a suggestion to the gang boss down the line.

'Your stepson or whatever he is, is a great shot. Some of the better hunters can also handle themselves. Don't write them off just yet, boss.'

'I'm not. It's just, I'm afraid it's going to be a bloody business.'

'They know that. We've talked a lot, long into the night when we should probably have been resting. This is deep for them, boss. This is their home, their history, their heritage.'

Gabriel smiled wryly. 'Home, heritage, history. Ever the poet, Sparrow. I wish you could give the speech tonight instead of me.'

'Has to be you, boss.'

Gabriel nodded. 'I know. Listen, Johnny, we need to change the plan.'

Sparrow's eyes narrowed. 'You only call me "Johnny" when something's seriously fucked up. What wrong, boss?'

As Gabriel spoke, Sparrow nodded, made the odd suggestion, asked pertinent questions. But mainly, he simply listened. When Gabriel finished, Sparrow nodded a final time.

'I think it'll work. What are you going to do between now and then?'

'I need to get over to Teguz and back. Tell them I've gone for extra ammunition.'

48

For the trip into Teguz, Gabriel borrowed one of his neighbour's produce trucks. The high-mileage three-tonner had a closed-in load bay. Perfect for transporting crates of mangos, papayas and bananas.

Several hours later, kidneys complaining, Gabriel approached a dilapidated-looking warehouse. Two shaven-headed men carrying submachine guns, appeared to his left and right. Their bare torsos were covered in blue-black tattoos. He'd been expecting them.

'Relax, fellas,' he called out, 'I'm here to see Óscar. Client,' he added.

Wordlessly, one searched him while the other pointed the snub nose of his submachine gun at Gabriel's face.

Satisfied he wasn't carrying, they marched him inside. The warehouse echoed with the sounds of wood and metal crates being stacked, unloaded or broken down. It smelled, not unpleasantly, of gun oil, greased steel and brass, and sawdust

If any of their contents had been used, the noise would have been significantly louder. Ex-Soviet munitions? American carbines? Chinese pistols? Syrian bombs? You wanted it, the man sitting counting hundred dollar bills on an upturned beer crate at the centre of the organised chaos could supply it.

Gabriel approached, flanked by his escort.

The arms dealer looked up and beamed.

'Terry! You're back already. Hey, boys, stop pointing guns at my friend. And bring him a beer. And a cigar. Cuban, not one of those Honduran pig-turds.'

Gabriel took the proffered chair and explained what he needed.

49

Gabriel stared out at the sea of faces.

They'd constructed a rudimentary speaker's dais out of planks resting on upturned bar crates and he stood atop it now.

His heart was racing and for once he let it. No flight, but there would definitely be a fight. And right now, his job was to prepare the whole of Santa Rosa for what was to come.

Pera stood in the front row, her eyes bright, shining. Beside her, his arm around her waist, was Santi, a rifle slung over his shoulder. He went everywhere with it now. The sight reminded Gabriel uncomfortably of child soldiers he'd seen in war-torn countries: Congo, Afghanistan, Kosovo.

His men, the six who'd dropped everything to join him to protect a village they'd never heard of a month before were clustered on his right, halfway towards the back. Like Santi, they carried their weapons. A formidable array of longs and shorts, grenades clipped onto cross-belts, daggers stuck through belts, machetes, whatever they felt comfortable wielding when the ammo ran out. As it always did.

Gabriel spoke. His voice caught in his throat. He tried again.

'I was born in England. I grew up in Hong Kong. I travelled

around the world. And finally I found a home, here in Santa Rosa. I was a broken man when I arrived here. You helped heal me.'

He looked down at Pera at this point. She blinked furiously and placed her right hand over her heart.

'Men are coming to try and take Santa Rosa away from you. From us. I will not let that happen. These are not cartel thugs with gold-plated pistols. They are not roadside bandits demanding protection money. They are well-trained soldiers. They are used to killing. They *enjoy* killing.

'You have been training hard to fight these killers. To protect what is yours. Because Santa Rosa isn't just houses and fields, a bar and a cafe. It is your home. Your history. Your heritage.'

Gabriel lifted his gaze and locked eyes with Sparrow, who nodded his acknowledgement of the stolen phrase. Murmurs in the crowd grew. Whispers. He knew why. When was Gabriel going to switch from the doom-mongering and give them the rousing speech they needed?

'But now that I know what we are facing, I know that fighting isn't enough. So, there's a new plan. My sister, Tara, is going to join the sharpshooters. That gives us two sniper-spotter teams on the hill. They'll provide overwatch. My men and I will engage the enemy and draw them away from the village, onto the beach near the old shipwreck. Everybody else will hide in Snakehead Canyon until it's safe to come out.'

The crowd erupted into shouts of protest and querulous complaints that they hadn't been training all this time to hide like children. Gabriel held his hands up for quiet. When the shouts and questions had died away, Gabriel spoke again.

'Listen to me. This man, Kalt, who was behind the offer to buy us all out? He wants Santa Rosa and all the land around it. But he knows he won't get it until every last one of you is dead. If you fight, you'll be slaughtered. This way, we stand a chance.'

The dais creaked and swayed. Gabriel looked to his left. The woman he'd collected at Teguz airport had joined him.

'Gabe is right. There's no point dying for nothing. I know my brother. I have fought alongside him in other places. If he says you should take cover in the canyon, that's what you should do.'

Further protests surged up from the crowd, but Gabriel could hear the will draining out of them. That weird, gut-clenching mixture of paralysing fear and pre-combat nerves was curdling into something less exciting, less scary but also more reassuring. Resignation. Reassessment. Relief.

They weren't going to fight. They weren't going to die. They were farmers, fishermen, shopkeepers, cafe and food truck owners, homemakers.

They weren't soldiers. How could they ever have allowed themselves to believe it?

50

At 6:31 a.m. the next morning, after a five-second phone call from one of the early-watch sentries posted back along the coast road, the alarm sounded. The church bell rang continuously, its discordant pealing rousing everyone who wasn't already awake.

As agreed at the end of the previous night's meeting, all but a handful of the villagers gathered in the square and climbed aboard fruit trucks, pickups, tractors pulling trailers, whatever vehicles they could press into service.

The convoy of two dozen vehicles pulled out, heading for Snakeshead Canyon.

And safety.

51

Ten miles west of Santa Rosa, the commander of the sixty-strong mercenary force answered his phone.

'Talk to me.'

'There's a new plan. You're going to love this. All but a handful of the villagers are hiding out in a place called Snakehead Canyon. It's half a mile outside the village on the south-western corner. I'm texting you the grid reference.'

'You're sure?'

'He told them himself last night. Thinks they're going to be slaughtered if they try to fight.'

The squad commander laughed around his cigar.

'Well, he got part of it right. We'll fucking massacre them. Any way out?'

'It's a box-canyon. You can just drive in, block the entrance then take your time.'

'They armed?'

'Maybe a few shotguns. Hunting rifles.'

'No problem. How about the Brits?'

'The plan is to lure you down to the beach. Maybe take a few guys from the main force to wipe them out.'

'Leave the tactics to me, OK? You've done your job. Just stay out of trouble.'

52

Gabriel watched through binoculars as the plume of red dust drifted south to north, thinning out until it vanished entirely in the blue haze over the hills.

He counted ten vehicles. Some lightly armoured personnel carriers. Others SUVs. From his vantage point high above the road he could look straight across the village to where Santi lay in his sniper nest. Santi's orders were clear. Aim for the windscreens. Disable the drivers.

Bilbo and Kylie were based one side of the road, with the Javelins. Tiny and Bullseye had dug in on the other side, each equipped with an RPG and a couple of grenades.

Johnny had gone with the villagers to help them hide in the crevices of the steep rock walls that enclosed the canyon.

It was almost time to join him. No need for binoculars now. Gabriel could see the armoured convoy clearly with the naked eye.

In ten seconds or so the lead vehicle would be in range of the Javelins. He watched as Bilbo and Kylie separated and prepared to launch the guided missiles.

Nine … eight … seven …

On the far side of the road, movement. Tiny and Bullseye had risen to their knees and were shouldering the RPGs.

Six … five … four …

The lead vehicles were well within range now and only a quarter of a mile from the village.

Two bone-white smoke trails blossomed from the scrub. The roar of the missiles reached Gabriel a second later. The lead missile streaked towards an armoured personnel carrier.

And sailed harmlessly over its roof, curving mid-flight and deviating towards the distant hills. The impact when it hit the steep escarpment looked like a flower opening. Orange, yellow and red petals inside a sooty-grey cloud. The explosion, a deep, bassy rumble inside a crackling chatter like gunfire, reached him several seconds later.

The second missile, only half a second behind the first looked to be on target. The high-explosive warhead would turn the target vehicle into a couple of tons of metal shards, along with a few hundred kilos of vaporised human flesh and bone.

Then, within fifty feet of its target, a white SUV that must have held a half-dozen fighters, it swerved into a vertical flightpath. It detonated in mid-air, a starburst of white smoke trails with that blazing flower at its centre.

What the hell? One faulty guidance system he could just about credit. But both? No. He'd seen them being taken from their crates. They were the genuine article. No way would Óscar Gutierrez have attempted to cheat him on that kind of merchandise. It wasn't worth his reputation.

The answer came to him in a flash as bright as the dying explosion. Kalt must have installed radio-signal jammers in the vehicles. And Gabriel knew how he'd known to do it.

But Kalt hadn't reckoned with the RPGs. These were altogether more primitive weapons. Unguided, except by the human being aiming the ungainly but deadly weapons.

In unison, Tiny and Bullseye got to their feet, shouldered the RPGs and pressed the triggers. The grenades shot from the launchers and sped towards the convoy, trailing greyish-white smoke.

The second vehicle took a direct hit to its left side. It flipped up and over, landing on its roof at the side of the road, blazing like an inferno. The boom of the explosion rolled outwards, echoing off the distant hills.

Two places behind it, an armoured personnel carrier swerved off the road as its driver tried desperately to avoid the incoming grenade. He succeeded, but the front of the vehicle dipped down suddenly. He must have hit a dried-out gully. Men spilled from the back, assault rifles up and firing in the direction of the RPG launchers.

Two more grenades were zeroing in on the convoy but then, in a coordinated and almost balletic move, the remaining eight vehicles separated to all points of the compass, leaving the road in speeding curves that threw up great rooster tails of red dust. The grenades passed harmlessly between them before detonating in the distance.

None of the vehicles headed towards the village. Instead, they all headed on the same bearing, though the drivers maintained a big gap between them and the next vehicle.

Straight towards Snakehead Canyon.

Behind them, a couple of villagers activated the deadfall trap. In vain. The two trees collapsed in towards each other, blocking a road nobody was using.

53

Riding a small dirt bike he'd commandeered from Santi, Gabriel raced towards his observation point, five hundred metres south of Snakehead Canyon on the crest of a hill.

Waiting for him were the two snipers he'd picked. Violeta and Alfonso. They'd provide cover while he observed the initial targeting of the mortar bombs. Then he'd phone corrections through to Sparrow and the mortar fire teams, who were set up and awaiting his call two kilometres back.

He kicked out the side stand and dismounted.

'They are coming?' Alfonso asked in English.

Gabriel nodded, his stomach tight with anxiety. It had to end here, or he knew he'd be digging a mass grave.

The road of the remaining vehicles in the mercenary convoy reached the canyon. Gabriel counted eight. He couldn't discount the possibility that some of the men had dismounted, but at least they'd be able to destroy their transport.

Thirty seconds later, the mouth of the canyon filled with armoured trucks. Then the SUVs. They drove in three abreast, at speed. Two stopped at the canyon mouth. A smart move. Gabriel would have done the same. Protect the back door at all costs. Shame for them it wasn't going to work.

On the vehicles came. Gabriel observed them through the binoculars. Close enough he could see the drivers as they drove their vehicles towards what they believed would be a massacre.

In that belief, they were at one with the eight men waiting for Gabriel's order to commence firing.

He had to hold his nerve. He wanted the convoy deep enough in that they'd have no chance of retreating.

'Come on, come on,' he murmured.

Then the lead truck stopped dead. Behind it the rest skidded to a stop, sending dust flying ahead of them. Had they realised their mistake? The driver of the front vehicle leaned out of the cab. Then disappeared inside again. The last vehicle hurtled backwards before executing a fishtailing slide until it was facing out again.

Gabriel called a mobile phone number. The phone didn't belong to anybody. It was taped to a C4-based IED buried a foot deep in the centre of the entrance to the canyon. The bomb detonated with a roar that echoed off the walls of the canyon. The two vehicles blocking the canyon flipped up in the air. One landed on its roof, the other on its wheels, where it promptly burst into flames. A huge cloud of smoke and dust boiled up out of the canyon. Inside, realising they'd driven into a trap, the other vehicles began manoeuvring frantically.

Too late.

While the shockwaves from the IED explosion had been smashing everything in their path, Gabriel called Sparrow and gave a one-word order.

'Fire!'

A handful of seconds later, the first four mortar bombs Gabriel had bought in Teguz arced in, high overhead, on a steep parabolic trajectory that ended with them landing inside the canyon. His calculations were fine. No need to call in corrections. Instead another short call.

'On target!'

The devastation was vast and immediate.

Gabriel could picture the scene back at Sparrow's firing station and the other three he commanded. Each centred on a Soviet-era PM-38 120 mm mortar.

Sparrow yelling, 'Hang it!'

The loader gripping the bomb by its bulbous midsection and placing it in the barrel up to the painted yellow line at the widest point.

'Fire!'

The mortar bomb drops into the barrel. The loader ducks away, hands over his ears.

A loud crack as the launch charge detonates.

The other teams would be following this simple drill, over and over again. Four teams with four bombs apiece. A devastating battery even aimed at enemy fighters in open ground. But kettled inside a rock-walled canyon, where the shock waves would bounce around, totally lethal.

A total of 24 KG of high explosives rained down on the mercenaries in the canyon. The blast damage would have been horrific on its own, but the thick-walled steel shells were designed for fragmentation and those flying scraps of cast iron would be equally devastating to human flesh and bone.

In that hellish period of time, which must have felt like eternity to the enemy fighters beneath the rain of death, but in reality lasted only fifty-nine seconds, Sparrow's team launched sixteen mortar bombs. Two struck home with direct hits to vehicles, obliterating them and their passengers instantly.

The point-detonating fuzes of the other fourteen struck the hard, dry ground and set off the main high-explosive charges. Anything, man or metal, within the thirty-metre blast radius was shredded.

The noise of the close-spaced explosions was immense. The hard rock walls of the canyon served as both amplifier and resonator chamber, multiplying and distorting the reports until Gabriel felt the detonations vibrating inside his body. Smoke boiled up out of the canyon before being caught by the breeze and drifting towards the sea.

And then. Silence.

Gabriel rode his bike down to the ridge and stared down into the hellscape at the bottom.

He'd seen photographs taken on the Somme. A blasted landscape of mud, barbed wire and the mangled remains of men and machines. The scene that greeted him as the smoke cleared was worse. The unyielding rock had intensified the sixty blasts and multiplied their effects.

Normally, on an open battlefield, the blast waves would be free to travel away from the point of detonation, dissipating their energy in the air. Here, in *Cañón Cabeza de Serpiente*'s close-fisted embrace, all that energy had been concentrated into a deadly field of destruction worthy of much more powerful munitions.

Nothing remained. The earth was churned and scarred, burnt black in places, in others a reddish brown-like flesh showing through charred skin. The large boulders dotted here and there were gone. In their places rocks no bigger than a football lay scattered.

Of the eight vehicles, one remained weirdly intact, though it burned fiercely, emitting yellow flames and a thick coiling column of greasy black smoke. The rest were reduced to tangled black metal members that might have been transmissions, body panels, axles or engines. A leg hung in a branch protruding from a tree growing sideways out of the canyon wall thirty feet up.

His nostrils filling with the stench of burning plastics and charred meat, Gabriel turned away, suddenly nauseated.

He had to get back to the village.

54

Carrying his M4, Gabriel led Violeta and Alfonso back to the village.

As they approached from the landward side, they heard machine-gun fire. So some of the mercenaries had indeed left the convoy early. Black smoke drifted east to west across the rooftops from the fire trenches, bringing with them the unmistakable, heady stink of burning petrol.

Gabriel signalled for them to spread out. He raised his rifle and approached the square.

From the direction of the beach, he heard three distinct bangs, followed by screams. The Claymores. He had no more time to think about distant casualties, The battle here was still raging.

Three mercenaries were pinned down behind a car. Armed with rifles similar to Gabriel's own they were maintaining discipline, taking turns to fire while the others reloaded.

He aimed and squeezed off a shot. The mercenary currently on his feet and firing over the car's roof took the round in the back of his head. Blood sprayed pinkly into the air above him and he toppled sideways, covering his companion with gore.

As the other two swung their rifles round and fired, Gabriel ducked behind a wall. Bullets thudded into the bricks right beside his head, sending sharp fragments spinning into his face. He spun round and squeezed the trigger, sending a burst of fire towards whoever was shooting at him.

His gun clicked. Out of ammo. He grabbed another magazine from his belt but it was too late. A huge mercenary emerged from the shadows aiming an assault rifle at his head.

'Fuck you, gringo,' he said in English.

Gabriel flinched as the man pulled his trigger. He heard the shot. Felt the wet spray of blood. No pain. He opened his eyes. The headless body loomed over him for a couple of seconds before slumping sideways, knees buckling.

Gabriel stood and looked around him.

Violeta stood. She lowered her rifle. Gave him a thumbs-up. And then the side of her head erupted in a spray of pink mist and her lifeless body fell sideways.

Gabriel spun round to see a mercenary advancing, his assault rifle at his shoulder. Then he too died from a single gunshot to the head, as Alfonso put a round between his eyes before ducking back down behind a low wall.

No more gunfire in the square. Was it over then? Cautiously, Gabriel advanced along the walls, scouring each side of the square for enemy fighters. But none appeared. He glimpsed a body between two buildings. Burly, clad in combat fatigues. He ran over and when he saw who it was, he knelt, moaning softly.

'Oh shit, Tiny. What happened?'

But the big man was beyond answering. Half his face was gone. Lying beside his corpse, the welded-up mace he'd selected on that first day of training.

Gabriel looked around. A sheet hung from a washing line strung between two rusting metal poles. He dragged it off and covered Tiny with it tucking the edges under his arms and legs so it wouldn't blow free. He signalled to Alfonso, who trotted over. When he saw the sheeted figure he swore.

'It's Tiny,' Gabriel said. 'Stay with him.'

Picking up the mace, he crossed the square to the village hall and knocked. Twice, then three times. Then once more. A precise, pre-agreed pattern. Inside, a wooden bar clonked as somebody dropped it to the floor. The heavy iron key scraped in the lock and the door swung inwards. The villagers were packed tight inside. Their faces were pale and the children wore dazed expressions, traumatised like so many before them by the chaos of war.

'It's OK,' Gabriel said, softly. 'You can come out now. It's over.'

Behind him, the villagers emerged, blinking in the sunlight. Several erupted into bouts of violent coughing as the stink of burnt propellant and smoke assailed them.

Pera was among them. She hurried over to Gabriel.

'Have you seen Santi?'

'No, but I'm sure he's OK. He'll be back safe.'

'Oh, thank god. And you? Are you hurt. Did they get you?'

'I'm fine. I need to find everyone. I'll be back. Can you set up a dressing station in the hall? We'll bring in the casualties.'

He left her there, giving orders for medicines and dressings to be brought to the hall from her place.

As he left the square, M4 slung over his shoulder, he caught a movement in the corner of his eye. He spun round. A mercenary emerged from the shadows between two buildings. No gun. Like Gabriel he'd run out of ammunition. But he carried a wicked-looking combat knife and he was intent on using it.

He rushed Gabriel, knife swinging left and right. Gabriel parried an incoming thrust with the handle of the mace. Then swung it upwards and jabbed it into the merc's face. Swinging a heavy melee weapon was a rookie's move. It might feel right, but its momentum wouldn't be gainsaid, leaving the wielder with an exposed flank as it completed its swing.

The merc dropped back, shaking blood from his eyes as it dripped down from a gash on his forehead. He came in again, switching the knife from hand to hand, just like the football hooligan in Liverpool. Only this guy was a pro, the moves practised in the field.

He feinted left, then came in low on the right. Gabriel jumped back out of range of the blade. He swung the mace down hard. The contact wasn't square-on. Just a glancing blow across the man's forearm, but the mass of welded scrap metal beat it down towards the ground. Now it was Gabriel's turn to attack. He lunged forwards and headbutted the merc right over the gash on his head, drawing forth a scream and a fresh wash of blood that sheeted down over and into his eyes, blinding him.

The merc staggered back, swearing and swiping at his eyes with his sleeve. Yelling a bloodcurdling battle-cry, Gabriel came at him fast, and brought the cross-welded gears down to the top of his head. Steel met bone with a sickening, wet crunch. The bright teeth, filed to wicked points, bit deep into the man's skull, caving it in and sending spurts of scarlet blood high into the air. He moaned incoherently, and reached up with a quivering hand. His knees buckled and he sank down into the position of a penitent. Gabriel kicked him in the chest and pulled back on the haft of the mace. It pulled free of the skull, leaving a flopping mass of hair and bone behind it.

Gripping the mace in both fists, Gabriel swung it hard at the side of the man's head. His face caved in on itself as several kilos of steel smashed their way through his sphenoid, zygomatic and temporal bones. Pinkish-grey brain matter spilled out in bloody globules and his left eye burst free of its ruined socket to dangle disgustingly on his cheek.

The now lifeless mercenary collapsed sideways, where blood hosed out from his shattered skull, forming a fast-spreading lake in the dust.

Gabriel turned and ran on.

He needed to find the others.

55

An hour later, Gabriel had rounded up his remaining men.

He stood in the centre of the square with Sparrow, Bullseye and Paddy. Santi had arrived five minutes earlier, his rifle slung over his shoulder, and now stood with his mother.

Kylie had taken a round to the leg. It had missed the femoral artery but he was incapacitated. He lay on a camp bed inside the village hall, a tourniquet cinched around his thigh.

Bilbo was also wounded. He'd been hit in the shoulder and fallen into a burning fire trench. The right side of his face was a mess. He'd live, but he needed specialist burns treatment.

Of the snipers, Alfonso and Santi had survived unscathed. Violeta had been killed with a single shot to the head when she'd watched her target go down instead of ducking.

'Where is Tara?' Pera asked.

'I'll go and look for her,' Gabriel said.

Sparrow joined him. 'I'll come with you.'

As they left the square, Gabriel turned to his number two.

'She's not my sister. She's a plant. Whatever happens, follow my lead.'

Sparrow frowned. But whatever questions he had, he saved them.

Together, the two men toured the village. Starting in the centre and working their way outwards. As they crossed the coast road, a farmer driving a flatbed truck passed them. He slowed down.

'I've got the casualties in the back. I'm taking them to Hospital Loma de Luzon. It's between Balfate and Rio Esteban. They've got an ER. Your friends will be fine, Gabriel.'

His exhaust smoke merely added one more flavour to the noxious blend of smells that didn't so much fill Santa Rosa as infect it. Blood, shit, gun smoke, burning chemicals and destroyed vehicles, spilled gasoline and diesel.

Gabriel pulled up short and pointed between two palm trees that separated the road from the beach.

'There she is!'

She sat on one of the blackened spars of the wrecked boat that poked up out of the sand like the ribs of a long-dead sea monster. She had her back to them. And she was on the phone, apparently oblivious to the mangled corpses of three mercenaries who'd caught blasts from the Claymores Gabriel had heard detonating from the village square.

Gabriel put his finger to his lips. Sparrow nodded. Gabriel led him between the trees and onto the soft white sand. It was another world on the beach. The fighting hadn't reached it. A squadron of pelicans glided above the waves, which lapped rhythmically onto the sand.

Gabriel looked down. The spiny pink and cream shell of a spider crab lay half-buried in the sand, a few metres away from a ball-bearing-riddled body of a dead mercenary. He raised his boot and trod on it carefully. It broke with a loud crack. The spy spun round, her face a mixture of emotions. Surprise, then joy.

'Oh, Gabe, thank god! I was trying to reach you.'

'What are you doing down here, Peachy?' he asked, walking over to her as she pocketed her phone. 'Why did you leave Santi alone on the roof?'

'They were getting ready to attack us. I circled round behind them. Got them all.'

'How many?'

She shrugged. Frowned. 'Four? No, five.'

'Nice work. Come on, let's go back into the village. You can help at the dressing station.'

'Sure,' she said, getting to her feet.

He readied himself to incapacitate her. He couldn't risk pulling a gun. This had to come out of nowhere. He needed her alive.

He couldn't draw a weapon. But she had no such qualms.

The tiny pistol that appeared in her hand barked, once, twice, three times. Sparrow's eyes widened in shock. He looked down at the holes in his chest, already blooming scarlet and soaking the front of his shirt.

Gabriel blocked her arm as it swung round towards him, but she struck him full in the face with the heel of her hand, crashing his lower jaw upwards and clacking his teeth together. He staggered but kept his focus on the pistol, already extending towards him.

The killer's finger curled around the trigger.

Less than a second remained before his death.

56

The woman screamed.

Blood fountained out behind her, spattering the white sand with jewelled droplets like scattered rubies.

From his supine position, Sparrow had shot her through the right shoulder. She dropped the little chromed pistol and took off up the beach, away from Santa Rosa, dodging in and out of the Claymores standing on their spindly wire tripods.

Gabriel glanced at her then down at Sparrow. He knelt beside his friend.

Blood gouted from his lips. He coughed a fine spray into Gabriel's face.

'Go after her, boss.'

Gabriel shook his head, stripping off his shirt and wadding it into a thick pad before driving it down over the wounds on Sparrow's chest.

'Shut up, Johnny. I need to keep pressure on these.'

Sparrow coughed. Grimaced as blood bubbled out of his mouth, foamy and bright scarlet.

'Go. I'm done.'

His eyes were rolling in their sockets. His face was waxy. Blood was soaking through Gabriel's improvised field dressing, covering Gabriel's hands.

'She can wait,' he grunted.

He gathered Sparrow into his arms and sat with him on the hot sand, now stained a deep red beneath Sparrow's torso. In a few seconds, it was over. Sparrow's head flopped to one side, lolling over Gabriel's right thigh.

He lifted his dead friend's head up and laid it back down, as gently as he was able, on the sand.

'I'm sorry, Johnny.'

He got to his feet and sprinted after the spy, who was a hundred metres or so up the beach, heading towards the blackened spars of the wrecked fishing boat. He passed the now-redundant clackers – the detonators for the Claymores. Even if she'd been in range, he wouldn't have used one: he wanted her alive.

Her steps were faltering. Sparrow had inflicted some serious damage with his final shot. Even if he hadn't had her in sight, Gabriel would have had no trouble following the trail of blood spatter.

She drew level with the wreck and turned left abruptly, realising that in the palms edging the beach she'd have a better chance of escaping. Gabriel fired on the run, not pausing to aim, but not needing to either. He aimed to her left, blowing splinters from one of the blackened spars and driving her back onto a straight path along the beach.

She staggered, then her leading foot caught in a thick tangled skein of red and green seaweed. More Mermaid's Rope. She threw her hands out and crashed to the ground, screaming as her right arm buckled. The scream rose in pitch as her bullet-punctured shoulder hit the sand.

Panting, Gabriel reached her a few seconds later. She rolled onto her back, her left hand gripping a thin-bladed knife. She swung it low, aiming for his right calf. He jumped back and then kicked it from her hand, stamping on her wrist, which broke with a loud, brittle crack.

She screamed, but he had no pity for her. Not after she'd killed Sparrow.

He raised his pistol and brought it down sharply on her skull, just above her left ear.

57

Sparrow's corpse lay a hundred and fifty yards away, Gabriel's blood-soaked shirt draped over his chest. If he half-closed his eyes, Gabriel could imagine he was looking at a piece of driftwood garlanded in seaweed.

He rested his booted feet on the woman's supine body and looked out at the sea, the gentle swell rising and falling.

It was peaceful on the beach. Brown seabirds the locals called beach-hoppers skittered back and forth just ahead of the incoming wavelets, stabbing needle-beaks down looking for food just beneath the surface of the wet sand. Gulls dipped low, gliding mere inches above the sea, occasionally diving down with hardly a splash to emerge seconds later, glittering silver fish in their beaks.

How many circuits had he run from his house out to this wreck and then back again? A hundred? A thousand? He knew he'd never run another.

His ears were ringing. Those mortars made a hell of a noise. The mercs would have known they were dead men the moment the first bomb detonated in the canyon. Forget snipers. Indirect mortar fire was the fastest and most efficient way to slaughter a body of fighters.

Something had happened to him. He felt distanced from reality. Almost as if he were asleep. But his eyes were open. Weren't they? He raised his hands and gently touched his own eyeballs. Winced at the contact. Three soldiers watched him, knee-deep in the surf. Smudge, Tiny and Sparrow. They weren't real. He knew that. He'd hardly be able to see through them if they were. But it was comforting, in a way.

The woman came round with a groan. She rolled to her side and threw up on the sand. He let her, then replaced his boot. He also trained the muzzle of his pistol on her face.

She looked up at Gabriel. Her face was a mask of hatred.

'You're a fucking dead man, Wolfe.'

He stood, drew back his right foot and kicked her in the ribs. She cried out. Amateur dramatics. It hadn't been a hard strike. She was still able to draw breath after all.

'Is that a nice way to talk to your big brother?'

'How did you know? What changed?'

He squatted next to her, though out of range of her teeth. Women like her, women like Tara, in fact, were trained to use any part of their anatomy as a weapon.

'I think I was just blinded by the changes to your appearance. At first, I mean. And you knew our history,' he said. 'It made sense you were Tara. And maybe I just needed to believe you were her. But you kept calling me Gabe. Pera calls me that. My wife called me that. But Tara never has. She calls me BB. For Big Brother. And your triad name? It wasn't Wei Tao. It was Wei Mei. Plum not peach, do you see? Two strikes. And when I drove you here from the airport, I mentioned Master Zhao, remember? You asked me how he was. When he'd been dead for years. Now, maybe Tara could have forgotten a detail like that, even though she knew how important he was to me. But the other things? Forgetting my nickname? Forgetting your *own*?'

'So you fed me the line about the canyon.'

'Who else could have planted a spy but Kalt? I'm guessing that's who you were calling when we found you. So he knows Mason fucked up.'

'Yeah, he knows. And he's not going to stop. You're not going to beat him. He's too powerful. He's too rich. He's too—'

'Shut up!' Gabriel barked. 'I'm going to ask you two questions. If you lie, I'll know. A lie gets a bullet. Ankles, knees, elbows, hips, belly. I'll keep you alive and you will suffer. Is my sister alive?'

She stared at him, hatred beaming out from her like a laser.

'Fuck you.'

He shot her through the left ankle. She screamed as bone fragments and blood sprayed out.

'Is my sister alive?'

She barely hesitated.

'Yes.'

'Where is he holding her?'

She clamped her lips. Though her eyes betrayed her. They signalled her fear.

'I'll take silence as a lie, as well.'

He pushed the muzzle hard against her right ankle.

'No! Don't. Yes, he's got her. He's got this compound inside a nature reserve on the Mexican coast. Reserva de la Biósfera Sian Ka'an. It's in Quintana Roo State.'

'Grid reference.'

'My phone. In my pocket.' She indicated the right hip pocket of her trousers.

'Unlock it.'

She dragged the phone free and held it up to her face then handed it up to him.

'Look in Contacts. Under Kalt. It's all there. Everything you need.'

Gabriel checked. She was telling the truth.

Kalt had kidnapped Tara partly to substitute his own spy. But Gabriel was sure there'd be play. Leverage. Now they each had something the other wanted. For whatever reason, Kalt wanted Gabriel. And Gabriel wanted Tara.

He had no choice.

He had to help Xander Kalt recover Peacemaker.

At his feet, the spy moaned softly as she clutched her ruined ankle. He knew he'd have to get her to the field dressing station. He'd let the villagers decide what to do with her.

Shouts startled him. Thoughts of rescuing Tara vanished. He whirled, pistol up, but it was one of the local women. Her long black hair tied back, she was running up the beach. Her skirt streamed behind her as she ran barefoot, leaping over rotted chunks of palm tree and skirting patches of sharp broken seashells.

But it was what she carried in her hands that had Gabriel taking a step back.

A black assault rifle.

When she was thirty yards out, he recognised her. Julimar. The woman who'd flirted with Tiny.

She came to a halt in front of him and looked contemptuously down at the woman who'd posed as Tara.

'Is that her?' she demanded, chest heaving. 'Did she betray us?'

'Give me the gun, Juli,' he said, holding his hands out.

She swung it out clumsily, so that the barrel wavered right in front of his gut.

'Is that her?' she yelled in his face.

'Yes, it's her,' he said, anxious not to take a killing burst from an M4 into his midsection.

Juli glared at him.

'Go.' He didn't move. 'Go!'

So he turned and started walking. Behind him, he caught Juli's words.

'*Esto es para* Tim.'

The gun roared. A red-hot shell casing hit Gabriel on the back of the neck, searing the skin. It took Juli two seconds to burn through a full magazine. The gun fell silent.

Pungent smoke drifted past Gabriel on a light breeze that had sprung up, as if Nature herself wanted to cleanse the village of the stink of slaughter.

It carried Juli's sobbing to him, too.

Gabriel kept walking. The dead needed burying.

58

Enraged by the call he'd just ended, Kalt hurled a stone at a black-and-white monkey regarding him sagely from the rail of the ornately carved wooden balcony.

Why couldn't they just fuck off into the jungle and leave him be? Little bastards.

It screeched, baring white fangs, but stayed put, mocking him with its weird little face and those disgusting hands like a fuckin' human's.

He grabbed the oversized chrome-plated pistol he'd left sitting on the wicker table between two brass-bound steamer chairs. A Desert Eagle. Fuckin' righteous weapon.

Pointed it at the monkey.

'Do you feel lucky, punk?' he growled. Literally a perfect impression of Filthy Harry.

He squeezed one eye closed and squinted down the barrel.

'Well. Do you?'

He pulled the trigger. And screamed.

'Fuck!'

The recoil from the damn thing almost broke his goddamned hand. And the top bit, whatever the fuck George had called it, cut two deep parallel grooves into the web of skin between his thumb and forefinger. Jesus, they ought to fuckin' ban them. Totally not fit for fuckin' purpose. He wrinkled his nose as the gunpowder went up it. Sneezed. When he checked again through streaming eyes – his allergies were playing up – the monkey was gone. So was a sizeable portion of the handrail.

'Fuck, yeah!' he crowed. 'Now who's the fucking boss? Huh?'

A distant chattering seemed to mock him and he caught a flash of black-and-white in a tree.

Never mind. Next time, he'd be ready. He sighed. The brief elation dissipated as rapidly as it had arrived.

The girl he'd spent so much money on, training her up to be Wolfe's sister, what was her name, Sara? Kathy? Didn't matter. The point was, she'd just called. George's plan had failed. No, failing would have been recoverable. Like the mantra said, fail big, fail fast.

What the plan had been was vapo-fuckin-rised. He whacked the heavy pistol's barrel down on the remaining portion of handrail.

How had a bunch of mango-farmers defeated George's squad of seasoned paramilitaries? Even with Gabe's hand-picked little bunch of tin soldiers, the mercs should have just massacred them all. After all, that was what Sara-Kathy had told him was going to happen.

The villagers are in the canyon. The squad heads to the canyon. The squad kill all the villagers in the canyon. Xander gets to own the canyon and all the land around it.

Lorne appeared on the balcony beside him. Crystal goblet of Xander's eighty-year-old tequila in his pudgy fist. Not that Xander drank alcohol. It reduced life, when the only nutrients he allowed to pass his lips extended it. Xander could smell the alcohol coming off him in waves. He'd been drinking since breakfast. One of Xander's Cohiba 55 Aniversario 2021 Edicion Limitada cigars smouldered aromatically in between two sausagey fingers.

'Hey, Xander. Y'all all right?'

Fuckin' lawyer. Worse than the fuckin' monkeys.

'How is this even possible, Lorne? I mean, tell me. You're my legal adviser. Advise me. How did he do it? He can't keep thwarting me. He can't! I demand an answer.'

'Oh, now look here, Xander. Y'all gotta expect the odd setback. You gotta look at the big picture. What you're tryin' to achieve, well, let's just say Rome wasn't built in a day.'

He smiled ingratiatingly. Xander wanted to punch his smug, self-satisfied face. Ram that six-hundred-dollar cigar down his greedy throat.

'I know, Lorne, why don't we just *not* say that? Why don't we just say, I thought Gabe was on *my* side?'

'So he double-crossed you. Y'all still got his sister, haven't you? Maybe it's time to bring her into play.'

'No. Maybe it's time to kill him. I could do it myself. Trick him somehow then blow his fuckin' head off. That'd teach him a lesson.'

The lawyer laughed. A big, wet, tarry sound lubricated with expensive vintage tequila. He puffed on the Cohiba and blew a stream of fragrant blue smoke out over the balcony. Followed it with a smoke ring that wobbled as it expanded before breaking apart.

'Well now, Xander, and how exactly are y'all planning on achieving that? The man don't *want* your money. And he musta seen through your little spy gal's cover somehow. Seems to me you're tied up tighter than a hog at slaughterin' time. Hell, boy, if sixty combat-hardened motherfuckers can't do it, what else you got?'

Xander felt it then. That familiar unpleasant tightness in his head. Like at school when they used to take him somewhere quiet and beat him up, and he'd take it for so long before somehow detaching himself from what was going on, what was happening to him.

'Well, I've got this,' he said.

His gun felt weightless as he raised it. He pushed the barrel into Lorne's right eye and pulled the trigger.

The Texan's head exploded. Bits of bone flew in all directions. Animals squealed and shrieked, hooted and whistled in the jungle. Blood and brain matter sprayed out in a sphere, coating Xander from the top of his head down to his shins.

The headless corpse hit the rail at the point where Xander's previous shot had smashed through the woodwork. It gave way with a loud crack and the dead lawyer plummeted into the undergrowth beneath the balcony.

Frowning at the thought of three hundred dollars' worth of Cuban cigar being wasted, Xander put the gun down on the wicker table and called his recovery mission director.

'Angela, we need to talk.'

59

Gabriel stood, head bowed, heart heavy, at the graveside.

As four men from the village lowered the plain wooden coffin into the ground, Juli cried out. Her friends gathered round her and hugged her, but her cries still broke free of their collective embrace, intensifying Gabriel's guilt.

If he'd picked someone else, Tiny would still be alive. Or maybe if Gabriel's tactics had been better thought out, he'd have survived the paramilitaries' murderous onslaught. He could have courted and then married Juli and become a proud father to a bunch of babies.

He'd offered to pay for the funeral, but Juli had insisted.

And then, just an hour later, it was time to leave.

He drove the four remaining members of the team to Teguz, and a flight back to the UK. Paddy, Kylie, Bilbo and Bullseye. Each man with ten thousand pounds in his account plus another ten as a success bonus. Though to Gabriel's ear, 'success' rang hollow given he'd also had to arrange for Sparrow's body to be shipped home. He'd called Sparrow's parents and broken the news to them as gently as he could. His mother's wails stayed with Gabriel long after the call had ended.

Amid swirling groups of excited travellers and watch-checking solo flyers, most toting briefcases and laptop bags, the five men huddled, arms around each other's shoulders.

'Those that have fallen, we will remember,' Gabriel said. 'They fought bravely, and died with honour. We will keep them in our hearts. Tiny. Sparrow. Goodbye, boys.'

'Goodbye, boys,' the others murmured in unison.

None was afraid to cry in front of the others. Despite the curious looks from passing travellers, they let their emotions out. Then, they cleared their throats loudly, smiled through their tears and broke apart. Gabriel stood back as the others grabbed their bags and went through security.

Back in the truck, he made a call to the UK.

'Hi, this is Sal, who's this please?'

'Hi, Sal, it's Gabriel Wolfe. We met at your office when I came to talk to Johnny.'

'Oh, yes! Hi. Is your top secret mission over, then? Johnny was super tight-lipped about it. Just said he was taking some annual leave. What was it, a big boys' adventure week somewhere thrilling? White-water rafting in Colorado? Rainforest trekking?'

Gabriel swallowed hard. It did nothing to shift the lump threatening to choke him. Her bubbling enthusiasm was unbearable. He had to stop her.

'Johnny's dead, Sal. I'm so sorry.'

Silence bloomed on the line like the black shadow of a storm cloud overwhelming a sunny Welsh hillside.

'What do you mean, dead? How?'

'He was helping me defend a Honduran village from a paramilitary attack. He survived that, but we were infiltrated and the spy killed him.'

She sobbed. A brittle, broken sound that had Gabriel flinching from the raw emotion.

'Did he, I mean, was it bad?'

How to explain to a civilian that bleeding to death from gunshot wounds was always bad. About as far from an easy death as you could imagine.

'It was quick. Instant, really. He felt nothing. Look, I've arranged for him to be flown back to the UK, to his mum and dad. But I thought, you could handle things on the work side.'

Yes. Of course.' Her voice was brisk. Business-like. Emotionless. She was in shock. 'Leave it to me. Thanks for letting me know, Gabriel. I have to go. Goodbye.'

She hung up, cutting a sob in half, leaving Gabriel hearing that bitter sound in the silence of the truck's cabin all the way back to Santa Rosa.

A second voice joined Sal's. This one, his sister's.

A simple message, spiralling round in his head like a carousel of black horses.

Save me, BB. Save me.

He vowed he would. Whatever the cost. He was coming for Tara.

60

Angie Espinosa found her boss frightening.

But he paid well and she needed to rescue her mortgage which was deeper underwater than the Kashalot-class Soviet research sub Xander Kalt had hired her to recover.

Her old salvage business had been doing great. Then Hurricane Katrina had swept across the south and wrecked her boat. Just one more casualty among thousands. And, like a lot of her neighbours, her insurance didn't cover the loss. Act of God? Act of fucking corporate cowardice more like.

So now she was employed by this billionaire man-child with a fixation on his great-grandpop's prototype computer. Why he was willing to spend so heavily to recover Peacemaker was beyond her understanding. But these tech bros had all the shit they wanted, so if they need to go to Mars or down the Marianas Trench, it was nothing to her. Just as long as the pay cheques cleared at the end of every month. Besides, this was hardly on that kind of scale.

She knew the marine chart like the back of her hand. But still, every day, she pored over it, tapping her index finger on the spot, circled in red, on the Mesoamerican Barrier Reef where the sub lay on her side. A whale beached underwater.

Kalt had told her the whole story. Much of it made no sense. Why were the Soviets sending a computer to Cuba by submarine? She knew her history. Khrushchev had sent nuclear missiles to Cuba, but that made more sense. They could hit every American city from there. Kennedy had done well to face the enemy down and get the nukes off his back door step. But a computer?

She shrugged, not for the first time. Ours is not to reason why, blah bah. Except Angie had no intention of doing or dying. OK, doing, fine. But not the other thing.

Besides, from what Kalt had told her, plenty of men had already died. The entire crew had suffocated when a much earlier hurricane than Katrina knocked out the power and sent it to the bottom.

She pictured fish-cleaned skeletons still wearing Soviet naval uniforms. It wasn't the bodies themselves that perturbed her. Salvage was occasionally a grisly business and you got used to the sights after a while. It was just the idea of being enclosed in that tin can while the oxygen ran out.

At least on a ship, you could jump off. Try your luck in the open water, among the sharks that prowled the Caribbean like unleashed guard-dogs.

Her phone rang. Xander.

'Yes, Skipper?'

He insisted on that. She hated it. An unearned title.

'Join me in the lounge?'

He phrased his orders like questions. She'd learned the hard way it was merely a concession to politeness, and one he clearly resented having to make.

Five minutes later, she went in to join him. His hair was wet and standing up in spikes. A white linen shirt clung to his skin.

'Drink?' he said, holding up a one-quarter full bottle of tequila. She'd seen the lawyer, Packard, making free with it and wasn't surprised to see how little was left.

'Please.'

Xander poured half of what remained into a tumbler and handed it to her. He picked up a highball glass filled with one of his disgusting super-smoothies, this one a greyish mustard-yellow, and slurped some up through a straw.

He sat facing her on a squashy sofa covered in a woven native throw, jaguars in orange on a background of green foliage. She glanced past his right ear. Frowned. Beyond the open sliding glass doors, someone or something had taken a section of the balcony railing away. Bright scars of bare wood stood out against the dark-green paintwork. And was that blood?

She gestured with her glass.

'What happened?'

He twisted round on the sofa to follow her outstretched arm. Turned back to face her. Giggled.

'I had to let Lorne go. And there's a new plan. Well, I *need* a new plan.'

Angie sipped the spirit. Over the years she'd developed pretty sensitive antennae to all kinds of danger. Sharks on wrecks. Unstable loads that could topple as a big wave hit, trapping you under tons of immovable wreckage. Sly-looking gang leaders who promised you the location of a big haul before trying to double-cross you when the loot was on dry land.

They twitched now.

'Meaning what, exactly?'

'Meaning, we're not using Santa Rosa anymore. I need suggestions. Now. Go.'

She thought fast, parking the dawning realisation that if she went to the balcony and looked over to the jungle floor, she'd most likely see the lawyer's white-suited corpse splayed among the ferns and lianas.

'We could sail the salvage ship in from Miami. Round the north coast of Cuba, staying out of its territorial waters, and then in round Puerto Rico. Probably have to hand out bribes along the way. Coastguard, whatever. But we could have everything in position in a few days. Then we dive for it. Use a bell. But we'd need a specialist saturation diver. The sub's what, forty metres below?'

'Forty-one, to be exact, but let's not quibble.'

'OK, so there aren't many people who can make a dive like that.'

'You know them, though, right?'

'I know some of them. It's a pretty small community.'

'OK, get on it, I want a full crew operational in three days.'

'But, Xander, it could take longer than that just to track down the right guy.'

'"But, Xander",' he mimicked, adding an unpleasant whiny overtone. 'Three days, Angie, or do I have to find a new mission director?'

'No, Xander,' she said. 'Excuse me. I need to start making calls.'

Swearing in her head, she left her boss, who she was reasonably sure was a sociopath, to his own company. He was welcome to it.

With Angie gone, Xander finished his smoothie. Winced. Goddamnit, the stuff tasted foul. But his medical teams assured him it contained the exact balance of micronutrients to promote immune system resilience.

Gabe thought he'd won, but he'd not reckoned with Xander Kalt. He'd have to use the sister as leverage but, in the end, Gabe would come round. All that talk about killing him with Lorne? Joking. That was the trouble with lawyers. No sense of humour.

Every great man had his consigliere. Telemachus had his Mentor. The Prince had his Machiavelli. Bilbo Baggins had his Gandalf. And Xander Kalt would have his Gabriel.

For some reason, Gabe was holding out. And Xander did not appreciate being held out on. If Xander decided on something, then it was happening. End of.

61

After seeing off his comrades, Gabriel drove straight from the airport in Teguz to a much smaller field. *Campo La Masica* – La Masica Field – was one of many small private aerodromes dotting the country, many controlled or at least used by cartels.

La Masica Field had taken the concept of an airfield and reduced it to its most essential elements. A ragged orange windsock, tattered at the narrow point of the cone. A corrugated-iron roofed hangar painted white. And a grass runway. Beyond the field, thick scrub on the north and west sides, rocky desert to the south and east.

Today, as indicated by the flapping windsock, a breeze blew north to south, necessitating take-off towards the scrub. Gabriel was not reassured by the burnt-out wreck of a single-engined plane nose-down among the trees and bushes.

A man sat low in a picnic chair in the shade of the hangar. He wore a straw cowboy hat pulled down low over his eyes. And he appeared to be slumbering soundly.

Gabriel parked the truck and climbed out. The warm wind was pleasant after the hot interior of his un-airconditioned truck.

Low humidity today, so he could enjoy the prickling sensation as the heat dried the sweat on his face and arms.

'*Hola, señor. Es usted piloto?*'

Without shifting position, the man spoke from beneath the wide brim of his hat.

'Yeah, I'm a pilot. Where you going?'

American-accented English. Not rare in Honduras. But not usual, either.

'Mexico. *Reserve de la Biósfera Sian Ka'an*. Heard of it?'

'Nope. Got the grid ref?'

'I do, yes.'

'How far?'

Gabriel told him the round trip distance. The man grunted.

'Yeah, we can do that on a full tank. Take about two hours each way.'

'I only need a one-way trip.'

'Still gonna cost you for the return. Same overheads whether I fly back solo or with a passenger. This biosphere got a landing strip?'

'I doubt it. But we won't need one. I'm going to parachute in.'

At this, the man did, finally, shift in his chair. He sat straighter and tipped his hat back, revealing sunglasses and a straggling moustache-beard combo.

'You're going to parachute in? What are you, some kind of daredevil? A YouTuber, that kind of thing?'

'Something like that.'

The pilot shrugged as he pulled out a phone.

'Your funeral.'

'How much?'

The man looked him up and down.

'American?'

'British.'

'Eight hundred dollars plus fuel.'

'I'll give you five hundred including fuel.'

The pilot smiled. 'I just looked the place up. It's a fucking nature reserve. Protected by Mexican State and Federal laws. I don't know whether it's a no-fly zone but that's added risk, OK? Eight hundred *including* fuel.'

'Deal.'

'One last question. You carrying? Only that's a no-no as far as I'm concerned. Deal-breaker.'

Gabriel put the parachute down. Held his hands wide. 'No. I'm not carrying.'

Not yet, anyway, he could have added.

The man spat on his hand and stuck it out. Gabriel took it immediately and they shook hard. A waft of sweetish alcohol fumes floated across the short distance between them.

Ten minutes later, he was sitting beside the pilot as the Cessna rumbled down the grass strip away from the thick bank of scrub rising to maybe twenty-five feet above the ground. As the plane executed a tight turn at the southern end of the runway, Gabriel looked down for his harness. The straps of webbing were present, but there was no buckle.

'What happened to *my* harness?' he asked, noticing that the pilot's was secure over his skinny torso.

'Don't worry about it, it doesn't affect airworthiness.'

The plane accelerated gradually but the pilot made no move to pull back on the control column and the brush drew near enough for Gabriel to make out small birds flittering among the branches. Despite himself, he tightened his belly muscles and gripped the grab handle beside him.

The pilot was humming a tune. A lilting melody that in any other circumstances short of torture would be pleasant. As it was, it merely raised Gabriel's anxiety level.

Was the pilot on Kalt's payroll? Was he just going to throw the little Cessna straight into the trees, saving his own skin, while Gabriel flew through the windscreen to be impaled on a broken tree branch?

'I flew in the war against Nicaragua,' the pilot said as the end of the runway loomed. 'Had a bunch of Delta Force guys once. The Americans were on our side.'

'Oh, yeah?' Gabriel's voice was tight.

They had less than fifty yards to go. The plane's engine was loud in the cockpit but still the pilot kept the control column level. Gabriel jammed his feet against the bulkhead in front of him. Then he bent his knees. No sense breaking his legs in the initial impact. If he survived, though, he'd kill the pilot. Fuck, this was a bad mistake.

The engine note rose and the Cessna climbed high above the airfield before banking sharply to starboard. Gabriel looked down into the startled face of a black-furred howler monkey, its mouth opened wide.

'You OK, my friend?' the pilot asked, pulling a cigar from the flap-pocket on the front of his flying jacket.

'I'm fine.'

'You smoke?'

'No, thanks.'

'What's your name?'

'Terry. Yours?'

'Emilio. Like Emilio Estevez, you know? The movie star?'

'I don't really watch a lot of movies.'

'Me neither, but my mom? She's a big fan. She loves all them guys. Rob Lowe. Judd Nelson. The chicas, too. Molly Ringwald. Ally Sheedy. Demi Moore.' He shook his head and puffed on the cigar, releasing a cloud of blue-silver-grey smoke into the cabin. 'You said you was British, huh?'

'As fish and chips.'

'Funny place for a Brit to end up. Don't you guys all go to Australia?'

'Some do. Spain, too. I fancied Honduras.'

'Whereabouts you live then? If you don't mind me asking?'

'Santa Rosa.'

'Nice. You ever visit Frida's?'

He turned and grinned at Gabriel. Somehow, Gabriel knew he was winking behind the mirror shades.

'Only for a massage. And I got a haircut there once.'

'A haircut? What are you, man, a fucking faggot?'

Gabriel turned his head away and looked down at the jungle a few hundred feet below them. Honduran machismo was a constant source of irritation and this man's personal brand was even more unpleasant than usual.

'How about you fly the plane, and we'll leave the discussion of my private life out of it?'

'Oh, sure,' he said, raising his hands from the control column. 'No offence, Terry. Just making conversation. So, you married?'

'No.'

'Girlfriend?'

'No.'

'I'm married. Couldn't live without her. Wanna see the love of my life?'

'Sure.'

He took his right hand off the control column and delved beneath the flying jacket. Smiled. 'Keep her right over my heart. Here she is.'

Gabriel turned away from the view of the mist-wreathed jungle and looked across at the pilot.

The pilot grinned. 'Meet the love of my life.'

62

The pilot pointed the blued-steel revolver at Gabriel's face. Cocked the hammer with his thumb.

'I call her Alina. You like that name, Terry? Or I guess we can drop the fun and games now, eh, Gabriel?'

Gabriel's pulse elevated to ninety. He focused on breathing slowly, dropping it back a few notches.

'What do you want?' he asked calmly.

'Nothing from you, man. Señor Mason's already giving me everything I want.'

So the ex-spook had been watching the airfield. No, he'd been watching *all* the airfields. Probably dropped a couple of hundred dollars on every pilot in Northern Honduras.

'Where are you taking me? If it's to Xander Kalt, there's no need for the gun. That's where I'm going anyway. He's got a compound inside the reserve.'

'Who's this Kalt character? I told you, I work for Señor Mason. And where I'm taking you is way out over the sea. Then you're gonna get out, without your chute. Señor Mason told me to do it this way specifically. Says he used to do the same to leftists during the war. Only back in the day, the CIA used helicopters. You know, with those nice wide-open doors at the back.'

Gabriel processed this information. Mason must have parted ways with Kalt. Maybe it was personal. Had he had friends among the mercenaries? It was a possibility.

Gabriel stammered as he answered. 'L-look, Emilio. Whatever Mason paid you, I'll give you double. No, wait! Triple! I've got it in my bag. Thousands of dollars. It's just in the back there. I can go get it for you.'

He twisted awkwardly in his seat, though the lack of a harness made it easier to manoeuvre around in the thinly padded aluminium bucket.

'Sit the fuck down!' the pilot commanded, jabbing the barrel in the air.

'OK, OK!'

In a single move, Gabriel swung back round, shot out his left hand and grabbed the revolver around the cylinder. He curled his thumb over the top strap and shoved it down between the hammer and the exposed end of the cartridge.

The pilot swore, and pulled the trigger instinctively. As the plane heeled over to port, engine screaming, Gabriel felt the brief sting as the firing pin hit his thumbnail. Nothing compared to the bigger sting of a hollow-point .38 bullet.

He wrenched the pilot's wrist over sharply, and heard the snap of breaking bones. He howled and let go of the gun. Gabriel elbowed him in the face, snapping his head back while he flipped the gun round and lowered the hammer.

The plane dropped into a dive.

'You broke my fucking wrist, you fucking fag!' the man screamed.

Gabriel pushed the barrel hard into his ear.

'Use that word once more and I'll paint your brains over the windscreen. Now pull up.'

'Fuck you!'

Gabriel withdrew the revolver then whacked it down hard on the man's left knee.

'Pull up or I swear to God I'll kill you right now.'

The man grabbed the control column and eased the Cessna out of its screaming death-dive. Sunlight burst into the cockpit turning everything bright silver.

Gabriel lowered the gun a fraction. Then the pilot's left hand seemed to jitter in the corner of his vision. Sunlight glittered off something hard and metallic.

The switchblade came up like a snake striking. Gabriel recoiled as it sliced through the spot his face had occupied just a split-second ago.

He blocked the second strike, and swore as the razor-sharp blade sliced across his forearm. White-hot pain lanced up to his elbow.

A second counterstrike with the revolver sent the switchblade clattering to the metal floor. Blood was running down his arm and into his fist, making the gun butt slippery.

He jammed the stubby barrel of the Police Special hard against the thin bone of the pilot's left temple. Curled his finger around the trigger. Thumbed the hammer back.

'Don't shoot!' the pilot shouted as the plane veered sideways in a sudden crosswind, engine whining as it hit a pocket of empty air.

'Get up,' Gabriel said.

'What?'

Gabriel shot out the side window beside the pilot's right ear. The bang was enormous in the hard-surfaced cockpit. Acrid blue gunsmoke filled the cramped space.

'Get the fuck up.'

'OK, OK. Now what? You want me to go back there? You going to tie me up or something? Only this bird has no autopilot.'

By way of answer, Gabriel left his own seat, grabbed the pilot by the scruff of the neck and hauled him up to his feet. He shot out the door latch. The door swung and clattered as the air pressure changed in the cabin. Two more rounds obliterated the hinges. With a metallic screech and a bang, the door detached from the fuselage and span away.

Gabriel forced the pilot around until he was facing the open doorway.

'No!' the pilot screamed above the roaring wind. 'You can't kill me. You need me to fly you for the jump.'

Gabriel braced himself. Then he kicked the pilot in the small of the back, through the door and out into the void.

'How hard can it be,' he said, as he settled himself behind the controls.

63

Buffeted by the cross winds entering the cockpit through the blown-out door, Gabriel held the plane on a steady bearing towards *Reserva Biósfera Sian Ka'an*. His arm had stopped bleeding. Mainly because the blood had coagulated into the cloth of his sleeve, forming an untidy bandage.

Below him, pelicans flew northwards, a lazy V formation heading towards Cuba. Somewhere below them, beneath the sparkling green-blue surface, lay the Doomsday weapon. The thought of anyone, let alone a narcissistic madman like Xander Kalt, getting their hands on it was chilling.

As the minutes ticked by, his mind began to unravel. Numbed by lack of sleep and the carnage of the last few days, his grip on reality kept slipping. Sounds, smells, tastes and sights that had no place in the cockpit of a light plane made their presence felt.

The chatter of small arms fire. Smudge's South London tones. *Kudos, boss. Never knew you could fly a plane.* The roar of exploding petrol tanks in SUVs hit by Javelins.

Blood suddenly smeared the windscreen, making Gabriel jump, lurching forward to swipe his hand across the glass before the red slick vanished as sharply as it had arrived.

And a smell that sent his pulse skyrocketing. Lemon. And sandalwood. Her smell. Eli's.

He looked to his left. But she wasn't there. He craned round to look over his shoulder. No, not there, either. Suddenly he desperately wanted to see her again. Her ghost. In his darkest moments, when despair had taken him to the brink of ending it all, he'd found if he surrendered to the PTSD, let the tamped down fear and anxiety have its head, he could drive a wedge into the slim gap between fantasy and reality and admit her presence.

He closed his eyes, briefly, and whispered, 'Eli. Please. I need you. I *want* you.'

He altered the pattern of his breathing, gasping in and out, short, sharp inhales and stuttering exhales through his teeth that washed carbon dioxide out of his bloodstream, upsetting the delicate balance between that gas and oxygen. The first signs of respiratory alkalosis made themselves felt. He began to feel panicky, his fingers started tingling and his mouth dried.

He closed his eyes and willed himself back to every traumatic episode in his life, starting right back with the catastrophe in Mozambique during his last operation with the Regiment. A warlord's fighters ambushing them. A heavy machine-gun mounted on a truck opening up. Smudge taking a hit from one of the massive rounds that took his lower jaw off, killing him on the spot.

He gasped for breath. Leaned forwards on the control column, sending the plane into a gentle descent towards the ocean.

Who would willingly allow his PTSD to rise up from the depths of his mind like a surfacing sea beast, to rend and tear his sanity? A madman? Or simply a man who'd lost so much he felt he had nothing left to lose?

The scent of lemon and sandalwood grew stronger. Palpable. He imagined her skin, sand-speckled on the beach at Ha Long Bay during their brief, ill-fated honeymoon.

'Eli!' he cried out, as the engine note rose and the airframe juddered.

'I'm here, my love, my honey. I'm here.'

He opened his eyes. Turned to his left.

And she was there. Beside him. Looking as beautiful as she had on their wedding day. Her grey-green eyes a-sparkle, her mouth curving upwards.

He let go of the control column to reach for her. But his arms flopped uselessly by his sides as the plane's nose dipped lower and the engine protested.

'I miss you so much,' he said.

She smiled sadly.

You have to let go, Gabe. Let me go, my love. I'm dead. You can't bring me back.

'But I want you. I need you, Eli.'

The wind roared in the cockpit. The plane slewed sideways in another crosswind and the port wing dipped suddenly towards the horizon. The engine howled louder still.

'I'm coming, Eli. To be with you.'

No, Gabe. You have to pull back from me. Eli shook her head violently, sending her long hair flying around her face in a russet corona. *No, not back. Up. Pull up, Gabriel. Pull up, pull up!*

He looked away from her screaming face. Out through the windshield. At the expanse of blue-green water, crested here and there with white caps. Pelicans skimming low over the water. And a shoal of bright-silver fish that flashed dark and light as they turned en masse.

Eli screamed one final time.

PULL UP!

Gabriel coughed. His vision cleared. Visions of Pera and Santi filled his mind. Their faces. Pera's, delighted, when they'd gone to collect her food truck. Santi's, triumphant, as he put the football past Gabriel into the improvised beach goalmouth.

He gripped the control column and heaved back with every ounce of his will.

Engine howling like a banshee, the plane hurtled seawards, its angle of attack softening but nowhere near fast enough. Teeth bared, Gabriel leaned back in his seat, hauling on the wheel until his muscles were burning as if set alight.

His stomach floated free as with an unearthly noise the plane executed a roller coaster turn, dipping and rearing to starboard, its wingtip grazing the surface of the water and leaving a long white streak of foam. He yelled out his defiance and summoned every last ounce of his strength to straighten the plane up and send it spearing upwards.

The altimeter and airspeed indicators spun as if Devil-possessed and the artificial horizon swung wildly as the instruments struggled with the lunatic physics of the trajectory Gabriel had subjected the plane to.

After what felt like an eternity, he was able to level the plane out. His breath came in ragged heaves and white sparks wormed their way round the edge of his field of vision. A burning smell invaded his nostrils, though he could see no flames.

He sniffed violently. But it had gone. Her scent. He looked left, knowing it was fruitless. She'd left him.

Then her voice swelled into life between his ears.

You have to let me go, Gabe. Don't risk your sanity for a memory. You should go home. Back to England. See Fariyah again. Rediscover your purpose. I love you, my honey, my soul. I love you. I l…

Tears overspilled his eyes. He sobbed until it felt as though he might never stop. And the miles passed. And the Mexican coast drew nearer.

And from somewhere deep down, beyond memory, beyond love, he found the strength to go on.

'I love you, too,' he murmured. 'Goodbye my love. Goodbye.'

64

Feeling nothing but a grim sense of purpose, Gabriel flew on towards the drop zone.

Eli's spectral voice echoed inside his brain. And he knew that she – or, rather, the part of his mind that clung onto reason at times of heightened stress, even as it chose to use another's voice – spoke the truth.

If he survived this, he had to get it back together. Honduras had been a year-long bolt-hole. Or longer? He'd lost track of the weeks and months passing. Even the seasons had blurrier edges here.

But he'd been a fool to think he could live out his days playing at being a farmer. Who was he kidding? Trouble followed him around like a stray dog he'd fed once too often. The least he could do was to be prepared for it.

But all that lay in the future. One of many possible futures. One in which he wasn't machine-gunned, stabbed to death, or killed by whatever horrific weapon lay beneath the sparkling waters of the Caribbean.

He checked the grid reference. The reserve ought to be visible by now. But how would he recognise it if it contained no developments to fix on as landmarks? He leaned sideways and craned his neck to see out of the window. A river wound through the forest, a sinuous silver strip reflecting the sun. Dark shapes like floating logs lay across it.

Then he saw it. A cluster of buildings in the centre of what appeared to be landscaped gardens, in a stretch of otherwise virgin rainforest. A track leading away towards the distant highway. He saw vehicles. A kidney-shaped swimming pool, the water tinted turquoise by the tiles. It had to be Kalt's private compound. He widened his search, looking for a landing site.

Found it. A clearing to the north of the compound. Maybe half a click.

He made a final circuit out to the west and then came back in again on a south-west bearing of 112 degrees 30 minutes. The plane's nose pointed out towards the Caribbean. He checked the fuel gauge. It was showing three-quarters full. The full-tank range was 500 miles. And they'd flown 200 hundred up to the reserve. So, 300 remaining. Perfect.

He lashed the control column and then clambered into the back. He unsnapped a flap on the chute's outer wrapping and extracted a pistol. It would have been useful up front a while back.

He stuck it into his waistband and left the pilot's revolver on the floor. With a grunt, he hoisted up the chute and buckled himself in. No time for ceremony. He just slid the door back and jumped. As he tumbled free of the plane's cramped embrace he watched it fly off. The fuel would run out at a point roughly half-way between Jamaica and the easternmost tip of Honduras at the place where the Rio Coco emptied out into the Caribbean.

He pulled the ripcord. Felt the old familiar tug as his harness tightened around him. Looked up. The canopy opened flawlessly, bellying outwards as it caught the air. The ripstop nylon wobbled and snapped before settling into the fluted hemisphere that would carry him safely to Earth.

His trip to the ground wouldn't take long but he was still able to relish the silence and the sense of weightlessness as he steered the chute towards the clearing to the north of the compound.

As the ground loomed up towards him, Gabriel realised his mistake. What had looked like a flat grassy clearing from the air now revealed itself to be dotted with thorny scrub. The last thing he wanted was to land in the centre of a mess of vicious spines and have to spend an hour digging their tips out of his flesh with a knife.

He pulled on the cords and swung wildly left to right, coming in hard enough to knock all his wind out, but mercifully avoiding a dense patch of orange-flowered shrubs bearing dagger-like thorns sturdy enough to remove an eye.

He got to his knees and freed himself from the harness. The parachute was snagged on the thorns, flipping and bellying as the wind tugged at it. Gabriel felt bad, screwing up the pristine look of the place and spent ten minutes he couldn't really afford cutting it free before rolling it into a fat sausage and shoving it out of sight at the foot of a tree.

He checked his compass and the map he'd bought in Teguz before leaving. Just under a kilometre to the compound. He set off.

I'm coming, Tara.

65

After the brief silence of the jump, the jungle at ground level was alive with noise. The hooting calls of howler monkeys boomed everywhere although when he looked up, he could never see them.

The humidity must have been nearing saturation point. Within a minute or two his clothes were soaked with sweat and clinging unpleasantly to his skin. Mosquitos whined about his face and he slapped one off when it bit him just below his left eye.

Something small and hard hit him on the top of his head, bouncing clear and landing on the forest floor with a soft crunch. A half-eaten fruit, green like a lime but with bright-orange flesh inside the hard-looking rind. He looked up. A long-limbed monkey with straggly black hair draping from its arms regarded him with curiosity from its perch some twenty metres up in the tree.

'What are you looking at?' Gabriel said.

The monkey cocked his head on one side as if to say, *Are you talking to me?* Then it got to its feet and swung away, hand-over-hand, in search of more fruit.

Another sound grew in volume as he made his way through

the jungle towards Kalt's compound. The chuckle and rush of moving water. It had to be the river he'd seen from the Cessna.

Pushing through a tangle of vines, Gabriel emerged onto the bank. He checked the compass against the map. Shit. His destination lay on the other side. The water was a deep jade green. No telling whether it was shallow enough to wade across. But the lack of ripples in the centre suggested not. No rocks or fallen trees lying on the bed to create turbulence.

Downstream it curved around overhanging trees and disappeared. Upstream it offered a better option. As it elbowed its way north, the inside curve enclosed a crescent of gravelly beach. The river was no more than ten metres across and white foam breaking over protruding rocks, slimed green with algae, suggested it was shallow enough to wade across.

The vegetation along the bank was too thick to permit him to simply follow it up to the beach so he headed inland for thirty metres until he found an animal track he could use.

He emerged onto the little patch of stones. And came face to face with another creature from the Mexican rainforest. Not a monkey this time. Nor a frugivore. The animal facing him was definitely more into meat. It raised its broad, scaly head as he stumbled from the undergrowth onto the gravel. Opened its huge mouth wide, revealing two-inch-long yellow pointed teeth. And hissed.

Gabriel's blood ran cold.

The crocodile must have measured fifteen feet from its scaly snout to the tip of its saw-toothed tail.

He stood perfectly still while he calculated his odds. How fast could an adult crocodile move? He realised he had no idea. But he didn't fancy finding out the hard way. At the moment, as he locked gazes with the yellow-eyed reptile, it seemed more confused than aggressive. The mouth stayed wide, giving him an excellent view of a surprisingly pink tongue and, less surprisingly, the kind of dental work designed to turn muscle into meat and bones into crunchy snacks.

This close he discovered something else about crocodiles he'd never appreciated before. They stank. A mouldy stench like stagnant water in which something had died and rotted down.

Keeping his movements slow and deliberate, and praying the huge reptile wasn't hungry, he inched his hand around to the back of his waistband and retrieved his pistol.

He brought it around to his front and racked the slide. The metallic rasp startled the creature. It backed up half a step and clopped its jaws together with a wet snap.

'Please don't make me shoot,' Gabriel said. 'I don't want to hurt you.'

He was more worried about enraging it, somehow doubting a few 9mm ball rounds would do much against a prehistoric beast that must weigh at least a ton and a half.

His heart was racing and there was nothing he could do to slow it down. Didn't want to, since if the creature made a single step towards him, he'd turn and sprint for the jungle, finding out the hard way whether he could outrun an adult male American crocodile.

The noise from the water behind the croc changed. Gabriel looked past it. The surface was undulating and breaking harder off the submerged rocks. He looked upstream and saw why.

Approaching slowly were another half-dozen crocodiles. The beast in front of him turned its head. Gabriel had no more time. If the rest of the beasts arrived it was game over. He aimed wide and fired three shots, simultaneously shouting at the top of his lungs.

The crocodile swished its tail and shuffled sideways before slithering off the tiny gravel beach and into the water, where it swam upstream to join its friends.

No time to lose.

Gabriel ran for the water, gun raised. Spray lashed up, but to his immense relief the river was shallow, no more than knee-deep. He high-kicked it across the stretch, dodging the larger submerged boulders. To his right he could just make out the seven dark-green crocodiles undulating towards him.

Just a couple of yards to go and he'd reach the safety of the other bank, where he could dive into the undergrowth and hopefully shake them off.

Then his leading foot dropped deep into a hole. He stumbled, going thigh-deep. He flung his hands out and lost his grip on the pistol which splashed into the opaque water and vanished from sight.

He glanced over his shoulder. The leading croc was only metres away, its greenish-yellow eyes signalling its deadly intentions.

He yanked his leg out of the hole and dived towards the bank. He scrabbled from grip on the slippery vegetation fringing the river. Behind him the croc was splashing closer. He imagined those wide-open jaws lined with yellow fangs seizing his leg and dragging him back into the water to drown him.

'No!' he screamed, grabbing a twisted root and hauling on it with all his strength.

He flopped out of the water onto his belly. No time to lie there gasping for breath. He was up and on his feet, thrusting through the dense growth. He caught movement beside him and turned just in time to see the croc's vast, armoured back rising from the water.

He plunged through the branches, ferns and creepers that grabbed at him and seemed hell-bent on holding him back where the crocodile could catch him.

With a convulsive effort that involved every muscle, he slid through a gap between two mossy tree trunks and rolled over and up onto his feet. He ran at a crouch, aware, as he did that his arms, pumping by his sides, were streaked with blood. Fat black S's undulated on the skin at the top of each scarlet stream.

Behind him, the undergrowth crackled and swished, but no crocodile emerged. The criss-crossing branches were simply too thick to admit its massive body.

Gabriel ran on until he reached a small clearing bisected by a fallen tree. He jumped onto its upper surface and swung up from there into the lower branches of a living example growing up between two rotted limbs.

He waited five minutes. The air was alive with the whistles and pops of florid red and yellow parrots and the ever-present calls of the howlers. But he couldn't make out any hissing or dragging that would indicate the crocodiles were still on his trail.

Gabriel lay his head back against the branch.

'Oh, fuck,' he murmured.

His left arm itched. He brushed at it absentmindedly. Then recoiled with horror as his fingers encountered something soft, pulpy and slimy to the touch.

A fat black leech clung to his skin, blood leaking from the point where its jaws were attached to him. Three more had made him their midday meal and when he pulled up his trouser legs, he found five more of their fellows stuck to his calves and shins.

He shuddered as he watched their pulsating bodies filling up with his blood.

Back when he'd trained for jungle warfare, and then in the field, opinions had varied as to the best method of getting rid of leeches. Some swore by a lighted cigarette. Fine if a) you smoked b) you happened to have a spare smoke on you and c) everything you owned wasn't sodden. Others claimed that the liberal application of salt and/or vinegar would do the trick. Yes, because every soldier carried a full range of condiments in their kit. But the most popular method, and the one Gabriel had found worked best from him was mechanical. You just had to break the suction between the leech's mouthparts and your skin.

He pulled out his pocket knife and opened the smaller blade. Inserted the tip at the point where the creature's mouth was fastened onto him. And twisted. You had to be careful unless you wanted the creature to leave mouthparts under your skin, so he employed a deft little lift-and-flick manoeuvre to simultaneously loosen and detach the evil little thing.

Blood flowed freely from the tiny circular wound, a consequence of the leech's anticoagulant saliva.

Gabriel repeated the disgusting process eight more times. At the end, he retched, nauseated by the slime clinging to his fingers.

Leaking blood like a mediaeval visionary afflicted with stigmata, he descended to the ground.

He walked away, anxious now to get to the compound, find Tara and get the hell out of Dodge.

66

Xander Kalt had to be stopped. But Gabriel had to rescue Tara first.

Night fell as Gabriel made his final approach to Xander Kalt's illegal compound in the Mexican rainforest.

As he waited for the sun to dip behind the topmost edge of the forest canopy, he had time to wonder about the size of the bribe Kalt must have paid to the Governor of Quintana Roos State. The phrase, 'one rule for them, another for us' had never seemed more true.

Men like Kalt saw the rule of law as an inconvenience. Something that could be ignored at best and bought off at worst. And if he was to be believed, he now intended to replace it on a worldwide scale with a far simpler and more brutal diktat. 'What I say, goes'. All thanks to the Doomsday weapon his great-grandfather had designed. A man who'd lived during the time when the Soviet Union was the number one threat to Western security, and not fanatics with a holy book in one hand and a bomb trigger in the other.

The moon was full, but even without its silvery light, Gabriel would have had no trouble finding the compound. Its periphery was illuminated with security lamps on poles strung out around the boundary fence.

He pulled out a pair of wire-cutters as he approached the fence, then put them away again, nodding with satisfaction.

Ten feet from where he'd emerged from the undergrowth, the earth at the foot of the fence was darker than the surrounding ground. A deep black shadow in a semicircle abutting the fence. Peccaries were known for their tenacity when on the trail of food. One or more had burrowed under the fence, leaving a short tunnel easily deep enough for Gabriel to squeeze through. He emerged on the far side and rubbed some of the loose dirt over his hands and face.

A curved track, its surface flattened and smoothed by numerous tyres, led towards the main house. Its white plaster brightly reflected the moonlight.

A crack alerted Gabriel to another presence besides his own. He'd been expecting guards, and here was the first.

The man was dressed in the internationally approved style for hired muscle. All black, from the tactical boots to the long-billed cap. He had the regulation curly-wire earpiece, too, which meant Gabriel would have to be fast. A Heckler & Koch MP5K submachine gun dangled from its webbing sling. Not much good to its owner if he was the subject of a blitz attack. A pistol was holstered on his right hip. Strap over the butt.

The man had got complacent. Probably happy to pick up a fat pay cheque from Kalt every month for doing little more than a night watchman would do. Endless middle-of-the-night patrolling and occasionally shooing away of an over-inquisitive wild pig.

A second man emerged from round the corner of the house.

'Hey, Jorge! Any action?'

'Oh, yeah, sure. I got action, all right. I got two mosquitos a minute ago and I think I might have seen a capybara.'

The second guard laughed.

'Think we should tell the boss we're under attack from giant rats?'

His companion joined in before gesturing at the other man's pockets.

'You're a real comedian, Filipe. Got a smoke?'

'Sure.'

The two men went through the time-honoured ritual of offering, lighting, inhaling, then split up again.

Gabriel followed the newcomer as he continued away from his partner and round to the back of the house. He was muttering to himself and chuckling at his own joke.

'Fucking giant rats.'

The final word turned into a wet gasp as Gabriel's blade slid across his neck from left to right. The cut was swift, deep and precise. The windpipe opened, preventing him from screaming. The major blood vessels followed, sending arterial spray arcing away to spatter the foliage hemming them in with a noise like sudden rainfall.

Gabriel only had to hold him for a few seconds before his plummeting blood pressure sent him briefly into unconsciousness before death claimed him.

He lowered the body to the ground and removed the submachine gun. He checked the magazine. Full. Two spares in narrow pockets on the tactical vest. The guard was roughly his size. Gabriel took the whole thing, plus his cap, and slung the submachine gun over his shoulder. For now, he needed silence. Or as much silence as he could personally sustain.

As he dumped the body in the undergrowth and scattered leaves over it, the noise from the nearby nocturnal creatures paused for a few seconds. Then it resumed in full force.

The creatures who hunted, foraged or searched for a mate at night were much noisier than those during the day. As if compensating for the lack of light, everyone seemed to be staking out a sonic claim.

Insects buzzed and creaked, cicadas loudest of all. Frogs called in a symphony from fluting chirrups to trebly warbles all the way down to bassy rumbles. Howlers, never the most reticent of animals, maintained a deafening chorus of calls that had earned them their name. Apparently they could be heard a mile away. Gabriel thought that was something of an underestimate. He reckoned the Cubans would be able to pick up their signal. And, somewhere deep in the forest, a jaguar coughed menacingly. A good night for predators.

He found the second guard leaning against a swing-bench, smoking as he stared out at the jungle. He'd rested his submachine gun on the seat, propped up against the arm-rest.

Gabriel stole up behind him on silent feet, avoiding the twigs and sticks that might snap underfoot. If the dry leaves were rustling beneath his feet, the susurration was drowned out many times over by his friends in the orchestra.

He drew nearer. Just a foot or so from the guard's back. He unsheathed his knife and then felt an unexpected pang of guilt. Another dead man to add to his tally. But the man was part of a crew who'd kidnapped Tara. And right now that was all that mattered.

Gabriel waited for him to take a long final drag on his cigarette. He struck, hard and fast. Wrapped his left forearm around the guy's head and hauled him back, exposing his stubbled throat. A swift, sure slice with the knife and the windpipe was severed. Smoke jetted out from the gaping wound as the dying guard struggled, witnessing six-foot arcs of his own arterial blood piercing the fog of silvery-blue smoke.

Gabriel lowered him to the ground.

'*Lo siento*,' he murmured, as he laid the body in the rich deep humus that covered the forest floor. He kicked a thin layer of rotting vegetation over it. He took the second submachine gun and slung it over his shoulder. Stuck the guard's pistol into his belt.

For the next ten minutes, he waited to see if another pair of guards were on duty. The place was still. Maybe out here, Kalt felt safe. His mistake.

At the rear of the property, waste bins clustered beneath a reed-roofed shelter. Water butts were ranged along another wall, corrugated plastic hoses leading from the gutters screwed into their black plastic tops. To the right of this little facility a door stood open. Maybe the guards used it. Maybe Kalt did. It didn't matter. He'd been careless. And Gabriel would have been inside anyway.

First, he needed to shorten the odds of finding Tara before the two dead guards were either missed or discovered.

Kidnappers, in Gabriel's experience, came in two flavours. Sadists and negotiators. Sadists had no intention of returning their victims. Their goals were personal, deviant, often sexual. Islamist militias in Africa. The Taliban in Afghanistan. Cults in Japan. It was all about power. Self-gratification. Denigration. They tended to keep their victims in deplorable conditions. Humiliating them with a lack of basic sanitation. Room to move around. Even natural light. He'd experienced it personally, more than once.

But negotiators weren't interested in their victims themselves. They saw them as currency. They took things other people loved, and then traded them back in exchange for money, arms, safe passage, the freeing of comrades in a wider struggle. And they tended, though the rule didn't always hold, to treat their captives with more decency.

Kalt was a member of the latter group. Gabriel was sure of it. He'd taken Tara first to learn about Gabriel but then to trade her. But for what? He'd already asked Gabriel to join him. Was it that simple? Was he hoping to use Tara as leverage so Gabriel would help him recover Peacemaker? It made a twisted kind of sense.

In which case, it would make sense that he'd not mistreat her. The wood-framed house was big. Gabriel couldn't afford to spend hours searching for Tara. If a new shift of guards came on duty at, say, dawn, they needed to be gone by then.

He doubted the house would have a cellar. The rainforest would be too soggy underground. In any case, there was no need. Why go down when you could just spread out? So Tara would be either on the ground or the upper floor. A guest room, then, modified for the prisoner. Locks on the door, bars on the window.

He began a circuit of the house, checking each of the windows in turn. None had curtains, though a few had Venetian blinds. He paused below a window where light spilled through the slats of the blind, painting irregular stripes of bright green on the closest trees. A shadow moved across it. But the glass was unobstructed. He moved on.

On the rearmost elevation, he found her. Or at least he found a barred window. No light. But the metal grid screwed onto the outside of the window frame was plain to see.

He looked around for a pebble. But the ground around the house was just tamped flat dirt. Any stones were most likely way back on the river bed. He slid a magazine out of one of the pockets on his tactical vest and pushed the topmost round free with his thumb. Repeated the process until he had five of the little brass projectiles in the palm of his hand.

He gauged the distance and then flung a round at the window. It bounced off the glass with a crack and landed somewhere in the darkness. He threw a second. Another impact. Another bright, hard sound. Metal on metal this time, as it glanced off one of the bars. He frowned. Was she here at all? He'd invested a lot in the idea that the bars signified something. She could just as easily be locked up in an internal, windowless room on the ground floor. These billionaire-types all had panic rooms, didn't they?

'Come on, Tara,' he murmured, as he launched a third round up at the window.

It smacked against the glass just as a light flicked on behind the blind. A shadow appeared. Gabriel stood back, unshouldering the MP5K. The slats closed and rose towards the top edge of the window, letting yellow light spill out into the night.

A woman. His heart sank. Not Tara. But then he remembered. They'd switched her for a ringer, but Tara had told him herself about her surgery. She lifted the sash.

'BB,' she whispered. 'Is that you?'

Oh, thank God. It was her. Elation filled him and despite the precariousness of the situation, he found himself smiling.

'Yeah, it's me. You OK?'

'I'm fine.' She grabbed the metal bars. 'It's bolted in, you won't shift it.'

He shook his head. 'Wasn't planning to. I'm coming in. Get ready.'

67

Gabriel used his knife to spring the lock on the door near the recycling hutch at the back of the house. Security was minimal. More evidence of Kalt's hubris.

Before going inside, he unshouldered one of the submachine guns and pulled back the charging lever.

Inside, the house resembled a movie director's idea of a Spanish colonial villa. Polished dark wooden furniture, hand-woven textiles on the walls, the floor, draped over trunks. A suit of armour complete with long, polished sword resting point-down on the mahogany plinth. Ornate, gilt-framed mirrors and, over a fireplace, surely the most unnecessary design detail ever placed in a rainforest dwelling, a six by four-foot portrait of Xander Kalt.

In the painting, he posed regally in front of a glittering palace composed entirely of glass. His outfit was truly bizarre. It was as if he'd briefed the artist to look at Renaissance images of princes and then instructed them to 'bring it up to date'.

Flowing cobalt-blue drapery that reflected the light like sunlit silk flowed down over riding boots fashioned from chrome. A sword hung from a gilded belt, but its blade was a beam of light, white at the centre, fading to turquoise at the edges. At his booted feet, their curved bellies kissing the ground, two greyhounds, one black, one grey looked up at their master, a traditional touch rendered surreal by the exposed viscera visible through transparent panels on their ribcages.

Nuts, was Gabriel's artistic and psychological read on the image. *Just like its subject.*

Voices floated down a corridor towards him. Male, more than one. He sprinted for the stairs, running on the balls of his feet, and took them three at a time. He arrived on the upper floor just as the three men entered the square reception hall. Each carried a pistol at his hip and a submachine gun on a sling over his shoulder.

They obviously found the image of their boss as *fascinating* as Gabriel had. They stopped in front of it.

'If *I* had his money, I wouldn't get something as crazy as that,' one said.

'Yeah, we know what *you'd* get. You taking Olivia Garcia up the ass. Not that she'd ever go for you unless you lost thirty pounds and grew your hair back.'

He shrugged. 'Hey, if I had Kalt's money, why not? Some crappy actress like her? She'd beg me for it.'

The other men laughed. The third chipped in.

'You know what I'd have? Me with all the greats, you know? Pinochet. Galtieri. Batista. Trujillo. Stroessner. Noriega.'

'Don't forget Castro,' the first man said with a wink at his companion.

'Fuck you! Castro can suck my dick.'

'Castro's dead, idiot.'

Their voices faded as Gabriel backed away, aiming for the corner of the house where they'd confined Tara. Something about the way the men were talking suggested Kalt wasn't on the premises. That was OK. Gabriel planned to catch up with him before too long. And certainly before he'd brought Peacemaker up from the depths.

Sweeping the H&K's barrel from side to side, he made his way down the corridor, pausing to listen as it doglegged. But whatever men Kalt had guarding Tara, they all appeared to be on the ground floor. From their laughter, still finding amusement in their artistic fantasies.

It wasn't hard to pick out the door to the room where they were holding Tara. A sturdy padlock-barred entry.

He drew his knife and inserted the tip of the blade into the first screw holding the hasp in place. Exerted a little force. Nothing happened. He pushed harder, fearing that if he overcooked it, the tip would break off. The screw remained immovably in place.

He tried the others. None budged by as much as a hair. If he had longer, he could maybe dig the hasp out of the wood. But the door looked to be made out of some sort of tropical hardwood. He could be there for hours.

He scratched his fingernails across the wood. Tara's voice answered immediately.

'BB?'

'Yeah,' he murmured. 'I'm going to have to shoot the lock off. Be ready.'

'OK. Count to five.'

He heard feet scuffing on the far side of the door. He knew his sister would take cover well away from any possibility of ricochet or flying splinters.

One ... two, three...

He aimed at the lock.

Four ...

Squeezed the trigger.

Five.

The gun spat flame. The bullet smashed the padlock, which fell to the floor with a clunk. The report was immense in the tight-walled corridor. The guards would be on their way. He thought he heard their shouts over the ringing in his ears.

He booted the door in, splintering the flimsy original lock and tossed the second H&K to Tara, who was emerging from an en suite bathroom. She caught it and pulled back on the charging lever. She joined him and they ran into the corridor. Better to fight in a confined space with a way out than get bottled up in a room with barred windows.

She dropped to one knee, submachine gun raised. He stood behind her, ready to fire over her head. The guards' yells echoed as they stormed up the wooden stairs. The dogleg prevented Gabriel or Tara sighting on the onrushing guards, but it did the same favour to the men currently charging up to the top floor.

The first man rounded the dogleg, jinking left and right and almost slipping as he emerged into the straight portion of the corridor.

Then Tara opened fire. Bullets tore him almost in half, spilling silvery-purple intestines from his midsection and sending sprays of blood and tissue back into the face of the second man.

Gabriel opened up. A short burst that shattered the following man's skull, exploding it in a welter of bright arterial blood that sprayed up to the ceiling. His headless corpse staggered on for two more steps before collapsing over the body of the first guard.

No way would the third guard follow his friends.

'Come on!' Gabriel shouted.

Tara jumped to her feet and they retreated, she facing the way they'd come, he facing forwards, their backs pressed tight together.

He opened the next door he came to. A small bedroom housing little more than a double bed and a wooden wardrobe.

'In here!'

They ducked inside and together pulled the wardrobe over with a crash that released a strong scent of camphor. They heaved it into place across the doorway.

Tara went to the window and opened the sash. She leaned out.

'There's an extension. Flat roof. Six-foot drop, maybe eight.'

Gabriel nodded and was halfway across to join her when the door behind him shuddered under the impact of a boot or shoulder charge. It banged loudly against the toppled wardrobe.

'*Mierda!*'

The man on the far side didn't bother with another attempt, or even wasting breath on further swearing. Bullets slammed through the door, sending razor-sharp splinters flying out in a hemisphere.

Tara was already out the window and dropping onto the flat roof. Gabriel had one leg out when something like a punch hit him in the back, sending him face-first against the window. No time to investigate, and he had the dead guard's tac-vest on, so any damage would be minimal.

He was out the window and beside Tara a second later.

They dropped to the ground simultaneously. Above them they heard another burst of gunfire. Sustained this time. The guy had burned through an entire magazine.

'We need wheels,' she said. 'They're all at the back.'

He followed her in a crouching run as she led him around two corners of the massive wooden building. Behind him a burst of machine-gun fire drowned out the noise of the jungle.

'*Volved! Hijos de putas!*'

Gabriel stopped. *You want me to come back? OK. You get your wish.*

He turned. Crouched. Waited.

The third guard rounded the corner, red-faced, gun swinging wildly.

Gabriel hit him high in the chest with his first burst. Then removed the top of his head with the second. Blood misted around him and drifted away from the house, borne on a current of warm, humid air to dissipate in the undergrowth.

'BB, come on!' Tara yelled.

He found her, submachine gun raised, standing beside a brand-new Jeep, its engine idling. Kalt must have enjoyed playing at soldiers when he specified the jungle camo paint job, but now Gabriel and Tara would be the ones to benefit.

He swung up into the passenger seat while Tara took the wheel and slewed the 4x4 round in a circle before flooring the throttle and heading back down the dirt road leading away from Kalt's compound.

Heckler & Kock cradled in his lap, Gabriel shook his head. If only all extractions were that simple.

68

Half a click away from the house, in a black-painted pickup, George Mason lit a cigar.

He puffed contentedly, enjoying both the flavour of the smoke and the way the tip glowed red in the dark. You could do a lot with a glowing cigar tip. If you knew how. And you weren't squeamish.

In the load bay behind him lay a hundred and twenty-pound, five-foot-long *arapaima*, its luminous eight-inch-long lure still lodged in the giant fish's gullet. Almost extinct in Mexico, they'd been recently reintroduced into the reserve by the state government. There was a strict ban of fishing for them, let alone cooking them. Mason thought that a pity, given how succulent the white flesh was when you blackened it on a barbecue with a little Cajun seasoning.

His phone rang.

He glanced down and tutted. Brought it to his ear.

'What?'

'Get over here. We're under attack.'

The unmistakable sound of small arms fire crackled in the background. Mason swore. Called out.

'Jerome! Get your fucking Chicano ass back here. We gotta roll.'

69

High beams blazing, Tara was taking the road through the jungle as fast as she could, but progress was still slow.

She swept round a long shallow bend and shrieked as she slammed the brakes on. A herd of deer the size of large dogs scattered in panic. Three headed straight for the oncoming jeep before breaking sideways into the jungle. One bounded almost vertically, landing on the hood with a clatter from its hooves, before skittering off sideways, almost rolling before regaining its balance and disappearing into the green wall that enclosed the track.

On the move again, she maintained a more cautious thirty, slowing to twenty or even ten when the track narrowed or they had to skirt a fallen log.

'How far to the highway?' she asked, letting the wheel spin through her hands as the Jeep hit a patch of mud.

'The Chetumal-Cancún Highway's about twenty miles from the compound.'

'So about an hour unless we risk turning this bugger over?'

'Something like that.'

'How many more troops do you think Kalt has here?'

'No idea. But the sooner we're out of Mexico, the better I'll like it.'

On a straightish stretch of track, Tara glanced across at Gabriel.

'Thanks, BB. For coming to get me, I mean.'

'I could hardly let that nutjob kidnap my baby sister and get away with it,' he said. 'Did they mistreat you?'

'No. That's what was funny. Kalt spent time with me explaining all about his plans. Made sure I had my favourite food. Plenty to drink. Clean clothes. If it wasn't for the bars on the window I'd have thought it was a nice little rainforest Airbnb,' she said. 'The funny thing is, I think he wishes you were working for him, not against him.'

'He said that?'

'Pretty much. Why?'

'I had dinner with him. He made the same offer. Unlimited pay, whatever I wanted.'

'Why, do you think? A man like Xander Kalt can hire anyone he wants.'

'Thanks for that vote of confidence, Sis.'

'That's not what I meant! Sorry. I meant, why not pick someone more pliable? Someone who'll happily do whatever he's asked to without raising objections?'

'He gave me this line about every great man having a sort of adviser. I think he sees himself as a cross between Machiavelli's Prince and Alexander the Great.'

'So, certifiable, then.'

'Totally.'

Tara laughed. Gabriel found her laughter infectious and soon the Jeep's cabin rang with the siblings' slightly unstable hysterics.

He pointed ahead to a bend. 'Better slow down.'

Wiping her eyes, Tara took her foot off the throttle and eased the Jeep into the curve. The high beams illuminated the wall of green that hemmed in the track.

Half-way round she screamed and slammed the brakes on hard, bringing the Jeep to a sliding halt, half-slewed round across the track. Coming towards them at a rate of knots was a black pickup riding high on oversized tyres. A rack of halogen lamps mounted on a roof bar flooded the cabin with white light.

'Out!' Gabriel shouted.

In a move so synchronised they might have practised it, the Wolfe siblings grabbed their submachine guns, threw their doors wide and rolled out.

They dropped to the ground and pushed their way through the undergrowth out of sight of the truck and its occupants.

'Stop them!'

The man's voice carried the edge of command. And Gabriel recognised it. George Mason, the former CIA paramilitary. One of the guards must have called for backup.

No wild bursts of automatic fire though. Whoever Mason had with him was well trained. No trigger-happy cartel gangbanger, then.

Tara was on the far side of the track. He knew her moves. She'd be trying to circle round to get behind the pickup. How many men would Mason have with him? The pickup wasn't a crew-cab, so probably only one. Two at most. Reasonable odds.

He crouched by the foot of a twisted tree, its fat trunk covered in thick, soggy moss. To his left he heard footsteps. Tara? No, too heavy a tread. And Tara was too savvy to make such a racket. She hadn't been brought up by Master Zhao, but in its place she'd been trained as a child-assassin by the Chinese state's best operatives. Stealth was one of their main weapons. That and anything lying around, from pencils to vegetable peelers.

His pursuer emerged from a patch of thick ferns. A white guy. Six-five, two hundred pounds. Shaved head. Neck as thick as his head. Full-size Glock gripped in a fist like a bear's paw that made the pistol look like a sub-compact.

'Hey!' Gabriel hissed.

The man spun round and presented Gabriel with an easy target. Three rounds centre-mass. Blood sprayed from the exit wounds. He sank to his knees and fell face down into the leaf mulch. Gabriel put another round into the back of his head.

He stayed in a crouch.

Mason would have heard the shots. And he'd be waiting for a triumphant call that their target was down. When it didn't come, he'd know he was down a man.

'Wolfe, you better get your ass out here,' Mason called. 'I found your little sister trying to act like a forest mouse.'

He sounded confident. Relaxed. A bluff? Gabriel couldn't be sure.

'Tara?' he called out, then scuttled away from his position. No sense in allowing Mason to get an auditory fix on his location.

'Go, BB! Leave m—'

Her final word was cut off abruptly in a muffled shout. Gabriel clenched his jaw. He could picture it all too clearly. Mason standing behind Tara with his hand clamped over her mouth. He must have a gun or a knife dug hard against her back, though. She'd have disarmed him easily otherwise.

'Thirty seconds, Wolfe. Follow my voice,' Mason called. 'Don't be too long. If I see anything that looks like a weapon she's dead. And don't think about coming up behind me. I got that angle covered.'

'OK, Mason, I'm coming. Don't hurt her.'

Tuning in to the direction of Mason's constant taunting, Gabriel pushed his way through the undergrowth. He'd need to lose the submachine gun and the pistol but he decided to wait. Mason would want to see him drop them.

He put his hand out to push a broad-bladed leaf aside when he froze. Lit a silver-grey by the full moon, with the red bands on its multi-jointed legs turned a dull orange, a huge spider hung from its underside. Gabriel fought down a wave of nausea. Ever since he could remember, he'd had an unreasoning terror of spiders. All through his military service, he'd dealt with it as best he could. Jungle warfare was the worst and he'd simply had to face his fears and avoid the usually harmless creatures as far as possible.

'Fuck,' he murmured as he stilled his trembling hand.

The arthropod remained utterly motionless. He could see the

moon reflected over and over again in its beady black eyes. Heart pounding, he stretched out his fingertips a little further until he was within touching distance. It moved suddenly, the two front legs lifting from the surface of the leaf and waving at him menacingly. Adrenaline flooded his system, jolting him to a whole new level of high-alert terror. He thought he could see two glossy black fangs reflecting the moon back at him along their curved chitinous lengths.

But the spider didn't move away. Or advance on him.

In a single move, he swept his hand out and closed his fingers around it in a cage. The sensation of eight hairy legs scuttering against his palm and the insides of his fingers almost made him lose it altogether. A shudder convulsed him as he closed his hand a little tighter. He didn't want to kill it, but quieting it would enable him to go on.

No such luck. The spider was panicking. He looked at his caged fist in horror as one then two hairy feet poked out through the gaps between his fingers before withdrawing.

Then his hand flared with pain as if speared with red-hot needles. It had bitten him. Pera had told him once that the really big spiders weren't that dangerous to humans. Their bites were painful but no worse than the sting of one of the invasive Asian hornets that had begun appearing on the Honduran coast. He hoped fervently she was right.

His hand was throbbing painfully and the giant spider was going crazy in its prison, spinning around, rubbing those hairy limbs between Gabriel's knuckles.

He pushed on, wanting to scream out his disgust and hurl the innocent captive as far from him as possible.

Instead he emerged onto the track about ten feet from Mason. He stood beside the pickup, his back pressed to the tailgate. Tara knelt before him, head bowed. He had a pistol pointing down at the nape of her neck. An executioner's stance. The round would destroy her brainstem. Death would be inescapable and instantaneous.

He looked over at Gabriel and smiled triumphantly.

'Well, well. If it isn't Xander's would-be mentor. You know, Gabriel, I don't know if it's the British accent or what, but that man has got such a hard-on for you it's embarrassing.'

Gabriel didn't bother responding. Instead, using his left hand, he unslung the submachine gun and tossed it over towards Mason. It landed at his feet. Still using his left hand, he reached across his own body and drew the pistol, using just his thumb and forefinger on the butt so the gun dangled uselessly in his hand. He swung it back and then forwards, releasing it at the end of its swing so it, too, fell in the no-man's-land between them.

'OK,' he said, walking closer to Mason. 'No weapons. Now let her go. You want me? Fine. Here I am.'

Mason tipped his head on one side.

'Aw. Now, Gabriel, that is so sweet. And hold it there. Not another fucking step. But you know I have to kill you both, don't you?'

'No!' Tara shouted from her kneeling position. 'Let me live. Xander likes me. He'll be mad at you if you kill me. Shoot Gabriel.'

Gabriel took another step closer. His right hand felt like a tautly inflated balloon and he desperately wanted to check it. But he kept his gaze locked onto Mason.

Mason swung his gun arm up and pointed it straight at Gabriel. In the same instant, Gabriel flicked his right hand up and out in an underhand throw that sent its enraged captive flying, spraddle-legged, straight towards Mason's face.

Mason yelled out as the spider hit him over the right eye. His gun arm jerked spasmodically and he fired wildly, sending three rounds smashing through the forest. The spider got caught in his collar then scuttled free and bounced to the ground. Mason screamed. This time because Tara had reared round and sunk her teeth into his groin. He staggered back against the tailgate, blood spreading across the front of his trousers. He swung the gun down towards the crown of her head. Which was no longer there. On her feet already, she chopped him viciously across the right wrist.

He dropped the pistol. Gabriel reached them and smashed a fist into Mason's exposed throat.

Then a gun barked twice and the left side of Mason's face disappeared. Blood and bone exploded outwards, spattering the giant fish that lay in the load bay.

Tara stood off by a couple of feet, the still-smoking Glock in her extended hand.

'I thought you hated spiders,' she said.

A whole-body shudder rippled through Gabriel as he held up his right hand, which was red and puffy.

'I do. Can we go now, please?'

Forty minutes later Tara swung out onto the Chetumal-Cancún Highway and took the jeep up to ninety. Seven minutes after that, they reached *Aeropuerto Internacional de Chetumal*.

Despite giving the appearance of being closed for the night, it turned out there was a well-resourced night-flight programme operating out of the airport. Provided, that was, the passengers had sufficient funds.

After agreeing a price for flying them down to Aeropuerto de Trujillo on the north coast of Honduras, Gabriel made the necessary transfer to a man who seemed unfazed that the latest drug traffickers to use his charter service should look so unlike his normal passengers.

'No bags?' he asked.

'Just these,' Gabriel said, raising a jacket flap to reveal the butt of his pistol, as Tara did the same.

The pilot shrugged. 'It's a three-hour flight. Make yourselves comfortable.'

70

Elated, Kalt stared out of the diving bell's thick, circular, Plexiglass porthole.

Forty-eight metres below the surface of the Caribbean, the light was minimal. The water around them a deep blue compared to the sun-pierced turquoise nearer the surface.

Lit bright yellow by the specialist diver's lights and those beaming across the twenty metres of open water from the bell, the submarine lay on its side. The coral in which it nestled seemed to Kalt like an open-palmed hand, extending from the Mesoamerican Barrier Reef specifically to catch the sub.

Without its cradling grasp, the Kashalot-class submarine's 1,390 tons would have disappeared forever into a trench that Kalt's research director had assured him was well over 2,000 metres deep. At that depth, the pressure would have crushed the *Ozersk* like an empty soft drinks can in a giant fist. The unimaginable forces would have rendered it, and everything inside it, not just unrecoverable but compressed into a hard, dense lump of scrap metal.

His heart was beating fast like a drum and his mouth was dry.

He pressed his face to the glass, frowning with irritation as his breath misted it briefly.

This was it. The moment he'd dreamed of for so many years. Somewhere inside that long tubular steel coffin lay the machine that would ensure history ended then began anew on the day he, Xander Kalt, recovered Peacemaker for the world.

The diver who'd just flipped over from the bell to the sub, returned, hanging outside the observation window. He shook his head and tapped his dive watch. Then pointed upwards. The message would have been perfectly clear even without the tedious safety briefing he'd subjected Kalt to. Jesus, it wasn't as if he wasn't a qualified diver himself.

But they were standing, well, swimming – haha – on the brink of a momentous discovery. Forget the pyramids. Forget the wheel. Forget space travel, electric cars, social media and toothbrushes made of fuckin' bamboo. Xander Kalt was about to institute a new paradigm for human behaviour.

War was over and the human race would finally achieve its full potential. And with him at its head, because legacy states and legacy governments would be as obsolete as fossil fuels, it could reach far beyond the narrow goals it had always set itself.

Aliens observing earth – because, oh, yes, Xander knew full well they existed – would marvel. The species they'd long despaired of, despite giving them mathematics, medicines and machinery, now revealed in all its glory. *Its* glory? OK, Xander's glory.

Xander refocused on the diver. He was jerking his finger upwards again. Tapping his watch. Then pointing at the hatch for Xander to let him in. Xander regarded him with curiosity. And a thought struck him. A very worrying thought. Xander Kalt was not a man to allow negative emotions into his life. They were ageing, science had proven it. So the jittery feelings in his gut were as unwelcome as a jelly doughnut in his carefully calibrated dietary regime.

The thought was this.

What if the diver gets the credit for recovering Peacemaker?

The mainstream media would obviously be all over the story. And they'd want first-hand testimony from the man who'd brought the weapon out of its decades-long hibernation.

He frowned at the thought of the former SEAL's made-for-Netflix handsome face filling screens across the world. Even his name was annoying. Chuck Driver. Chuck! Like some fuckin' Norman Rockwell newsboy.

He stared out through the two-inch-thick Plexiglass. Maybe Chuck was running low on air. He was certainly acting pretty agitated. He was actually hammering on the outside of the porthole and then gesturing frantically to his left, where the hatch was located.

Kalt leaned away from the porthole. He swivelled in his chair to consult the compact digital panel that controlled everything that happened on and outside the bell. Power. Light. Stabilisation. Oxygen. Emergency procedures.

It was amazing what you got for your seventy-seven million-and-change. A state-of-the-art, AI-equipped diving bell capable of withstanding pressure down to 300 metres. But it still had a big red button labelled 'EMERGENCY'. He smirked. Like something out of a Looney Tunes.

Depressing it would seal the bell off from the outside world. Explosive bolts would detach all external links bar the main steel hawser. The main computer would send an automatic retrieve command to the winches onboard the research ship so many metres above them.

Xander stretched out his hand and gently pushed down on the button. The smoothly milled, red anodised aluminium disc was cool to the touch. He left his hand there.

Outside, a burst of frothy white bubbles burst outwards from several points on the hull as the bell began to rise to the surface.

The diver, arms waving, eyes wide behind the thick plastic visor of his helmet, dropped away, his weights dragging him down, past the cradling ledge of coral, into the black abyss of the trench beyond the reef. He could drop his belt, of course. But then, as he'd explained at totally boring length in the safety briefing, he'd bob up to the surface like a cork out of a bottle where he'd die in agony from the bends.

Xander turned away and picked up the comms handset.

Poor Chuck. He'd get a hero's funeral. *After* Xander had made the announcement about Peacemaker.

71

They'd set out tables and chairs outside the *Café Cielo Azul* and placed Gabriel and Tara as the guests of honour with their backs to the door, looking out across the candlelit square.

Even though it was late, well past 11:00 p.m., all the village children able to stay awake were playing happily in the dust. Some chased chickens across the square. Others sat at the tables, pulling meat from chicken wings or sneaking sips from their parents' beers and guifiti.

A band played mariachi music and everywhere people danced.

Pera came and sat next to Gabriel. Her eyes glistened and, as she spoke, he realised she was drunk.

'Come and dance, Gabe. I love this song.'

He allowed her to pull him up from his chair, stumbling a little and realising that Pera wasn't the only one unsteady on her feet. To cheers from their neighbours, she led him out into the centre of the dancing.

As they arrived, the band switched seamlessly from an upbeat tune into something slower and slinkier, the Latin beat digging a groove deep enough to swallow a man whole.

'I don't know how to dance to this,' he said helplessly.

She grinned.

'It's easy. You put your hand here,' she placed his right hand on her left hip. 'And you hold my hand like this. No, this!' she laughed as he messed up the simple grip.

'Then what? I don't know any steps.'

'Just feel the music, Gabe. Don't be a stiff Englishman. You're part-Honduran now.'

So, concentrating hard on feeling the beat, which felt like a contradiction in terms, but there you were, he started to move in time with Pera. She was an excellent dancer, as, it appeared, was everyone over the age of eight in Santa Rosa. Without seeming to, or at least not too obviously, she led him through some basic steps, twirling away from him with just their fingertips touching, before coming back into a hold, each time a little closer until he could feel her breasts pressing against his ribcage.

He looked down at her face, which was upturned. Waiting.

Would it be so bad? Really? Her lips were parted. He knew what she wanted. Suddenly, he wanted very much to lose himself completely. Mentally, emotionally, physically. Yes, he had to find a way to stop Kalt getting his hands on the doomsday weapon. But right now he wanted – needed – to think about something else. Just for one night.

He bent his head and their lips met with an electric charge.

She wrapped her arms around him tightly and moaned softly as the kiss deepened.

Gabriel found the beat inside the music and let it penetrate his soul. And for the first time in a very long while, he began to relax.

72

By the time Kalt had depressurised, he was unable to stand still, much less sit down. Adrenaline was making him feel like every muscle, every bone was flooded with electricity.

He paced up and down in his rosewood-panelled state room while his mission director Angie Espinosa sat waiting for him to speak.

'Look, Angie, obviously it's bad news about Chuck,' he began. 'And in the fullness of time I will spring for a fuckin' great funeral. A really beautiful ceremony. Probably the most beautiful funeral ever in the diving world. But right now, I need you to focus.'

'On what, Skipper?' she asked. 'Without a diver, we're screwed.'

He spun round. Why was everyone always so negative?

'No. We are not screwed, Angela. I'll do the diving myself. I'll go into the sub and I'll find and recover Peacemaker. The plan stands.'

Her eyes widened.

'No offence, but you're not qualified. You can't.'

He turned to face her.

'If I could build Kaltium up from a single PC in my parents' garage, I'm pretty sure I can do this. And you're wrong. I am totally qualified to dive.'

'Yes, for shallow water scuba. But we both know you falsified part of your PADI records.'

Anger flared bright and hot in Xander's breast. How *dare* she?

'I falsified nothing!' he shouted, enjoying the way she flinched at the power of his voice. 'All I need is someone in the bell as my point man and we're good to go. So get everything ready and no more quibbling.'

She was shaking her head. Incredible. Actually defying him.

'Well, it won't be me. I'm not going down there to watch you commit suicide.'

He exerted his will and calmed his breathing. Just another of his amazing skills. Part of a bio-hacking system he could probably sell for millions if he could be bothered to take it to market.

'No, you're right. It won't be you. I've got someone else in mind.'

73

Gabriel woke from a dream in which he'd been dancing the tango naked in front of his old Sabre Squadron. Then someone close by cocked a rifle with a loud click.

He opened his eyes. His head was throbbing gently in time with his pulse. He turned to see Pera's face inches from his own. As she slept, her breath caught in her throat on each inhale with a soft click. That must have been the sound that infiltrated his dream.

The window smashed and something hard and metallic bounced off the bed frame and landed on the floor beside him. His unconscious mind took over, honed by years of training.

Grenade!

He flung back the covers and dived out of bed, smothering the lethal little bomb with his torso.

It detonated with an oddly quiet hiss. Thick white smoke enveloped him. He gasped for breath, drawing a great gust of the stuff deep into his lungs. It coated the back of his tongue. Acetone. Like rotting melons.

Gabriel rubbed his eyes and sat up in bed. What a nightmare! He turned to Pera, thinking to offer her coffee.

Pera was gone. So was his bedroom.

He was lying in a narrow cot, bolted to a metal wall studded with rivets and coated in thick, matte, pale-blue paint. The ceiling was low, and curved over his head. On the far side of the tiny room, a round-cornered, rectangular bulkhead door. Three sturdy-looking hinges, a plain metal handle, a circular porthole.

He stood. The floor seemed to undulate beneath his feet. The realisation hit him. He was onboard a ship.

He flashed on the nightmare. The grenade. The smoke. A gas canister hurled through his window. Not a nightmare, then. The perpetrator's identity. No thought required.

Xander Kalt.

But Gabriel was alive. So this must be yet another of the billionaire's obsessive attempts to bring Gabriel round to his side.

Nausea overwhelmed him as the floor pitched sharply and he turned, grabbed the plastic bucket placed beside the cot and emptied his stomach. The sharp smell of part-digested *baleadas* and too much guifiti made his eyes sting. He turned away, and rested his forehead against the cool metal wall.

What now?

74

More for form's sake than any realistic expectation of escape, Gabriel tried the door handle. It swung by a few degrees before stopping suddenly, jarring his wrist.

He returned to the bed to wait.

An hour passed.

A loud metallic ratcheting sound came from the door. The handle swung down, slowly, almost tentatively, as if whoever was on the other side had been told to expect fireworks.

Gabriel sat perfectly still. The time for blitz attacks was over. This was all about psychological tactics. For now.

Standing in the round-cornered doorway, Xander Kalt cut an unassuming figure. He wore a black baseball cap, a K in a circle embroidered in gold. A zip-up hoodie over a plain white T-shirt. Navy cotton chinos and black deck shoes.

'Hi, Gabe,' he said, diffidently. 'I brought you some tea. It's English breakfast. And some biscuits. That's what you Brits call cookies, right?'

He reached to his right and brought a tray into view. On it rested a black mug, also bearing the gold Kaltium logo, and a plate of digestive biscuits.

Gabriel reached for it, forcing Kalt to come into the little cabin.

'Thanks, Xander. I'm gasping.'

The Englishism was deliberate. If Kalt wanted to play at 'two nations separated by a common language' Gabriel would ace it.

Kalt frowned. He actually looked nervous, biting his lower lip.

'You're not mad at me?'

Gabriel took the mug from the tray and brought it to his lips. The tea was hot and, amazingly, delicious. He dunked one of the biscuits and ate it in two bites. Making Kalt wait for an answer was another small play in what promised to be a long battle.

'Why would I be mad? You gassed me in my own home in the middle of the night. Is Pera all right?'

'She's fine. She slept longer than she might have but the gas is a special formulation of my own. I minored in chemistry at Princeton. No lasting side-effects.'

'Good. Because I'd have had to kill you otherwise.'

Gabriel smiled to let Kalt know he was joking.

The laugh, when it came, carried an edge of anxiety. Was Kalt actually scared of him?

'But we're cool now, right?'

This was bizarre. Like some kind of courtship. Gabriel played along. He patted the hard mattress.

'Come and sit by me. I have questions.'

Kalt's mouth screwed over to one side. 'You're not going to do some evil SAS shit on me, are you? I mean, I know I could be dead already but you won't get off the ship without my OK, so you ought to at least hear me out.'

Gabriel held up the index and middle fingers of his left hand. 'Scout's honour. Now sit.'

Kalt complied, putting the tray on the metal floor at their feet. This close, Gabriel could smell his aftershave and a strange vegetal odour, like freshly-chopped salad leaves.

'Ask your questions, Gabe. I promise I'll do my best to answer them all.'

'Why me?'

Peacemaker

Kalt furrowed his brow. He looked genuinely puzzled.

'What do you mean?'

'You had Mason. You had the lawyer, Packard. I assume a man like you can afford the best in the world in every field. Yet you keep coming after me. I want to know why.'

Kalt snickered quietly.

'I had to let Lorne go. Permanently. And you gave George his papers yourself. I was impressed with your little stealth attack, by the way. Kinda sorry I missed out on the action.'

'Yeah, sorry about that. But he was trying to kill me and my sister. Whom you kidnapped by the way.'

'Yes, and I'm sorry, too. If there'd been any other way, you have to believe I'd have taken it. As for George, forget it. He was useful for a while. But he had his chance – no wait, chances, plural – and he blew them. I don't tolerate failure in myself, Gabe, and I certainly don't tolerate it in others.'

'I'm just an ex-soldier. How do you know I'll do better?'

'You're being modest, Gabe. I know you better than you know yourself. I researched you when you first popped up on my radar screen. Not literally. Radar's such a bogus technology. Legacy tech is going the way of linear TV and paper books. But using some stuff I developed myself, I researched the shit out of you. We're literally like twins. The way we see the world? Our backgrounds? Yours in Hong Kong, learning at the feet of Zhao Xi? And then serving your country. Me forging my own path without any help from anyone? OK, so I didn't serve. But I wanted to! I really did! And I'd have been brilliant. I'd have led totally beautiful missions. Believe me, with my natural aptitude for strategy plus off-the-charts levels of courage, I'd have got the Silver Star for sure. Loads of other medals. 9/11? Never would have happened on my watch.'

Gabriel tried to avoid shaking his head in disbelief. The last person he'd met who came anywhere close to Kalt's level of self-delusion was a cult leader named Christophe Jardin. But he'd turned out to be a dyed-in-the-wool gangster-capitalist, whose interests were of the basest and most mercenary kind.

'So why didn't you?' he asked.

'In the end I realised the world needed my intellectual talents. I sacrificed my own desire to serve for the greater good. But that's the brilliant thing about this plan, Gabe,' he said, raising his voice excitedly. 'Instead of fighting wars, we'll end them. Together.'

'With Peacemaker.'

'Yes! With the weapon my great-grandfather developed. We are this close,' he held up thumb and forefinger a millimetre apart. 'The *Ozersk* is about forty metres directly below us. She's waiting for us, Gabe. You and me. You turned me down before. But when you see what's down there, I swear to you on all that's holy, you'll thank me for inviting you to be a part of this.'

And that was when Gabriel realised. Kalt simply couldn't bear being told 'No'. He pictured a spoiled brat in a private school uniform somewhere in Manhattan's Upper East Side. Doting parents who indulged his every whim. How he'd fly into a tantrum at the merest whisper of that forbidden word. The man was a sociopath. A clever sociopath with a talent for developing technologies at the right time. But a sociopath all the same.

He turned to face Kalt, uncomfortably close on the narrow cot. Tried to avoid inhaling that odd vegetal aroma.

'What's the plan?'

'You're in?'

'Of course I'm in! You don't think I'd pass up an opportunity to literally change the course of history, do you?'

Kalt's eyes were bright. He was nodding furiously.

'You won't regret it, Gabe. I promise you that. There's just one small thing I need to ask you. You can dive, right?'

'Absolutely. If you researched my record you'll know I'm qualified.'

'Awesome! Me too!'

As Kalt began talking, speaking rapidly and seemingly forgetting to breath except for the odd punctuating gasp, Gabriel started formulating a plan of his own.

75

It turned out that between Kalt's first attempt to retrieve Peacemaker and this one, Kalt had changed his mind several times about the best way to reach the sub.

His mission director, a stern-faced Latina called Angie Espinosa, explained the latest idea to Gabriel over breakfast.

'Xander found out about this company in France. They make state-of-the-art deep-diving equipment,' she said, arrowing a bladed hand from the tabletop down towards the floor of the mess. 'They're developing a new gas combination and a specialised suit that means you can go deeper for longer without days-long depressurisation. Xander bought two and flew them down here on one of his jets.'

'And when you say, "developing", they're fully tested, yes? I mean otherwise how would he get his hands on them?'

Her habitual scowl deepened, grooving deep lines each side of her mouth.

'No. They're prototypes. They've tested them in the Med, but everything beyond standard dive depths has been done with modelling software. Have a guess whose?'

The penny dropped. 'Kaltium's?'

'Exactly.'

'Shit.'

She fixed him with a green-eyed gaze.

'You're going down to the kind of depths that can kill professional divers, Gabriel. In a rig nobody knows anything about.'

'But Xander's using it, too.'

She looked around, but they had the mess to themselves. The rest of the crew were on deck, prepping the dive equipment.

Still she lowered her voice to a conspiratorial murmur.

'My opinion? He's insane. You know why he wants it, right?'

'Yes.'

'You think it'll work?'

'No.'

Her eyes flashbulbed.

'Then why are you doing it?'

'I could ask you the same question.'

'Me? Oldest reason in the book.' She rubbed her thumb and forefinger together. 'I'm underwater on my mortgage – no pun intended – and I lost my livelihood when Katrina struck. I was struggling to make ends meet when Xander appeared like the money fairy saying I was the best salvage captain on the eastern seaboard and did I want to help him make history.'

He regarded her for several seconds, trying to determine whether to bring her into his confidence.

'So you don't buy his messiah complex?'

She fished inside the collar of her shirt and brought out a gold crucifix on a fine chain.

'I know who my saviour is. And it sure as shit isn't Xander Kalt.'

'I have my reasons for helping him,' Gabriel said quietly.

'Yeah? Well I hope one of them's to stop him. He's going to get someone killed before long. I mean this whole plan's got more holes in it than a trawl net. How's he even going to get this thing working? It'll be corroded or rusted the fuck away, or damaged when the sub went down.'

He leaned his head towards hers.

'If you help me get down there, I'll help you get away clean. Who's your contract with, him or the company?'

'Kaltium.'

'Good. They'll honour it. Look, there's something I need you to do. And then, maybe you should show me these diving suits.'

76

Gabriel took the five multi-coloured capsules Angie was holding out to him in her cupped palm: two were pink and green, two were black and yellow, one was all gold.

He swallowed them down with water from a fresh bottle he'd watched her crack the seal on. That represented excessive, if not redundant, zeal for his own safety, given Kalt could have killed him multiple times since gassing him back in Santa Rosa.

'They'll alter your blood chemistry for the next twelve to eighteen hours,' she said. 'Supposed to negate the risk of nitrogen narcosis and decompression sickness.'

He didn't care for that 'supposed'. But it was far too late to turn back now.

'Tip your head over,' she said.

'Why?'

'I have to administer an injection.'

'Can't you do it into my arm?'

'Not according to the protocol that came with the suits.' She sighed. 'We doing this or what?'

Gabriel forced himself to relax, despite hating the idea of a long metal needle probing among major blood vessels like the jugular vein and the carotid artery.

She placed cool fingers against the skin and applied counter-tension to stretch it tight where the needle would go in.

'You might feel a pinch,' she said.

'Fuck!' he grunted, gritting his teeth as what felt like a meat skewer punctured the skin. His entire neck turned ice-cold as Angie depressed the plunger. As the hypo emptied its cocktail of drugs into his system right next door to his brain stem, he saw tiny red lights spark into life in the centre of his vision. He smelled ozone, like after a lightning storm. Light-headed, too.

'Thith ithn righ'.' His tongue felt huge in his mouth. Why couldn't he speak? What was happening? 'Dop!'

Angie's face swam into view right in front of him. Her eyes were enormous and cartoony, giant black pupils in oval whites stretched up to her hairline.

'Breathe,' she said. 'You have to breathe. Deep. In-out. Come on. Do it with me, Gabriel.'

It seemed like the stupidest thing, taking orders from a cute Latina Disney character, but he complied anyway. Slowly, his vision returned to normal. The smell of electrical discharge faded. The world shuddered and snapped back into pin-sharp resolution. He smelled diesel oil, sea water.

'What the fuck was that?'

'You all right, Gabe?'

He looked sideways. Kalt was grinning at him. Fucking lunatic.

'Quite the rush, huh? Listen, don't worry. We're protected now. Those Frenchies have developed bleeding-edge biopharmaceutical technology. I'm a major investor.'

Gabriel turned away. Angie was beckoning him over to a rack where his diving suit hung.

Compared to the flexible wetsuits he'd used before it looked more like something for exploring outer space than the depths of the sea. Bulbous-jointed sections of yellow plastic moved over each other around black ball-joints.

It took Angie and an assistant thirty-five minutes to assemble the suit around him. Closing the seals alone took ten.

Gabriel took a step forward and immediately stumbled as the squared-off toe of one of the weighted boots caught on the deck. Strong arms grasped him. The burly crew members on either side righted him and gave him a slap on the back.

'Try again,' one said.

He lifted his right foot, feeling every gramme of the seventy-kilo suit, and planted it down with a clonk on the wooden deck. Another. Gradually he got the feel of it and made it over to the electric hoist where Angie stood ready to load the rebreather onto his back. She'd explained it weighed another thirty kilos. Punishing on land – or deck – but weightless underwater.

He'd be breathing a proprietary blend of oxygen, helium and 'a couple other gases you don't need to know about' according to Kalt, who was currently undergoing a similar fit-out a few metres away.

Gabriel braced his legs as Angie hoisted the rebreather onto his back. As its weight settled on his shoulders his knees still sagged a little. It was like having a safe strapped to him.

'Helmet next,' Angie said. 'You ready?'

The helmet was all planes and angles. More thick yellow plastic, bristling with stubby black rubber transmitter masts, video cameras, circular seals, and depth-activated lights. And a curved visor in which he saw a miniature version of himself, an obese wasp, waiting to be closed off from the outside world.

She lowered the bulky construction over his head and settled it into the neck ring. One by one, she closed the seals with a series of dull clacks. His head was jerked around a little as she attached the gas pipes to the back of the helmet. A distant hum filled his ears and he inhaled as she'd told him to, drawing the first breath of the gas mixture into his lungs. It tasted vaguely metallic, but within a few breaths that had faded. There was too much else to concentrate on.

Like hanging onto the yellow and black thruster Angie handed him. They'd practised operating them beside the ship, but now they were doing it for real. The controls were deliberately oversized to allow for the restricted movements of the suit's gloves. He gripped it firmly and placed his thumbs over the large red control buttons.

One after the other, the two men were lifted up and over the side of the boat on an electric hoist with a swinging boom.

As the water closed over Gabriel's head he took another deep breath of the gas mixture. He turned his head, an oddly effortful move in the constraining bulk of the suit.

Beside him, Kalt's bulbous form dropped into the water. Gabriel raised his thumb and finger and made a 'C', as near to the 'OK' sign as the gloves would allow. Kalt responded in kind. A hum filled Gabriel's helmet as the winch began paying out line and his descent towards the *Ozersk* began.

Somewhere, forty metres below his weighted boots, lay a weapon of such immense power its creator had shot himself rather than live with the knowledge of what he'd done.

And Gabriel's only task was to prevent it falling into the hands of Professor Kaltrov's great-grandson.

The waters darkened.

77

The first sharks appeared at the twenty-metre mark.

A pair of hammerheads, their crazily distorted heads a tribute to the mysteries of evolution. Or God after dropping acid, your choice.

They circled the two divers, one even coming close enough to bump its flattened snout against the belly of Gabriel's suit. It flicked its long, scythe-like tail and darted away, apparently unhappy about the hard plastic interloper to its domain.

Protected by the suit, Gabriel felt no fear, just an intense sense of wonder as he caught the shark's eye on the right side of its wide, flattened head. Its partner moved in next, but this time there was no gentle exploration. A fast sweep of its tail and open-mouthed pass directly in front of him that did set Gabriel's pulse jumping.

'You OK, Gabe?' Kalt asked over the intercom. 'I think she likes you.'

'I'm fine.'

'Look behind you. You've got more company.'

Gabriel paddled himself in a half-turn by swinging his arms.

He wasn't ready to use the thruster yet, and Angie had instructed them both to wait until they were within sight of the sub.

Emerging like ghosts from the gloom, three deep-bellied sharks were approaching the slowly descending pair. Gabriel recognised them from the pale, mottled ends of their fins. White tips. According to the safety briefing Angie had run through with them, among the most dangerous of the Caribbean sharks.

They were big. He estimated their length from snout to tail at eight to ten feet. And unlike the hammerheads, their mouths were both wide and easily placed to take chunks out of people in the water.

Angie kept the line paying out, so as the sharks approached him and Kalt, swimming lazy circles and figure-eights between them, the light continued to dim. Soon, the ever-shifting streaks of sunlight that illuminated divers and sharks alike faded until the water assumed a deep-cerulean hue in which the sharks vanished until they rolled into their turns, exposing pale bellies.

Gabriel kept his breathing steady and tried to stay calm, reminding himself that the suit encasing him was designed to withstand extremes of pressure higher than the pressure exerted even by a Great White's jaws.

He did not find the thought comforting.

The three sharks turned in unison and swam off, their powerful tails creating turbulence that set his suit shifting laterally, producing a momentary sense of nausea.

His helmet lights came on automatically, triggered by the dive depth sensors. He felt better being able to see clearly, although all the illumination revealed were particles eddying crazily in the subsurface currents.

Out of nowhere, a torpedo-like shape rocketed straight at him. He had no time to react before the white tip banged into his visor, jaws open so wide he had a terrifying sight of the ridged interior of its mouth. For one horrifying moment, as he came eye-to-eye with it, he thought the shark had cracked the visor. Visions of water flooding in and drowning him crowded out rational thought and he screamed.

Then the shark broke off its attack and hurled itself at Kalt, rocking his suit over by thirty degrees.

Over the intercom, Gabriel heard Kalt's oddly emotionless voice.

'Fuck off, you dope. Don't you get it? This suit's impact resistant. You'll only hurt yourself. Go on, git!' he added in a cod western accent.

Maybe the white tip understood him. Maybe it realised it wasn't going to get to the meat of this vast yellow crustacean. Either way, it rolled away and streaked off into the darkness.

Slowly Gabriel's pulse settled. He looked down. Somewhere in the gloom, beyond the toes of his yellow boots, he thought he detected a darker shape. Was this it? Had they found the sub?

He looked left and right, scanning for recognisable features. Yes. As the metres ticked off, its outline sharpened. It was huge. Maybe it was technically classed as a small boat, but down here, it looked enormous, like a dead whale, drowned underwater.

Forty-seven seconds later his boots clonked down onto the hull of Soviet research boat, Kashalot-class, *Ozersk*. The helmet mic picked up the contact – a dull clang – then two more, fainter this time, as Kalt landed a few metres away from him, closer to the conning tower.

Kalt gave the OK, then turned and activated his thruster. Heading for the conning tower. Gabriel depressed the thrust button on his own unit and his feet lifted free as its powerful motor pulled him over the surface of the sub.

The circular hatch was open. The captain must had blown it at the last minute. A desperate, hopeless attempt to save his crew when he realised all other options were exhausted. What a horrible way to die. Forced to choose between suffocating in a metal coffin, drowning in open water or becoming shark food.

Kalt interrupted his morbid imaginings.

'Come on, Gabe. We're going in.'

He followed Kalt as he rose up and then angled his thruster downwards towards the waiting hatchway.

Gabriel did not suffer from claustrophobia. Tight squeezes,

metaphorical and literal, had been very much the order of the day on many ops in the SAS. Had he been a sufferer, being locked into a plastic, body-shaped coffin, albeit a jointed one with a window to see out of, would have been bad enough. But compared to the tight squeeze as he descended, head-first, into the submarine's narrow conning tower, it would have felt like a walk on a prairie.

His shoulders kept banging on the walls, which ran with pipes and riveted joints between the steel plates. At one point his cable snagged on a protruding piece of metal and he had to back up, no easy exercise in a three-foot wide tunnel, to free it.

Eventually he found himself in the sub's control room. There was more room to move about but now there were seats, the periscope and chart tables to navigate around.

He encountered the first skeleton on the floor behind what must have been the captain's chair. It still wore the peaked cap and uniform of the Soviet navy, although the cloth had largely disintegrated, revealing disarticulated ribs and a sagging spinal column. Scavengers had picked it clean decades ago, and the bleached-white bones looked more like a medical exhibit than the frame of a once-living human being.

As he moved cautiously through the space, more skeletons came into view. He counted twenty-three. Maybe the crew had decided collectively to face death together, down here, in the boat they'd have called 'she' rather than leave for certain death and die alone.

'I honour your lives,' he murmured.

'What was that?' Kalt quacked into the intercom.

'Nothing. Did your great-grandfather say where Peacemaker was stored?'

'No. We have to find it for ourselves. I bet you a thousand bucks I find it before you.'

What was wrong with him? Forty metres down, in a dead submarine full of corpses, he wanted to bet over childish competitions.

Gabriel ignored him and moved on.

Where would the captain have kept Peacemaker? Professor

Kaltrov had been curiously vague about Peacemaker's technical specs, preferring to indulge a very Russian appetite for lushly romantic language exploring the very worst things that could happen. But it wasn't a missile or any kind of warhead.

Gabriel had formed the distinct impression they were looking for a suitcase-sized item. Some sort of dirty bomb was his best guess, although that didn't really square with the apocalyptic terms Kaltrov had used to describe its effects.

Then he heard five words that chilled him to his core.

'Gabe! Buddy? I found it!'

78

Gabriel manoeuvred himself around in the tight space and used the thruster to pull him through the narrow waist of the sub to Kalt's location.

He found him in a small room off the main corridor. Lying on a metal table before him was an olive-green steel container about the size of a weekend suitcase.

What the hell could fit inside such a small space and have such devastating effects? Maybe it wasn't a dirty bomb at all. Could it be a gas of some kind? Gabriel knew the Soviets had invested heavily in developing all kinds of chemical, biological and nerve agents. Maybe this was the ultimate iteration of that deadly process.

Whatever it was, it would have to be capable of spreading its effects at least continent-wide for it to work as the ultimate chip in the geopolitical poker game where ten million lives were table stakes.

Kalt stood reverently in front of it, his blocky yellow helmet angled down so he could gaze rapturously at his latest acquisition.

Gabriel moved closer, standing beside the billionaire so he

could see what was stencilled in yellow paint onto the upper surface.

Just a single word.

Миротворец

Peacemaker. And a crude graphic: a skull and crossbones.

The case had a handle on the side. Kalt slipped the fat fingers of his right glove through it and clutched it tight before dragging it off the table. It sank slowly through the water before coming to rest, bouncing gently off his leg.

'Time to go,' Kalt said, his voice alive despite the flattening effect of the helmet's comms module. 'We did it. Oh and, Gabe?'

'Yes?'

'I trust you. You know that right?'

'I do.'

'But, anyways, I'm going to need to keep sending the ship a series of pre-agreed codewords on the ascent. If I miss one out or give one out of sequence, or stop transmitting completely, Angie's under orders to cut us both loose.'

'No need, Xander. I've got your back. Let's just hope the sharks have gone.'

Together the two men eased the suitcase-sized weapon through the sub's narrow corridors, up through the conning tower and out through the hatch, back into the open water.

Their helmet lamps projected tight white cones into the dark waters that pressed in on all sides. A fleet of tiny luminescent squid flitted away as the beams caught them.

Kalt raised his free arm and extended a pointing hand directly above his head.

Gabriel nodded.

Somehow he had to get Peacemaker away from Kalt. But he needed Kalt alive to give the sequence of codewords or he'd die down here, the twenty-fourth body to lie among the ruined hopes of a once-great empire.

79

Breathing steadily, as Angie had advised in the pre-dive briefing, Gabriel kept Kalt in his eyeline all the way to the surface.

No sharks this time. Just a school of silver, torpedo-shaped kingfish that came to investigate the two bulky yellow and black creatures swimming up through their part of the water column.

After twenty minutes, bright sunlight began arrowing down through the water, dappling the surfaces of their suits with bright yellow spots. A dark shape loomed over them: the ship's hull.

Angie's voice came over the intercom.

'You guys OK?'

'OK?' Kalt said. 'We're fucking fantastic.'

'I'm good,' Gabriel added.

'Good job. You both surface then I'll send the sling in. You first, Gabriel. Then you, Xander.'

'Why him?' Kalt sounded petulant. 'It should be me.'

'I've got the videographer standing by, Xander. You'll look better without Gabriel in the background.'

The comms went silent for a moment.

Gabriel looked across the five metres of water at Kalt, his

right hand clutching the handle of the Peacemaker crate. The man's ego was the size of Manhattan. He'd bite. He had to.

'Yes. Get Gabriel out of the water first. No need for any film of him. Tell the video guy to wait till I'm ready.'

'Aye, aye, skipper.'

Gabriel's helmet broke the surface. The white hull of the ship loomed over him. The sling attached to the hoist splashed down next to him. A crewman in Bermudas jumped in after it and swam around Gabriel like a pilot fish beside a shark, looping the webbing around his arms and legs. When the sling was secure the motor hummed, sending vibrations down through the rope, webbing and into Gabriel's plastic suit.

Turning gently in the air, he rose from the water and swung over the side and onto the deck. Angie left the two men flanking her and came over to him. She raised a hand and they bumped fists. Then she unhooked him from the sling and sent it over the side again to collect Kalt. And Peacemaker.

While Angie loosed the webbing straps around him, the men who'd been standing with her went to look over the side. She moved on to his helmet, unsnapping the seals and finally lifting it off him.

He took a huge gulp of fresh air, relishing the almost perfumed aroma of sea salt and ship's grease. He didn't think he'd ever smelled anything so sweet or so welcome.

The hoist operator – a woman – swung Kalt over the side to deposit him on the deck right between the two men who'd watched his ascent.

'You OK, Gabriel?' Angie asked.

'Yeah. And, Angie? Thanks.'

'No problem.'

She got him out of his suit, then left him and went over to Kalt, running through the same precise sequence of movements to detach his helmet from the neck ring on his suit. As soon as she lifted the bulbous contraption clear he swung his head between the two men who'd been flanking Angie, the hoist operator and three others armed with assault rifles.

'Who the fuck are these people?' Kalt demanded, wild-eyed. 'Where's José and the rest of my crew? And where's my fuckin' videographer?'

'I'll explain in a minute, Xander,' she said, removing the suit in its predetermined sequence of sections until he was standing there in a pair of swimming trunks, still gripping the Peacemaker crate.

The six people who'd brought them onboard were all dressed alike. Dark-blue short-sleeved shirts with epaulettes. Blue trousers. Black boots. Each had a neat rectangular name-badge sewn above the left breast pocket.

One of the men walked over to Kalt. He was dark-skinned. His epaulettes each bore two gold stars.

'*Buenos dias, Señor Kalt*. Allow me to introduce myself. My name is Captain Ibrahim Sandoval, of the Cuban Revolutionary Navy.' He pointed astern where a sleek grey warship sat a few hundred metres away. 'That is my ship. She is a Rio Damuji-class frigate.'

'I don't give a flying fuck who you are!' Kalt exploded. 'But you should know I'm Xander Kalt. And I want you off my ship. And where the fuck are my crew?'

The Cuban captain drew his pistol and pointed it in Kalt's face, making him choose between stepping back or standing there with its muzzle denting his nose. He stepped back.

'Your crew are under arrest. *You* are under arrest. And *that*,' he nodded at the olive-green case in Kalt's right hand, 'is now the property of the Cuban government.'

Gabriel looked down as someone gripped his right forearm. It was one of the Cuban sailors. Clearly, they weren't taking any chances. Angie had been similarly restrained. Nothing too aggressive, but the Cubans didn't need to be, given they had all the guns, not to mention a ship equipped with enough heavy weaponry to send the research ship to the bottom.

Kalt dropped to his knees and levered open the catches on the green steel casing. He was muttering to himself, much to the Cubans' amusement.

'No fuckin' way. You tangled with the wrong guy. Just you wait and see.'

He wrestled the lid open and pulled out an aluminium case about the size of an office inkjet printer. He stood, and brandished it at the Cuban captain.

'Back, the fuck, off,' he said. 'Throw your weapons over the side or I will annihilate you. I will destroy you, your ship, your whole country. I will rain down hell!'

Gabriel looked on, amazed. Kalt had lost it. He was literally staring down the barrel of a gun, and there were plenty of others now being unshouldered and pointed in his direction. How could he even think of opening that case, let alone threatening to detonate Peacemaker? His breath caught in his throat and a chill ran through him. If Kalt was insane, that was *precisely* the sort of thing he could do.

To hell with everyone, to hell with the world. It was like watching a toddler being given the nuclear codes.

The Cubans all burst out laughing. The captain holstered his pistol, stepped back and folded his arms.

'With that, *Señor Kalt*?' He shrugged. 'Go on, then.'

Kalt grinned, a cockeyed expression that reinforced the notion in Gabriel's mind that the billionaire was deranged.

'Fine.'

He opened the case. His eyes widened and his mouth dropped open.

Gabriel craned his neck to see what had so shocked Kalt. And then he smiled.

80

Kalt emitted a strange noise. Somewhere between a cry and a cough.

He looked at Gabriel. His eyes were wild, flicking left and right. His face seemed unsure what expression it should be bearing. Gabriel detected puzzlement, rage, horror. Fleeting signals of the emotions crowding in on Kalt one after the other, each barging to the front of the queue to have its voice heard.

The man was clearly unable to mentally process what he'd just seen. His brows drew together and he shook his head.

He looked down again, at the contents of the sleek aluminium case.

'No, no, no. It can't be. Where is it?' He glanced over at Gabriel again. He was shaking. 'This isn't right. What the fuck did you do? Where is it? Where's Peacemaker? Where's my fuckin' weapon?'

He reached in and took hold of the object inside the case, holding it up, dropping the case onto the deck with a sharp clang.

The Cubans guffawed.

'He's going to write a letter to the president!' one cried.

The object in Kalt's hands was painted a dull, flat shade of grey. On the front a metal logo, riveted to the metal frame, read *MOCKBA*. In English, 'Moscow'.

Below the logo, stubby plastic keys were arranged in four rows. They bore, on their upper surfaces, numbers, punctuation marks and Cyrillic characters. Above the logo, a roller, ink ribbon and carriage return lever.

Poleaxed, Kalt dropped the Soviet-era portable typewriter to the deck. A piece of paper fluttered free from the underside of the typewriter. The captain bent to retrieve it.

He straightened. 'It's in Russian.'

'I speak Russian,' Gabriel said. 'Let me read it out for you.'

The captain handed him the note. Gabriel scanned it then, finally understanding the grim irony of the situation and the events of the preceding few weeks, began reading.

'My name is Vladimir Kaltrov. I am the senior research scientist and developer on the Peacemaker project. This weapon is a crime against humanity. A nightmare. I cannot allow it to exist. I have destroyed it and all our records. I intend to end my life now rather than face torture when Comrade Andropov discovers my betrayal. I hope whoever discovers this will understand one thing. The only hope for mankind lies in words, not weapons.'

Gabriel caught a sudden movement in the corner of his eye. By the time he'd looked up, Kalt had darted forwards, punched the Cuban captain in the face and snatched his pistol. Seemingly at the same time, he stuck his arm out, fired three shots at point-blank range into his body and then hurled himself sideways and dived off the deck.

The remaining Cubans snapped to their senses and rushed to the side and began shooting down into the water, while Angie bent to the wounded Cuban and tried to stem the bleeding. The noise of the assault rifles was deafening. Kalt had vanished below the surface.

Gabriel grabbed a knife from a fish box. The man whose insane greed for power had cost Sparrow, Violeta and others their lives would not escape justice this time.

81

Filling his lungs, Gabriel plunged over the side and into the water. Above his head, bullets lanced down through the water, leaving trails of bubbles like white spears.

Without the bulk of the dive suit, he felt fishlike in his ability to twist and kick sharply down after Kalt.

Kalt was ten feet down, his back striped by the rays of sunlight penetrating the crystal clear water. He was kicking strongly, though where he thought he was going baffled Gabriel.

It didn't matter. Kalt was going to pay for the havoc he'd unleashed on the people of Santa Rosa and the friends Gabriel had brought from England to protect them.

Stroking strongly, Gabriel chased down after Kalt. He entered a stream of cold water that shocked him before the temperature jumped back up. Kalt looked over his shoulder. Eyes wide, he doubled up as if in pain. Then he lashed out his feet, knocking Gabriel's left hand aside just as he made a grab for Kalt.

The adrenaline that had powered Gabriel's dive and descent now made its presence felt in his lungs, as they ran through the last remaining oxygen. Kalt would have to follow suit, or drown, so Gabriel kicked up to the surface and gulped down a breath. No shots: Angie must have convinced the Cubans to hold their fire.

As he turned, ready to submerge again, Kalt surfaced right beside him. His mouth wide open, he drew in a huge breath and duck-dived before Gabriel could get to him.

Still gripping the knife, Gabriel upended and kicked out strongly, following Kalt's trail of bubbles. Dark shapes cruised just at the edge of his vision.

He caught Kalt by the left ankle. But as he brought the knife up, Kalt parried the blow and then grabbed his right wrist. Kalt was strong, and they tussled in the churning water, each trying to gain an advantage over the other.

Lungs bursting, Gabriel stabbed out the fingers of his left hand, aiming for Kalt's eyes. He missed, as Kalt jerked his head back. Then Kalt pulled himself towards Gabriel, using his grip on Gabriel's right wrist as leverage. He jammed the fingers of his other hand into Gabriel's throat then withdrew them before lancing them out in a grip designed to crush his windpipe.

Gabriel desperately needed another breath. His vision grew spotty as dark clouds gathered in his vision. His pulse roared in his ears as he drew his knees up to try and dislodge Kalt. With a convulsive arch of his back he got his knees between their torsos and shoved outwards with every last remaining ounce of his strength. It was enough to break Kalt's grip. But Gabriel was still on the point of losing consciousness.

The dark shapes grew larger, more definite, as he fought to keep his mouth closed and not give into the panic. His brain was shrieking an insistent alarm. It needed oxygen and any moment now was going to triggersharks the age-old reflex to breathe, underwater or not.

Kalt was lunging towards him, mouth stretched wide in triumph, bubbles leaking from his nostrils. His clawed hands were coming for Gabriel's eyes. Gabriel had one final chance. He had to take it or drown.

He closed his eyes, and forced himself to go limp.

As Kalt hit him, he simply allowed his head to move

backwards under the water-baffled impact. Kalt swam above him and in that moment, Gabriel, weakened almost to the point of defeat, raised his right fist and let Kalt's own momentum drag his exposed chest over the point of Gabriel's knife.

A long wound unzipped from Kalt's sternum down to his navel. A red cloud blossomed obscenely into the water as the blade sliced into the superficial blood vessels just beneath the skin. Kalt clamped his hands over the long wound, but he had already lost.

Gabriel fell away, rolling onto his back and kicking for the surface.

The sharks that had been tracking them moved closer. Their upper surfaces were dark, their lower, greenish grey. Some had beautiful mottled stripes on their flanks. Other, white tips to the dorsal fins.

One had a wide, flat head that protruded grotesquely on each side.

The hammerhead made a complete circuit around Kalt's flailing form before lunging in, rolling onto its side and hitting him hard in the belly. Kalt's arms and legs splayed as the shark thrashed, before departing with a chunk of flesh in its jaws. Blood issued forth in great cloudy gouts, staining the water a deep scarlet.

A tiger shark, twelve feet long at least, moved in next, its striped flanks curving. The huge predator arrowed in before ramming its gaping, tooth-ringed jaws into Kalt's midsection. A stream of silvery bubbles burst from Kalt's mouth as his panicked eyes locked onto Gabriel's.

The last sight Gabriel had of Xander Kalt was his face disappearing behind the greyish flank of an onrushing white tip. And then vanishing in a red cloud of his own blood and viscera.

More sharks joined the feeding frenzy, streamlined missiles intent on claiming their own share of the booty. With his last remaining strength, Gabriel kicked away from the roiling mass of predators as they reduced Xander Kalt to so many scraps of flesh drifting in the currents of the Caribbean.

His head broke the surface just as he was on the point of blacking out. Two Cuban sailors hauled Gabriel aboard the research ship by his unresisting arms.

He collapsed onto the deck, gasping for breath, then spewed a thin stream of seawater onto the planking. Through the oval scuppers he saw pink foam boiling on the surface of the water.

Behind him he heard a pistol slide being racked.

'Señor Wolfe. You are under arrest. Stand up.'

82

Gabriel and Angie were transferred to the Cubans' ship.

From there, they were taken to Havana and thence to the basement cells of the headquarters of the National Revolutionary Police Force.

The Cubans were puzzled by Gabriel's lack of ID. The fact he spoke to them in Cubano, the Cuban dialect of Spanish further confused them, although it did mean he could at least try to negotiate his freedom.

Thankfully, Angie, as an American citizen, not only had ID, she also had a hotline to the American embassy in Havana.

After talking to Angie at length, and relaying the details of their conversation to the Director of the CIA, the American ambassador in Havana held urgent talks with Cuba's ministers of justice, foreign affairs, defence and public health.

He laid out the potentially devastating impact on Cuba had Kalt actually secured and detonated the real Peacemaker. And encouraged them to see the actions of Angie Espinosa and the Britisher Gabriel Wolfe as those of friends of Cuba.

In the end, and thanks to corroborating testimony from the Cuban sailors who'd captured Kalt's research ship, the minsters agreed. Word reached the Havana chief of police, and Gabriel and Angie were duly released after paying a nominal fine of 23.95 Cuban pesos – one dollar – each.

Angie opted to return to New Orleans, and Gabriel was put on a flight to Tegucigalpa.

At the airport, having taken possession of their tickets, they stood facing each other, surrounded by Cuban security at a discreet distance of three feet.

'Well that was intense,' Angie said.

Then she cracked up. Gabriel followed suit, the two of them laughing madly under the baffled looks of the black-clad heavies.

'Goodbye, Angie,' Gabriel said. 'I hope your next voyage is slightly less stressful.'

She frowned. Then smiled. 'Oh. That's British irony, right?'

'Something like that.'

'I hope you make it home OK. Goodbye, Gabriel.'

They hugged awkwardly, it was hard to be natural when three armed internal security agents are watching you like hawks. Then parted and headed off to their respective departure gates. He spent the wait staring out of the huge plate-glass windows. On the horizon, the mountain tops were shrouded in grey cloud that rolled in towards Havana.

Half an hour later, as his plane taxied down towards the end of the runway, Gabriel took a last look at Cuban soil. But deep down, he felt a troubling lack of enthusiasm for returning to Honduras.

What did he have there, really?

83

Festival candles flickered in the windows of the houses facing the square. Strings of multicoloured lights looped between the houses, rising to TV aerials on roofs or the flagpole in the centre, before arcing gracefully to their next stop. A band comprising guitars, drums and double bass thrummed out a driving, drum-heavy Honduran dance beat called punta.

People drank heavily from plastic flagons of guifiti, swigged from bottles of the local beer, or sucked brightly coloured fruit drinks through straws.

The air was heavy with perfume, both natural from the garlands of flowers mounded on the long trestle tables groaning with food, and as applied to the pulse points of the village women, who laughed, danced and sang along to the punta beats.

The men were no slouches either, having switched from farming or fishing clothes into suits that, if not quite the latest cut, made up for their lack of timeliness with swagger and bright colours.

Pera had cooked all the previous day, aided by her former workmates at Frida's. Now trestle tables were crowded with earthenware bowls heaped with tortillas, rice and beans, or filled to the brim with rich meat stews. Barbecued beef ribs and *baleadas* stuffed with chicken, beans and guacamole jostled for table space with whole grilled kingfish and the giant prawns called sea rabbits.

Gabriel was dancing with Pera and Tara, taking turns to swing them round as they held coconut shells filled with a local cocktail mix high above their heads.

As he danced, he scanned the square, unable to fully relax. Alert for dark-clad figures, warning shapes like long narrow tubes, the glint of light of steel. As he swung away from Pera his heart jittered in his chest. Standing on the far side of the square were two men in British army camouflage. One black, one white. Smudge. And Sparrow.

He shook his head. And repeated a new mantra. Not real, not real, not real, not real.

'You all right, Gabe?' Pera shouted close to his ear.

'I'm fine. Just tired.'

'Tired?' She widened her eyes comically. 'You cannot be tired! This is fiesta! It's early. Only two o'clock.'

But suddenly Gabriel Wolfe *was* tired. In fact, 'tired' would have been a relief. 'Tired' he could have coped with. Danced it off. Drunk it off. Found someone who'd make him a coffee. He was exhausted. And not just from the events of the previous few weeks.

Ever since the Cubans had put him on the plane in Havana, a feeling had been settling over him like the cloud drifting in towards the airport from the mountains. He was running. But the thing he was running from? Was it 'out there'? Or was it 'in here'? He massaged his chest, where an ache had settled over his heart.

Someone spoke close to his ear. Raspy, papery, seemingly bypassing his ears to make itself felt inside his head despite the music, which had grown in volume as people sang along to a popular tune.

He turned. Staring up at him was the old woman, *Abuelita* Leda, who'd fixed his gunshot wound. She wore a frilled black dress of lace that swept the ground as she danced in front of him, her ropy arms twisting around each like snakes. An old woman pulling moves he'd expect to see from a twentysomething.

'What did you say?' he asked.

'I fixed your bullet wound, but the *susto* still lies across your heart like a sleeping jaguar. Come with me.'

Gabriel looked around. He wanted to tell Tara and Pera he was leaving the party for a bit. But they'd disappeared, swept off to dance.

He followed the *curandera* out of the square and along a narrow street towards the western edge of the village. As they walked the music faded, and lights from the fiesta dimmed until they were walking in silence beneath a waning moon.

Gabriel became aware of a heaviness inside him. Not fear, but apprehension. A sense of time being limited before he'd be called upon to act. Like the hours before combat. You checked your gear. Then you rechecked it. Checking magazines, working bolts or charging levers. Stroking a blade along a whetstone a few more times. Testing the edge against a thumbnail. But however you chose to distract yourself, the knowledge of what was to come hovered over you like a spectre.

It's coming. The moment when you will be tested. Again.

Abuelita Leda stopped. They'd left the village behind them and Gabriel hadn't even noticed.

To his right, a dune, its top spiky with the stiff-leaved grass the villagers used for weaving baskets. A breeze set the needle-like leaves rustling and clicking against each other as it brought the salty tang of the sea. To his left, a ramshackle wooden cottage, its roof surmounted by a satellite TV dish.

'Come in, then,' Leda said, pulling the plain wooden door open and disappearing into the gloom.

Gabriel took one last look at the sea. Out there, somewhere between Honduras and Cuba, and many, many fathoms down, in the inky, lightless depths where only grotesque fish with transparent, glassy bodies and hideous teeth swam, what was left of Xander Kalt lay. There also lay his dreams of world domination. Dreams that had ended with the discovery that his ancestor had something he would never understand. Principles.

'Gabriel!'

Leda's voice was sharp. It had lost its papery quality and now radiated that hard-to-define quality every good leader wanted to possess: command.

He ducked his head under the low lintel and stepped inside.

Leda lit a candle, then another, and another until the small living space was washed with their yellow flicker. He looked around frowning.

Leda laughed as she lit another of her homemade cigarettes, this one pungent with the sweet, cloying stink of cannabis.

'You look disappointed. Were you expecting dead birds hanging from the ceiling? Cat skulls under glass? Dried lizards tied in pretty bunches like herbs? This is Honduras, Gabriel, not Hollywood.'

She turned and pulled open the top drawer in a chest of drawers, made from a rich, deep red timber and inlaid with mother-of-pearl and slices carved expertly through sea shells to reveal their inner helices and whorls.

She brought out a small cloth roll tied with a leather thong and set it on a low table.

'Sit.'

He sat.

She joined him, descending from a standing position to a low squat without a single knee-pop or groan over protesting muscles.

She loosened the thong and unwrapped the cloth roll. Inside lay a few small yellow-white objects Gabriel suspected might be human knuckle bones. But equally they could have been carved whale bone.

She nudged them towards him. 'Pick them up.'

He scooped them up. They were cool to the touch. Oddly comforting as he rolled them around his palm.

'Now what?'

She raised her sparse eyebrows, wrinkling the tobacco-brown skin of her forehead.

'Now what? Here. Try this.'

She proffered the cigarette. He took it from her fingers and placed it to his lips. Drew on it, and then took the sweet smoke down into his lungs. Held for and then released it with a cough.

'Is this part of your practice?' he asked as he felt some of the anxiety he'd been feeling since arriving back in Santa Rosa leave him.

'No. But it's good shit, right? I grow it myself. Dry it, cure it, everything. Again.'

Gabriel sucked more of the smoke down. Felt the seat beneath him softening, shifting, drawing him closer.

Gabriel laughed. God, she was funny. Why hadn't he met her before? They were practically neighbours on the beach road.

She rose to her feet and switched on an electric kettle.

'I'll make tea.'

Some minutes later, she handed him a small china cup filled to the brim with a dark, bitter-smelling brown liquid. Mushrooms? Herbs? Not English Breakfast, he was sure of that.

'Drink.'

'Why am I here, *Abuelita*?' he asked, leaning back in the embrace of the armchair.

'Drink your tea and I'll tell you.'

He complied, slowly, sipping the foul-tasting liquid until only dregs remained.

She drew deeply on her roll-up. Regarded him with narrowed eyes. He found he was holding his breath, waiting for her to exhale. Finally she let the smoke go, opening her mouth and allowing the smoke to boil forth in a thick white cloud that curled upwards, obscuring her face.

It cleared. Gabriel sat up straight.

'Eli?'

'Why are you here, Gabe? You know why.'

He went to hug her but his body wouldn't obey him. It weighed a ton. A thousand tons. His arms wouldn't even lift from his sides. The tea.

'I couldn't live there without you, El. I had to go. I needed to disappear. It was all over. Us…the Department. My life ended that day on Scalpay.'

She shook her head. Her auburn hair floated free, swirling around that perfect face as if she were underwater.

'No, my honey, my soul. Your life did not end. Mine did. You ran from your grief. But it followed you here. You cannot escape grief, Gabe. You must learn to live with it. To accommodate yourself to it. Grief starts as your enemy, then it becomes a companion. Not a friend, never that. But your life shapes itself around it until you find a way forward. It's time to come back to your life, Gabe. To your purpose.'

'I have no purpose anymore, El. I lost that too, when I lost you.'

She shook her head, setting her hair waving in the current.

'Without purpose, a person is nothing. Find it again, Gabe. Find your purpose.'

His vision darkened. He could hear *Abuelita* Leda talking, but the words were in a language he couldn't understand. Then a single phrase revealed itself to him.

'It's time to go.'

84

Gabriel rose from the hammock slung between two palm trees outside his house. Dawn was breaking and he stood on the veranda to watch the rising sun gilding the Caribbean, first a pale-yellow gold then deepening to a burnished copper. He had no memory of getting home after his visit to the *curandera*'s beach house.

He made coffee and then walked down the beach, intending to thank *Abuelita* Leda for her counsel the previous night.

At some point between taking that first puff on her homegrown weed and waking, something had shifted inside him. He could still feel his grief, but overnight it had grown a thin protective shell around itself. He could sense it, examine it even, but he no longer felt that power it held over him, driving him to stay hidden out here on the Honduran coast.

He walked on, his sandalled feet crunching on the millions of bleached-white shells littering this part of the beach. A flock of pelicans zoomed down low over his head, their flypast making him duck instinctively.

He lifted his hand to shade his eyes and scanned the beach. Looking for the dune with the spiky basket-grass. It lay a little further up the beach, just beyond the wreck with its black wooden bones sticking out from the sand.

Had it really only been a week or two since he'd sent the guys on that training run to the wreck and back? Time had become elastic and he found it hard to count the days between then and now. All he knew was that Tiny and Sparrow lost their lives fighting to protect a village halfway round the world.

He reached the wreck, stooped and selected a smooth white pebble. Hurled it at the nearest spar. The stone clonked off the wood and ricocheted into the air drawing the momentary attention of a gull, which swooped before screaming in disgust and flying on in search of actual food.

The dune rose in a gradual slope on his left and he turned inland to climb up its grass-spiked side and on to Leda's house.

Panting a little from climbing the sandy slope, which seemed intent on resisting his efforts, he reached the ridge and looked down on the far side. He frowned. Turned through one-eighty degrees. Beyond the dune was a vast brackish lagoon, matted with floating clumps of weed. Narrow pathways snaked through it, rising at the most to a few inches above the water, dividing the main body into smaller ponds and rivulets that petered out in marshy land that stretched away towards the road.

He turned back. He'd had some beer with the meal, but he hadn't been drunk. The *curandera* had led him here. To the western edge of the village. He looked back towards Santa Rosa. The land between his elevated position atop the dune and his own house was either marsh, dry scrub or farmland. *Abuelita* Leda's house had simply vanished.

He shook his head.

'No,' he said aloud. 'We're not doing this. She was there. She was real.'

He slid down the landward side of the dune and splashed his way through the lagoon and onto firmer terrain.

For the next two hours he quartered the land, investigating every copse, every dip in the ground, working his way out from his start point until he'd ascended the hill where the coast road rose up before sweeping southwest and on towards La Masica.

Finally, thirsty and hungry, he conceded defeat and walked back into Santa Rosa. *Abuelita* Leda was real. But whatever she'd given him in the tea had messed with his memory, and his sense of direction, Her house was just … somewhere else.

But her words, and the feelings they'd kindled? Those were lodged in his mind, their power undeniable, directing his actions. By noon, he'd made all necessary arrangements, which involved, among other things, a trip to talk to Julio, the bar owner, about certain items in Gabriel's cellar.

He was eating lunch on the veranda when Pera appeared from the door behind him, her face bearing a wide smile.

'Good morning, Gabe. How are you feeling?'

'I feel good. Yes. Really good. You?'

She winced and touched the pads of her fingers to her temples.

'Oh, Mother of God, I drank too much guifiti.'

'Listen, Pera, did you see *Abuelita* Leda there last night?'

'The *curandera*? No, why? Did you?'

'Yes! She was right there when you and Tara were dancing. She took me back to her house and gave me a joint to smoke. Some sort of tea, as well.'

Pera laughed. 'Sounds like the two of you had quite the party. So, what do you want to do today?' She turned and waved a hand towards the sea. 'It looks beautiful out there today. We could take a boat out.'

Then she looked down at the rucksack leaning against the railing at the end of the veranda. The straw cowboy hat atop it. The battered leather courier bag beside it.

'Do you have other plans? Are you going hiking?'

Gabriel sighed. He'd been dreading this moment. And now it was here.

'Pera, I'm leaving.'

'Yeah, I get that. Looks like you're ready for a camping trip.'

She kept her voice bright, but he saw it in her eyes. The way they tightened. And her mouth. How the lips trembled briefly before she clamped them together into a thin line. Her chin wobbled. She raised a finger and pushed the tip hard against the little dimple.

'I'm leaving Santa Rosa,' he said. 'I'm leaving Honduras.'

She took a step towards him, then back, shaking her head. She raised her hands.

'No. You can't. We're safe now. You saved us. You have no reason to go.'

Gabriel struggled to form the words he'd been rehearsing in his head.

'I'm sorry, Pera. But I have *every* reason to go. I've been hiding here. Running. This?' He swept a hand to encompass the beach, the sea, the trees behind his house. The village. The *life* he'd been living. 'This isn't me. It's not *for* me.'

Tears sprang to her eyes and she let them stay, tracking down her cheeks and plopping onto the warm dry wooden deck boards where they blossomed briefly into dark-grey flowers before drying and disappearing.

'But what about us, Gabe? The other night? Did that not mean something to you? Because it did to me.'

He drew her to him, but she pushed him away with a hard shove from the heels of her hands.

'Of course it meant something, Pera. It meant a lot. And everything I said, I meant, as well. But I can't stay. I'm sorry. This has been like a dream, living here. But it's been a nightmare, too. That business with El Rey kidnapping Santi? And all the shit we've gone through in the last two weeks?'

'But that wasn't *you*, Gabe. You were the one who made it right!'

'That's what I'm talking about. If my life means anything at all, it has to be about something more than just growing mangoes and beans and chillies. I need to find my purpose again.'

She stuck her hands on her hips. Anger flashed in her eyes.

'So I don't mean anything? You fuck me and forget me, is that

Peacemaker

it? Just a whore from Frida's you felt pity for so you bought her a food truck.'

Her pain was so close to the surface it unmanned him. He couldn't bear the distress etched into her face.

'Pera, you know that's not true. Please, let me hug you.'

He held his arms wide and, after a moment's hesitation, she stepped into his embrace. Suddenly she was squeezing him so tightly he had to gasp for breath. Tears came then, too. From his eyes as well as hers.

He spoke into her hair.

'I love you. And I love Santi, too. I'll never forget you.'

She sobbed against his chest.

'I love you too, you bloody Englishman.'

She held him for another minute. Then she turned and left, without a backward glance. And shortly after that, Tara arrived.

'Ready to go, BB?'

He nodded, not trusting himself to speak.

Heart far heavier than the meagre possessions he loaded into the back of the truck, Gabriel gave a final glance at the beach, and turned the key in the ignition.

As they drove to the airport, Gabriel realised something had shifted inside him. The grief he had shouldered since Eli's death on Scalpay had settled into something different. Weighty, but no longer agonising. Like a fully loaded Bergen.

He knew he would always carry it with him, but now, at least, he had made peace with it.

READ ON FOR AN EXTRACT FROM PURITY KILLS...

...the story of Gabriel's sister.

1

1998 | A SMALL VILLAGE IN GUANGDONG PROVINCE, CHINA

The fish was a giant: Wei Mei had first seen it when her gang had been swimming in the river. An expanse of silver scales that flashed in the sun as it rolled over a few centimetres below the surface and dived for the bottom.

She planned to catch it and then sell it at the market. Think what she could do with the money someone would pay for it.

'You're twelve, Mei,' her best friend, Ping, had said when she'd shared her plan. 'You can't have a stall. The authorities won't permit it.'

'Who cares about the authorities? I'll do it anyway,' she said, folding her arms. 'By the time they find out, it'll be too late.'

Squatting by the edge of the slow-moving water, she pictured the fish snaking along the bottom looking for something tasty to eat.

'Come along, beast,' she murmured, eyes fixed on the softly rippling surface of the river. 'Come and get your dinner.'

So engrossed was she in the hunt that she failed to notice the

1

older boy creeping up on her through the reeds and broad-leaved plants that thronged the bank.

Tan Hu was fifteen. A good head and shoulders taller than Mei and all of her friends except Beanpole. But Beanpole was too skinny to defend himself against the village bully.

Because that's what Tan Hu was. Actually, Wei Mei thought 'bully' wasn't strong enough to describe the kind of boy who would beat up little kids for fun. Throw sharp-edged stones at them when they were playing quietly in the dirt. Or steal their snacks right out of their hands and run off laughing as they cried.

Mei kept the line nice and taut against the current. Behind her, Tan Hu grinned as he manoeuvred into position. Keeping low, he slid a knife from a nylon sheath on his belt. As he watched her, he pressed the palm of his left hand against his groin, enjoying the hot, fluttering sensation it produced in the pit of his belly.

Mei blinked as a flash of sunlight bounced off the water. When she looked again, the tip of her fishing pole was dipping sharply.

With a cry of triumph – 'Got you!' – she jerked the rod up to set the hook in the beast's great bony-lipped mouth. Immediately the rod seemed to fight back, almost pulling free of her hands.

'Oh, no you don't!'

She heaved back and felt the fish resisting her, a surge of power like when you tried to lead a mule with a rope and it didn't feel like coming with you.

Straining every muscle, she levered the rod upright and was rewarded with a flash of silver as the fish broke the surface, rolling and thrashing in the dull green water.

She leaned backwards, and the combined strength of her arms, the bamboo pole and the heavy fishing line brought the beast curving and bucking towards the bank.

Leaning over and trying to avoid the gaping mouth with its double row of ugly, needle-pointed teeth, she stuck her thumb and fingers into its gill slits and clamped down hard. It was cold in there and slippery, but she squeezed tighter and readied herself to yank it out of the water.

She could already imagine what she'd shout at the weekly market.

'Come on, ladies and gents! Who wants this beautiful fish? One-hundred-and-fifty yuan and it's yours.'

She knew she'd have to haggle, but even a hundred would be a fortune.

Then another hand gripped the rod and pulled the giant fish closer. She whirled round, ready to thank whoever was helping her land the beast. And a cold tremor flashed through her.

Still holding the rod, Tan Hu swept his knife out in a wide arc and cut the line.

The fish folded itself double then disappeared back into the green-dark depths, showering the two children with water from its scimitar-like tail fin.

'What did you do that for, you idiot?' Mei shouted.

She punched Tan Hu in the face, drawing blood from his lower lip.

In response, he brought the knife up where she could see it.

'Do what I say or I'll cut you open like a fish belly,' he said. 'Take your clothes off.'

'No!'

He grinned; an oddly disjointed expression as if his lips had forgotten to tell his eyes something was funny.

'My friend here says you will.'

The knife was small, but the blade looked sharp. If she tried to take it off him, he'd probably stab her or give her a good cut. Mei wanted neither. Instead, she meekly said, 'OK, Hu.'

His eyes widened. 'Really?'

'Yes, really. Just turn around.'

'You'll run.'

'No I won't. Anyway, you can run faster than me, you know that,' she said, holding her hands wide. 'So what would be the point?'

He nodded. And, like the stupid brute he was, he did just that.

1

Mei launched herself at him, grabbed a handful of his thick, shaggy hair and pulled back hard. His head snapped back and he howled with pain. Then she dug her fingers into his throat, choking off the sound.

'Try that again and I'll come to your house at night and castrate you with your own knife. I mean it,' she muttered into his ear.

Then she shoved him, hard between the shoulder blades. With a cry, he pitched forwards into the swirling green water of the river they all called Little Mekong, even though the real one was way, way, *way* over to the west.

But as Tan Hu toppled in, Mei's foot slid in a patch of clay where the weeds had been torn away in the scuffle. She went in straight after him.

His head broke the surface a few seconds later. Ten metres downstream from where she was treading water.

'I'll kill you!' he screamed, spraying river water from his mouth.

'Try it!' Mei yelled back. 'Next time maybe I'll slit your belly open.'

He opened his mouth to shout something back but swallowed river water instead. Coughing, he went under again, only to reappear another twenty metres downstream, now facing in the direction of the current and striking out towards an overhanging tree branch.

Mei reached the bank easily: she was a strong swimmer. She hauled herself out and clambered to her feet, careful not to slide straight back in on the slippery red mud.

Laughing, she ran back the way she'd come, through bamboo and the pink-berried plants with long, sharp-pointed leaves that had earned them their nickname: Devil's Tongue.

Halfway back to the village she looked over her shoulder, just to check Tan Hu wasn't after her. Maybe he'd try it on again later, but she'd be ready for him this time. Probably she ought to take a knife from the kitchen just in case.

She looked forward again and crashed into Ping, who was running the other way.

Mei jarred her ribs as she tripped and fell onto the hard-packed red earth of the track. Ping stumbled, but stayed upright. Hurriedly, she pulled on Mei's wrists, dragging her to her feet.

'What is it?' Mei asked her friend as she rubbed her elbow. 'You look like a demon's chasing you.'

Ping's eyes were wide. 'There's a man at your house. He's got a gun! He was pointing it at your mum and shouting.'

Mei's heart was thumping in her chest. She'd forgotten all about the pain from the collision.

'What about? What was he shouting? Tell me!'

'You!'

'What do you mean, me?'

'He said she had to tell him where you were. He said he was taking you away. And he's wearing a suit!'

This was bad. Nobody from round here wore suits. The only people who had guns *and* suits were Party officials. Mei had seen them now and again when Mummy had taken her into Shenzhen. Mummy would delight in pointing them out.

'See those two over there? They're Party. Secret police, most likely. If they don't like you, you just disappear. Turn up three weeks later in a ditch outside the city limits with a bullet in your brain.'

At the time, Mei thought Mummy Rita was doing a poor job of frightening her. But one was actually here, in the village. And looking for her.

Mei took Ping by her narrow, bony shoulders.

'Listen, Ping. Listen to me really carefully,' she said. 'Go back to the village. Just act normal. If he asks you, say you haven't seen me.'

'Why? What are you going to do?'

'I'm going to get a better look at this guy without him seeing me.'

Ping's eyes widened.

'That's a really bad idea. What if he spots you?'

Mei grinned.

1

'He won't!'

With Ping gone, Mei turned off the track. She knew the woods round the village like her own skin. Every animal track, every fallen tree, every patch of boggy ground that would swallow you whole if you fell in.

She started working her way back to the village using every bit of her skill. She'd come out in a stand of bamboo just behind the house. Dense enough to hide in, but with enough light coming in between the thick green stems to spy on the house.

She wanted to get a good look at whoever was threatening her mum. Eventually he'd leave and then Mei would have a think about what to do afterwards. But, for now, she just needed to see him.

Reaching the house meant pushing through some dense patches of spiny shrubs. They had inch-long thorns hidden amongst gaudy orange flowers with black centres. It didn't seem fair that such pretty flowers concealed those evil little spikes.

By the time she reached the stand of bamboo, her arms, legs and face were scratched and bleeding. But that was fine. Scratches healed.

She peered through. At first she couldn't see either Mummy Rita or the Party man. Then she heard him. A deep, boomy voice riding over the top of Mummy's higher one.

'Where is she?'

'I told you already, Jian! I don't know. She's a naughty girl. Always running off. Never in school when she should be,' Mummy said, repeating the complaints she usually threw in Mei's direction. 'She spends every day by the river or in the forest. Why don't you look there?'

'Oh, I will. Maybe for now I'll just sit here. Bring me some jasmine tea.'

Mei frowned. Not at his rudeness. In her experience, men were usually rude to women. Party men, especially. But because Mummy Rita had called the man by his name. Jian.

That was weird. As far as Mei knew, the village headman was

the only Party official Mummy knew. And this wasn't him. And why did she sound cross with him and not frightened?

She decided it didn't matter. She'd ask Mummy later. What mattered was making sure the fat Party man with the gun didn't catch her.

And anyway, she had no idea what she might have done to attract the attention of the Party in the first place.

Sure, like Mummy said, she skipped school most days. But honestly, what was she going to do with all that stuff about fractions and minerals and the history of the People's Republic of China?

The stuff she really needed to know? How to fight off boys like Tan Hu? How to snap a chicken's neck? How to milk a goat or tell which berries in the forest were OK to eat? Those, she either knew already or could ask real people in the village, like the blacksmith or one of the farmers.

She took one last look at the man with his shiny silver gun and his slicked-back hair. *See you later, Mr Party Man!*

Something crackled in the dry grass behind her. Maybe a rat. Too loud for a mouse or one of the big purplish-black beetles that trundled around the place pushing balls of cow dung. She prepared to go.

The pincers that suddenly clamped on the back of her neck made her scream. A giant stag beetle had got her! She felt herself rising to a standing position without using her legs.

'Got you!' a man said from behind her.

With his fingers still digging into the soft flesh at the sides of her neck, the man marched Mei over to her house.

The fat man got to his feet, a broad smile on his face revealing flashing gold teeth. He put the gun away in a leather holster inside his suit jacket.

Mei was terrified. She started gabbling.

'Look, I don't know what I've done, OK? But I'm sorry. I love the Party. I love Chairman Mao. And all the ones in charge now. I know I've skipped school, but I can explain. Just, please don't hurt

1

my mum. I'm a disobedient girl. I never do what she says, it drives her mad, she can't control me. I'm—'

The torrent of phrases, most of which had come originally from Mummy Rita's own lips, dried as the fat man burst out laughing.

'Wait! You think I'm with the *Party*?'

He laughed harder, only stopping when a fit of coughing seized him. Bending double, hands flat on his wide thighs, he shook his head until the coughing stopped.

He pulled a red handkerchief from a pocket and wiped his streaming eyes.

'You hear that?' he said to the man gripping Mei's neck, 'She thinks we're with the Party!'

'Fat chance,' the man said, chuckling deep in his chest.

The first man cleared his throat and sighed out a big breath.

'Listen, Mei, I'm about as far from being a Party man as you can ever imagine,' he said. 'You won't remember me, but I've known you since you were a baby. I'm here to take you back to Hong Kong.'

'What?'

Mei couldn't believe what he was saying. Hong Kong? Why? And if he wasn't a Party man, what was he?

'Hong Kong,' he said. 'A place of opportunity, still, despite the handover.'

Mei had no idea what he was talking about. What handover? But she did know there was no way she was going to Hong Kong with him. She wasn't going *anywhere* with him.

She slapped at the man's hands around her neck.

'Get off me.'

Mei watched the fat man signal something with his eyes over her head. The other man let go of her neck.

'Do you need to get some things before we leave?' the fat man asked.

'I need to pee. Your bully-boy frightened me,' she said.

Fat man laughed again. 'Fine. But don't even think of running off. We'll only catch you.'

Mei shrugged. 'Who said I was going to run? Hong Kong sounds fun. And I hate it here anyway.'

Mummy Rita reappeared just as she said this. Mei watched her face crumple. Her lips trembled as she handed the small china cup of tea to the man she'd called Jian. Mei felt guilt wash through her. But she couldn't explain she'd only said it to get the fat man to relax.

'Fine,' he said. 'But be quick. We've got a long journey ahead of us.'

Mei nodded. She walked off around the side of the house. As soon as she was out of sight, she ran. She ran as fast as she'd ever run in her life.

She found Ping playing down by the stream that fed the Little Mekong.

'Ping!' she hissed. 'I have to go.'

'What? Where?'

'Shenzhen. That guy's not from the Party. I don't who he is, and I don't care. But he's not taking me to Hong Kong.'

Ping's lower lip trembled.

'You're coming back, though, right? When they've gone, I mean.'

Mei smiled. 'Of course, silly.' She had an idea. 'Look, if you really, really need to find me, leave a message somewhere only we know about.'

'But where?' Ping asked, crying properly now.

Mei looked up. Where would be a good place for a secret message? Mummy always took her to the big city on the bus. Yes! That was it.

'The bus station,' she said. 'Where the bus from here pulls in. Queue number seven. There's a stand selling *People's Daily*. All decorated with red-and-yellow banners. The hammer and sickle.'

Ping smiled tearily, wiping her snotty nose with the back of her hand.

'I know it. We went to Shenzhen last year. Dad bought a copy off the sales lady.'

'Put your message inside an empty drinks can and squash it

1

flat,' Mei said, 'then leave it at the back of the stand. I'll check every week.'

Ping nodded, gave an almighty sniff, then turned and ran back towards the village. Just before she disappeared out of sight, she turned and raised a hand in a farewell wave.

* * *

Three months passed. As did Mei's thirteenth birthday. Every week for her first month in Shenzhen, she checked round the back of the *People's Daily* stand at the bus station.

But soon after arriving, she fell in with a group of street kids and found she enjoyed the life. Stealing food from stalls, and wallets from head-swivelling tourists. Running from the cops if a daring raid caused too much commotion. Sleeping on the top floor of an unused carpark, warm in the humid night air of high summer.

Little by little, her memories of the village faded as the thrills of city living took hold of her.

2

THREE YEARS LATER, SHENZHEN MEGACITY, CHINA

With her practised thief's eye, Wei Mei spots the three rich kids before Binyan does.

She picks out her mark. The one on the left, nearest the road. She can hit him, snag his wallet, chuck an apology over her shoulder – '*Sorry, mate, wasn't looking where I was going!*' – then escape through the traffic.

He won't follow. His threads look too new, too fancy, too damned expensive. No way he's going to risk a chase across nine lanes of traffic. He might fall down and get his wuvvly wittle blazer dirty and then what would Mummy and Daddy say?

She snorts. Who is she kidding? They'd probably buy him two more to replace it. His mates'll cluster round him, when any fool knows you leave the fallen man and go after the attacker.

Has Binyan even noticed? Probably not. He's probably daydreaming about setting his next fire. It's how he got his nickname.

Spark just about sums him up. Show a normal kid an empty

2

car or an abandoned building and they look for stuff they can sell on. Spark starts looking for matches.

Weirdo! But she likes him, just the same. They hang out together every day. Binyan calls her Juice.

'Because you've got the juice. You know, the rush, the swagger,' he exclaims, when she presses him for an explanation. 'The juice!'

But Mei knows better. She heard him once, talking to another member of their gang. 'Plum juice, man. It's my favourite.'

Her name means Beautiful Plum. Spark's in love with her. Or so he thinks. That's OK. He never tries anything. Good job, too, 'cause he'd have to learn to piss like a girl if he did.

She nudges him.

'I spy dinner,' she murmurs.

Spark nods. 'I got your back,' he mutters.

It's a tried and tested routine. She goes in for the kill, Spark lingers, ready to trip a pursuer or generally get in the way: whichever'll give Mei time to get away with the loot. Then they find somewhere quiet to divvy up the spoils.

The snazzily-dressed trio are about five metres away now. They've got that look. Not just the money. The confidence.

It comes from knowing they're protected. Not by bodyguards, nothing so obvious. Though she and Spark aren't averse to rolling the odd executive or tourist dogged by some shaven-headed goon with a bulge on his belt.

No. These kids have *protection*. The only kind that really matters. Their parents are high-ups in the Party. You fuck with them, the Party fucks you straight back. But, like, a thousand times worse.

Last year a girl – who they called Panda, on account of her striking black and white hairdo – pulled a knife on a Party kid and took his wallet.

'Total result,' she crowed later, round the fire on the top of an abandoned building as she showed them the genuine dollar bills the kid'd been carrying around.

Panda turned up dead three days after that. Slung onto a pile of stinking rubbish behind a cafe. Eyes crudely gouged out. Fingers removed. A Party pin hit so hard into the skin of her forehead it had lodged in the bone beneath. Her mouth stuffed with a crumpled sheet of glossy, coloured paper that, when they hooked it out, depicted a smiling Chairman Mao.

In blood-red writing, someone had added an unofficial slogan:

THIEVES NEVER LAUGH FOR LONG

Poor Panda. Mei had stretched out a hand and stroked her cheek. The dried blood gave her skin a sandpapery feel. They couldn't bury her. It wasn't their style, in any case. They just left her and moved on. You had to.

The Party kids are only a couple of metres away now.

Mei's heart is racing. It's mostly excitement. She's never been caught and doesn't intend to start now. Mostly excitement, sure. Maybe a little jag of fear running through the middle of it all like a guitar string vibrating.

'Ready?' she hisses.

'Ready,' Spark hisses back.

Mei takes a step to her left and then, as the Party kids draw level, stumbles sideways and gives the nearest one a hefty bump on the shoulder.

'Hey! What the fuck?'

He spins round. Shiny, well-fed face a mask of righteous indignation. *Where do they learn that expression?* she has time to wonder.

'Sorry, man,' she says holding him by the shoulder with her left hand, while her right snakes inside his Burberry bomber jacket. This style has the inside pocket on the right. 'I tripped. Are you all right? Did I hurt you?'

He sneers. Behind him, his two friends are watching with smirks on their faces.

'Yes, Ren,' one says sarcastically, 'did the street rat hurt you? Shall we call a private ambulance? Shall we get her friend here to fetch you a glass of water?'

2

'Piss off, Ching!' he snaps. He glares at Mei. 'Of course you didn't hurt me, you little street whore. Now fuck off.'

Which Mei is happy to do, his fat leather wallet nestling inside her own jacket. She and Spark are halfway across the road when a shout goes up.

'Hey! The little bitch stole my wallet!'

'Get her!' the one called Ching shouts.

Without turning her head, Mei shouts, 'Run!'

It's force of habit: Spark doesn't need telling. Together they dart through the traffic, zig-zagging between cars, motorbikes, vans and trucks.

Ignoring the parps and toots from the drivers' horns, Mei streaks for the pavement on the far side of Shennan Avenue, almost bumping into a drably-dressed woman fiddling with oversized sunglasses.

Mei's grinning. The Party kids won't dare chase them into the stinking, smoking traffic; once she and Spark are safe on the other side, they can dodge into an alley and make their way home via the back streets.

There's a loud bang. And a scream. A boy's scream.

Spark's scream.

She looks back, just for a second. Through a gap in the traffic she sees her friend lying in the road. Something's happened to his neck. His head's at completely the wrong angle.

Beyond him, she sees the three rich boys charging towards her. The leading boy, the one she rolled, actually leaps over Spark. His teeth are bared.

'Come here, whore!' he yells.

Tears streaming down her cheeks, Mei sprints away. Poor Spark. She hopes he's just injured. That some kind person will gather him up and take him to hospital.

Yes. That's what will happen. And once he's better, he'll discharge himself and come and find her. But for now, she needs to put some serious distance between her and the rich kids.

Mei reaches the safety of the pavement, although it's choked with people and keeping ahead of the rich kids is proving hard.

412

2

Now she can feel it. Fear. She doesn't want to end up like Panda.

She weaves through the oncoming shoppers like a snake, twisting and turning her body while keeping her balance as she races down the street. She's got a destination in mind. A place where she knows every square centimetre: every climbable fence, every blind alley, every elevated walkway, every nook, cranny and hidey-hole.

She reaches the side street that leads to the building site and – *Oh, thank you, thank you!* – it's almost deserted. Just a couple in drab, much-washed, old-people clothes gumming their way through coconut cakes they're eating out of a paper bag.

She skips round them and hurtles through the gates into the deserted site. The workers have all been redeployed to another city project. It's why she and Spark like to hang out here.

She risks a look over her shoulder.

Shit! The lead boy is only twenty metres away.

A lump of concrete the size of a mango whizzes past Wei Mei's head and bounces harmlessly off a corrugated-iron sheet with a loud clang.

'Come back here, bitch!' he screams after her. 'I order you!'

Yeah, like she'd follow *his* orders.

Mei runs on, deeper into the huge building site.

A fire is burning in a blue-painted oil drum. Three peasants from the countryside are gathered round it. They're passing a bottle from one brown hand to another.

They look over, mouths agape. Like they've never seen a sixteen-year-old girl fleeing three Party kids for her life before. Idiots!

Another lump of concrete flies past her head and strikes the oil drum with a boom like the world's most out-of-tune gong. She laughs. He might be rich, he might be protected, but he's got a shit right hand.

Mei streaks around a huge red-and-yellow crane and through the slit in the chain-link fencing she and Spark cut last month. This is the supply yard and it's the perfect place to lose them.

2

Huge piles of stone slabs, bricks and bamboo scaffolding poles everywhere.

She vaults a stack of wooden pallets and skids sharp-left down a narrow corridor between two temporary cabins the workers use.

Then her heart stops. One of the rich kids appears at the far end, turning the light to dark.

'Got you now, bitch,' he says with an evil smile.

Mei turns, intending to run back the other way. Then her hopes explode. Ching is standing at the other end. She's trapped.

3

They advance on her. Walking. More of that confidence they get spoon-fed from the moment they're born.

'I bet she's a virgin,' Ching calls out to his friend.

'Not for much longer!' he calls back.

Mei looks up. The cabins are about two and a half metres tall. Their sides are smooth.

She turns sideways onto the two boys, braces her back against one cabin and her left foot against the other. She's done this before, in the hills where she and Spark found a really cool cliff for practising being famous mountaineers.

With a grunt, she lifts her right foot off the ground and sticks it against the wall at her back.

Now she starts climbing. Push up, reposition left foot. Lift hands and stick the palms against the hot metal. Push up again. Reposition right foot.

The boys have reached the spot where she was standing a moment ago. The one called Ching stretches up a hand and manages to grab her dangling right sneaker. She jerks her knee up, pulling her foot free of his grasping hand, then kicks out and catches him a glancing blow across the face.

3

'Shit! You broke my cheekbone, bitch. You're going to pay for that,' he screams up at her.

What is he *talking* about? She's wearing knockoff Nike Air Jordans. How the fuck does he think she broke his bone with a squishy lump of foam?

He's jumping up, but she's safely out of range. Another couple of pushes and she's on the roof of the cabin.

She runs to the far side and looks over the edge. It's a big drop to the ground, but there's a pile of empty sacks about two metres out from the cabin. In the distance, she sees the peasants still round their oil drum. The rising heat makes their faces wobble. One looks over, smiles and waves. She sighs. How do they ever think they're going to survive in the city, acting like dumb cows?

The boys are shouting. Calling out. The usual names. Bitch. Whore. Cunt. Mei grins. They're down there and she's up here.

She backs up a few paces, gets into a sprinter's crouch, then hurtles towards the edge, leads with her right foot and leaps, arms outstretched, sailing over the gap, over the hard concrete strewn with cigarette butts and broken glass, and lands with a perfect roll on the pile of sacks.

She rolls to the edge and stands…and comes face-to-face with the third boy. Who she totally forgot about.

He's holding a stave of wood. He swings, but he telegraphs the move with an exaggerated backswing and Mei ducks as the club whistles towards her face.

The wood glances off the side of her head, spinning it round. Her vision darkens and tiny red fireworks pop around the edge of her vision. She staggers, but then is on her feet and running.

'Come back here, you!' he shouts.

Now she hears two more sets of running footsteps. The side of her face is warm. She puts up her hand and her palm comes away covered in blood. It's fine. She's had worse.

Hoping to throw them off by a metre or two, she tips her hips to the right, then suddenly jinks left, scooting round the back of a cute yellow dumper-truck, its scoop full of red sand.

But she's miscalculated.

3

She's boxed herself in between tight-packed pallets of bricks. She leaps towards the first stack and starts climbing. The toe of her Air Jordan misses the lip where one brick stands proud of its fellows and drags her fingertips painfully out of the crack she's wedged them into.

Searing pain shoots up her left arm, all the way from her fingers to her shoulder. She looks. Two nails have torn down to the quicks.

Then a hand grabs her right shoulder and spins her round. The incoming blow knocks her over, her head narrowly missing the edge of a column of bricks. A kick to her midsection drives the wind from her and she curls into a little ball.

'I've got her,' her attacker shouts. 'Here! I've got the little bitch.'

Groaning with the effort of pulling air into her bruised chest, Mei levers herself into a sitting position, but he kicks her arm out from under her.

'You're going nowhere, cockroach,' he says with a triumphant smile.

Sweat sheens his round face, which is the bright red of a ripe tomato like the ones Mummy Rita used to grow back in the village.

For a second, Mei wishes she'd never left. That she was back there now, wandering the hard-packed red-dirt roads, singing to herself, or helping one of the farmers drive oxen to a new paddy.

The two other boys arrive, out of breath. Panting. Their sleek haircuts are properly mussed up now and they've got smudges on their soap-washed faces. As for the clothes, Mei reckons Mummy and Daddy might have a few sharp words on *that* score.

'You stole Dalei's wallet,' the boy says.

She's identified him as the leader. That makes him the most dangerous. But also it makes the other two vulnerable. They'll look to him for a steer on how it's going to go down. And they get their courage from him, too. So he's the one she needs to deal with first.

3

'He can get more money. I can't,' Mei spits back, pushing herself away from them with her hands and heels.

He puts his hands on his hips.

'Do you know who we are?'

She thinks of the famous clowns from the State Circus. 'Are you Piggy, Ducks and Uncle Sam?'

He scowls. 'Ha, ha. Our fathers are members of the Shenzhen People's Governing Committee. They're very powerful. You picked the wrong boys, men, I mean, to tangle with.'

The one called Ren looks at his leader. 'Come on, Dalei, I thought we were going to fuck her. I'm as horny as a goat.'

That's when she pulls her knees up to her chest in a lightning-fast crunch, braces her hands against the gritty concrete beneath her and shoots her right leg out. Her heel connects square-on with the front of his expensive American denims. He emits a high-pitched squeal, like a pig when the village butcher draws his long, sharp blade across its throat.

He falls sideways and Mei rolls onto her belly and is on her feet in a second. There's nowhere to escape to, and she's had it with running, anyway.

The one called Dalei looks panicked. His eyes are wide and Mei sees the fear in them. Good. He's not used to his victims fighting back.

He swings wildly at her. She doesn't even have to duck, the blow is so poor. She just leans back a little as his fist passes harmlessly in front of her face. Then she lunges and gives him a faceful of clawed fingers, aiming for the eyes, but content to hit him anywhere on that expanse of fat, pork-fed flesh.

She catches him across the nose and one fingertip slips, disgustingly, inside, but the real damage happens when her index finger, tipped with a torn and dirty nail, scrapes across his eyeball. He screams and his hands fly to his face. Mei shoves him hard and he trips over his own feet and tumbles to the ground.

She turns and meets Ching's incoming fist which chops her across the neck: a vicious blow that sends a spear of agony lancing across her chest and making her feel sick.

Staggering, she lets herself stumble sideways as if she's hurt worse than she is. She crashes against the nearest pallet of bricks, but the sound is mostly where she shoves them with her right hip. She straightens and swings her right hand across in a fast, tight arc.

When she connects with the side of Ching's head, he emits a short, grunting groan. His eyes roll up in their sockets. Mei drops the sharp-cornered brick to the ground. Blood is coursing down his face from the wound to his temple. He is still on his feet.

He groans again; an odd, disconnected sound as if it's coming out of his body and not his mouth. Then he falls sideways, slamming into the pile of bricks before coming to rest on the ground. A pool of dark-red blood the colour of ripe plums spreads out beneath his head.

A hand grabs her ankle. She looks down. Dalei, is it? The one whose eye is closed and weeping a slimy mixture streaked with red. He's trying to pull himself to his feet using her leg as a support.

'I'll kill you, you little whore,' he croaks.

'Not today,' she says.

She stamps hard on his other hand and hears a crackle like dry twigs snapping.

Yowling like an alley-cat, he lets go of her ankle. Mei turns to see Ren, still rolling around, both hands clutching his private parts. Funny. She'd have thought he'd be feeling better by now. But time slows down when you're fighting. She thinks about braining him with a brick, then shakes her head. They've learned their lesson.

She's about to go, then smiles. Taps her forehead. *Silly me!*

Bending, she relieves the other two boys of their wallets and sprints away from them. She stops briefly at the group of peasants round the improvised brazier. Hands them one of the wallets.

'Here. No need to go to work today,' she says with a grin, then runs off back towards the street.

She fails to notice the new arrival among the group, a woman dressed in a dowdy blue smock and loose matching pants. Perhaps

3

because the adrenaline is messing with her perception. Or maybe just because the woman seems so utterly insignificant, even among a boring group of country bumpkins.

NEWSLETTER

Join my no-spam newsletter for new book news, competitions, offers and more…

Follow Andy Maslen

Bookbub has a New release Alert. You can check out the latest book deals and get news of every new book I publish by following me here.

BingeBooks has regular author chats plus lists, reviews and personalised newsletters. Follow me here.

Website www.andymaslen.com.
Email andy@andymaslen.com.
Facebook group, The Wolfe Pack.

© 2024 Sunfish Ltd

Published by Tyton Press, an imprint of Sunfish Ltd, PO Box 2107, Salisbury SP2 2BW.

The right of Andy Maslen to be identified as the author of this work has been asserted by him in accordance with the Copyright, Designs and Patents Act 1988.

All rights reserved

No part of this publication may be reproduced, stored in a retrieval system or transmitted, in any form or by any means, electronic, mechanical, photocopying, recording or otherwise, without the prior permission of the copyright owner. Requests for permission should be addressed to the publisher.

This is a work of fiction. Names, characters, businesses, places, events and incidents are either the products of the author's imagination or used in a fictitious manner. Any resemblance to actual persons, living or dead, or actual events is purely coincidental.

Cover illustration copyright © Nick Castle

Author photograph © Kin Ho

Edited by Nicola Lovick

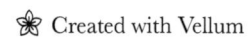

❦ Created with Vellum

ACKNOWLEDGMENTS

I want to thank you for buying this book. I hope you enjoyed it.

As an author is only part of the team of people who make a book the best it can be, this is my chance to thank the people on *my* team.

The serving and former soldiers whose advice helped me to keep the military details accurate: Giles Bassett, Mark Budden, Mike Dempsey and Dickie Gittins.

For his insightful first read and suggestions, my first reader and sternest critic, Simon Alphonso.

For their brilliant copy-editing and proofreading Nicola Lovick and Liz Ward.

For his super-cool cover, my designer, Nick Castle.

The members of my Facebook Group, The Wolfe Pack, who are an incredibly supportive and also helpful bunch of people. Thank you to them, also.

And for being an inspiration and source of love and laughter, and making it all worthwhile, my family: Jo, Rory and Jacob.

The responsibility for any and all mistakes in this book remains mine.

Andy Maslen
Salisbury, 2024

ABOUT THE AUTHOR

Photo © 2020 Kin Ho

Andy Maslen was born in Nottingham, England. After leaving university with a degree in psychology, he worked in business for thirty years as a copywriter. In his spare time, he plays the guitar. He lives in Wiltshire.

Printed in Great Britain
by Amazon